A Viking Legend:
The Descendants of Odin

Ainsley Bloomer

Edited by Ryan E. Johnson, Helle Wilson, Dustin Geeraert,
Craig Gibb, John Robin, Sanford Larson, and Tim Haughian

Prairie Heart Press
Winnipeg, MB

Published December 2023 by Prairie Heart Press, an imprint of Story Perfect Inc.

Prairie Heart Press
PO Box 51053 Tyndall Park
Winnipeg, Manitoba R2X 3B0
Canada

Visit http://www.prairieheartpress.com for more great reads.

Contents

Acknowledgements and Dedication

I have been fortunate and grateful to have family members and friends that have helped edit this manuscript. Many thanks to my sons, Jamie and Brett, and my husband, Vaughan, who have been supportive and positive throughout the years of this project. To my sister, Kathi, who has aided and encouraged me to keep going. To Deb Nielsen, Kristín Jóhannsdóttir, Lauren Carter, Marilyn Ekelund, Jeffrey Olsson, Sonja Lundstrom, and anonymous for reading, sharing valuable comments and supporting my work. To Eleanor Farrant, who inspired me to write the first three chapters of this book. A special thank you to Helle Wilson, who provided valuable discussions, insights and edits. I would like to thank John Lindell, archive assistant with the Eskilstuna City Museum, Sweden, for his help with the Ramsund Stone.

I would like to thank the University of Manitoba Icelandic Language and Literature Department, especially Ryan E. Johnson, for his acceptance and long time support of my work, for his attention to detail, for sharing his vast wealth of expertise, special insights and guidance within the editing process, and for writing the Foreward. Thanks to Dustin Geeraert for his long time support, editing suggestions and the inclusion of my project into his online symposium, "Transforming Old Norse Literature-Literature," on the University of Manitoba Department of Icelandic Language and Literature's YouTube Channel (https://www.youtube.com/watch?v=YbmAHgNnA60), I would like to thank Mackenzie Lynne Stewart, for reading my manuscript, writing an essay on it, and providing valuable questions and feedback. Also for giving her permission and providing a picture of her diorama called, "A Viking Burial" for inclusion. I would also like to thank P. J. Buchan, Catari Gauthier, and Karla King for their help. The Icelandic Department's support helped make this project a reality.

Special thank you to my editors at Prairie Heart Press: Craig Gibb, John Robin, Sanford Larson, and Tim Haughian.

Finally, I would like to thank a colleague who inquired about a replica of a viking art brooch I wore, a story I reflect on in the Afterword to this book.

Any errors in this manuscript are mine.

This work is dedicated to my family, my ancestors, and those who have walked this way before.

List of Images and Permissions

Original Photographs:

Title Page. "The Viking Ship" (Woodcut by Walter Crane). Photograph taken in 2011 by Dustin Geeraert, of University of Manitoba Archives' copy of William Morris, The Story of the Glittering Plain (Kelmscott Press, 1894, held by the Dysart Memorial Collection of Rare Books).

The photograph of brooch on page 286 was taken by author, 2020.

Other Images:

All other images are in the Public Domain and appear by a Public Domain License. The titles of some paintings have been translated or abbreviated.

Page 1. Richard Dybeck, "The Runestone Sö 101 (aka The Ramsund Runestone)" (1855). Wikimedia Commons.

Page 5. Lorenz Frølich, "Oðinn Consulting the Seeress" (1895). MyNDIR.

Page 20. Oluf Olufsen Bagge, "Yggdrasil" (1847). Germanic Mythology; also on Wikimedia Commons.

Page 21. Ainsley Bloomer, "Yggdrasil the World Tree" (2023).

Page 25. H.L.M., "Óðinn the Allfather" (1901). MynDIR.

Page 35. John Charles Dollman, "The Ride of the Valkyries" (1909). Wikimedia Commons.

Page 45. Johannes Gehrts, "Sigmund's Sword" (1885). Germanic Mythology.

Page 61. John Charles Dollman, "Werewolves" (1909). The Norse Mythology Blog.

Page 71. Johannes Gehrts. "Helgi and Sigrun" (1885). Germanic Mythology.

Page 75. Johannes Gehrts. "Sigrun Goes to Helgi's Grave Chamber" (1885). Germanic Mythology.

Page 77. Mackenzie Lynne Stewart, "A Viking Burial" (2023).

Page 284. Rotox, "Dwarf" (2006). Wikimedia Commons.

Page 287. A panel at Urnes Stave Church, Norway, a UNESCO World Heritage Site. Wanda Marcussen.

Page 291. Carvings on Medieval Church at Hylestad, Setesdal, Norway. The Sigurd Portal Door, by Professor D. L. Ashliman, University of Pittsburgh.

Page 292. The 11th century Ramsund stone carving in Södermanland, Sweden. The Ramsund Runestone: The Wonders of Runes, by Karen P. Foster. The diagram of the Ramsund carving, created by anonymous and published on 22 February 2021, is from The Ramsund Runestone: World History Encyclopedia.

A Viking Legend:
The Descendants of Odin

Foreword
An Exodus of Northern Legend
By Ryan E. Johnson

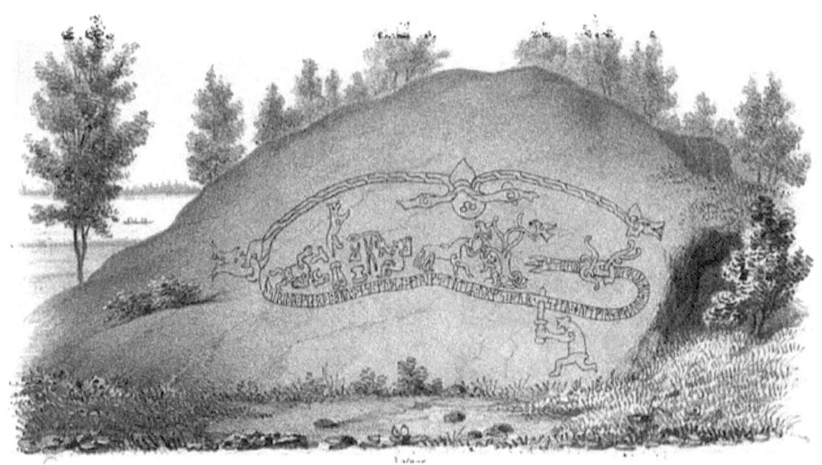

The Ramsund Runestone in Sweden by Richard Dybeck

What you are about to witness is a testament to a culture's long memory. Our story, in large part, is about the legendary people of a past world when the nations we know today were yet to form. A multitude of tribes ruled over areas that would be shaped and reshaped. Political borders, if they existed, quickly changed. Northern tribes ruled over kingdoms far from their homeland, such as the Vandals, who ruled over a kingdom in Northern Africa, in 439 taking the Roman province of Africa along with other Roman areas like Sicily, known in the Old Norse tongue as Sikiley. Closer to modern day Germany, in 411, the Burgundians under King Gunnar staked a claim along the River Rhine but were driven west in 443. The area of France called Burgundy still bears their name.

These people faced adversity but ultimately had their voices heard. They speak to us from the past despite suffering slaughter at the hands of Flavius Aetius, a Western Roman general and statesman. He, along with a cohort of Hunnish forces, slaughtered the majority of the Burgundians, while the survivors resettled in Eastern Gaul. Here they found a way to blend in, and they assimilated well with other cultures. By 451, the Burgundians formed a contingent as part of Atli's Hunnish forces, a man known to Anglophones today as Attila the Hun.

It is possible that parts of today's story were originally crafted in oral forms by this group of people. They, among others, have a place in this mythological tale. Such a tale involves unique individuals, both men and women, the harsh warlike realities that they lived with, and with their equally dangerous love affairs. Although these stories have been passed down to us by our forebears as testaments to a time we no longer understand, they provide insight into our past. What they left us may be a fleeting memory of a feeling about a time long ago, but these tales are imbued with the essence of the legendary characters discovered inside, providing a glimpse of our ancestors and bringing us ever closer to ourselves.

These narratives in oral form were cherished by some of the most seafaring people of their age. Some brought them to a land that fostered artisans for generations, some of them becoming great skaldic poets of the Norwegian royal court. In the year 874 of our Common Era they arrived on the shores of a more distant land in the North Atlantic, a land that has met with a multitude of names: Klaki, Frón, and Thule are among the more exotic. The island known to us today as Iceland, was settled by various groups, and chief among them were Norwegian shepherds and Irish slaves. In about 60 years, roughly between 870 and 930, the island was fully settled, and a small band of farmers began to form the aristocracy that would lead the country on its fated path. In the year 999 by our reckoning but 1000 by theirs, with the threat of societal upheaval, a pagan chieftain laid under a cloak to consult the old gods. It was in this solitary reflection that he determined the fate of all Icelanders thenceforth. Upon his return to Middle Earth, it was proclaimed into law that all Icelanders shall be Christian.

He threw the idols of the old gods into the falls, now known as

Gods' Falls, so that Icelanders would always drink from the cup of their arcane knowledge.

It was then that Icelanders turned themselves toward the written word. A culture rich with a treasure trove of oral history began to put quill to calfskin, an expensive medium to be sure, but one less rare than the wood upon which they had carved their runes. Certainly, wood could be harvested from the fallen trees of distant lands that washed ashore or the small scraps that could be mustered from the scraggly birch bush covering the island, but nothing of any length to tell a real story could be preserved. Vellum was less painstaking to write upon than to carve rock, and better preserved than the easily eroded basalt of that geologically youthful land. Before the written word on vellum and the introduction of the Latin alphabet, the only thing that kept our stories alive through the centuries was memory and word of mouth.

And so our medieval brothers and sisters began to create another treasure trove that would stand the test of time and preserve their tremendous ancient memory. By the 13th century, the Icelanders were known as a Nordic culture of long memory by their peers from Greenland, the Faroes, Shetland, the Hebrides and Orkneys, to Jutland and the Scandinavian peninsula, and further on to the east and south. Current cultural memory has become so entwined with the written page that understanding of the oral culture has become but a distant feeling that we stretch out for in the dark. But the narrative on the written page has been a mainstay of Icelandic culture until this very day. Icelandic people met with successive natural disasters and desperate economic plight during the last half of the 19th century. Over the course of the exodus period between 1875-1915, many Icelandic manuscripts came to Turtle Island, now known to Anglophones as North America, where we still gratefully accept the hospitality of our indigenous brothers and sisters. Along with those manuscripts came a thriving manuscript production culture, some of the resulting manuscripts being written in multiple camps and long-term settlements. Such manuscripts were often composed of multiple related narratives grouped together, and these pages continue this tradition. The following narrative is a recreation of an ancient Nordic tale that was fostered in the land that birthed our people. It has appeared in a variety of sources, but in pieces here and there. The purpose of this book, as explored in the Afterword, is to bring the larger story together into one text.

For those new to Old Norse legend, all names and special terms are explained in an Annotated Glossary, and we begin with an overview of the Norse universe. We look to the Old Norse World Tree, Yggdrasil, that houses the nine mythological realms. Although there are nine realms in the Old Norse cosmos, only the three realms called Asgard, Midgard and Svartalfheim, are featured in this story. Some events in this story take place in Asgard, home of the gods and goddesses and some in the world of dwarves, Svartalfheim, but most occur in Midgard or Middle Earth, the realm of humans. Our tale is, for the most part, not about the gods but about legendary mortals descended from them, yet it begins, mythologically, at the beginning of time and the creation of the AllFather, Odin.

Chapter One
A Creation Saga

Odin Consulting the Seeress, by Lorenz Frølich

Ár var alda, þar er ekki var,
var-a sandr né sær né svalar
    unnir.
Jörð fannsk æva né upphiminn,
gap var ginnunga en gras hvergi.
—*Völuspá*

Young were the ages, when
    nothingness was,
There was no sand, nor sea, nor
    cool waves,
Earth was found nowhere, nor
    the high heavens,
Only the great primeval void,
    but no meadows.
—*The Seeress's Prophecy*

This tale begins with a brief introduction of the origin of the nine realms of the Old Norse Mythological world. It then delves into Midgard, or Middle earth, the land of the humans, and records the first six generations of the lives and loves of the descendants of the god Odin and his human wife, Katrin.

In the beginning there was nothing. Nothing, but the endless expanse of ceaseless and continuous landscapes frosted over by the freezing and the frigid penetration of raw ice and snow that bitterly burned and bit in endless and relentless storms of a winter-like state. This came to be known as the great Ginnungagap, the extensive chasm of space and time that faced north, and from which existence eventually would spring forth.

In the many ages of the realm of time, long before any remnant of the earth was formed, the dark abode of Niflheim came into being. The dark world, one of the nine realms, is a cold and foreboding place. This realm would eventually house the giantess Hel, and the world of the dead also called Hel. Within Niflheim were great dark mists of frosty haze and a dazzling omnipotence of a massive, sturdy well of waters that sprung forth heaving and pitching its way. The primordial well was called Hvergelmir which burst forth screaming and scorching with freezing and burning cold waters. Great gargantuan torrents of gushing waters forcefully flowed from Hvergelmir, forming eleven raging rivers that raced, rushed, gushed, and cascaded in all directions over the great Ginnungagap. These eleven enormous rivers that formed and flowed were known as the Elivagar, yet each river carved out its own path, and received its own appellation.

Fimbulthul was known as the mighty one, while Fjorm was the lively river. Gjoll flowed between the living and the dead realms, finding its way in Niflheim, to where Hel's dead were to dwell. A bridge was formed over Gjoll, called Gjallabru, and the newly dead passed over this bridge and through Hel's gates on their way to the realm of Hel. Then there was Gunnthra, the river that vigorously illuminated her pathway. The river Hrid swirled, curled and hurled itself along. Leiptr, with its brilliant beams of bountiful waters, shimmered and sparkled in plentiful pathways of frosty, freezing waters. When gargantuan glaciers gushed forth from the freezing fiery well of Hvergelmir, they plunged into the waters of the river Slidr and meanwhile. underneath these waters, there were monumental swords that turned and churned in a circular formation in the racing and freezing waters, while grinding the glaciers. Slidr would eventually race right through the realm of the goddess Hel. Then there was the river, *Svol,* who ran her course with cool satisfaction and relieved all those with a great and mighty thirst. The river Sylg gurgled along, as it gorged its way through its course. Vid crashed and thrashed, while Ylg dashed and splashed.

The eleven rivers ran far and wide in all directions. Some rivers flowed over pure and clean lands increasing their sheer delight and clarity. Some flowed over and through poisonous plains, and these waters were infected with a vile venom. The coursing, poisonous flow ebbed on and on until succumbing to the freezing biting frost, and thus they began to freeze. It oozed on, until it solidified and turned into a slag-like ice, a frosty frozen mass of poisonous slime. When this massive poisonous slag of ice finally seized up and came to a halt, it clunked, clanked, wrenched and groaned. A venomous vapour rose from the poisonous mass and froze some more until it became a frosty freezing rime of grime. This frosty rime formed layer upon layer upon layer that spread across parts of the mighty and yawning Ginnungagap, the great and powerful void. It became filled with the weight of the frozen poison.

To the extreme far south of the great Ginnungagap, was the realm named Muspelheim. It was thought to have been formed long before Niflheim ever came into being. Possibly the oldest of the old and the most ancient of the ancient realms. Muspelheim was the southerly world that was formed of furious masses of endless ferocious flames forcefully scorching, burning, and bellowing. These legions of flames were livable to only those who were native to this furious and curious realm. The ones known as the fire-beings dwelt there. There was one named Surt, who was situated, stationed, and ruled there. He was in possession of a magnificent, huge, and powerful flaming sword. He was to use this sword to defend and protect the realm of Muspelheim. Although Surt and his sword offered a definite defence, if any life form found a way to pass through into Muspelheim from any other realm, one would find the ferocious flames impossible to pass, because they would burst into flames and become apart of the burning masses of molten fire. The core of Muspelheim was a continuous burning fire and, along its outer edges, a burning crust tried to form but never could, as molten particles and sparks would blast forth from the centre to the edges of the blaze and through the crust.

From Niflheim, there arose the crisp chill of all things cold and grim, yet throughout other parts of Ginnungagap there was a mild and windless otherworld. To the most southerly end of Ginnungagap, the frozen frosty ice made of the poisonous rime of grime met the sizzling sparks and the flaming molten particles that blazed and flew out of the world of Muspelheim. The blazing heat of Muspelheim created a thawing and a dripping within the frozen grime and poisonous rime of Ginnungagap. Whisperings within the thawing, crackling, and dripping produced an energized quickening, where a new life form began to grow. The drippings grew and grew and grew, and continued growing into a massive form of an atrocious man-like creation, who was made from the thawings, and drippings of the poisonous rime and from the sparks and molten particles that had blasted forth from Muspelheim. The form grew into what we have come to know as the great and powerful frost giant called Ymir. He was thought of as the first creation…a primeval evil creation. From Ymir all the frost giants and giants are descended, as it says in the poem called Völuspá (the Seeress's Prophecy). The giants would know him as Aurgelmir.

The frosty ice in a clear, and clean area of the great Ginnungagap continued to thaw and drip, and another quickening began. The quickening grew and grew and grew into the form of a mighty she-cow that we know as Audhumla. The cow was humongous, with four nurturing rivers of milk that flowed from her teats, as she fed the young frost giant, Ymir, like her calf.

And it has been said in all the many stories of Ymir that when he was sleeping, he became so hot that he began to profusely sweat. He sweated such an enormous abundance that, under his left arm, grew the forms of a male and a female. And when the forms ripened, they detached themselves from his underarm and the descendants of Ymir began. We have called these creations the frost giants. They multiplied, and some were made of the poisonous frost rime, while others were made from the clean frozen frost.

Audhumla, the she-cow who fed mighty Ymir, grew hungry herself, and she searched the great Ginnungagap for food. She found an area pure, clear and clean of the poisonous rime, and she began to lick the ice. The icy mass was grainy, salty and tasty. The cow licked and licked, licking all day long. By the end of the first day, she had uncovered what looked like a long hair. The second day, Audhumla continued to lick the salty, clean and clear ice and, by the evening, she had licked out what appeared to be the head of a man. Audhumla continued to lick and, by the end of the third day, she licked out a complete and charismatic-looking man. Then, a massive storm brewed and spewed, and intense lightning crackled through the air. When lightning shot through the man-like creation, it electrified and energized him. He awoke and slowly arose, and he felt the great power of the electrified storm through him and all around him. He walked, and he understood. He was big and beautiful in appearance, powerful in strength and quick in agility. His consciousness grew. We came to know him as Buri, the first of the old Norse mythological gods. Buri also fed from the mighty and nurturing she-cow, Audhumla. He lived separately from the gargantuan frost giant. Buri eventually begot a son that he named Bor, and the son grew and grew and grew. Bor met Bestla, the beautiful daughter of the giant Bolthorn, and he loved her. Bolthorn was of the pure and clear frosty ice waters of the great Ginnungagap. Bor and Bestla betrothed themselves to one another and in time, they had three healthy and hardy sons, Odin, Vili and Ve.

As the descendants of the frost giants procreated, a great difference developed among them. Some were of an evil and vicious nature, while others were pure, peaceful, and natural in nature. There were the frost giants, the giants, and varieties of both. As the frost giant clan grew, Ymir became more and more maliciously cruel, and wickedly vicious. He was feared and hated by many, even within his own kind. Ymir's evil vein brought forth violence, fights and killings. It was said that being made of the mixture of poisonous rime of Ginnungagap and of the molten fires of Muspelheim was too much for any living creature to endure within themselves. He went mad with raging fury and deep-rooted evil. He growled and beat on all the frost giants, giants and gods. He beat Bor, and he beat Bor's wife, Bestla. He howled and stomped and spewed cruel words. He beat Odin, Vili and Ve.

Finally, one day, Bor's sons had had enough. They could no longer stand to see their father, mother, themselves, the frost giants both good and bad, the giants and the gods being beaten. The brothers joined together with the intention of seeking a way to end the tyranny of Ymir. They spoke with the original frost giant and tried to reason with him, but Ymir was to cold and quick, and while full of putrefied poisonings and vulgar viciousness, he beat the brothers again and again. Odin, Vili and Ve defended themselves as best they could. Ymir was quick from the icy quickening and cruel from the vile poisonings, and generous with his beastly bashings. By the end of the day, Odin, Vili and Ve had grown tired, but the fighting continued until Ymir tired and fell. The brothers laid themselves down and fell into a deep sleep from the sheer exhaustion of battle. They slept on the higher grounds of Ginnungagap. When the young gods awoke, they discovered that Ymir had bled out had succumbed and subsequently died.

Ymir's body was so immense and so monstrously massive that, when he fell, the vile blood that flowed within his body burst forth from all his wounds and drowned out the entire race of frost giants and the giants that lived on the lower grounds of Ginnungagap. All were drowned except for the one called Bergelmir, along with his family and household. He was a carpenter and had built many creations that were scattered all over his home and property. He had built a big box that he was thinking of using for a house. He had not carved out any doors or windows in it yet and, since the poisonous and vile blood had rushed in and was drowning all those around him, he had to think fast. While yelling and screaming for his family to come, and with all his might he turned the box upside down and threw his wife, children, and his household into the box. They had made it in the nick of time, as they floated away on the vile blood in their box-like boat. They were all in shock as the blood gushed and groaned, and all those around them had drowned. Bergelmir was humbled as his family and all his household were saved. It was from Bergelmir, his family and his household, that all the other frost giants and giants were descended.

As the flowing flood of blood continued, Bor's sons woke and secured the god clan to higher ground. When they pondered the massive body of Ymir, they decided to honour the first creation and dragged his body to higher ground. They took Ymir's body to the middle of Ginnungagap, and out of him they made the earth. The earth was made from his flesh, and the mountains, cliffs and rocks were made from his bones. From Ymir's teeth, molars and broken bones, the brothers made the rocks, stones and gravel of the earth. From the unconfined flow of blood, they made the sea and the lakes, and they placed this sea around the outside of the earth, so that the sea encircled and contained the whole earth.

The brothers set the skull of Ymir up over the earth to make the sky. The four corners of the sky were held up with four points and, under each corner, they placed a creature who was later to be known as a dwarf. The names of the four dwarves holding up the skull that formed the sky were Austri, Vestri, Nordri, and Sudri; or East, West, North and South. The three brothers took Ymir's brains and threw them into the skull (sky) to make the clouds. Next, the brothers gathered the molten particles and the sparks that were shooting out of the world of Muspelheim and flying uncontrollably around. These were set in the middle of the firmament, with the sky both above and below, to illuminate the heavens and earth. They made fixed places for most of these burning elements, but some moved in a wandering course beneath the sky. They found places for all the sparks and molten particles and established their courses. These were the stars and the planets and from then on, times of the day were differentiated, and the course of years were set.

Around the circular edges of the earth flowed the deep and bloody sea. The brothers gave the surviving giants the east shores and mountains along the coast in which to live. They called this area, Jotunheim (Giantland). Different kinds of giants and frost giants developed there. There were giants of many shapes, sizes, colours and temperaments, as this rhyme describes:

Some were as tall as a mighty yew,
   and some different shades of blue.
Some were small,
   and some were all the colours of fall.
Some were thin,
   and some wide as a mountain.
Some were green,
   and some mean like a wolverine.
Some were blue,
   and some with a purple hue.
Some were pink,
   and oh! how they stink!
Some were born ogres or trolls,
   with eyes like blackened sink-holes.
Some were silvery white,
   and some dark as a pitch-black night.

As you can see, there was a great variety of giants and frost giants.

The gods took counsel and decided to build a stronghold for themselves high up in the middle of their whole creation. They called their home, Asgard (God Earth) or the city of the gods. It was considered a god heaven. Some generations after, some people thought this was Troy. The gods also determined that Odin, the first-born son of Bor and Bestla, would be their leader.

Asgard was where all the gods and their kinsmen lived and had their halls. In the very centre of the city of Asgard was the hall of Odin, and in the middle of this hall and to the edge, a special seat was designed. This seat was called Hlidskjalf. It was magical and made for only Odin to sit on. His wife, Frigg, could also sit upon it, but no one else. This seat enabled Odin to see into and over all the other realms. He could see into Niflheim, Muspelheim, Jotunheim, Midgard, and the other realms yet to come into being. Odin sat in Hlidskjalf and looked out, and he was contented.

As Asgard was being created, all agreed that Odin, the oldest son of Bor and Bestla, would be the main ruler of all the gods. Although he was the ruler, Odin preferred to share the responsibility of leadership with others. He assigned rulers to oversee the arrangements of their stronghold and to judge with him on all the matters and fates of the other creatures. This was done in a place named Idavoll, (Eternally Renewing Field) which was in the middle of the stronghold. They built forges and made hammers, tongs and an anvil. With these tools, all other tools were fashioned. After their tools were made, they worked on stone, on wood and on all things metal, including great quantities of gold.

Another task that required planning and preparation was the building of the living quarters for each god. This took time and precision. Then there was a temple built where the gods would take counsel and decide an all matters concerning them. There they placed twelve seats in addition to Odin's throne. This temple, made of pure gold, is called Gladsheim (Home of Joy). Another great hall, a serene and sacred sanctuary, was built for the goddesses. It was big and beautiful, and it was called Vingolf (Friendly Quarters). Many things, such as their furniture, household items and even utensils, were crafted of gold. This was truly a golden age for the gods.

In the inner high ground below Asgard, the brothers designed and made Midgard or Middle Earth, and they fortified this area with Ymir's eyelashes. This fortification surrounded the whole of Middle Earth and was there to guard from any hostility that any giant or any other creature may wish to do upon the land.

As the sons of Bor strolled along a sandy seashore in Middle Earth, they came upon two fine, modest and honest-looking pieces of driftwood resting side by side. Odin, Vili and Ve meditated upon them awhile, and saw something of themselves within the two logs. They decided to give the wood life and thus created a man and a woman, the first two humans.

Odin held the wood pieces and breathed into them giving them life and breath. The humans awoke and breathed-in the spiritual and life sustaining essence of Odin's breath. Vili touched the would-be humans giving them each a consciousness and the ability of movement. They became aware, moved their arms and legs and turned their heads side to side. Ve looked upon the humans. When he touched them, he gave them each a friendly face and all the senses. The sense of hearing, of seeing, of smelling, of tasting and of touch… He also gave room for a sixth sense to develop as needed or desired. The humans were overwhelmed with these new abilities, yet spoke out loud to the gods and to one another and understood. They became curious.

The brothers looked upon their creations, the man and the woman created in a likeness of themselves, yet designed and destined to be mortal, unlike themselves. The god brothers gathered some materials from the seashore and wove them together and made clothing for the man and woman and dressed them. The grateful humans thanked and honoured the three gods.

Odin decided on names for them. The man he named Ask (Ash), because the man was created from the remnant of an Ash tree, and the woman he named Embla (Elm), as she was created from a piece of an Elm tree.

While the great spirit of Odin carried Ask and Embla, he showed them all the lands of Midgard and told them that this would be their new home. The god brothers told the new humans about their home, Asgard and the other realms. They told them all that had come before them and all that would come after them. They told and showed Ask and Embla that they were protected from the giants, frost giants and other creatures by the fortification of Ymir's eyelashes all around Midgard. They insured that Ask and Embla knew their history and would share their stories of the gods with their descendants. When the gods had told them and shown them all they knew, they rested the humans in a secure and life sustaining area of Middle Earth. Ask and Embla thanked the gods and the gods went back to Asgard. Ask and Embla lived and prospered in their new surroundings and had many children. Communities of villages sprung up and spread out across the Middle Earth landscapes. Odin visited the human realm from time to time.

The gods noticed that there were living creatures in the form of worms or maggots living in Ymir's flesh in the deep earth below Middle Earth, therefore the gods took counsel to decide on this matter. They met in Gladsheim and each took their seat. They realized that these living forms were recreating there, and they wished to set some controls over this rapid growth. They decided that these life forms would be transformed and be given an understanding and a likeness of themselves. They were creatures small in size and lived deep in the earth and the rocks. The gods decided to make the area their home and gave it the name of Svartalfheim (meaning dark-elf-home or home of the dwarves). These creatures have been known as dark elves or dwarves, and can grow from three to five spans. Some become wide in the middle, although most are lean, muscular and even-tempered. Dwarves eventually became skilled as major smiths and artisans working with gold and other metals found in the earth. They became so skilled that they eventually took over the smithing and artisan work the gods had previously done.

All the areas spoken of were all housed within the great World Tree, known as *Yggdrasil.*

Chapter Two
Yggdrasil the World Tree

In the world of the Old Norse, there is a sacred and central tree that encompasses all nine realms. The cherished tree has always been and will always be, and is named Yggdrasil, (Odin's horse). It is the largest and best ash tree of all trees. There is a sacred space within the tree, and each day the gods hold court there. The branches of Yggdrasil spread out over all the world and sky, and there are three large roots that spread themselves far apart. All nine realms are touched by one of the three roots.

The first root grows upwards, toward the heavens, traveling into and through Asgard, the city of the gods. Asgard is considered one of the realms of Yggdrasil. Under this root lie many things, most importantly an honoured well, called the Well of Urd. There are two pure white swans who swim and nourish themselves in the sacred and revered well. There is also a hall under the Ash root beside the well, and living in this hall are three extraordinary maidens called norns. Their names are Urd (meaning: past; "had happened"), Verdandi (meaning: present or becoming; "happening"), and Skuld (meaning: future or obligation; "will happen"). They are also known simply as Past, Present and Future. These norns take special care of the tree. They nourish the ash tree every day by drawing the life-sustaining water from the well and then mixing the water with the mud that lays beside the well. They spread the nourishing mud mixture all over the ash tree. This prevents the tree and its branches from withering or decaying. The water from the well is considered so sacred that all things that come to the spring are washed with the restorative spring water and become as white as pure snow, or as white as the membrane called skjall (skin), which is similar to the inside of a white eggshell.

There are also a variety of other norns that are descended from various lineages and determine the fate of all living creations. There are norns who come to each human at their birth to decide the length and fate of their life. These norns are related to the gods. Others are descended from the elves or from the dwarves. All creatures of the realms of Yggdrasil have their own norns. Norns of a noble and distinguished stock may grant a good life, while unfortunate and forsaken norns may grant a life of misfortune.

There are other areas in the heavenly places of Yggdrasil where the first root grew. These beautiful places in heaven are divinely protected until the forces of Muspelheim are unleashed.

Following is a closer look at the nine realms, starting at the top of the World Tree and working our way through to the three roots of Yggdrasil.

1. The first realm is known as the Heavens and contains nine heavenly realms. The realms of Asgard and the Heavens intertwine with one another with some heavens located in Asgard and the rest located exclusively in the Heavenly realm.

2. In the second realm in the upper branches is Asgard, where the gods called Aesir (male gods) and Asynjur (female gods) live. They are known as Asgardians. There are many great halls dedicated as homes of the gods and goddesses. During the creation of Asgard the gods took significant care in its construction, as the roof is made of pure silver. Valaskjalf is the name of the hall that belongs to Odin. Inside this hall is Hlidskjalf, the throne where only Odin or his wife, Frigg, can sit. This exclusive chair is where one can sit and see into all the nine realms.

3. Alfheim is in the upper branches of Yggdrasil and is where the light elves and fairies live. Elves are said to be beautiful and more brilliant than the sun. They adhere to nature and listen to the wind, the rain and the earth. They are also careful and sensitive with themselves, each other, and all earthly matters. They can appear in a variety of pastel like colours or pure white

and even invisible. Some inherent darkish colours of purple, green, blue, brown and black and may glow, yet can blend into their surroundings. They have roundish eyes and pointed ears. These enlightened senses aid them in hearing and in seeing great distances. The fairies, similar to the elves yet smaller, live amongst and beside the elves. Some fairies have wings with which they can fly, while elves may ride swiftly on horses, some traditional looking, some winged and some are unicorns. While fairies have been known to be kind, some are mischievous, and some can be outright nasty. Yet, most elves and good fairies can keep the troublesome ones at bay.

4. Another realm, also situated in the upper branches of Yggdrasil, is Vanaheim, where the creatures called the Vanir live. Some are peaceful and yet some are war-like. They are known as deities, associated with fertility, with the ability to see into the future, through a specialized magic named Seithr. Most are tall, lean, and hardy. The war-like vanir are skilled fighters, and some have the specialized pointed elf-like ears that aid their hearing in hunting and in warfare.

5. In the fifth realm, we find Midgard or Middle Earth, the land where the humans live.

6. Underneath Midgard, we find Svartalfheim, the land of dwarves, where the second root of Yggdrasil runs through.

7. The second root also grew through the realm of Jotunheim, the region of the giants where a part of the great Ginnungagap used to be. Under this root lies the Well of Mimir. There is wisdom and intelligence hidden there, and Mimir is the name of the well's owner. Mimir was the one among the Aesir who was full of wisdom and intelligence, because he drank from the well with the Gjallarhorn, a large, beautiful and sacred horn. Odin, in his quest for wisdom and knowledge, went to Mimir and asked for one drink from his well of wisdom. But, Mimir refused him, until Odin gave up one of his eyes as a pledge.

8. The third root of the mighty tree is divided between the realms

of the rulers, Hel and Surt. This root extended out to the eighth realm called Niflheim, the dark home, where Hel ruled. Under this root was the well of Hvergelmir, the original well from which the eleven mighty rivers flowed. A variety of serpents lived there, along with a huge and gruesome one called Nidhogg (Hateful Striker). All the serpents gnawed at the root of Yggdrasil.

9. Muspelheim is the ninth and most southerly realm of Yggdrasil. This is where Surt and his family of fire-beings live.

Yggdrasil, by Oluf Olufsen Bag

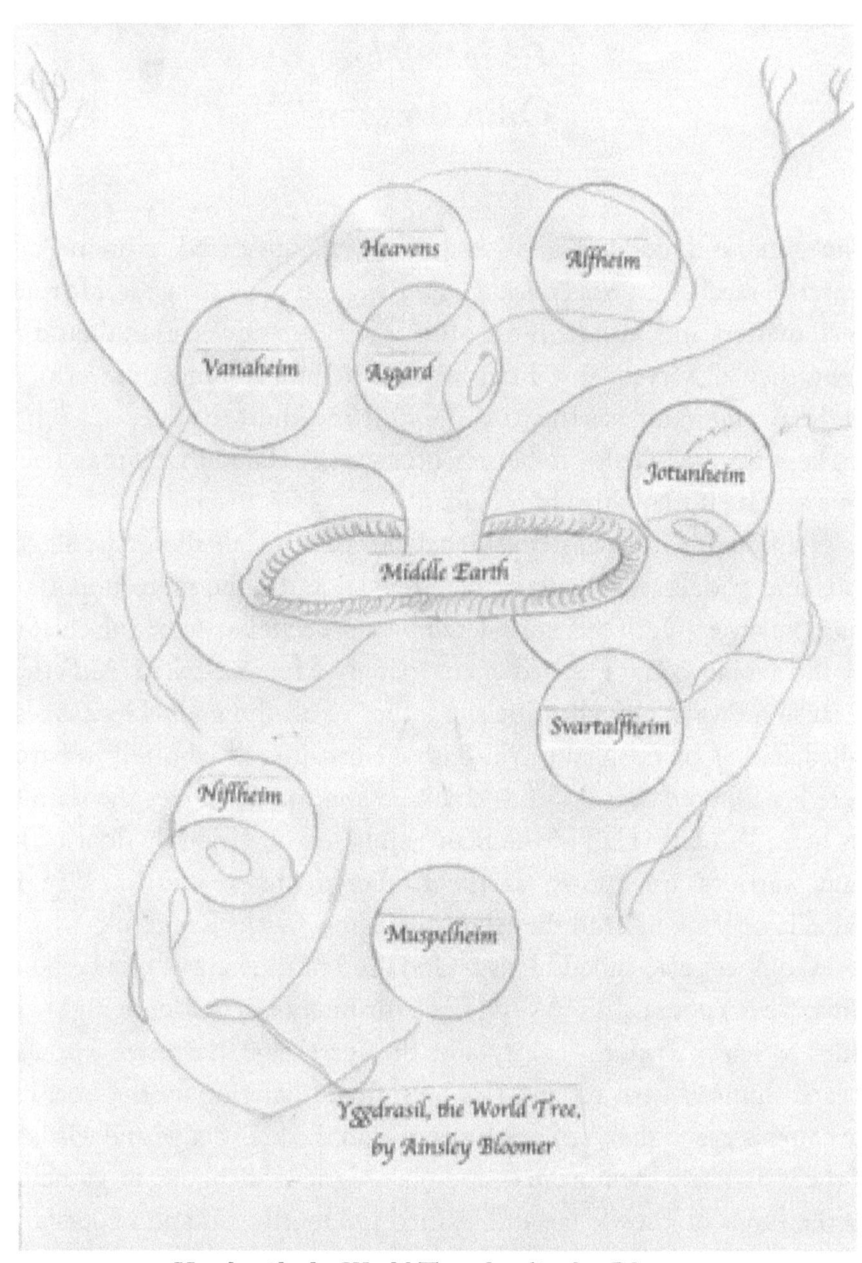

Yggdrasil, the World Tree, by Ainsley Bloomer

Chapter Three
Odin Borsson

The gods and goddesses of Asgard were considered a divine and powerful race. Odin was considered the highest of all the gods. He ruled in all matters and, although the other gods were powerful in their own right, they all served him. Frigg was considered the most powerful of all the Asynjur and was the wife of Odin. She knew the fates of all men but kept this knowledge to herself, because she feared that if man knew his own fate it may drive him mad.

Although Odin was considered the ruler of all the gods, all the gods and goddesses were considered equal and none more important than the other. Odin was considered by most scholars to be the chief of all the Norse gods. He had many names. He was called AllFather, because he was believed to be the father of all the gods. He was also called Father of the Slain (Val-Father), because all who fell in battle were his adopted sons. With them, he mans and welcomes the slain to his halls, Valhalla (Hall of the Slain) and Vingolf (friendly floor). The slain warriors are known as the Einherjar. These warriors live in Valhalla or Vingolf until they fight their final battle, Ragnarok.

Odin was also called Hanga-God (god of the hanged), as he hung himself on Yggdrasil the World Tree for nine days and nine nights in order to learn wisdom, poetry and the secrets of the runes. He also speared himself with his spear as he suffered hanging on the tree. He gave up his eye to the Well of Mimir to gain the knowledge and wisdom of the well. After the nine days and nine nights of hanging, he gathered up the runes of knowledge and learned to identify, cut and understand them.

He was also called Hapta-god (god of prisoners) and Farma god

(god of cargoes). He was also called Grim, Gangleri, Ygg, High, Just as High, and the Third. He also named himself Harbard, the ferry man.

Most of Odin's names were given to him because of all the different languages in all the worlds. Odin's name changed to match the different tongues of the different beings, as they needed to know his name to worship and to pray to him. Also, some of his names derived from some of the events that took place in his travels. Since Odin liked to travel incognito to all the nine realms, he would give those he met in his travels a pseudonym, so that beings would treat him like they normally would anyone else without recognizing him as the AllFather or ruler of all the realms.

Odin's father was Bor, who was the son of Buri, who was licked out of the ice by Audhumla, the she-cow. His mother was Bestla (an ancient giantess), who was the daughter of the giant Bolthorn. Bor and Bestla had three sons: Odin, Vili and Ve. When the young god brothers were older, they took the body of Ymir, the original ancient giant and created earth, sea, sky, and clouds. With his body the brothers formed the earth (Miðgard or Middle Earth) making the land, mountains, rocks, gravel, the sky, and the clouds. They also used Ymir's eye lashes to form the barrier around Middle Earth, to protect it from the frost giants, giants, trolls and other beings.

Odin owned the spear, Gungnir, which never misses its target.

Odin has with him two ravens named Huginn and Munnin (Thought and Memory). These two ravens fly daily throughout all nine worlds and return to Odin's seat, Hlidskjalf, to report the happenings in each realm. He fears for his two ravens every day. His fear for Thought was that he may not return to tell him the happenings of the day. But if Thought did not return, then Memory would have no thoughts to remember. Therefore, Odin feared more for Memory.

Odin also owned an eight legged horse named Sleipnir, which was a gift from Loki, but this is another story. He also owned two wolves named Geri and Freki. Odin fed his wolves his portion of food from the magic boar Saehrimnir, as Odin himself did not eat, but only drank from the mead of poetry.

Frigg, the wife of Odin, was the daughter of Fjorgyn. From this family and Odin's came the god clan that we call the Aesir. Odin fathered numerous children. Jord (Earth) was both Odin's daughter and his wife. With Jord (the personification of the earth), he had his first son, Asa-Thor, who was powerful and strong. With his wife Frigg, he fathered a son named Baldur and a blind god named Hod. With the giantess Gridr, Odin fathered Vidar, and by Rinda, he fathered Vali. And we learn that with a human named, Katrin, he fathered, Sigi. Some believe that Odin fathered all of the Aesir and some of the other races.

One day, as Odin and his brothers were walking along a beach in Middle Earth, they came across two logs, an ash and an elm. They fashioned the logs into the likeness of a man and a woman, and Odin gave the logs breath and life. Vili gave them brains and feelings, and Ve gave them their senses. The gods then clothed them. These logs became the first man and woman, and they were named Ask and Embla (Ash and Elm). Humanity's story begins with the creation of a man and a woman who recreated themselves and spread across Middle Earth. Humans eventually named Wednesday (Woden's day) after Odin, who was known as Woden in Old English.

Odin the AllFather, by H.L.M.

Chapter Four
Sigi Odinsson

One day Odin, the AllFather, was sitting on his magical throne, Hlidskjalf, that provided him the exclusive ability of seeing into all nine realms of Yggdrasil. He enjoyed his chair and the knowledge that the great dimensions revealed to him. He not only saw into all of the domains, but he also journeyed into worlds of his choosing.

One sunny day, Odin was surveying Midgard when a glitter caught his eye. He examined the sparkling light, and realized he was looking at a fair, young maiden. The light that had caught his eye was from her long, brilliant hair, which shimmered and shone in the midday sun. He was drawn to her and beheld her for a while. His gaze lingered, until he made a decision. He called upon his trusted companions and prepared a journey to Midgard, to meet with the radiant human female.

When Odin found the woman, he appeared before her in human form. She was more pleasing than what he had seen from Hlidskjalf. She was beaming and full of cherished life. He expressed his love for her. Her name was Katrin, and she fell in love with him. They spent memorable months together and, in due time, she gave birth to a fair and glittering, golden haired, healthy son. He was considered the finest of his kinsfolk. Katrin and Odin had a name-giving ceremony for their son. He was sprinkled with water and named Sigi, Sigi Odinsson. Children's last names were made from the father or mother's first name with a son or daughter at the end of the first name. Since Sigi was the son of Odin, his last name was Odin's son or, in Old Norse, Odinsson. Although we know him as Sigi Odinsson, Odin used another name for the tribespeople and they knew him as Gangari, or wanderer, because he was always wandering in and out of their lives. The norns came to visit and chanted over Sigi. Odin loved the beautiful young human woman, Katrin, and their son, Sigi. As Sigi grew, he became a skilled huntsman and warrior, as all of the youth in his village were trained. Odin travelled back and forth from Asgard to Midgard.

In the same village, a man called Skadi lived and owned many thralls. One thrall, named Bredi, was well known as an accomplished huntsman. Skadi relied on Bredi to bring in game as food for his family and household. Some villagers said that Bredi was the best huntsman in the village.

One day, when Sigi was leaving the village to go on a hunting expedition, he saw Bredi leaving with his hunting gear. Sigi said, "I see you are fitted for hunting, Bredi."

"Yes, I am going hunting, as I see you are, too."

"Well, we may as well travel together."

They journeyed together for a little while, then decided to separate and meet again later in the day. Bredi, the exceptional huntsman, caught a generous amount of game, while Sigi also caught an admirable amount of game. By the end of the day, Bredi and Sigi met and spread their game out over the snow. It was apparent that Bredi had caught more game than Sigi.

When Sigi realized that Bredi would be bringing more game back to the village than he had, he was shaken. He had been outhunted by a thrall! As Sigi was the son of a Katrin and Gangari, how could a slave outhunt him? His pride swelled and reared an horrendous head. He became extremely upset, jealous, and angry. The thought that his village would know that he had been outhunted by a thrall ravaged his mind. He was embarrassed and flew into a blind rage. Bredi was unprepared, when Sigi assaulted him with his sword and killed him. As Sigi stood over Bredi, another uncontrollable shaking struck through him when he realized what he had done. He let out a horrifying scream. He had not meant to kill Bredi, and was unsure what to do next. On impulse, he hid the body of Bredi. He found a snow drift and buried him there. Sigi was sweating and shaking from his deeds. He cursed himself for his own weakness. He had to concentrate and steady both his mind and his body. He covered all his tracks, gathered up all of the game and, by late evening, returned to the village.

That night, Skadi was concerned, because Bredi had not yet returned. He visited Sigi and asked, "Where is my thrall, Bredi? I know he went hunting with you this morning."

Sigi stammered and said, "Bredi? Oh, yes… Uhh… He accompanied me this morning, but we soon parted. If I can recall, the last time I saw him, he chased a buck over a hill. I do not know where he went, because I have not seen him since. I thought that he must have returned to the village."

"No, he has not returned, and it is not like him to be gone this long."

Skadi went back to his lodgings, but he was suspicious of Sigi. He felt there was more to the story than what Sigi had told him. That night, Skadi arranged a search party to leave in the morning if Bredi had not yet returned.

The following morning, Bredi was still missing. Skadi gathered his men and went to search for his trusted and trained thrall. They searched all day and, by evening, had not found any trace of him. When gathering to return, some went out to have one last look, when a man called from a distance. Since the sun had been shining and warm during the day, some of the snow had melted. In the snowbank where Bredi lay, a part of his boot had become exposed. It had been difficult to see, because it was brown and blended in with the colour of the trees. Skadi and all the men gathered to dig the body out. They identified the deceased person as Bredi, retrieved his body and took him home. Before they left, they named the snow drift, Breðafönn, meaning Bredi's drift.

Upon returning home to the village, the men carefully examined the body of Bredi, because they wondered how he had died. They thought that he might have been attacked and killed by a wild animal. Upon investigation, they discovered that his wounds were not made from animal bites or claw marks, but by a blade. Bredi had been stabbed with a sword. Sigi was the only person known to have been with Bredi that day, and so it was determined that Sigi had slain Bredi. Skadi displayed the body of Bredi, with the blade mark, for all the villagers to see.

Skadi stated, "As you can see by the state of Bredi's body, he has been slain with a sword. Sigi was the only person with Bredi and the only person who could have killed Bredi. Since Sigi has not declared that he killed Bredi, I charge Sigi with the murder of Bredi. I offer Sigi one more chance to confess his crime and pay a wergild in compensation or be exiled."

When Sigi was confronted with the charge, he could not acknowledge the murder, and refused to pay the wergild for the death of Bredi. Therefore, the death was considered a murder, and Skadi declared, "I declare Sigi an outlaw and cast him out of the village."

To his mother's horror, Sigi was exiled. Sigi was now an outlaw, who would wander the land and have to hide if anyone came near. As an outlaw, he could be killed, on-sight, by anyone. In sheer grief, Katrin beseeched her beloved Odin for help.

Odin, was in Asgard when the events occurred, had seen everything from Hlidskjalf, and was not pleased. He had also seen and heard Katrin's sorrowful pleas for help for their son. Odin saw Sigi's actions and believed Sigi needed a path change. Odin seldom intervened in human affairs but, when he did, there was always a good reason. Sigi was one of his sons. He loved Sigi. Therefore, Odin, the AllFather, intervened.

Odin's first order of the day was to protect Katrin from harm. In Midgard, once a person was exiled, all his or her property could be confiscated. Since the property was rightfully hers and not her son's, she would be protected, but Odin wanted to make sure she was safe. He instilled respect into the minds of all the villagers with the thought to leave the woman in peace. Once he saw that Katrin was safe, he looked upon his son. He called some of the creatures of Yggdrasil and sent them into the realm of Midgard to help guide Sigi in his journey. Ratatosk, the squirrel, gnawed a passageway through an overgrown forest, and Sigi followed it. The stags, Dain, Dvalin, Duneyr and Durathror locked their horns and blocked the passageway after Sigi ran through. The dragon, Nidhogg, and the serpent sons of Grafvitnir, scared away any potential hunters of Sigi. The eagle and falcon guided him through safe passages, forests, rocks, valleys, mountains and plains. Along his journey, Sigi was subjected to tasks that the AllFather wanted him to master. Sigi learned honour, humility, gratitude, courtesy and compassion. He became stronger and grew spiritually, mentally and physically. When Odin saw Sigi's readiness, he supplied his son with troops of brave warriors and *stallions of the sea*, (ships).

Sigi had worked and trained hard to become a leader for his warriors. He and his men were able to take over kingdoms that needed a strong and courageous ruler. Upon settling, he sent for his mother, who came and stayed with him. Sigi was a great and compassionate king, and he ruled over a region of Midgard, known as Hunaland.

Sigi met a beautiful young woman named Sigurros, and they fell in love with one another. They decided to marry, and Sigi made a formal visit to her father, Bjorn. He asked for her hand in marriage. The father was delighted and prepared a grand and glorious marriage feast. He invited his family and Sigi met all of his in-laws. The couple was genuinely happy and, in time, a son was born to them. They had a naming ceremony, sprinkled their son with water and named him Rerir. Norns came and chanted over the boy. He had white-golden hair like his father and grandmother.

To Sigi's dismay, he discovered that his in-laws were jealous of his position, power, land, wealth, and kingdom. Everything that he owned… Although Sigi was generous to them, it was not enough.

Sigurros informed Sigi, "My beloved Sigi, it grieves me to tell you that I have heard my brothers' banters and, although they appear to be joking, they express that they are not satisfied. They see your generosity as a form of charity and, rather than taking charity, they want to own everything that you own and to rule the land without you."

Sigi found this news hard to believe, "Sigurros, your family has been good to me, and I cannot see that they wish me any harm."

Time passed, and her brothers spoke louder and longer about their displeasure. Sigurros pleaded again with Sigi. "I fear the worst from my family. Let us leave the kingdom and find another home where we can live in peace."

Sigi responded, "Although I am saddened by your brothers' threats, I believed they are idle threats, and that they mean me no harm."

Behind Sigi's back, the brothers kept up with their threatening words. Sigurros heard them, and she was convinced that they meant her husband harm. She tried again to persuade Sigi that they should move, and Sigi said, "I am not leaving our home, and this life that I have worked hard to create."

Soon the brothers' whispers and chatter stopped, and Sigurros seemed relieved. She thought that her brothers had decided that they were content with their way of life and would let them live in peace. She began to relax and sleep more easily. Then, one night while the whole household was asleep, the brothers betrayed her and her husband. They snuck in and slew Sigi and all his loyal men as they slept.

Chapter Five
The Tale of Helgi Hjorvardsson

Taking possession of all the lands, the brothers ruled over Hunaland. They allowed Sigurros to live, undisturbed, in her halls. She was horrified by the betrayal of her brothers. She hid Rerir for fear that her family would kill the son of Sigi, as well. As a youth, Rerir was heavily protected. He was raised privately with the protection of his grandmother, loyal maidens, scribes, scholars, skalds and trained warriors. Sigurros provided entertainment for Rerir, as skalds would visit and tell the youth many stories, including his favourite, The Tale of Helgi Hjorvardsson.

The tale of Helgi Hjorvardsson began with King Hjorvard, who had four exceptionally attractive wives. He favoured the wife named Alfhild. The king and Alfhild had a son they named Hedin, who pleased Hjorvard. Even though the king had four beautiful wives, he deeply desired to have the most outstanding woman known to man. This powerful craving made him swear an oath that he would have the most exquisite woman in all the known world. He later learned of a stunning woman named Sigurlinn, the daughter of King Svafnir. He decided he was destined to have her.

There was an earl to King Hjorvard named Idmund, who had a son named Atli. The king sent Atli on a mission to King Svafnir with the task of asking Sigurlinn's hand in marriage, for King Hjordvard. Atli journeyed to the kingdom of King Svafnir. When he arrived, the winter weather turned ferociously stormy and bitter cold, and he had to spend the whole winter within the realm of King Svafnir.

In the kingdom of King Svafnir, a trusted earl called Franmar, had a daughter named Alof. Earl Franmar was also the foster father of the king's daughter, Sigurlinn. For an unknown reason, he advised the king not to betroth Sigurlinn to King Hjorvard. The following spring Atli had to make the journey home with words of defeat.

On his way home Atli experienced an enlightening encounter, when he set up camp in an enchanting, mystical and magical forest. As he listened to the songs of the birds, he was astonished and bewildered, because he could understand the words the birds were singing. Initially, he thought he had entered into a realm of madness, but the birds assured him all was as right as rain, and that they understood him, as well. He spoke with his new flock of friends and revealed to them the quest of King Hjorvard. He asked many questions about what he should do. A bright and beautiful bird chirped and cheeped, "If you get what you want, then Sigurlinn will marry King Hjorvard."

Atli was betwixt and between about the answer, but it was an answer, nonetheless. The following morning, he bade farewell to his new feathery friends and continued home. Once home, Atli explained to King Hjorvard that the winter weather had made him stay longer than planned, and the marriage proposal had been declined. The king listened carefully, but was undeterred by the news. For a second time, he sent Atli to the courts of King Svafnir to ask for Sigurlinn's hand in marriage. So, Atli set off on his second journey.

Upon arrival, Atli was aghast. All he could see was fields and fields of blazes of flames with huge clouds of dust swirling all around. He stopped and studied the sight. What caused this, and who caused this? He needed to find answers and also to see if anyone was alive. He thought that the swirling clouds may have been caused by running horses, as their hooves kicked up the earth.

Atli was unsure as to what to do. Was anyone still alive? Did some get away? Where were they? Where was Sigurlinn? Was she still alive? He pondered these thoughts and decided to set up camp close by in a hidden area of the forest. If someone was responsible for the burning, they may still be lurking around. Also, if there were any survivors, he may be able to help them. He settled himself into a secluded area and waited and watched. No one appeared to be anywhere around. The flames were burning themselves out. He decided to investigate what was left of the halls of King Svafnir. He searched for clues as to what had happened. He searched around the area and found nothing. Finally he saw a little hidden home with a huge unfamiliar-looking bird asleep on the roof. He puzzled over the sight. He had never seen anything like it. Was this a good or bad omen? He did not want to take any chances. He silently approached the giant bird and slew it in its sleep. Upon entering the house, he found Sigurlinn and the earl's daughter Alof. The women explained to him that Earl Franmar possessed the special skill of *shape-shifting*. He had changed himself into the form of a huge bird that rested upon the house. He had been keeping Sigurlinn and Alof safe through his mystical illusions. The daughters also explained about a king called Hrodmar, who had also visited King Svafnir and asked for Sigurlinn's hand in marriage. Her father had rejected King Hrodmar's proposal.

Hrodmar was humiliated, insulted and outraged by the refusal. In his rage, he killed King Svafnir. He began raiding and burning King Svafnir's lands. Earl Franmar changed his shape and protected the king's daughter and his own daughter through his powerful magic. Since the attackers had left, Earl Franmar had fallen into a much needed sleep, as he was exhausted. Atli, unknowingly, killed the earl.

Atli confessed to the women for the slaying of the giant bird. He had not known what or who the bird was and did not want to take any chances. He was honestly remorseful and vowed to look after Sigurlinn and Alof. They gathered what belongings they had, and Atli took them home with him. King Hjorvard was extremely delighted when they arrived and provided a feast and a celebration. King Hjorvard married Sigurlinn and Atli married Alof. The enchanted forest birds had told him the truth, as when he got what he wanted, which was to marry Alof, King Hjorvard married Sigurlinn. Their lives were all enriched.

Sigurlinn bore a son to the king and both were happy. But, to everyone's surprise, it soon became apparent that the boy could not, or would not, speak. His silence was very distressing for the king, and he could not think of a name for the boy. Therefore, the boy became the son with no name. As the years went by and the boy grew older, he attached himself to a burial mound. He would sit on it for hours. Others wondered at the young man's odd behaviour, but they let him have his way.

One day while sitting on the burial mound, a group of nine valkyries on horses rode in the sky above him. The most beautiful of the valkyries stopped and called out to the silent young man, "Helgi, I foresee that you are destined to become a great and noble warrior."

As she spoke, something deep within him awoke and stirred. The presence of her words enlightened him. A spirit of life blossomed within him and colour rose to his cheeks. She had given the nameless boy a name and an identity. She called him Helgi. He was Helgi! Helgi inhaled the music of life that flowed from her words. Sparks of life and love flickered into flames, as he fell deeply in love with the young woman before him. For the first time in his whole young life, he spoke these words, "I can accept this name you have given me only if you marry me."

The Ride of the Valkyries, by H. A. Guerber

The music of the valkyrie's words continually streamed, as she revealed to Helgi his destined life. He was in awe, as he learned he was to own a great and gallant sword, that was resting and waiting for him in a place called Sigarsholm. She revealed to him the secret location where he would find it. Helgi was electrified by her words, mesmerized by her beauty and transfixed by his strong feelings for her. He slowly spoke to her again and asked, "What is your name?"

"I am Svava, the daughter of King Eylimi. I have come to you as your valkyrie, to protect and guide you in battle."

When King Hjorvard and Queen Sigurlinn learned their son had spoken, they were ecstatic with happiness. Sigurlinn and Hjorvard's son was given the name of Helgi by a valkyrie, which was highly unusual and an extremely noble honour for the family. Hjorvard was glad he had not given a name to the boy, and was grateful for the name the valkyrie had bestowed upon his son: Helgi, meaning pure, holy, blessed, revered and sacred. Helgi was a great and glorious name! Hjorvard and Sigurlinn gave a celebration in honour of their son and his new name, Helgi, of his identity, and of his relationship with the mysterious and beautiful valkyrie, the woman named Svava, daughter of King Eylimi.

In due time the king gave a mighty army to Helgi, with which to avenge his grandfather, Sigurlinn's father, King Svafnir. Helgi vowed to avenge his grandfather, but first he needed to find the great and magnificent sword that the valkyrie, Svava, had disclosed to him. Atli accompanied Helgi on his journey to find the sword. They trekked up a mountain top. Svava and the valkyries were riding above, so they knew they were in the right area. Once on top of the mountain, they saw a mirage of treasures. The sword had been placed into the ground with the hilt straight up. In a wisp of colours encircling the sword lay warriors' gear. There were swords, shields, axes, spears, halberds, helmets and armour. Helgi and Atli approached the one sword that stood out of the ground. Helgi walked through the treasures and colours and grasped the golden hilt of the sword. He looked up at Svava, who motioned for him to retrieve it, and Helgi pulled it out of the ground. The sword hummed and the wisp of colours that encircled the sword slowly slipped into it. Helgi was enchanted, and both Helgi and Atli chose other warriors' gear from the treasures that had surrounded the sword. Helgi thought he must ask Svava how the sword and all the gear came to be there.

Helgi and his army journeyed to the land where King Hrodmar lived. Hrodmar was unaware of Helgi, and when he heard that Helgi was there with his army, the king quickly called his men to arms. As the battle ensued, Hrodmar had little time to prepare. When Helgi confronted Hrodmar, the magnificent sword of Helgi was raised and brought down slicing right through Hrodmar and his armour. Helgi avenged his grandfather, King Svafnir.

On their journey home, Helgi was surprised by a grizzly and gruesome giant named Hati. Hati had been sitting on a cliff. He was so still, that he looked like part of the rock face, until he jumped out in front of Helgi and engaged him in battle. Fierce fighting unfolded between Hati and Helgi. Hati was killed. Helgi did not know why the giant chose him to attack, but he did not have time for words with Hati, because he was too busy fighting him.

Helgi and Atli fought side by side in many battles, and they also accomplished many brave deeds together. One evening, Helgi's ship was harboured in Hatafjord with Atli on the first watch. A huge, dark cloud came and hovered over the ship. As Atli looked up to the sky, he realized the cloud was a gruesome and huge troll giantess. She had waded through the water up to the ship. Atli had not seen her at first, because she was dark blue, like the sea and sky, with darker spots all around her big body. Her hair sprung out in dark wisps around her head. As she hovered over the ship, her smell nearly knocked Atli out. Her name was Hrimgerd, daughter of Hati, whom Helgi had killed in battle. Atli and the giantess engaged in a verbal battle known as a *flyting*.

The ogress growled at the ship. She bellowed and berated Atli. "None of you on this ship are brave warriors. Do you have a king?"

Atli responded, "The man you speak of is Helgi, as he is our king and we are protected from the likes of you ogresses and trolls."

"And, what is your name?" The ogress screeched.

Atli yelled out his name, and the ogress scowled her name, and they both called each other belittling names. She wanted to physically fight

Atli, and invited him to dry ground, called Varinsvik, but Atli could not leave the ship while Helgi was away. Hrimgeld informed Atli that she was the daughter of the great giant Hati, whom Helgi had killed. She screamed out for Helgi and demanded compensation for the death of her father. For compensation, she wanted to sleep with Helgi.

Atli bluntly told Hrimgerd that King Helgi would never sleep with her, and they continued to bicker back and forth. He told her, "You ought to be nine leagues underground with fir-trees growing from your breast."

She told him, "Your heart and head are in your hindquarters, though you have a strong steed's voice." Throughout the bickering, Atli learned from her that there were valkyries guarding the ship. The ogress boasted to him how she could have killed everyone on board the ship, if it wasn't for a "sea-golden girl," who was protecting the ship and everyone on it. Atli was curious if their protectresses were Svava and her valkyries.

"Are there one or more creatures protecting the ship?" Atli asked.

Hrimgerd said, "There was one girl guiding many girls all riding on flying horses. I could not catch any of them, as they are all wretched."

Atli kept the giantess talking with him all night long. They were so engaged in verbal battling and trying to get the better of one another, that the troll woman did not notice the light of the morning sun beginning to peek in the sky. As the sun rose and silently shone on the troll woman, she screamed and realized what Atli had been doing. However, it was too late for her. As the sun shone on her, the troll giantess turned into stone.

Atli was relieved when Helgi came back, and he informed him about the happenings throughout the night. Helgi listened intently about the story of the troll woman and the valiant valkyries protecting his ship. Afterward, he and his kinsmen went on another journey to visit King Eylimi, where he asked for Svava's hand in marriage. The king was contented with this proposal and agreed to the marriage. He supplied a wonderful wedding feast for the couple. Helgi and Svava were happy together.

Years later, while Hedin, a stepbrother to Helgi, was riding on a Yule evening, a huge and husky troll woman came upon him and blocked his pathway. She believed that any offspring produced by Hedin would be beautiful, valiant and strong like Hedin and huge like her kind. She demanded, "Strong and beautiful one, produce babies with me, and our children will have all the exceptional qualities of you and the enormity of me."

Hedin was surprised and shocked by the proposal. He thought the troll woman too grotesque, gruesome and putrid-smelling to go near. He countered her comment with, "My dear giantess, this idea of yours may have merit, but what if the children look like you and are small like me?" He could not stomach the thought of being with her and refused the rest of her advances.

They ended up quarrelling, until the troll woman growled, "You'll pay for all your cruel words and for rejecting me, when it comes to your drinking and pledges."

Hedin stopped giving the troll attention and got away from her. That night, when the ale flowed and men were getting drunk, they started making their pledges, as was the custom. They placed their hands on a sacrificial boar and made their vows with the pledging cup. All the men drank and pledged. Hedin had imbibed too much mead, and he made pledges that he would regret.

"I pledge to have Svava, my stepbrother Helgi's wife!" He hiccuped, laughed and pledged this over and over all night long. The next day, he was extremely upset and remorseful that he had made such horrible pledges. He went and confessed to Helgi what he had done. Helgi thought aloud that, "Truth resides within pledges."

Helgi believed in the old ways and the old customs. He considered that the troll woman who visited Hedin was his fetch.

The next day Alf, the son of Hrodmar, came and visited Helgi. He demanded compensation from Helgi for the death of his father. Helgi asked him what he wanted.

Alf responded, "I challenge you to an island duel."

Helgi agreed. Unknown to Helgi, Alf had planned the duel for the past three days and prepared it in his favour. At the duel, Helgi was standing where the sun shone in his face, and he could not see Alf well enough. With his sword, Alf lashed forth at Helgi and delivered a deathly gouge. Feeling the immense power of the strike, Helgi knew he was dying and called Sigar, his trusted friend. "Quick, my friend! Ride to Svava, and tell her she needs to come right away, if she wants to see me alive for the last time." With that, Sigar rode off and informed Svava of what had transpired, and she came right away.

"Svava, you are the love of my life, but I am dying. I want for you to live and be happy, so take Hedin as your husband now."

"Oh Helgi, these words you speak are too hard for me to hear. I love you, Helgi, not Hedin. My heart is yours and forever will be. I cannot do as you ask."

Hedin told Svava and Helgi, "I will avenge your death, my fair brother, and join you in *Valhalla*."

Helgi died in the arms of his beloved, Svava. Svava was so heartbroken and stricken with grief, that she died a short time after Helgi. The tale of Helgi and Svava's tragic love story has been told from generation to generation and has been a favourite story for many. People believe that the spirits of Helgi and Svava are reborn through other couples, generation after generation.

Chapter Six
Rerir Sigason

Rerir's favourite story was the tale of Helgi Hjorvardson. Growing up, he wanted to be a strong warrior like Helgi. As Rerir grew older, he wanted to avenge the death of his father, like Helgi wanted to avenge the death of his grandfather. And, he wanted to have a beautiful, loving wife like Svava. For years, Rerir secretly gathered an abundance of strong warriors who displayed a variety of fighting skills. These men trained many more men, and soon Rerir had a mighty army. When he felt he was ready, Rerir stormed his maternal uncles' homes and killed all of those who participated in the killing of his father. Then Rerir took possession of all the lands and all the wealth accumulated by his father and his maternal uncles. Rerir became king and ruled all of Hunaland for many years.

Rerir met and married a wonderful woman named Sigrid. She was tall and thin, with long brown hair and brown eyes. Rerir saw her as the most beautiful woman in the world, and felt like he was fulfilling his place in his world, like Helgi had. Rerir and Sigrid loved each other deeply, but no children came from their love. The couple was dismayed and prayed to the gods for a child. Frigg, the wife of Odin and goddess of home and hearth, heard the couple's prayers. She informed Odin of his grandson's prayers, and they discussed it at length. Odin decided to intervene into human affairs. He sent a wish-maiden by the name of Hljod. She was the alluring and beautiful daughter of the great giant Hrimnir. She had long silken hair, black as a raven. Her eyes shone with a forest green that sparkled with blueberries. Besides her alluring qualities, she had many special abilities. One of her abilities was that she could change her shape to that of a raven. As a raven, she flew to Rerir and Sigrid with a special apple clutched in her talons. As she hovered over them, she dropped the apple into Rerir's lap, while the couple sat together outside enjoying the day. Rerir looked upon the apple that had fallen into his lap, then gazed up at the sky and saw the raven flapping her silken, black wings. Both Rerir and Sigrid believed this was a sign from the gods and ate some of the apple.

A little while later, to their happy surprise, Sigrid was with child. The couple was overjoyed and celebrated. They prepared for the coming baby by designing and decorating a room. They had a white crib in the centre of the room covered with sheer linen sheets that draped from the ceiling. They had handmade stuffed animals and carved wooden toys lined up inside a shelved area along a wall. Hand-woven pictures adorned the walls. They were content awaiting the arrival of their child. When her pregnancy came to full term, they expected the birth of the baby, but all was quiet with the child and the birth did not occur. The baby remained within the mother for a year and well after. Meanwhile, Rerir had been called away to fight in a battle. When he came back, the baby was still not born. He was called away to many more battles and, all the while, Sigrid grew in size. The baby was alive and kicking, but did not come into the world. On the last occasion Rerir was away, Odin chose him as one of his warriors for Valhalla. Sigrid was devastated. Although a widow, she was reassured that Rerir was walking the halls of Valhalla with Odin. She was happy for her husband, yet she grieved his loss. Along with her saddened emotional and mental state, she found her physical state unbearable. Taking counsel with her most trusted healers and advisors, she decided that the child was to be cut from her belly. She knew she would not be able to survive the ordeal. With Rerir gone, she deeply desired for the child to be born, to survive, to live and to prosper. During the years of her pregnancy, she prepared for the coming of the child. She now prepared for the removal of the child from her body, as well as for her own departure from Middle Earth.

Chapter Seven
Volsung Rerisson

Sigrid's family and household made her as comfortable as possible and prepared her as best they could. She knew the power of the god-given apple had made her pregnancy last for such a great length of time. A fertility apple of the gods had undetermined effects on her human nature. She made all the arrangements for the caring, nurturing, rearing and fostering of her child, whether male or female. Finally, she bid farewell to her loved ones and her household. When she was ready, her trusted healer prepared her as best he could, then slowly sliced open her belly, placed his hands on either side inside her belly and brought out a boy child. He was five years old when he came into the world and, as a young boy, he raised his arms and hugged and kissed his mother and said these words, "I love you, my dear mother."

She told her son, "I love you my son and name you Volsung." She hugged and kissed her son and departed from this world.

Volsung Rerisson had made a vow to himself, while he was inside his mother's womb. "I will never fear or leave a battle."

The family and household held a funeral feast in honour of Sigrid together with the naming ceremony for the boy. He was sprinkled with water and officially named Volsung, as his mother had called him. The norns paid him an enchanting visit. He had the white golden hair of his father, with fierce blue eyes. He was raised with the love and care his mother had prepared for him. He grew up big and strong. In young adulthood, he became a great warrior and leader, as he followed in the ways of his father and grandfather, and ruled over Hunaland. He was victorious and daring in battles and considered one of the greatest warriors.

The giant Hrimnir, hearing of Volsung and of his many noble

deeds, sent his daughter, Hljod, to visit with him. Hljod was the beautiful, ageless and timeless "wish-maiden," who was sent by Odin, in the form of a raven to give the fertility apple to Volsung's father and mother. Once Volsung set his eyes on Hljod, he fell in love with her, and she fell in love with him. Volsung visited Hrimnir and asked for the hand of his daughter. He agreed and Volsung and Hljod were married.

The couple enjoyed many fruitful years together. Hljod gave birth to twins. The eldest was a girl, and a boy came a few minutes later. The couple held the name-giving ceremony, where their firstborn daughter was sprinkled with water and named Signy. The boy, their firstborn son, was sprinkled with water and named Sigmund. The norns visited, chanted and sang over the babies. Volsung and Hljod loved one another dearly, and their family grew. Over the years, she gave birth to nine more sons, each strong and healthy. When each of their name-giving ceremonies were held, the norns visited and chanted over each son in a language only they could understand. The second born son was Rerir, after Volsung's father, then came Sigi, named after Volsung's grandfather, then Helgi, David, Bjarni, Fridrik, Thor and the youngest was Metusalum, who was nicknamed Silas. All the children grew in strength and knowledge. Volsung invited warriors to educate the children in warfare, teachers to teach them to read and write in runes and skalds to share their stories and poems with the children. Everyone loved the tale of Helgi Hjorvardsson. The children worked hard in their training and education and accomplished many achievements. Volsung and Hljod were pleased with their growing family, and Volsung continued to build the household. He built a grand palace around the tremendous tree, Barnstock.

Volsung's wealth and prosperity was heard of throughout all the lands and soon he was visited by King Siggeir of Gautland. King Siggeir wanted to form an alliance with King Volsung by marrying his only daughter, Signy. Signy had turned into a pleasing young woman. She had long brown hair with golden streaks. Her eyes shone a blue-green. She was as strong as she was athletic, and she had delicate qualities, as well. With a very pleasant presentation, Siggeir offered glorious gifts and formally asked Volsung for Signy's hand in marriage. Volsung was pleased with the gifts and the arrangement of marriage. A magnificent wedding feast was prepared in the hall that surrounded the huge tree.

During the celebrations, an unidentified man appeared at the feast. He was tall, with a patch over one eye, and wore a plain-grey, hooded cloak. He carried a long silver and gold sword, shining and finely engraved. He strode into the hall and walked right to the middle of the room, where the tree, Barnstock, stood. He held the sword high and, with one thrust, he plunged the sword deep into the tree. He then turned and, with a deep voice, addressed the wedding party. "This sword is a special gift from me, and only the owner of this fine sword will be able to draw it from the tree. You will soon learn who the owner of this gift is, and he will never know a finer sword." Then the man disappeared.

Sigmund's Sword, by Johannes Gehrts

Everyone at the wedding party was surprised and amazed by this gesture. Everyone cheered with wild emotion, and thought that this was a well-prepared part of the wedding celebrations. But, Volsung was silent and bewildered. He said that he knew nothing of this procedure, and did not know the man who plunged the sword into the tree. Many rushed to the sword to try to pull it out of the tree. Some suspected that the mysterious man was Odin. Although this event was not part of the planned wedding arrangements, soon all the men and women, eager to try their hand at the sword, were gathering around the tree. Men and women lined up and took turns trying to pull the sword out of the tree, but the sword would not budge.

King Siggeir was determined to make the sword his own and had a burning desire festering within him for the coveted sword. He felt that the sword was truly his, and that it would come out of the tree easily for him. When his turn came to pull the sword out, he pulled like an ox, but the sword would not budge. He pulled with all of his might, but there was not even a single movement. He tried and tried, but the sword stayed strong and solid in the tree. Many said, "You have had your turn. Let someone else try."

Many strong men and women tried to pull the sword out of Barnstock, but none were successful. After everyone had their turn, King Volsung put his hands around the sword handle and pulled with all his might, but it still did not budge. All of Volsung's sons, one by one from youngest to eldest, tried their hand at the sword to no avail. The last to try was the eldest son, Sigmund. He placed his hand on the sword and pulled. The sword shimmered, shone and sang as it slid out of the tree, as if slicing through butter.

Everyone was amazed at the sight and cheered for Sigmund, son of Volsung, who was now the owner of the mysteriously engraved and gifted sword.

King Siggeir was furious. His burning desire to own the sword drove him face-to-face with Sigmund. "Sigmund, sell me the sword and, as payment, you will have triple its weight in gold."

Sigmund slowly replied, "Siggeir, you heard the man as well as everyone. Only the owner of the sword could draw it from the tree. If this sword was destined for you, you would have drawn it. Now that this silver and golden mystery has come into my hands, I will never sell it, even if you offer all the gold you own."

Siggeir was gravely insulted and angered by Sigmund's words but took great caution to compose himself and conceal his seething, flaming rage. He pretended not to care. "As you wish, Sigmund." He bowed to Sigmund and left the celebration.

That evening, Signy was reluctant to go with Siggeir to their wedding chamber, but her father encouraged her to go. She went unwillingly, but the couple consummated their marriage vows. The next morning, Siggeir announced, "I believe it is best to leave while the weather is still good. If I wait any longer, the weather will turn. Then, I will have to stay here longer than I thought, and I do not want to outstay my welcome."

Ending a wedding ceremony after one night was unheard-of and definitely not a custom of the people. A wedding feast usually lasted for several days. To atone for his shortcomings, Siggeir suggested to Volsung and his family, "Come for a visit to my home in Gautland in three months. When you visit, you are welcome to stay as long as you wish, and I hope that this will help make amends for our untimely departure from this elaborate Hunnish wedding feast."

Signy wished to speak to her father alone, and they went to discuss the matter. Signy was disturbed, dismayed and distressed and confided in her father, "Father, I know it is right and fitting for me do my duty and be married and stay with Siggeir, but I am beyond distressed with going away with him. My thoughts do not laugh with his thoughts, and my heart does not beat with his heart. I am also sensing, through our kynfylgja, a forewarning that great harm will come to us through this marriage contract."

Volsung replied, "Daughter, these words should not be spoken. For us to break this agreement without solid cause would bring great dishonour upon us and upon him. We would no longer have his friendship or his alliance, and he could unleash a treachery of war upon us. Our only path is to keep the agreement."

Volsung agreed with the invitation to visit Gautland in three months' time, as specified by Siggeir. Although her heart was stricken with grief, Signy prepared for her journey. She left with Siggeir and his men that same day, only one day after the wedding feast.

In three months' time Volsung, along with his sons and some of his men, sailed to Gautland to visit his daughter, Signy, and his new son-in-law, Siggeir. Upon their arrival Signy ran out and greeted her father with a warning. She cried out to him, "Father, this is a treacherous trap! Siggeir has gathered a fierce and frightful army these past three months, and he plans to kill you and all who have come with you! I beseech you, father, do not place yourself on these lands and risk your life. Return at once to your own kingdom, assemble your own army, and then return to avenge yourselves. There is only treachery and death here."

Volsung, by this time an elderly man, calmly replied, "You know, my beautiful Signy, when unborn I made the vow to myself that I would neither fear nor flee a battle. I have upheld my vow all my life, fought in hundreds of battles, and I plan to keep my vow now in my old age. One cannot escape death. Today, we will act our bravest and fight this battle. It will not be reported that my sons or I feared or fled a battle or asked for peace."

Signy burst into tears and cried bitterly. She said, "Father, I cannot return to him."

Volsung said, "Daughter, go to your husband and stay with him, no matter what happens."

Volsung refused to return home, because he believed that would show fear and also would show he fled a battle, which was the one thing he vowed he would never do. He could not break his vow to himself. Volsung, his sons and the group of men who accompanied them were prepared for wedding celebrations and unprepared for fighting. Since Siggeir and his men were ready, they quickly overcame and killed Volsung and his men in this battle of betrayal. Although the sons of Volsung and Hljod were well trained in warfare, they were heavily outnumbered by Siggeir and his men. One by one, Siggeir had all the sons captured and mercilessly bound. Seizing all of the weapons, Siggeir screeched and howled in delight when he spied the sword of Sigmund, the coveted gift from Odin. Siggeir snatched Sigmund's sword, held it up high, and laughingly proclaimed it as his own possession.

Chapter Eight
Signy and Sigmund

SIGNY VOLSUNGSDOTTIR
AND SIGMUND VOLSUNGSSON

Signy knew the day would come when her husband would kill all her brothers. She wanted to make a plan to save them, but needed time. She suggested to Siggeir, "I beseech you, husband… Let me look upon and speak with my brothers a little longer. Do not do away with them so soon. If you must bind them, then place each one in a stock."

Siggeir laughed out loud. "Ha! Your madness becomes you! You ask for a worse death for your brothers than I had planned. Yet, this thought of yours gives me great pleasure. It is better to let them anguish in agony longer, before they die. Your request will be granted!"

Siggeir ordered a huge tree trunk to be brought in. The ten brothers were attached to it by their feet, and their hands were bound behind their backs. Signy thought of ways to try to save her brothers. On the first night of their capture and entrapment, a grim she-wolf came at midnight and ate one brother. The brothers were terrified, because they could not defend themselves and could only hear their brother's screams and the sounds of him being eaten. It was horrific… Signy came out the following day to see that her youngest brother was missing, and blood was all over the area where he had been. Each night, Signy put a plan in place that she thought would protect her brothers, and each midnight the she-wolf appeared and ate one more brother. Signy and her remaining brothers were in shock. She tried a number of things to free her brothers, but nothing worked. Eventually, her twin brother, Sigmund, was the only one left. Not wanting to attract attention to herself, she asked her trusted servant to put honey all over Sigmund's face and also in his mouth. The servant did as she requested. At midnight, when the she-wolf appeared, she was particularly pleased with the honey.

The she-wolf licked the honey from Sigmund's face and, when she put her tongue into his mouth to lick the honey, he bit down hard on her tongue and would not let go. The she-wolf struggled violently. She braced herself against the stock and pulled hard, with so much force that her tongue was ripped out of her mouth, and the stock broke. The she-wolf died. It was said that the she-wolf was Siggeir's mother who knew witchcraft and sorcery and was able to shape-shift into the she-wolf shape.

As soon as Sigmund was free of the stocks, he ran. He ran as far and as fast as he could. He ran into the dark and forbidding forest and, focusing on his freedom, he vowed never to place himself completely in any position of trust again.

In the morning when the stocks were inspected, the body of Sigmund was nowhere to be found. Siggeir laughed, because he believed that the she-wolf had eaten Sigmund, and that all of the brothers were dead. But, he was alarmed and grieved, when it was discovered that his mother was found dead with her tongue ripped out of her mouth and blood everywhere. He thought the she-wolf had somehow killed his mother. He was unaware of all her powers in magic and her shape-shifting abilities.

Signy sent some of her trusted men to find out what had happened to Sigmund. They searched the area and forest but found nothing. She asked them to keep searching. Sigmund saw Signy's trusted men, so he made himself available to one of them. Signy was overjoyed when informed that Sigmund was still alive and living deep in the forest. She went and met with him. They discussed at length what to do and decided to build an underground dwelling, where Sigmund could live and hide deep in the forest. Siggeir's men were everywhere and, if Sigmund was discovered, he would surely be killed on sight. Signy brought him what was needed, and Sigmund's underground home was built. Meanwhile, King Siggeir delighted in the knowledge of what he thought was true. That King Volsung's men and all of his descendants were dead...

Signy played the part of a dutiful wife and lover for King Siggeir, but she secretly plotted vengeance for the death of her father and her brothers. Although she did not love the king, she bore him a son. He was given the name Vili, named after one of the brothers of Odin. At his name-giving ceremony, the norns chanted a short while and left. Signy's seething for revenge never subsided, and she raised her son with the purpose of him contributing to the killing of his father, Siggeir. With vengeance in her mind and soul, she managed, for the same purpose, to bear another son with King Siggeir. Her second son was named Ve, the name of another brother of Odin. The norns visited, chanted a short chant and left.

Signy continued to rear her sons for revenge, and it consumed her day and night. When she thought her eldest son, Vili, was old enough to help Sigmund avenge her father, she gave him a test. She stitched the cuffs of his kirtle to his hands, passing a needle through both material and skin. Vili screamed in sheer agony and continuously cried. Once she completed the task of stitching, she tore out the stitches. The boy wailed and wept in torment. She knew Vili was not ready. She believed the boy could learn from his uncle and her brother, Sigmund. After a while, she packed up Vili and took him to Sigmund.

Sigmund looked deeply into Vili and analyzed him. Soon he gave the boy a sack of flour and commanded, "I am going out to gather wood for the fire. While I am gone, make a loaf of bread from this sack of flour."

Then Sigmund left the boy alone in his underground home. Sigmund stealthily gathered up some firewood, and some nuts and berries. He waited and watched and, when he thought the boy would have made the bread, he returned.

"Is the bread ready?" Sigmund queried.

Vili replied, "I have not made any bread, because there is something moving and alive in the flour sack, and I was too afraid to open it."

Sigmund scowled at Vili. Although the boy had been honest,

Sigmund determined that he was much too cowardly in his character and too feeble in his physical frame. When Signy came back to the underground hut, Sigmund confided with his sister. "I do not trust this boy and do not want him as a companion, for he is not adventurous, nor bold, nor lionhearted, nor fearless."

Once Sigmund spoke these words, without hesitation Signy said, "The boy has only one purpose in this life, and that is for you to use him. If he is of no use to you, then kill him. His destiny is death." And so, Sigmund killed the boy.

Signy went home. Soon it was discovered that Vili was missing. Siggeir sent out a search party for Vili, but the boy was never found. Siggeir grieved the loss of his first-born son and had a memorial service for him, but he had hopes that, one day, he might return.

Signy let Ve grow a little more and, in the wintertime, she took the boy to her sewing room. She gave him the same test that she had given to Vili. She stitched the cuff of his kirtle to his hand and sewed through both material and flesh. Ve whimpered in pain. Once the cuffs were sewn, she ripped out the stitches. The boy, like his brother before him, howled in agony. Signy waited for him to grow stronger. When she felt Ve was hardier, she took him to Sigmund. Ve was also given a bag of flour and instructed to make bread, while his uncle went out for firewood. When Sigmund returned, he asked, "Have you made the bread?"

The boy said, "There is something moving in the sack, and I am too terrified to touch it!"

When Signy came, Sigmund told her, "This boy is of no use to me, as he shows no bravery."

"Then kill him, as he is of no use to us," was Signy's cold response. Sigmund killed the boy.

When Siggeir realized his only surviving son was missing, he went into a frenzy. He ordered men to search night and day, but the boy was never found. Siggeir grieved the loss of his second son, and again had a memorial service for the boy with the hopes that, one day, he might also return.

Chapter Nine
Sinfjotli Siggeirsson

Signy was consumed with conniving ways to avenge her father and brothers. She also lived with the fear that, since her twin brother and her were the last of their immediate family, they would have no worthy heirs. She planned to remedy that. She sent for a sorceress and, when she arrived, Signy saw that the woman was strangely beautiful and mysterious. The sorceress had long, thick, black, curly hair with white, gold and silver streaks running through. Her head was adorned with an elaborate headdress, decorated with feathers, beads and gemstones. She wore a red dress ornamented with embroidery and gemstones. Her deep-purple cloak cascaded from her shoulders. A wooden staff filled with gem stones was in her right hand. She stood gazing upon Signy. Her voice chanted, "You sent for me, my queen?"

The sorceress, who called herself Sybil, stood silently still. Signy motioned her to come closer. As she admired the sorceress, Signy asked, "Do you have the special ability to change your shape to my shape and change my shape to your shape?"

"Yes, my queen, I do have this ability."

Signy explained her inner desire to Sybil. "I want the two of us to change shapes. I will change into your shape, and you will change into my shape."

"It shall be as you wish, my queen," the sorceress said. She began to sing a soulful song, chanted words only known to her and used other magical ways. She raised her staff, and a whirling wind blew around and around the whole room. It became dark with streaks of purple and gold whirling around and around. When the wind ceased and the room cleared, all was the same, as if no wind had appeared. Signy had turned into the shape and likeness of the sorceress, and Sybil had turned into the shape and likeness of Signy. Signy was standing holding onto what appeared to be the staff of the sorceress. She was dressed in the clothing of Sybil. When looking upon her reflection in a metal cup, Signy saw the likeness of Sybil, the sorceress, and she was satisfied. Signy instructed the sorceress in all the queenly mannerisms and ways. When Sybil was ready, Queen Signy left her. When the sorceress met with King Siggeir, he was completely unaware that the woman beside him was not Signy, because she behaved in all ways befitting the wife of the king.

Signy, in the form of the sorceress, ventured into the forest and arrived at Sigmund's underground home. She purposely stumbled loudly around, so that he would hear her. When he peered out to investigate the noises above him, he saw the most alluring and appealing woman he had ever seen. He waited, and realized that she was all alone. He was mystified. When he approached her, she pretended to be surprised by his presence and said, "Oh, I am so happy to see someone. I have been traveling and have lost my horse and my way."

"Come have some food and rest yourself," Sigmund said. He took her into his home and offered her rest, food and shelter. He was soon overcome by her bewitching beauty, dazzling delicacy and exquisite elegance. Signy had no trouble seducing Sigmund. He had been alone for a long period of time. They loved one another for many nights in a row. When Signy felt she had been impregnated, she left as mysteriously as she had arrived. She returned to the halls of King Siggeir, met with the sorceress and, without anyone knowing, they changed back to their original shapes.

In nine months' time, Signy gave birth to another son. A son of her twin brother, Sigmund... She named him Sinfjotli. King Siggeir was overjoyed to have another son and thought the boy was his. Like his true father and uncles, Sinfjotli grew to be big, strong and courageous. Signy secretly taught many things to Sinfjotli. He learned all about his lineage, his grandfather Volsung, his uncles and how they were all mercilessly slain by Siggeir, whom he thought was his father. When she felt the boy was ready to meet Sigmund, Signy gave him the test. She stitched the cuffs of his kirtle to his hands and passed a needle through both flesh and material. Then she ripped out the stitches. Sinfjotli remained silently calm and did not flinch, twist, scream or cry, as his half-brothers before him had.

Surprised, she said, "This must be painful for you!"

Sinfjotli replied, "Such pain would seem nothing for my grandfather, Volsung."

Signy was satisfied with Sinfjotli. He showed strength and courage, and she took him to meet her brother. Sigmund studied Sinfjotli, yet could not see a fault within him. Like with the others before, he gave the boy a bag of flour and commanded, "Make us bread for supper, while I go out and gather firewood."

Sigmund gathered the firewood and, when he came back, he could smell the scent of fresh bread. He was surprised and asked, "Did you discover anything in the flour?"

Sinfjotli admitted, "I watched the flour carefully and saw something alive and moving in it, but once I kneaded it into the bread and baked it, the form stopped moving."

Sigmund laughed heartily and said, "Well done, my boy! We will make a meal of something else tonight, for you have kneaded into the bread a vile and venomous viper!"

Sigmund had a strong constitution and had prepared himself for many years and in many ways to be immune to many kinds of poisons. He could eat or drink a poison without any consequence, but on the other hand, Sinfjotli could only tolerate poison externally, but not internally through eating or drinking it.

Chapter Ten
The Testing of Sinfjotli

Sigmund looked deeply into Sinfjotli and saw something of himself, and that was something that he had not seen in his other nephews. The boy showed signs of bravery, strength and intelligence beyond his age. Sigmund also felt that Sinfjotli could prove to be a potential companion in the avenging of his father and brothers. Therefore, he spared the life of the boy. Sigmund also saw that Sinfjotli was young and had great potential to be taught, trained, hardened and shaped into what Sigmund wanted. Sigmund prepared and hardened Sinfjotli by accustoming him to extreme hardships, and many strange and extraordinary situations.

During the summer months, Sigmund and Sinfjotli travelled widely through the forests and neighbouring kingdoms. They found themselves in situations in which they killed many men and gathered their various treasures. Sigmund believed that Sinfjotli was the son of King Siggeir, and felt the lad could not be fully trusted. Yet, he saw in Sinfjotli the fierce strength and zeal that was characteristic of his father and of his brothers. Sinfjotli had been brought up with the stories of his grandfather and uncles, and how they had been brutally betrayed and killed by Siggeir, who he thought was his father. The idea of vengeance had been cultivated into Sinfjotli's mind since his birth. Sigmund continued to mentally and emotionally prepare Sinfjotli for the killing of Siggeir.

One day, while Sigmund and Sinfjotli were hunting, they came across an old and dilapidated log cabin. When they burst through the door, they were transfixed by what they saw. There were two furry, grey, strangely sparkling wolf skins, asymmetrically floating in the air, hanging over the heads of two men, princes, who appeared to be in a deep, enchanted sleep, for they did not flinch from the sounds of the door bursting open. Royal clothing and treasures were strewn all over and around the hut. The sight was bewildering. Sigmund and Sinfjotli became mesmerized by the wolfskins. Spellbound, they reached for the skins floating in the air and put them on. Once dressed, they realized they were trapped within the wolfskins. They wrestled with the skins, snapped at them and howled like wolves. To their horror and amazement, they understood their wolf sounds. As they were howling, the sleeping princes awoke.

The princes looked upon the horrified men wearing the wolfskins. One prince explained, "Try to calm yourselves, my good men, and let me explain. We are the sons of kings and were entrapped by a sorceress's spell. I am Prince Sam and this is Prince Traci. At one time, a sorceress looked upon us, and she desired what she saw. Our youth, our wealth and our looks… She demanded that one of us marry her daughter, but we were both betrothed to other women, so we refused her request. The sorceress was furious and became ferociously angry. She said, 'If neither of you marry my daughter, then neither of you will ever marry!' With those words, she cast the spell of the wolfskins upon us. The lure of the skins was too powerful to resist. Once the wolfskins are on, they cannot be taken off. We became wolves for nine days and, on the tenth day, we were able take the skins off and rest. The cycle would continuously repeat itself over and over again, and we were slaves to the skins. We have been unable to break free from the spell, until you two donned the wicked wolfskins. For nine days, you will howl and hunt like wolves. Then, on the tenth day, you will be able to take off the wolfskins and rest. After the tenth day, the enchanted cycle will begin again. We are sorry that you have taken on this misfortune, yet we are forever grateful to you for releasing us from the spell. We cannot remember how long we have been living like this, and we hope our betrothed have waited for us. But, we do not expect much. Our only wish is to return to our homes and live out our lives in a normal way. We will search a way for you to be released from this relentless spell, but for now we need to go home and find our loved ones. We bid you farewell." The two released princes dressed, gathered up their treasures and left the old shack.

Sigmund and Sinfjotli were aghast at their predicament. They barked at one another, each understanding the other. They both decided they would investigate a portion of the area around them on their own and meet at the old hut later. It was agreed that if either of them got into trouble or into a fight with seven or more men, he would howl for the other to come and help him. Sigmund growled at Sinfjotli, "You are young and fearless, but if you are reckless and abandon our agreement, you may become seriously wounded, for there are many hunters who want to kill a wolf."

Sinfjotli agreed and they parted.

Alone on his journey, Sigmund was surrounded by seven savage-looking men intent on harming him. He howled for Sinfjotli, who came as soon as he heard the call. All seven men were killed.

Later, Sinfjotli met eleven fierce men during his travels, and a great battle ensued. Sinfjotli managed to kill all of the men, but he was seriously injured in the process. When he felt he was near death, he dragged himself to rest under the protection of a big ash tree. Sigmund soon came and saw that Sinfjotli was in mortal peril. He questioned the boy. "Why did you not call me, as I had said? If one of us was attacked by seven or more hunters, we would call to the other one for help!"

"I am a child next to you, and you howled for my help while fighting seven men, but I did not need help fighting off eleven men."

Sinfjotli's arrogant answer angered Sigmund. He snapped at his son and unintentionally bit him in the windpipe. Upon realizing what he had done, he placed the boy over his shoulders and raced him back to the old dilapidated log hut from which they had come. He desperately tried to get the wolfskins off, but he could not. He cursed the skins and told treacherous trolls to take them.

Sigmund searched for help for the boy he-wolf, but found nothing. He howled out to the AllFather for help. Sigmund was unsure how to help Sinfjotli. Then two lively weasels appeared before the cabin and caught Sigmund's attention. As he watched, he saw one of the weasels bite the other on the windpipe. The bitten weasel lay down as if lifeless, while the other weasel ran into the woods and soon returned with a special leaf that he placed on the wounded windpipe of the weasel. In a little while, the wound of the weasel was healed, and they both went running into the surrounding forest. Sigmund realized he was being shown how to heal Sinfjotli. He jumped and howled with this knowledge. He wondered, what was the healing leaf and where could he find one? He stirred and whirled around, as he heard the flapping of great wings coming towards him. He sprang back, when he saw a huge black raven approaching him. A strange and mysterious leaf, like the one the weasel had, was in the bird's beak. The raven dropped the leaf in front of the wolf-shape of Sigmund, who then placed the leaf on the windpipe of Sinfjotli. The next morning, Sinfjotli was healed. Sigmund thanked Odin, and his raven, for hearing his pleas and helping.

Sigmund and Sinfjotli went back to Sigmund's underground dwelling close to Signy and stayed there until the tenth day. On the tenth day, the two men took off the enchanted wolfskins and stretched their human bodies back into shape. Sigmund collected some firewood and, when he returned, Sinfjotli was in a deep sleep. Sigmund built a fire and threw the wolfskins into the fire. The spellbinding skins sprang up and fought, snapped, howled, growled, screamed and squirmed, but Sigmund held them down with two huge and heavy logs until they crackled, hissed and withered in the cleansing flames. Sigmund was determined that the evil wolfskins would never again be donned by a human being. They were finally free. Free from the enchantment of the wolfskin spell… During this time, Sinfjotli had grown bigger and stronger. Sigmund looked upon his nephew with deep satisfaction. He knew that Sinfjotli had been thoroughly tested and was now ready to aid in avenging the deaths of his beloved brothers and of his father, Volsung.

Werewolves, by John Charles Dollman

Chapter Eleven
Vengeance, Truth, and New Beginnings

Signy had two more children with King Siggeir, the man she hated, detested and was betrothed to. She used all her strength to play the dutiful and loving wife, while seething thoughts of revenge burned through her soul. The deception was exhausting. The day finally came when Sigmund and Sinfjotli secretly entered a room in Siggeir's hall and hid from view. Signy became aware of their presence.

At that time, the children were giggling in play and rolling a golden ball back and forth in the hallway. The ball rolled into the room where Sigmund and Sinfjotli were hunkered down. Laughing out loud as they ran into the room to fetch the ball, the children saw the two men. To Signy's horror, they screamed and ran into the room where their father Siggeir sat. "Father, there are two fierce-looking men in the room wearing long helmets and shining mail coats!" Siggeir laughed and paid them no heed, as he thought that his children were playing a game.

Signy was shocked when she heard her children betray Sigmund and Sinfjotli. She whispered, "Because of my children's betrayal, you may kill them."

Sigmund said, "I cannot kill any more of your children."

Without hesitation, and with lightning speed, Sinfjotli drew his sword, slew the children and flung them in front of Siggeir. The horrified father screamed and ordered his men to come. A vicious battle ensued, as Sigmund and Sinfjotli fought all of Siggeir's men. Although Sigmund and Sinfjotli hewed through many men, there were too many of them. They were finally subdued and captured. Siggeir arranged to have Sigmund and Sinfjotli fettered and restrained. He wanted a slow and excruciatingly painful death for them both, and he pondered upon this.

In the morning, Siggeir ordered his men to build a cairn for the two prisoners. In the middle of the grave-like cairn, Siggeir had a stone slab placed. Sigmund was placed in the cairn on one side of the slab and Sinfjotli was placed on the other side. Siggeir had designed it so the two men could hear one another, but not see or help one another. He then ordered the cairn to be completely covered. Sigmund and Sinfjotli were to be entombed in the cairn unable to help one another and only able to hear each other die. Siggeir laughed, as he thought this was a perfect death trap.

Before the enclosure, Signy secretly threw some cooked meat and Sigmund's sword, wrapped in straw, to Sinfjotli. She told her trusted servants to not let anyone know. Sinfjotli felt through the darkness, found the sword and sliced the bonds free from his wrists. He then felt the top of the cairn, where he found a little opening and thrust the sword through. Sinfjotli whispered to Sigmund, telling him to feel at the top of the cairn for the sword. Sinfjotli had the hilt side of the blade, while Sigmund had the blade side. Sigmund felt for the sword and cut the bonds from his hands with the blade. He wrapped his shirt around his hands and grasped the blade. Although the sword sliced his hands, he and Sinfjotli sawed at the stone. When there was enough of an opening between the two, Sinfjotli passed some of the meat to Sigmund. They both sat and ate, thus increasing their strength. Sinfjotli also passed his shirt and some straw through the opening to Sigmund. Sigmund rewrapped his hands with Sinfjotli's shirt, the straw and his blood-soaked shirt. They continued to saw until the stone was cut in half. Sinfjotli passed through to Sigmund's side, and then they cut themselves out of the cairn. During the night, they were free from their cairn grave. While everyone was sleeping, Sigmund and Sinfjotli secretly gathered up supplies, clothes, armour and weapons. They dressed themselves in fresh clothing and armour. When they had all they wanted, they went into King Siggeir's halls and started a blazing fire.

The king awakened and screamed, "Who has done this? Who has set my halls on fire?'

In a deep and dark voice, Sigmund replied, "In your pride and arrogance, you thought all of the descendants of King Volsung were dead, yet here I stand before you, Sigmund, son of King Volsung, with Sinfjotli, my sister's son."

Siggeir was aghast, because he believed the cairn where he entombed the two men was impenetrable. How did they break free? Was this an act of the gods? Had he been wrong this whole time?

As fire ravaged through the halls, men raced to the doors, where Sigmund and Sinfjotli stood and killed anyone trying to get out. Sigmund yelled, "Signy! Come out from the flames, as I wish to help heal your great sorrows. Come and receive the gift of a new life!"

He knew that Signy had suffered for years with King Siggeir. Signy had been living in the scorching flames of her own personal hell of hatred and revenge ever since her marriage began. The life of conniving, the hatred and the killing of her own children for the sake of her seething vengeance had taken a tremendous toll on her. She solemnly came before her brother and son, hugged and kissed them and said, "Sigmund, I am drained of life. I foresee my death and it looks good. Memories of the slaying of our father and our brothers by Siggeir have tormented me all these years. My whole life has been about vengeance. I had my own children killed, when I thought them too fainthearted and spiritless in the avenging of our father and our brothers. I feared we would have no honourable heirs and, because of this fear, it was me who came to you in the form of the sorceress that seduced you. Sigmund, Sinfjotli is your son, not the son of King Siggeir. Sinfjotli is the child of both a son and a daughter of King Volsung and, for this reason, he has so much zeal, strength and courage. In all my married life, I have striven towards the killing of my husband, King Siggeir. I connived relentlessly and mercilessly to bring about this vengeance, so much so that I am no longer fit for life. To be consumed by the natural flames of this fire will be a relief from the raging storms of vengeance that have scorched my mind and soul all these years. It is time for you both to let me go. Sigmund, meet your son, Sinfjotli, and Sinfjotli, meet your true father. I have loved you both and loved our family. Go, live your lives and have children of your own. Remember, Sigmund, how you wanted to call your son Helgi, like in the tale of the beloved warrior, Helgi Hjorvardsson. Go and do that. Although I unwillingly married King Siggeir, I am willing to keep him here, to make sure he dies, and to die with him. I am ready for death."

Signy turned and walked into the unforgiving, fiery flames. Sigmund tried to prevent her from fulfilling her fate, but Sinfjotli stopped him. Sigmund stood helpless and horrified, as his twin sister died in the flames. She died with her husband, Siggeir, whom she hated, and upon whom she finally got her vengeance.

Sinfjotli contemplated this new knowledge about himself. That's why he learned so much about his mother's family rather than Siggeir's family. That was why he was trained to kill Siggeir. With this knowledge, everything seemed to make more sense to him. King Sigmund was his true father, not King Siggeir. Bewildered, father and son knowingly looked upon each other for the first time. They grieved the loss of their sister and mother. Yet, they were awestruck, knowing that one had a new son and one had a new father.

That night, Sigmund and Sinfjotli went back to the underground house. They rested and regained their strength, while Sigmund's hands healed. Sigmund prepared for the journey back to Hunaland where he had grown up and where King Volsung had ruled. They gathered up their belongings, found the trusted kinsmen of Signy and, with the ships of Siggeir, made their way to Hunaland. Upon arrival, they were informed that a man named Eirik had set himself up as the ruler. Sigmund confronted Eirik, thanked him for ruling in his absence, and relieved him of his duties. Sigmund took over his rightful claim as ruler and King of Hunaland after his father, King Volsung. With wisdom and fortitude, King Sigmund, with Prince Sinfjotli at his side, brought prosperity and wealth to the kingdom. King Sigmund and Prince Sinfjotli were admired and beloved.

Sigmund sat and looked upon Sinfjotli. He had always thought that Sinfjotli had been the son of Siggeir. The words of his sister had vibrated in his mind and had made his whole body quake. He remembered the female he had encountered near his home in the woods, but he did not understand. He found her fumbling around, and he had been attracted to her. However, she did not look anything like his sister. He had been mystified by her and had allowed her into his home. He gave her food, shelter and later his bed. He had loved her. He was thankful for her companionship, because he had been alone and lonely. Their time together was brief, as she left as mysteriously as she had appeared. The encounter seemed a dream. A lifetime ago… He realized the zeal, stoutheartedness, bravery and fullness of Sinfjotli were all characteristics of his late father, Volsung. Sinfjotli was his own son and rightful heir to the kingdom of Hunaland. Sigmund realized more deeply the extent to which Signy had gone to produce a worthy heir for their father. She had plainly seen the defects of character within her own husband and in her own children with Siggeir. She had deemed them unfit and unworthy of being an heir of King Volsung. She loathed her children's father, Siggeir. Signy knew that every day, Sigmund's life was in danger and any future for him was sketchy and unknown. She had to produce a worthy heir, and the only man alive whom she deemed worthy was her own surviving brother, Sigmund.

Sigmund was humbled and grew in wisdom and strength in his new life. He was a gifted and skillful ruler. He was loved and admired. When he turned his thoughts to producing another heir or heirs, he knew he had to find a trustworthy and noble bride. He thought that when he had another son, he would name him, Helgi, after the beloved tale of Helgi Hjorvardsson, the tale he heard around campfires and halls while growing up with his siblings. He remembered the words of his twin sister, Signy: *Go and have children of your own. Remember, Sigmund, how you wanted to call your son Helgi, like the beloved warrior Helgi Hjorvardson. Go and have children of your own...*

Chapter Twelve
Helgi Sigmundarson

The tale of Helgi Hjorvardsson was one of Sigmund Volsungsson's favourite stories of all the tales, poems, and songs shared in his time. He had pledged that if he had another son, he would name him Helgi. One day Sigmund noticed a beautiful young woman. Although Sinfjotli did not share his enthusiasm for her, it did not deter Sigmund. He learned that her name was Borghild of Bralund, and he courted her as was fitting for a king. Soon Sigmund and Borghild were married. Then, Sigmund did what no other man from his culture had ever been recorded doing. Rather than follow the custom of having his wife live with him in the country of his kin, he chose to move and live with his wife in the country of her kin. Although this was contrary to the traditions of the time, Borghild and Sigmund were happy. Sigmund left Hunaland in the capable hands of two warriors, his trusted friends and brothers-in-arms, James and Brett. Both these warrior-kings had come to Sigmund from other lands. The two men ruled in consultation with experienced elders and with one another. Although some thought that Sinfjotli would be made king, Sigmund felt that he needed more time with his son/nephew and wanted to keep him close. Sigmund chose to take Sinfjotli with him to the land where Borghild and her family lived.

The family settled into their new home, and soon the couple had a son of their own. They named him Helgi, as Sigmund had vowed, after the tale of Helgi Hjorvardsson and in memory of the last words he had heard from his sister, Signy. When the norns knew of the birth of Helgi Sigmundarson, they visited the new baby. They wove the golden threads of the boy's destiny and chanted, in unison, "Helgi Sigmundarson will be a wise warrior, the best prince, a kindly king, and beloved by all."

Sigmund bequeathed similar land to Helgi to what he had given

Sinfjotli. He granted a royal Danish residence called Hringstead on the Island of Zealand. The territories gifted were Snaefjall, Solfjall, Sigarsvoll, Hatun and Himinvangi. Sigmund also gave a brilliant blood snake (a sword) to Helgi.

Helgi was deeply loved by all. He grew strong and wise for his age and became an accomplished young man and warrior. As was the custom, Helgi and Sinfjotli were appointed a foster father, and Sigmund chose a man by the name of Hagal, who had a son named Hamal. Helgi, Sinfjotli and Hamal trained side by side and Sinfjotli, being the elder of the boys, was one of their guides. The young men became skilled in warfare. When Helgi was fifteen, Sinfjotli and Helgi became commanders of armies and they both faced and found triumph in many battles.

Sigmund and Borghild had a second son they named Hamund. The norns visited and chanted over the baby. While Hamund grew not to be warrior-inclined, he grew wise in the knowledge of the ancestors and law and literature.

King Sigmund and another king, by the name of Hunding, were having trouble agreeing on many issues, and minor disputes began to erupt between their two kingdoms. Over time, the disputes grew to feuding and then to bloodshed, as each leader's kinsmen were slowly being killed off. Helgi, the warrior son, was upset by the killings and wanted to help his father, so he came up with a plan. He disguised himself as an elderly man and slowly walked the courts of King Hunding. As he made his way around, he studied the habits and the comings and goings of Hunding's warriors. He wanted to discover their weakness and bring about their defeat. Unfortunately for Helgi, a suspicious soldier that confronted him, recognized him through his facade as Helgi, son of King Sigmund. Helgi ran.

King Hunding was informed of the imposter and immediately ordered the capture of Helgi. His troops stormed the home of Hagal, Helgi's foster father, in order to detain and capture Helgi. King Hunding's men were all around the house of Hagal, and Helgi was trapped with no escape. He had to do something fast, because he did not want to surrender to King Hunding. He disguised himself a second time but, this time, as a servant woman. He threw on a gown and cloak and covered much of his face. While keeping his head down, he began to softly hum a tune while grinding barley into flour. He pretended to pay no attention to the men, as they stormed through the halls, rooms, huts and cabins in their search. With his head down, Helgi quietly focused on the grinding, not wanting to draw any attention to himself. But, as Hunding's troops passed the room, one of the men noticed the woman fiercely grinding, stopped and commented, "Look at that woman with piercing eyes and powerful grinding! She should be wielding a sword rather than grinding corn."

Hagal realized the predicament they were in, as he too had witnessed the fierceness of Helgi's grinding. It was also true that Helgi had piercing eyes and was grinding ferociously. Hagal kept his poise and calmly responded saying, "Oh yes, our servant girl…" Hagal paused and gathered his thoughts. "She was a valkyrie, a strong and strange one, as you can see. But, that was long ago, before Helgi captured, tamed and trained her. Now she is our obedient, loyal servant, who grinds for us all day long."

Hunding's men accepted Hagal's explanation without question, as they were in a rush to capture Helgi and did not want to waste time with a servant girl. They quickly moved on and continued their search by looking into all the other rooms. Once Helgi realized they had passed and that he was in the clear, he slipped out and ran to the warships that Sinfjotli had secured by the sea shore.

Sinfjotli, Helgi, and their kinsmen made their way to King Hunding's kingdom where they engaged in a long and fierce battle. Valkyries were riding in the air, and a beautiful valkyrie, named Sigrun, took Helgi aside and asked him a series of questions. Helgi answered without revealing his identity to her. She already knew who he was and was in love with him. As the battle raged on, she used her shield-maiden abilities in Helgi's favour. Helgi fell in love with the sword-wielding valkyrie, Sigrun. When Helgi struck down King Hunding, the battle ceased, and Hunding's men surrendered. Helgi earned great renown from the winning of this battle.

The sons of King Hunding were saddened and angered by the death of their father and patriarch. They visited Helgi and demanded compensation for the death of their father, but Helgi refused to acknowledge them or their claim for any compensation. The Hunding brothers were angered even more, so they vowed to avenge their father. They quickly planned a battle strategy, besieged Helgi, and another fierce battle ensued. The valkyries rode within the second battle and again favoured Helgi. He fought valiantly and was again victorious in battle against the Hundings. The sons of King Hunding realized they were not as skilled in battle techniques as were Helgi and his men. They soon lost their lives. After this battle, Helgi received the nickname of Hundingsbani, meaning the bane or killer of Hunding. He was then known as Helgi Sigmundarson Hundingsbani.

Helgi and Sigrun, by Johannes Gehrts

Chapter Thirteen:
Helgi Sigmundarson Hundingsbani

After the battle of the Hundings, the valkyries gathered themselves alongside the forest, checking their blood-strewn shields, armour and weapons for any damages and cleaning their weaponry with the grass, hay, leaves and other foliage from the forest. Helgi looked upon the magnificent women warriors with awe and reverence. He owed the warrior women his life, as they helped secure his victory in the battle. His eyes beheld one that, for him, stood above all the rest. He was transfixed. He approached the armour-clad woman, and he realized that she was the same one that had taken him aside during the battle. She was the woman of his dreams. He asked her name.

"I am Sigrun, the daughter of King Hogni."

Helgi replied, "Sigrun, daughter of King Hogni, I am Helgi, son of King Sigmund. I am indebted to you and the valkyries for my victory. I am at your service, my lady."

The young woman smiled graciously at Helgi, but she appeared somewhat troubled. Helgi questioned her. "Forgive me, my lady, but have I done something to displease you?"

Sigrun replied, "Oh no, of course not, Helgi, son of King Sigmund. I am honoured to have fought by your side and to help secure this battle victory. What troubles me is that my father betrothed me to Hodbrodd, a son of King Granmar. Unfortunately, I think him worse than a troll, and I fiercely despise him. I have watched you in battle, and it is you that I have chosen from all others. Would you be willing to fight prince Hodbrodd and take me away with you?"

Helgi said, "You have my sword, and my word of honour, that I will do as you wish."

Helgi called all his troops of warriors, gathered up the warrior women, placed them on his ships and proceeded to sail home. Not long after, an unexpected storm broke loose upon them, and Helgi ordered all the ships to assemble together and row into the shelter of the nearest fjord. They all made it to shore. Sigrun and the valkyries used their preternatural powers to protect Helgi's ships from the storm and directed Helgi's men to a safe harbour.

Sinfjotli had also been guiding the ships, and once they had landed into a safe harbour, an unknown man came to a ship and asked them who they were. The man was guided to Sinfjotli's ship and was greatly impressed with Sinfjotli's presence, as he wore a shining silver helmet and a white tailcoat, and he carried a shield rimmed with gold and a spear adorned with a magnificent banner. The man expressed that he was Gudmund, the brother of Hodbrodd and a son of King Granmar. Sinfjotli and Gudmund engaged themselves in a furious flyting, until Helgi intervened, stating it was better to fight with weapons rather than to spar with words. Gudmund rode home and told his father and brother that Helgi, Sinfjolti and their men had come. King Granmar gathered an army that included Sigrun's father, King Hogni, and her brothers, Bragi and Dag.

A savage battle between Helgi and Hodbrodd unfolded. The valkyries favoured Helgi, and those who were observing the battle said, "It was like looking into a blazing fire!"

Sigrun, in valkyrie form, arrived and shielded Helgi from the blows of battle. Helgi and Hodbrodd battled, and Helgi gave the man his death blow, just as he had vowed to Sigrun that he would. He soon took over all the lands of King Granmar and Sigrun's father, King Hogni, who had both died in the battle, along with Sigrun's brother, Bragi. Her other brother, Dag, although wounded, survived the battle. In his heart he vowed to avenge his father and brother, but outwardly he swore oaths of allegiance to Helgi and Sinfjotli, the sons of King Sigmund.

Helgi became king and married Sigrun, and they ruled for a long time. They loved one another dearly and had many children. The first of their sons they named Viglundur. Then came Andres and Trausti. Their daughters were Ila, Steinunn and Julia. They were said to be of the Ylfings, or the wolf clan, descendants of the god, Odin. Helgi confided in Sigrun that it was he who had killed her father and brother in the battle. Sigrun was deeply in love with Helgi, and her heart and mind were free of vengeful thinking. She already knew and had forgiven him. Dag, on the other hand, knew it was Helgi who killed his family, but he was torn between the deep desire to avenge his father and brother, and of the brotherhood oaths he had sworn to Helgi.

For years, Dag sacrificed daily to Odin on this matter. He never heard anything from Odin, but he persisted in beseeching the AllFather every day. Finally, one day, Dag received an answer. A spear was resting against a wall in his hall. He approached the spear, and it radiated and vibrated. He realized he was looking at Gungnir, the mighty spear of Odin. Odin wanted Helgi to rule with him in Valhalla, but Helgi always won his battles, and the valkyries always favoured Helgi, no matter what Odin said. Odin lent Dag his spear. Dag was surprised by this! What an answer! What an honour! With the spear in his hands, Dag felt invincible. He visited the unsuspecting Helgi and placed the spear right through his heart. Helgi died instantly with the spear of Odin through him.

As Odin retrieved Gungnir, it disappeared from the site Dag had left it. Dag entered the hall where Sigrun was, and confessed that he had finally avenged their father and brother by killing Helgi. Sigrun was shocked and screamed in horror. "No! You have no idea what you have done!"

She loved Helgi and had forgiven him long ago for the deaths of her kin. She turned to Dag and openly cursed him. "From this day forward, you and all your descendants are cursed. You will live wretched and woeful lives, if you are given any life at all."

Dag said, "It was Odin who killed Helgi. Odin lent me his spear. It was his spear that killed Helgi. Sigrun, Odin wants Helgi to rule with him in Valhalla. I was only doing what Odin wanted. For the death of Helgi, I offer you whatever compensation you wish."

"There is nothing in this earthly realm that could ever compensate for the life you have taken. You have killed my love, my husband, the father of our children, and the father of your nieces and nephews, no less! You have killed me as well! All I want to do is die and be with my beloved Helgi. I curse you and any family you may have of your own."

Sigrun Goes To Helgi's Grave Chamber, by Johannes Gehrts

Sigrun ran to where Helgi was and cried over him. With the aid of her trusted folk, she gathered herself together and prepared the funeral feast for her husband, the father of their children. A burial mound was built for Helgi. She made arrangements for the fostering of the children, for she knew her time was near. She refused any earthly things for herself. She refused to eat, as she had lost her will to live. All she wanted to do was die and be with her beloved, Helgi.

To no avail, people tried to convince Sigrun otherwise. People tried to comfort her, letting her know that Helgi was now helping Odin rule Valhalla. Helgi was a great warrior, and Odin wanted him. It was also surmised that Dag, in helping to obtain Helgi, did just what Odin wanted. It was also said that, in Valhalla, Helgi found Hunding and humiliated him by making him do the work of a slave. All this talk and knowledge of Helgi being honoured in Valhalla gave Sigrun no comfort.

Meanwhile, in Midgard, a servant maiden of Sigrun said she saw Helgi riding outside of his grave. She ran and told her queen. The broken-hearted Sigrun rushed to the grave mound where Helgi had been sighted and, to her bewildered eyes, she too saw Helgi. She greeted him with all her love and affection, and the two embraced. Helgi was gentle and silently spoke with her. He let her know that he soon would be leaving for Valhalla and would not be able to come back to her. She was contented by resting in his arms on his gravesite, and she made her bed there. Helgi's men came for him when it was time to go to Valhalla. He said his last farewells to his beloved Sigrun and then rode away with his men. Hoping for Helgi to return, Sigrun visited the grave mound everyday. But, he did not return. While lying on the grave mound of her beloved Helgi, Sigrun died of a broken heart.

The families and households of Sigrun and Helgi honoured Sigrun with a Viking burial, burying her beside her beloved husband, Helgi, so that they may rest in peace together for eternity. Although she had been a wife and mother, she was also a vibrant valkyrie and a skilled warrior woman. Many believe that Helgi Sigmundarson and Sigrun Hognadottir were the spirits of Helgi Hjorvardsson and Svava Eylimadottir reincarnated.

A Viking Burial, by Mackenzie Lynne Stewart (2023)

Chapter Fourteen
Sinfjotli Sigmundarson

Although Sigmund was considered the King of Hunaland, he lived with his wife's family in Denmark. News spread of the great loss of Helgi and his wife. Sigmund was deeply grieved by the loss of his son, Helgi, and his daughter-in-law, Sigrun. A fitting funeral feast was prepared for them both. Many knew that Odin wanted Helgi beside him in Valhalla to rule over the einherjar and to prepare for the battle of Ragnarok. Although Sigrun had made arrangements for the fostering of her and Helgi's children, Sigmund wanted to shelter and raise his own grandchildren.

The children were brought to the halls of Sigmund, and he found that having them present was like a healing and nurturing balm for his grieving soul. After Sigmund's sorrow became bearable, he turned to his son, Sinfjotli. Sigmund knew that Odin wanted Helgi, and he felt that the AllFather would surely want Sinfjotli, as well. But, Sigmund hoped that Sinfjotli would outlive him.

While Sinfjotli was on an excursion, he met a lovely maiden, in whom he was captivated and charmed. Her name was Osk Sigurbjorg. Their friendship turned into love and they expressed the desire to marry. At that time, another man, named Vilheim, also wanted to marry the same beautiful woman. He told Sinfjotli that he was a better match for the young Osk, but Sinfjotli disagreed. The two men engaged in a battle and fought for Osk Sigurbjorg's hand in marriage. Sinfjotli was the victor. He had never met the man named Vilheim before, and did not know who he was or where he had come from. After his death, another man revealed to Sinfjotli the identity of Vilheim. Sinfjotli was distraught with the knowledge. The man he had killed was the brother of his stepmother, Borghild!

Osk and Sinfjotli were free to pursue their goal of marriage. Osk took her beloved to meet with her family, where Sinfjotli officially asked her father and mother, Thorstein and Terri, for her hand in marriage. Both her father and her mother were delighted and impressed with Sinfjotli and accepted the proposal. Sigmund and Borghild were invited, and a fine wedding feast was held in the home of Thorstein, where the two were betrothed. After the celebrations, Osk Sigurbjorg and Sinfjotli went to live in the halls of King Sigmund and Borghild. Sigmund was happy to have his son and his new daughter-in-law with him, along with the children of Helgi and Sigrun. Although there was happiness to share, Sinfjotli had to reveal to his father the sorry tale about Vilheim.

After Sinfjotli had been home a short while, he confided in his father about the events that brought about the death of his stepmother's brother. He offered to pay a wergild, and Sigmund agreed. Borghild had not heard anything about the comings and goings of her brother and, when Sigmund told her the fate of Vilheim, he offered her a wergild of anything she wanted. But, she was not appeased and flew into a furious rage. She demanded that Sinfjotli be cast out of the kingdom. Sigmund reminded her of their law and would not send his son away. Since Sinfjotli had confessed to the killing, the death was considered a manslaughter and the punishment was a wergild. If he had not confessed and was found out, then the death would be murder with the punishment of exile. Borghild wanted exile, but instead was offered a huge compensation for the manslaughter.

"We will compensate you with gold, wealth, and all you desire for the death of your brother."

Borghild was furious and would not be consoled. She knew she could not have her own way. Sigmund was abiding by the law. She turned to Sigmund and said, "I realize, Sigmund, that you are not only my husband but also my king. You have authority over me, and I must do as you wish."

The body of Vilheim had already been buried. Borghild spent time in contemplation and arranged for a proper funeral feast for her brother.

She let Sigmund and everyone know about her distress, and that her stepson, Sinfjotli, was the cause of her brother's death. Osk, being with child, remained in their own halls and did not attend the funeral feast. At the feast, Borghild began to serve the drink. With vengeance on her mind, she made a special brew and served a horn to Sinfjotli.

"Here is a drink for you, stepson." She smiled upon him with her eyes aflame.

Sinfjotli looked inside of the horn and was aghast. He said, "The drink is dusty."

Sigmund, an experienced drinker, said, "Then, give it to me." And, he drank the horn. Sigmund could handle poison both internally and externally. Sinfjotli could handle poison externally, but not internally.

Borghild turned to Sinfjotli and asked him, "Why do you let other men drink your ale for you? Are you not old enough to drink on your own?"

She then left and soon came back with another horn for Sinfjotli. This time she said, "Here… I brought another drink for you, stepson!" and she taunted him with many unkind words.

He took the horn from her and again looked inside. He saw that the drink was all grimy and messy and said, "This brew is blended with betrayal."

Sigmund again said, "Give it here, son." And Sigmund drank from the second horn.

She left again, returned and gave a third horn to Sinfjotli. She said, "You will like this drink. Refresh your thirst, son, if you have the heart of your grandfather, Volsung."

Sinfjotli again took the horn and saw that the drink was poisoned: "This mead is murky."

By this time, Sigmund was drunk, and he said, "With your moustache, filter the slosh, son."

It seemed a wise statement at the time, and Sinfjotli did what his father suggested. He drank from the horn while attempting to filter the poison with his moustache. As Sinfjotli drank from the third horn, Borghild looked on and smiled a gleeful and gruesome grin and then wholeheartedly laughed out loud. No sooner had Sinfjotli started to drink, when he keeled over, and fell to the floor.

Sigmund was shocked. He heaved and rose in horror. He held his son in his arms, as Sinfjotli took his last breath. Sigmund wailed in sorrow. He could not believe what had happened right in front of him. His son had died. He held Sinfjotli's body and groaned. He gently lifted his son into his strong arms and carried him out of the hall. He left his fortress and carried him for some time. He sojourned through a forest and to a long and narrow fjord. It was not known if Sigmund knew where he was taking Sinfjotli. He may have wanted to take him home to Hunaland. With Sinfjotli in his arms, he approached the waters of the fjord and saw a ferryman with a small boat.

Odin takes the corpse of Sinfjötli, by Johannes Gehrts

The ferryman asked, "Do you want passage across the fjord?"

Sigmund stooped over and answered, "Yes. And, what is your name, kind one?"

The man stated, "I am Harbard, the ferryman. As you can see my boat is small, and I can only take one person at a time."

Sigmund said, "That is good, my fine Harbard. Can you deliver my son first to the opposite shore? I will wait for you to come back or walk around the fjord."

"As you wish," said the ferryman.

Sigmund gently laid Sinfjotli into the boat, and the ferryman braced his oars and rowed his boat across the fjord.

The Death of Sinfjotli, by Jenny Nyström

Sigmund's eyes followed the boat as it departed, and he decided to walk along the shore and watch the boat as it carried Sinfotli across the fjord. As he was walking, a loud thunder cracked through the sky and massive splashing noises filled the fjord. He was momentarily blinded by a huge flash of light. As the light subsided, he saw the boat, the ferryman and his son all vanish within a brilliant stream of swirling coloured lights. A rainbow mist settled slowly over the fjord, as the sky and water grew quiet. The rainbow mists were the fine remnants of the rainbow bridge, Bifrost, that connected Midgard, the land of the humans with Asgard, the land of the gods. Sigmund fell to his knees. He was left alone watching over the waters. He stayed by the fjord awhile and beseeched Odin, the AllFather, to guide and accompany his son, Sinfjotli, in the world of the afterlife. He realized Harbard, the ferryman, was Odin in one of his many disguises. Sigmund was sorrowful to lose Sinfjotli, yet he was comforted in the knowledge that Odin had personally taken Sinfjotli with him over the Rainbow bridge to Asgard and then to Valhalla. He also realized that Odin was speaking to him in a calming deep voice, telling him that Sinfjotli would rule in Valhalla alongside him and with his other son, Helgi. This was truly an honour. Sigmund, in his sorrow, felt a sense of serenity in this knowledge and thanked Odin. He realized how much he had loved Sinfjotli, and now he could finally let his son go in peace, knowing he was with the AllFather.

Sigmund made his journey back home. He had gone further than he had thought while carrying Sinfjotli. When he reached home, the funeral feasting for Vilheim was over. He made his way to the woman he had called his wife.

Borghild stopped what she was doing and said nothing, as Sigmund glared at her. He tore the jewels and all the finery from her. She gasped. He threw her to the ground and said, "You, who I thought loved me, have betrayed me and my son. You are undeserving of being my wife and queen. I loved you and trusted you, when all you sought was your own vengeance against my son. You are nothing but a wretched and betraying witch of a woman."

Before Borghild could get up, he horsewhipped her. She screamed and begged for mercy. He had never treated any woman in this manner before. He stopped himself and declared, "You are no longer my wife. You are no longer queen. You have murdered my son with intent, and you have not confessed to your crime. Therefore, I declare you exiled.

You are no longer accepted here or in any other kingdom. You are cast out, never to return."

With that, he left her and let all the people of the kingdoms know of the cruel crime Borghild had committed with the intentional killing of his first-born son, her own stepson, Sinfjotli. He drove her out of the home and lands they once shared as a family. Before he cast her out, he held her up and declared, "My loyal people, I let it be known to you, of this day, that this woman whom you have come to know as Borghild, my wife and queen, has betrayed me and thereby has betrayed you. She has connived and poisoned and intentionally killed my son, her stepson, and your prince, Sinfjotli. She hereby is no longer my wife and no longer your queen. She is no longer queen of any land. She is cast out from them all. I tell you that you, nor any of your kinsmen, shall help or console her. You are to pass this message to all towns and villages, that no one is to help this wretched woman. She is an outcast. Be gone with you, woman."

With that, he let her go. Borghild, once queen, the woman who had it all, was exiled with nothing and no one to console her. All shunned her. She lived the rest of her shortened life in humiliation and shame. All adhered to what Sigmund had said. No one helped her, and no one consoled her. As an outcast, she could be killed by anyone who saw her. Yet, no one killed her, and she soon died a wretched outcast in her own homeland.

A funeral feast was given for Sinfjotli. Sigmund was grief-stricken. He had lost his son Helgi, his daughter-in-law Sigrun, his son Sinfjotli and was betrayed by the woman he loved and had thought loved him. He looked around and, finding nothing for him, he longed for home.

After the feast, he let it be known to all that his son, Hamund, who was knowledgeable in literature, law and the teachings of the ancients, would be the people's king and would rule the lands in his place. To Hamund, he gave the lands that he had given to Helgi, to look after while the children of Helgi were still young. While Helgi had been the warrior son, Hamund had been the learned son and had grown into a wise and beloved scholar.

A great ceremony and feast was held for the passing of the kingship to Hamund. He accepted the responsibilities that his father had bestowed upon him and swore oaths of honour to his father and to his new position as king.

Once all was done, Sigmund gathered up Sinfjotli's widow, Osk, the children of Helgi and Sigrun and their foster family, and left the land of Hamund's mother, and returned to his own kingdom of Hunaland. Sigmund was happy to be home in Hunaland, and soon Osk gave birth to a baby girl she named Emily. Sigmund was delighted with another grandchild, and the family had a name-giving ceremony for the new baby. The norns came and sang and chanted over Emily. The children loved the norns. Sigmund found a special love with his grandchildren, as they showered him with hugs and kisses. He focused all of his love, as he still had lots to give, on the young folk. They were educated and trained as was fitting for princes and princesses. They were especially interested when Sigmund told them the mighty tale of Helgi Hjarvardsson. And the tales of the lives of Helgi, Sigrun and Sinfjotli lived within their young hearts. Sigmund's love for all of his grandchildren and their love for him began to heal his broken heart. The children brightened his days.

His friends and comrades-in-arms, whom Sigmund had left in charge of Hunaland, were happy to see him return. King Jamie, King Brett and the elders had run Hunaland efficiently and peacefully in his absence. The kingship was given back to Sigmund with celebrations and feasts. Sigmund was known to have ruled Hunaland with fairness and peace, and he is remembered as the greatest of warriors and the wisest of all kings of the ancient times.

Chapter Fifteen
Hjordis Eylimadottir

While Sigmund was ruling his kingdom of Hunaland, he heard of a famous and powerful king called King Eylimi, who was married to a beautiful woman named Kimberlee. The king and queen had a refined young daughter considered to be the fairest and wisest woman in the land. Sigmund felt that she may be a good match for him, for although he had the love of his household and grandchildren, he desired a wife and companion. He gathered together a small group of trusted men and journeyed to visit King Eylimi. Upon arrival, he was treated with honour and respect. When meeting with Hjordis, he was enamoured by her elegance, delicacy, and exquisite beauty. She had long, flowing white hair, which was arranged in a refined manner. Her eyes sparkled a radiant blue. She wore a blue embroidered gown adorned with a necklace of amber. They sat together speaking of their lives. She was kind and gentle. Sigmund realized that all that he had heard about her was true and much more. He was pleasantly surprised and formally asked King Eylimi for Hjordis's hand in marriage. The King approved of the arrangement, as the family alliances were agreeable to him. Although King Sigmund was older, Hjordis was fascinated with Sigmund, and she also approved of the arrangement. Preparations for a grand marriage feast commenced for the betrothed couple.

Many came to the wedding feast, and amongst them was a surviving son of King Hunding by the name of King Lyngvi. This was a surprise, because most people thought that all the sons of King Hunding had been killed by Helgi, son of Sigmund.

Once King Lyngvi saw Hjordis, he was smitten and wanted her for himself. He boldly approached King Eylimi and asked for Hjordis's hand in marriage. King Eylimi was taken aback and said, "King Lyngvi, as you can see, this is the marriage feast for my daughter Hjordis and King Sigmund, with whom she is already betrothed."

King Lyngvi replied, "As the marriage has not taken place and has not been consummated, there is still time for a change of mind."

Lyngvi added, "King Eylimi, as we all can see, Hjordis is a young woman, and King Sigmund is an old man, much too old for her. I am a young man and more suitable for her. We can share a life together, have many children and grow old together. Also, the family alliances would carry impressive advantages for both our families."

King Eylimi stated that a new development had come forth that required some attention, and he would need to delay the marriage festivities. King Eylimi contemplated the new development. He decided that his daughter's marriage to either king would bring a good alliance.

King Lyngvi was pleased that King Eylimi gave him such attention and respect and continued to try to sway King Eylimi to his favour. He continued, "Why marry her off to an old man when she can have a young man more suited to her age?"

King Eylimi responded, "She is already betrothed to King Sigmund, but I have decided to bring the question to Hjordis and see what her thoughts are on this matter."

He turned to his daughter and said, "I trust you, my child, for you are a sensible and knowledgeable young woman. Although tradition states that the father shall choose a husband for his daughter, today I forfeit that tradition and allow you to make your own choice. Hjordis, you can marry either King Lyngvi or King Sigmund. I will honour the decision you make." Letting a daughter make her own decision of who to marry was a rare occurrence and, it was setting a precedent. For political reasons, marriage was usually arranged to form alliances between strong families. Since marriage to either king would be a good alliance, King Eylimi gave the decision for his daughter to choose. Which man could she love and live with?

Hjordis contemplated this new development and was grateful for the opportunity to make her own choice. She turned to her mother for counsel and spoke with her awhile. Then, she privately spoke with King Lyngvi for a while, and then privately spoke with King Sigmund for a while. She looked to herself, and envisioned who she could love and be devoted to. She made up her mind, returned to her father and said, "Father, I am grateful to you for this freedom to appoint my own companion. To decide between the two worthy men before me has been challenging. King Lyngvi offers his youth and a life together. King Sigmund offers his experience and the wisdom that comes with his age. Although I have found this decision difficult, I have deeply meditated upon this and have come to a decision."

Hjordis turned to King Lyngvi and said, "I see that you are a young and accomplished man. You hold great promise for any young woman that you may wed. I thank you for the great gift of your fond attention and your generous offer of marriage. I understand that such a union would benefit both our families, and I wish for the best for you and your family."

Hjordis then turned to Sigmund and said, "I see, Sigmund that you are an older and more experienced man. I have found it within myself that I could live with you and love you. I choose to be betrothed to you."

With these words, all cheered, and King Eylimi, again, gave his daughter, Hjordis, to King Sigmund. The wedding feasting and celebrations continued, as the music had never ceased, and many people had kept dancing and celebrating during the delay. The full wedding ceremony commenced, and King Sigmund and Hjordis were married. Celebration of their vows continued for three days. All were happy and rejoicing. People commented that this was the first time they had ever been to a ceremony where a father gave his daughter away twice, on the same night, to the same king!

King Lyngvi was not happy. He scowled and inwardly growled. He was extremely insulted, although Hjordis's words were kindly and calming, they were also true. She could live with and love Sigmund, but not him. He could not face the defeat, and he left the feast.

After the wedding festivities ended, Sigmund invited Hjordis and her family to live with him in Hunaland. They decided to go, and

Sigmund attended to his kingdom. King Eylimi set up a group of skillful people to manage his kingdom. King Sigmund recommended King Jamie or King Brett, yet King Eylimi stated the kingdom was in the capable hands of his son, Gripir, a great prophet and seer. With grand celebrations, the kingship was given to Gripir Eylimason and the elders. Upon the arrival in Hunaland, King Eylimi and Hjordis were thrilled to see all of Sigmund's grandchildren. They enjoyed a wonderful life and happiness in Hunaland.

In the meantime, King Lyngvi gathered an army to defeat King Sigmund in Hunaland. King Sigmund was warned of the coming attack and he gathered his men for battle. When King Lyngvi and his men arrived, King Sigmund was prepared. A battle ensued and raged on for days. King Lyngvi's men were merciless, and the fierce fighting continued. Queen Hjordis, the children and her bondwomen were driven into the forest for protection during the battle.

Sigmund's valkyrie maiden shielded him during the battle. One day, as all the men were fighting, a single man, tall in stature, walked unencumbered through the battlefield. He wore a grey hooded cloak and a wide-brimmed hat on his head that sloped over his face. One could see that he had only one eye, but that one eye pierced right through one's soul. He walked slowly and methodically, as if in slow-motion, right through the battlefield, untouched by the chaos of the men fighting all around him. He carried a mighty spear in his right hand. He advanced up to King Sigmund, who was fighting with one of Lyngvi's men. The unknown man raised his spear before King Sigmund. At that moment, Sigmund thought the man with the spear was another one of King Lyngvi's men, and he instinctively struck the man's spear with his sword. Once his sword clashed against the mighty spear, a huge clang erupted and vibrated all around. The electrified air made a crackling sound and flashing lights blinded the sky. When the light subsided, Sigmund's sword was broken into two pieces.

Sigmund stood stunned and motionless, as the grey-cloaked man who had been in front of him vanished. He realized that he had flung his sword against the mighty magical spear of Odin. He now stood with a broken sword with which to fight, and he was defenceless. The battle raged on and grew more savage. Sigmund's shield-maiden also knew that the man with the spear was Odin, and that Sigmund had been chosen by Odin to follow him to Valhalla. Sigmund quickly fetched the other piece of his sword and secured it. He had to battle with half a sword, and his adversaries took advantage of the man with the broken sword. Sigmund sustained a slew of injuries. When he fell, he was left for dead. King Eylimi also fell in the battle and died.

Once the two kings had fallen, King Lyngvi advanced to the royal estate. Searching for Hjordis, he tore through all the rooms, but he did not find her. He became furious, and thought that she could not have gone far. He stationed his men throughout the area to search for her. He believed that, since Sigmund fell, all of King Volsung's kin must be dead, and he had finally gotten revenge for the killings of his family. He felt relieved, because now his family would have nothing to fear from them. At first, King Lyngvi and his men stayed in the royal estate. They gathered their dead, buried them and then moved on. Lyngvi stationed some men in the nearby villages to keep a look out for Hjordis.

Under a blanket of trees and foliage, the women had been hiding in the nearby forest. When they knew King Lyngvi and his men were gone, they slowly began to emerge, searching for their loved ones on the battlefield. After making sure the children were securely hidden in the forest, Hjordis also slowly emerged from her hiding place. She silently searched the slain for Sigmund. When she found him, she discovered that he was still alive! Hjordis hoped that Sigmund would live and gently held him in her arms, resting his head in her lap. With hope in her heart, she whispered, "Sigmund, my love… Let me heal your wounds."

Hjordis goes to Sigmund, by Johannes Gehrts

Sigmund moaned, "Hjordis, my wounds are too deep, and I am beyond healing."

He looked to Hjordis and told her, "Odin came to me in the battlefield. I thought he was one of Lyngvi's men. He raised his spear at me, and I flung my sword to prevent his strike. As soon as my sword hit his spear, there was a loud clanging noise and a blinding flash of light. When the light vanished, the man was gone, my sword was broken in two, and I was standing there, defenceless. I know the man with the spear was Odin, the AllFather. He no longer wishes for me to fight for him. While it pleased him, in his name I have battled in many wars. But now, it is time for me to go to be with him and my sons in Valhalla."

With tears in her eyes, Hjordis cried, "Sigmund, you need to be healed and live and love me and take revenge for these killings, as my father lies dead not far from you."

It was believed that when one was close to death, one could see the future. Sigmund gave a sigh and said, "My love, the revenge is meant for someone else. Someone you love and trust… My time here has come to an end. Listen, my love, and look within yourself, Hjordis. You are a beautiful young woman, and you are carrying our son."

Sigmund slowly moved his battered arm to feel her belly and smiled. "Live, Hjordis. Stay alive, healthy and well, for yourself and for our son. Be strong, my beautiful young wife, and raise our son lovingly, thoughtfully and carefully. His name is Sigurd, and he will become a superior swordsman, and an accomplished and admirable warrior. I see him riding a magnificent horse and wielding this gift from Odin in the form of a reforged sword called Gram. Take the broken pieces of my sword, my love, and guard them well, for one day, our son, Sigurd, will come to you seeking them to reforge the new sword."

Sigmund gave the pieces of the sword to Hjordis, and she secured them.

"Hjordis, I have loved you, my fair and radiant queen. Go from this place, stay alive and live your life. Our son, Sigurd, will rule and be the champion of our family line. He will long be remembered, and I am happy and content with this knowledge."

Sigmund's eyes closed. Hjordis stayed with her love and held him, until he breathed his last breath. She knew he would find his way to Valhalla, as he had died of battle wounds.

Away to Valhalla, by Johannes Gehrts

Forlorn, she wept over him. She felt Sigmund's sword, broken in two. Her heart, like the sword, was also broken. A new day was dawning, and women began running and yelling for others to get off of the field, as ships were arriving. Some yelled that King Lyngvi was coming back. As the women ran from the battlefield to hide again within the forest, Hjordis gently laid Sigmund to the ground and, with the broken pieces of the sword secured, she got up and ran, as well. She had to move quickly, as she heard the warnings of ships landing on the shores.

Hjordis found the children, the foster family and a loyal bondwoman. She said, "Thora, help me. We must protect my unborn son. Wear my clothing, and I will wear yours. If we are caught, you will say you are the king's daughter and use my name. I will stay close by you, as your bondwoman."

Hjordis wanted to protect her unborn child and did not want anyone to know her identity. The two women quickly exchanged their clothes and accessories. The devoted Thora did everything that Hjordis asked of her.

The man who landed was not King Lyngvi, but a prince named, Alf, a son of King Hjalprek of Denmark. He had seen the carnage of men strewn about and the women rushing into the forest. He told his men to gather all the women and children and bring them to him. This was done efficiently and quickly, as most of the women had not enough time to secure their hiding places. When the women were brought before Alf, he noticed the woman dressed like royalty, and he told his men to bring her to him. As she stood trembling, he asked, "Who are you?"

Thora bowed her head and slowly glanced at Hjordis. The hidden queen made a slight nod that it was imperative she behave as a queen and tell her story. The bondwoman told Alf that she was a king's daughter and wife of King Sigmund, and then about the events that had taken place.

Alf asked, "Where are the king's treasures?"

Thora's eyes opened wide and again sought out Hjordis, who made an affirmative, hidden nod, and the bondwoman showed the way to the treasure. Alf gathered some of his men, and they secured the treasure to the ships. Once the treasure was loaded, they gathered all the women, children and survivors and placed them in the ships, as well. When all were ready, they set sail for Denmark. Alf kept the woman he thought was a queen and her bondwoman close to him. He examined the two women carefully and observed many inconsistencies.

Once in Denmark, the treasure and the women and children were all inspected by Alf's mother, Queen Kathi. She became curious about one of the bondwomen. In private, to Alf she commented, "The woman dressed as a queen does not behave as refined as the woman dressed as her bondwoman. It appears the bondwoman is the more enlightened one."

Alf agreed. "Yes, mother… I have noted this, as well. I must put these women to a test."

Alf called for the queen and her bondwoman to be brought before him. Hjordis, disguised as a bondwoman, and the bondwoman, disguised as the queen, came in. He first questioned the woman dressed as a queen. "As the sun appears over the horizon, how do you know when it is morning and time to get up, if you cannot see the heavenly bodies?"

Thora thought to herself, *I can answer that question*, and she said, "Since childhood, I was given ale and I would drink that and fall asleep. When I woke up, I would know it was daytime."

Alf made a little chuckle, as he was surprised by what she had said. He smiled and said, "That certainly is curious behaviour for a king's daughter!"

He then asked Hjordis. "As the sun peeks over the horizon, how do you know when it is morning and time to get up, if you cannot see the celestial bodies?"

Hjordis looked to her one little golden ring and responded, "Just before the first flush of the morning, this little ring that my loving father gave me chills my finger, and I know it is time to get up."

Alf was then convinced that Hjordis was the true queen and said, "I knew you were not who you have portrayed yourself to be, and I have rarely known of a maidservant having a golden ring. You are the true queen, and there is no need for you to hide from me. So, you must be Hjordis, and this other woman must be Thora, who is dressed in your clothes."

Thora made a little shriek and nearly fainted. Hjordis held her arms out to her, and she embraced the terrified maidservant. "Thora, my dear… Be calm, all will be well."

Alf then said to Hjordis and Thora, "You need not be afraid of me, for I have no intentions of harming you or any of the survivors of the battle. I have treated all of you with respect and dignity. In all honesty, I have been fascinated by you two women. Young Thora, you are a devoted and loyal maidservant, and for that you shall be greatly rewarded. Hjordis, I have studied you since I first saw you. Your mannerisms gave you away long before my test. You have shown that you are delicate, cultivated, elegant, refined and beautiful, even in your maidservant's clothing. Your voice is soft, yet confident, and you know how to treat and converse with royalty and warriors."

For a moment, Alf looked upon the two women and then turned

again to Hjordis. "Hjordis, daughter of King Eylimi, now that it has been confirmed who you truly are, I will treat you even better than when you first came. I wish to make you my wife and queen. I see that you are with child, and you will be cared for. When the child comes, I will pay for your dowry."

Hjordis and Alf sat beside one another, and she told him her life story. She told him about the children of Helgi and Sigrun, about Osk and her child Emily. Alf had all the family brought before him and introduced himself. The children were tired and scared. They had lost their mother and their father and, now, their grandfather. As children, they had witnessed the ravages of war. Osk and Emily fared a little better, as Osk was older and Emily too young to remember. Shelly, the sister of Alf, comforted the children. They were given baths, food and their own rooms. They were treated with honour, as was fitting for princes and princesses. Shelly and the kinswomen of Hjordis watched over the children, Osk and Emily. Their needs were attended to. Hjordis grieved the loss of her husband, father, kinsmen and home. She expressed her sorrow for leaving her deceased husband, father and kinsmen on the shores. She wished for them a proper funeral. Alf offered to help her and agreed that this would be fitting for the two kings.

He sent messengers to the shores of Hunaland. Lyngvi had already retrieved his dead warriors, buried them and left. King Alf, Hjordis, Thora, and trusted folk sailed back and gathered their dead. A funeral pyre was made. King Sigmund and King Eylimi were placed in a small ship that was set ablaze and let go from the harbour to burn out at sea. When Alf, Hjordis and Thora returned, they had a funeral feast for King Sigmund, King Eylimi and the fallen warriors. Hjordis, Osk, and the children felt more at peace.

During these times together, Alf had fallen in love with the exquisite Hjordis. He kept her safe and as comfortable as he could, as she was to give birth. She cared for Alf, as he was kind, decent, giving, sharing, loving and honest with her. She gave birth to a son, as King Sigmund had foretold.

Hjordis and her son were brought before King Hjalprek, and he was very pleased to see the boy with the piercing blue eyes. The boy was sprinkled with water and named Sigurd, as King Sigmund had called him. The norns visited and sang and chanted over the boy. The children were enchanted with the norns. King Hjalprek betrothed Hjordis to his son, King Alf, and her dowry was finalized. Alf and Hjordis were married, and they loved one another. Alf and Hjordis raised Sigurd and the children of Helgi and Sigrun as their own. Osk Sigurbjorg and Emily were also well taken care of. Everyone in the kingdom loved and accepted them all as royalty.

Chapter Sixteen
Sigurd Sigmundarson

Sigurd's early life was a good one. Along with his nieces and nephews, he was raised as a king and queen's child and given the many privileges of royalty. At the time, it was customary for all sons and daughters to have a foster father and Regin, the son of Hreidmar, offered to be the foster father to Sigurd. Although Regin was a man small in stature, he had impressive strength, was cultivated in many skills, knew the writings of the runes, spoke in many languages and was skilled in magic. The kings recognized Regin's extensive knowledge and excellent wisdom. When Sigurd was a child, Regin introduced him to an array of physical sports, the skill of wielding a sword, bending a bow, throwing a spear and riding a horse. He also taught mental sports, like playing chess, Hnefatafl (Viking Chess) and other mentally stimulating games. As was customary for a prince, he taught Sigurd to read, to write in runes and to speak in several different languages.

Regin revealed to Sigurd all the stories he knew of Sigurd's ancestors, from Sigi Odinsson to Rerir Sigasson, Volsung Rerisson and his father, Sigmund Volsungsson. Regin also chanted and sang the songs, poems and stories of Sigurd's half-brothers, Sinfjotli, Hamund and Helgi, and how Helgi was named after the mythological tale of Helgi Hjorvardsson. His brother, Hamund, was a king in his own right and ruled the area that King Sigmund once ruled and where Hamund's mother once lived. Sigurd played and trained with his nieces and nephews. Although they were a little older than him, Sigurd was a quick learner and began to shine with them. All the children felt secure and happy living in King Hjalprek and Queen Kathi's kingdom. Regin told Sigurd the life story of his mother, Hjordis, and how she came to be the wife of King Alf. Hjordis had also spoken to Sigurd about his ancestors, herself, the birth of his father and how he was the king of Hunaland. She told him the tales of his brothers, their journeys, their loved ones and the battles they had fought. Sigurd knew about the pieces of his father's sword that lay secure with his mother. He knew the stories of how his father was chosen to wield the gifted sword from the god, Odin, how many battles he had won and, finally, how the sword broke against the spear of the same god who had gifted him the sword. Sigurd knew all the stories.

As Sigurd grew into a young man, his foster father Regin became annoyed with Sigurd's attitude towards all his abundance. It bothered Regin that he would think so little of all his great wealth and fortune. Regin told Sigurd a little about himself and how he came to King Hjalprek's courts. He said that he came with nothing, because he had to flee from his brother's cruelty and threat on his life. When he came to the king's courts, he was grateful to be accepted and have a place to live. He was happy to be useful and, as a blacksmith, diligently worked everyday. He received recognition and respect from others, and that made him pleased with himself. Yet, within Sigurd, he saw a young man who had been given everything and paid little heed to his gifts. This demeanour of Sigurd disturbed Regin to the point where he confronted Sigurd about his behaviour. "Sigurd, do you know anything about all your wealth and how it is managed?"

Sigurd knew about the wealth of this father that was now in King Alf and King Hjalprek's halls and replied, "Yes, I know about the wealth, and I am content that the kings guard it."

Regin continued, "Are you positive that they are looking after it wisely?"

Regin believed that Sigurd should have more knowledge and access to his father's wealth, and also that he should be more active in the daily overseeing of it.

Sigurd had never really thought of these things and responded, "Foster father, I am young and my mother and I have trusted the kings to look after the treasures from my father and grandfather's kingdom. I believe they are more experienced than I am in these matters and can look after them better than I can."

Regin commented, "It mystifies me that you walk among kings and royalty and go around like an unsettled vagabond."

Sigurd corrected Regin, and told him that he saw himself, not as a vagabond, but as an equal to the other kings and his nieces and nephews. "What you have said is far from the truth. I am equal to the kings in ruling the land, and I am free to have all that I would want."

Regin challenged Sigurd on his last statement. "Well, then, go and get yourself a steady steed for your enjoyment and to ride throughout your lands."

Sigurd wanted to prove that Regin was wrong. "Yes, I will see the kings about this matter."

After the conversation with Regin, Sigurd went to see his father and grandfather, the kings. King Alf and King Hjalprek greeted him, "Hello, our dear Sigurd! What brings you before us?"

Sigurd said, "Hello father Alf and grandfather Hjalprek. I have come from a long conversation with Regin, and I believe I am ready to have a horse of my own. I would like to ride around the country and see our lands, as I wish to know more about our kingdom."

King Alf responded, "Of course, Sigurd. What is ours is yours. Go and see Fridsteinn, our man gifted in the knowledge of horsemanship, and he can show you the abundance of our horses from which you may choose."

Sigurd thanked the kings and went home. The next morning Sigurd was up at dawn and went to the horse stables to find Fridsteinn. The horseman informed him that the horses were grazing in the meadows past the forest. He walked along the green paths to the forest. In the quiet of the long and silent trees, an elderly man approached him. He wore a long, grey hooded cloak, and he had a long, grey combed beard. The man also had a grey patch over one of his eyes. Sigurd did not recognize the man.

The man addressed Sigurd. "Good morning, young man. And, what brings you to the fields and forest so early in the day?"

Sigurd subconsciously trusted the man and sought out his advice on horse choosing. "Good morning! I am on a personal quest to find a horse to call my own, and I would appreciate your advice in this matter."

Odin and Sigurd trekked a ways together, and Odin said, "All the horses are over yonder, and we can round them up and lead them to the Busiltjorn River." Sigurd and Odin gathered all the horses together and drove them into the deep river. The horses instinctively swam ashore except for one, and Sigurd knew that one was for him. The horse was large and grey, full of youth and vigour and genuinely handsome.

The old man informed Sigurd, "This young, handsome steed is descended from Sleipnir, the horse of the god, Odin. He will need specific care, befitting his special breed. This will include appropriate grooming along with conscientious raising. As well as being honoured, he is the best horse known to man, and will serve you well."

After the mysterious, grey-bearded man spoke these words, he vanished in a wisp of wind. Sigurd realized he had been walking and talking with Odin, the AllFather. He openly thanked Odin for his counsel and guidance. Sigurd secured his new horse, named him Grani and rode him back to King Hjalprek's courts. Everyone who saw Sigurd and his new steed praised his choice of horse.

Although Sigurd gained a new horse, Regin was still vexed. He expressed, "Having only one horse is not fitting for your position as a prince. You need to have more wealth around you and at your disposal. It displeases me to see you wandering like a wayward whelp in your own kingdom. Yet, I know a place, not far from this kingdom, where there is an overflowing of magnificent and luxurious treasures, all waiting to be claimed. I have heard it said, that the one who obtains these treasures will receive great renown and respect and be known throughout the kingdoms as a man of noble honour."

Sigurd was enthralled with Regin's words and grew curious. "You said all these treasures were not far from this kingdom… Well, how far is this place? And, if there is so much treasure, why, then, has no one claimed it?"

Regin responded, "The place is called Gnita-Heath, and it is filled with a magnificent accumulation of white, yellow and red golden objects, all spreading throughout the one wide area. There is no other place in the world that boasts to have so much gold. Once claimed, you will have your own wealth and would have no need of anything from anyone. You would no longer have to ask the kings for any of your father's wealth, because you would have your own wealth. It would last all your lifetime and the lifetimes of all your descendants. To answer your second question, no one has claimed this immense bounty, as it is guarded by a serpent creature named Fafnir."

Sigurd, aware of tales of an area filled with gold guarded by a dragon serpent, said, "I have heard these stories in my childhood and thought this serpent tale was just that... a tale and not real! I must tell you that all the stories that were told described this serpent as an enormous and ferocious dragon beast that rages and growls and blows scorching brimstone and poisonous fire all around him. Everyone who has ever gone before this beast has died an excruciatingly painful death. No one has ever survived an encounter with him or claimed one piece of the much sought after guarded gold."

Regin discredited the tales that Sigurd had heard, and suggested to Sigurd that he was not worthy of his forefathers. He said, "These tales you have heard are all wrong. The monster you speak of is no more than a grass lizard. Your forefathers would be ashamed to call you kin, if you believe everything you hear and are afraid of a worm!"

Sigurd was still a youth, but his curiosity urged him to find out more about the creature. Sigurd asked, "It is true that I am not as experienced as you or my forefathers, but you need not mock me for my youth. But tell me Regin, why are you telling me these things?"

Regin settled himself and said, "It is time for me to tell you a little about my youth, and how I came to be here. Then you will better understand."

Sigurd, wanting to understand what Regin was telling him, said, "Well, we have all afternoon Regin, so there is enough time to hear your story. You have told me some of your youth, and I am ready and willing to listen to your whole story."

Chapter Seventeen
The Saga of The Golden Curse

As Odin sat on Hlidskjalf, he noticed something he had never seen before, and that convinced him to enter an area between Midgard and Svartalfheim. He saw a sprawling, green forest sprinkled with sparkles of gold through which he could not see, not even a peek! This was unusual. Normally, on any given day, from Hlidskjalf he could see into every nook and cranny of every area of every realm. Not being able to see into this particular area made him curious.

Every morning, his loyal ravens, Hugin and Munin, flew throughout each of the nine great dimensions and gathered news of the current happenings of the day. On this morning, before they set out, Odin asked them to investigate the mysterious forest. He thought to himself, *Where did this forest come from and why can I not see into it? If this is magic, I want to know what kind and to whom it belongs.*

When his sleek, black ravens returned, Odin asked, "What is the news of the mysterious forest?"

Hugin crooned, "There was an old shack in the middle of the forest."

Munin cawed, "There were three gnarly and twisted dwarves living there."

Odin was surprised. "Is that all there is within the forest?"

"Yes, yes," squawked Munin and Hugin in harmony.

Odin pondered, "What is the rest of the news of the day?"

The ravens told Odin their news, and he was satisfied. Yet, he was still curious about the mysterious forest. He surveyed the area from Hlidskjalf and still could not see through the forest. He needed to know more, so he decided to pay a visit to the dwarf family.

Two of his companions, Haenir and Loki sojourned with him.

Odin loved to travel through the grandness of the nine worlds, and this journey was no exception. The three walked from Asgard to the Bifrost Bridge, where they met with Heimdal, the guardian of the brilliant blue, radiant red, and sunny yellow rainbow bridge. Once past Bifrost, they entered the realm of Midgard, the land of the humans. There they sojourned through to its edges and on to Svartalfheim. A ways in, they came to a vast, mysterious, green forest that concealed everything.

They walked through the magical forest a while and, when they came upon a wondrous waterfall, they stopped, listened, and watched. All of a sudden, out splashed a big, black otter that perched sleepily on a nearby rock in front of the sparkling waterfall. He had a long, slim body with relatively short limbs. As he sat on the rock, he wiggled and waggled his webbed feet. He then suddenly swooped a salmon up from the water and clutched it in his claws. He sat and slowly observed his catch.

Since the three sojourners had been traveling a while, the thought of supper came into all of their minds, and they looked at one another. Loki took it upon himself to catch both the salmon and the otter. Instinctively, and without hesitation, he threw a large rock onto the head of the otter. It instantly fell. Loki swooped up the otter and the salmon. The three companions were pleased with the catch and continued their journey. They came to the old house the ravens had mentioned. Upon knocking, a strange-looking gentleman opened the creaky door. He appeared to be half human and half twisted dwarf. Odin looked at the man and thought to himself, *Now this is the creature whom I could not see from Hlidskjalf, but where are the others?*

He heartily greeted the dwarf. "Greetings, my fine fellow! We have journeyed along this pathway before, and I do not recall seeing this forest or your house. But, here you are! We ask you for a night's lodging, and we can repay you with enough food for everyone in your household."

The strange-looking dwarf was named Hreidmar. He was the master of the household and skilled in a special kind of magic. Before

Hreidmar offered them entrance, he commanded, "Leave your spear and your shoes at the door."

The three entered into the home of Hreidmar, and they visited awhile.

Hreidmar explained, "For some reason unknown to us, we were chosen by an unruly and unreasonable norn, who decided to place a curse on all of us. We begged her to undo the curse and leave us alone, but she would not and now we are here."

As evening enveloped the farm and the forest, Odin, Haenir, and Loki became hungry.

Odin said, "Hreidmar, here is our catch from this afternoon. We offer supper to you and your family."

Odin brought out the otter and the salmon. Hreidmar recognized the catch, and let out horrifying screams that startled Odin, Haenir, and Loki, as his sons ran into the room.

"Fafnir! Regin! Your brother, Ottar, has been killed, and these are the men who have killed him!"

With lightning speed, the dwarf men bound Odin, Loki, and Haenir with an extraordinary magic unknown to Odin. They snatched Odin's spear and Loki's shoes, because they knew these belongings had special enchanting qualities. Odin, Haenir, and Loki were completely taken off-guard, shocked and surprised that they could be wrestled down so quickly and bound so easily. What had happened? This had never happened to them before on any of their journeys, and they did not understand the nature of any of this nor of any wrongdoing. The shocked look on their faces stirred Regin to tell the bewildered and baffled trio the story of his brother.

"Ottar is our middle brother and, as you can see, we are ugly and deformed dwarf men, because we have been cursed by a nasty norn. But, Ottar's curse was a little different. He looked and acted like a real otter. He is, or was, a great swimmer, fisherman, and hunter, which helped us immensely by supplying us with a plentiful amount of food from his catches. We used to live in the village but, after we were cursed, some villagers were terrified of us. Some beat us, or threw stones, garbage, anything at us. Some yelled at us to get out of the village, as they did not want us there. Soon, we left and found our way here. It is peaceful here, and we have lived in peace and under the protection of the forest our father created for us with his special magic. We know the three of you are some kind of immortal beings, because you would never have gotten this far into the forest if you were not. We thought we would be safe from any harm with the marquee of our magical forest. But, as you can see, you have come, and you have killed our brother, Ottar."

Hreidmar stepped in and said, "I welcomed you into our home, I placed trust in you, and I was thoroughly unaware of the death of my son. The penalty for his killing is death. Death for you all!" Hreidmar had turned a white-grey colour, and his facial expression emanated an icy dread, spiked with clear and cold thoughts of vicious vengeance.

Odin pleaded, "Dear Hreidmar, we had no idea the otter was your son. If we had known, we would have left him alone. We are truly sorry for our miserable mistake. We wish no harm or ill will to you or your family. We offer any amount of wealth to you as compensation for your son, if you spare our lives and return our objects."

Hreidmar and his sons looked at the three figures constrained by magic, then looked to each other. They went into another room and took counsel. When they returned, they agreed with Odin's plea. An agreement was made and oaths were sworn. Odin, Haenir, and Loki would give Hreidmar whatever he wanted and, once received, their lives would be spared and their objects returned.

Hreidmar carefully flayed his otter son and made a bag from his carcass. Once he had finished, he placed the bag in the middle of the room. Looking at Odin, Haenir, and Loki, he commanded, "This bag of Ottar shall be completely filled on the inside with red gold and completely covered on the outside with yellow gold. These are the terms of the compensation."

Odin agreed, "We have the means to fulfill your request, but how are we to fulfill these terms if we are all bound?"

Hreidmar thought a moment and said, "I will let one of you get the gold. When you return with the gold and the terms of the agreement are fulfilled, then you will all be free to leave."

Odin, Haenir, and Loki spoke amongst themselves and decided that Loki would get the gold. Hreidmar released Loki from his binding magic.

Odin instructed him, "Loki, go deeper into this realm of Svartalfheim and find the dwarf called Andvari. He will be swimming in his falls, Andvara Falls. He, too, has been cursed by a norn and will, most likely, be in the form of a fish known to many as a pike. He is the guardian of the dwarves' gold. Do whatever you need to do to get the gold from him, and bring it here as fast as you can."

Loki responded, "I will be able to complete this task quicker, if I have my running shoes."

Hreidmar agreed, and Loki slipped on his special running shoes and sped off. He raced to the sea and called out for Ran, the goddess of the sea.

"Oh, radiant Ran, please rise."

Ran heard Loki and rose from the sea. She queried in her soft yet clear, bubbly voice. "What brings you to the sea, Loki?"

"Radiant Ran, I have come on behalf of the AllFather, Odin, and our friend, Haenir, as they have been captured and bound, and I have a plan to free them. But, I need to borrow one of your nets."

Ran replied, "I can honour your request and be of assistance to Odin and Haenir. Take this net of many knots and gnarls."

And with that, she offered Loki one of her rare and enchanted nets.

Loki thanked her and sped-off further into Svartalfheim. He first heard the falls and then, following the sound, he found Andvara Falls. He spread the mystical net over the falls and waited. In a matter of moments, Andvari found himself caught up in Ran's magical net of knots and gnarls.

Once Andvari was caught, Loki bargained with him. He offered Andvari his life for all of the gold in his possession. Loki said, "Do you know who is the fish that swims these waters and does not know how to protect himself? Ha, ha! That is you, Andvari! Now, give me the fire of the well (gold), or I will eat you for my supper."

"It is true. I am Andvari and a son of Odin. In ancient times, a norn turned me into this pike that you see before you. I want my life, so I will bring the gold to you."

As Loki pulled him out, he shouted, "Andvari, if you value your life, you better fin-over all your gold, because I have a delirious desire to eat pike, my friend, and you look delicious."

There was no bargaining with Loki, and the agitated Andvari brought all the gold to him. Andvari struggled to conceal one golden ring, but Loki saw him do this and demanded what Andvari was concealing. "You are holding out on me, Andvari… Give it here!"

Andvari confided, "You have all of the gold, and I will be left with nothing for all my work, unless this one ring remains in my possession. With this one ring, I will be able to make more gold for myself." And with that, Andvari showed the ring to Loki.

When Loki saw the ring, he snatched it and began preparing to leave with all the gold. Andvari pleaded to keep the ring, but Loki refused and continued preparing. As he was about to leave, the devastated dwarf sourly snarled at him. "Since the ring and all my gold will not be with me, I put a curse on it. All the gold you carry will bring misfortune and death to whomever possesses it, and will be of no use to anyone."

Loki was more concerned with returning to Odin and Haenir with the gold in order to free them from the dwarf's magic, than he was to heed the words of Andvari that spouted a curse on the gold. Loki raced back to the house of Hreidmar, where Haenir and Odin were still bound. When Odin saw the gold and the ring, he was elated. He hoped to be finally free of the binds. Hreidmar ordered Odin, Haenir, and Loki to fill the bag of Ottar with the red gold. He unbound Odin and Haenir for this purpose. Somehow, Odin managed to slip the ring Loki had into his pocket. The three did as Hreidmar commanded. The empty bag of Ottar was filled on the inside with the red gold and covered completely on the outside with yellow gold.

When they were finished filling and covering the bag of Ottar, Hreidmar walked around inspecting it. He said, "One whisker is uncovered. If it is not covered, there is no agreement."

Odin felt the ring in his pocket. A reluctance that he did not fully comprehend pulled at him, as he took the ring out of his pocket and placed it on the whisker of the otter. The otter was completely covered. Hreidmar made another check around the otter and, this time, he was satisfied. "You are free to go. Odin, take your spear. But, if you or any of your kind set foot on my land again, you will feel the full force of my wrath."

Odin, Haenir, and Loki gratefully agreed to never return. They were free to go and free of the Ottar's ransom. Odin took his spear and, as they were about to leave, Loki recounted the words of Andvari. "All the red gold inside and all the yellow gold outside of Ottar, and the ring that covers his whisker, were cursed by the distraught dwarf, Andvari. He said the gold will be the death of anyone who owns it, and it will be of no use to anyone."

Hreidmar smirked and, although Odin was curious about the curse, he really wanted to learn the knowledge and the mystical magic of Hreidmar. But, due to the gruesome looks of the gnarled dwarf, Odin turned with Loki and Haenir, and they fled as fast as they could.

Hreidmar smiled and gloated over the gold. He obsessed over it. Fafnir finally confronted him. "Father, it is time for you to give us our share of the gold in compensation for our brother, Ottar."

Hreidmar growled, "I am not sharing any of my gold with you or anyone else. It is all mine!"

Fafnir argued, "We are in our rights to have our portion of the compensation. Ottar was our brother, as well as your son."

Hreidmar was angry, and they fought a heated battle, until Fafnir drew out his father's sword, Hrotti, and slew him with it. Next, Fafnir went and found his father's helmet, called Aegis-Helm (Helm of Dread). The helmet was so terrifying, that it brought fear into all living creations who placed their eyes on it. He placed it on his own head. He then went and stood beside Ottar, who was filled with gold inside and outside. The grimmest of grins lurked over his face and a strange sensation spread throughout his gnarled body, as he gleamed and gloated over the gold.

Regin suggested, "Brother, let us share the gold amongst ourselves and with our sisters, Lyngheid and Lofnheid, and our mother, Runa, as now we do not have to live with only this meagre existence. We can all live a better life. Let us share one-fifth of the gold, as we do not have to divide it into sevens, since Ottar and father are both gone."

Fafnir snarled and growled and laughed and bluntly said, "No!"

Regin went to find his sister Lyngheid, and he told her what had happened. He then asked her, "How can we get Fafnir to share the gold?"

Lyngheid suggested, "Well, go and ask him nicely."

Regin went back to his home and asked Fafnir, as nicely as he could, but Fafnir sneered and jeered at him. "If you think there is any hope of my sharing the gold with you, after I have killed father for it, then you are mistaken. I will never share this gold with you or with anyone else. Begone from here!" He let out a gruesome growl. "Or, feel the bite of the bloody blade Hrotti, as father did!"

Regin pleaded, "Fafnir, how can you say this? I am your brother!"

Fafnir rose Hrotti high in the air and was about to plunge the sword down upon the head of Regin, when Regin ran. As he fled the house, he snatched his sword, called Refill, that rested by the door. Running on fear, he raced and stumbled through the night and fell into the realm of King Hjalprek in Thjod. He had no idea where he was. He humbly came before the king and pleaded for a place in his service.

"What skills do you offer?" the king asked.

Regin showed him his sword, which was all he owned, and said, "I am a smith and a craftsman."

King Hjalprek closely inspected the sword, Refill, and he liked what he saw. He offered Regin the position of a craft-smith. Regin was grateful to be accepted and have a new home and a new place in which to work. He diligently fulfilled all of King Hjalprek's work orders.

Meanwhile, Fafnir drooled all day and all night over what once was his brother, Ottar. His form filled on the inside with red gold and yellow gold on the outside was still standing in the middle of the room, where Hreidmar had left it. The ring on the whisker produced more gold, as Andvari had said it would. Fafnir became obsessed with the gold and desired to hide and hoard the gold all for himself. He went to an area called Gnita-Heath, and dug out a huge cave for himself. He made doors and fastenings cleverly cast in strong iron. They were securely attached to the front opening of his lair. All the posts in the cave were also cast of iron and were sunk deep into the earth. He built his lair long and huge. He gradually placed all the gold there and, when he was finished, he lay on the glittering gold. Day after day, he sat on the gold and obsessed. As he sat, he began changing. He slowly grew one hundred times larger, and scales evolved on his outer skin. He growled and spit venomous flames, if anyone came near. He changed into a huge and fearsome dragon. People knew of him and his story, as he came to be known as the dreadful dragon, Fafnir.

The Dragon Fafnir, by Arthur Rackham

Chapter Eighteen
Regin's Story

Regin remembered and began to tell Sigurd the tale of his past. "My father, Hreidmar, was what I thought a great and wealthy man. He married our mother, Runa, a tall woman with long brown hair, brown eyes and a dimple on her cheek. Father would call her Cheeky. They had five children. Two daughters, Lofnheid and Lynheid, and three sons, Fafnir, Ottar, and me, Regin… According to father, I was the least accomplished and the least honoured of all their children. Our mother and father were unable to agree on almost every matter that came before our family. She became desperately unhappy. Finally, she packed up herself and our sisters' belongings, announced her departure and left. Then, only my father and brothers lived together. Being the least accomplished, I made myself useful and learned to work with iron, silver and gold. I would make things of use from any kind of metal. My brother, Ottar, had a different nature, as he was a great fisherman. Fafnir was, by far, the largest of all of us. He was the strongest and fiercest of the three sons, and he wanted everything for himself. Within him, my father had a cruel and angry streak which may have contributed to our mother leaving. Unfortunately for us, his behaviour caught the attention of a norn. Disgusted with father, Ottar, Fafnir and me, she wove a curse into our lives. We were transformed into what you see… gnarly dwarves. But, the curse took on a different form for my brother, Ottar. He was transformed into the likeness of the otter, an animal that waded the waters. During the day, he would roam the river waters catching fish in his mouth. He brought his catch to our father and thus greatly helped us, as he fed us very well. He was in many ways like a real otter. He would come home late in the evening and eat alone, with his eyes shut, because he could not stand seeing his food supply lessen.

One day some enchanted beings came to the river's falls where Ottar was. They killed him and the salmon he was holding. When they came to our home and asked for lodging, father invited them in. Later they showed father their catch of the day. When he saw our brother, his son, Ottar laying there, dead, father screamed for Fafnir and me. We bound the three killers with father's magic, and he was going to kill them, when they pleaded for their lives with an offer to fulfill anything we wanted. Our father said that the skin of Ottar had to be filled on the inside with red gold and on the outside with yellow gold, or else the guests would meet their deaths. The three wanderers agreed.

One of the three killers, Loki, went to obtain the gold. He captured Andvari, the keeper of the dwarf's gold and threatened his life. Andvari wanted his life and gave Loki the gold, but put a curse on it, saying that it would be the death of whomever owned it.

Loki brought the gold back to my father's house, and Ottar was filled on the inside and outside with the gold. Once the gods left, our father became obsessed with the gold and would not share it with the rest of us. Fafnir fought him for it and slew father. He would rather have the gold than have our father. Fafnir also became obsessed with the gold. When I suggested that we share the gold amongst our living family members, he became enraged and threatened to kill me. I was frightened. He was about to slay me, when I fled for my life with nothing but my trusty Refill. Fafnir became so obsessed and ill-natured, that he set out for the wilds and allowed no one to enjoy the treasure but himself. He has since become serpent-like and now, in an area called Gnita-Heath, lies upon and guards the golden hoard. I found my way to the kingdom of Hjalprek. The king saw my sword, praised my work and gave me the position of craftsman and sword smith.

This is what I remember of my family. Fafnir has taken over all the gold. I have yet to avenge my father and gather the compensation for my sisters, my mother and myself. Now, I have brought my story to you with the hopes that you would help me in the quest of recovering our family's compensation. There is ample gold and, as a reward for your help, you will receive your share of the gold."

Sigurd had listened to his foster father carefully. He contemplated the story and said, "Your tale is terribly tragic, Regin. You have lost your family members and your wealth. Your story also explains why you have treated me the way you have concerning my own wealth."

Regin agreed that his story was tragic and admitted being somewhat happy that Sigurd was finally beginning to understand him.

Sigurd contemplated, "The serpent who guards the gold is your brother, Fafnir?

"Yes, Sigurd, the lizard-snake sitting on the gold is my brother."

Sigurd asked, "And the gold he guards is Odin's compensation for the death of Ottar?"

"Yes, the gold he guards is our compensation for the death of our brother, Ottar."

"Regin, you not only have a strange and disturbing story, you also have dishonourable and shameful male kinsfolk," said Sigurd.

Regin agreed. "Yes, my male kin have been horrid and heartless to me."

Chapter Nineteen
The Forging of Gram

"Regin," Sigurd queried, "You say you are a worthy smith?"

"Yes, I have long been admired for my skills and workmanship," Regin beamed.

Sigurd made a request to Regin. "Well, then make me a sword that is strong and sturdy and has a steadiness that surpasses all others. If you accomplish this, I swear to you, I will be capable of carrying out considerable conquests and, among them, the slaying of your brother, the lizard serpent."

Regin replied, "I can make you a sword, Sigurd. With it, along with the slaying of my beastly brother, you will be able to fulfill all your adventures."

Regin left Sigurd and went to his forge and, with his skills, made him a sword. When it was ready, he presented it to Sigurd. Sigurd took the sword, held it high and studied it. He was not pleased and asked, "Is this your smithing, Regin?"

"Yes, Sigurd."

To test the sword, Sigurd swung the sword up and then down, striking the anvil. The anvil remained intact, but the sword broke into pieces. Sigurd scoffed and threw what was left of Regin's smithing to the ground. He ordered, "Get to work and forge another sword and, this time, a better one."

"Pardons my lord, Sigurd. I can do better, and I will."

Regin returned to his smith and forged a second sword. When he completed it, he approached Sigurd with the newly forged sword and said, "Here is your new sword, Sigurd. I am sure you will like this one, although you are a hard young man to forge for."

Sigurd took the sword, studied it like the first one and then swung it up and down upon the anvil. Like the first sword, it broke into pieces. Sigurd was furious, glared at Regin and said, "What kind of foolishness are you forging for me? Are you undependable and devious like your forefathers?"

Sigurd remembered his father's sword and that the remains were in his mother's keeping. He turned to Regin and said, "Stop now, Regin, and study your forging, for I am going to visit my mother."

He left Regin and made his way to Hjordis's halls. Sigurd asked her, "Mother, do you remember all the tales you told me of my father and all the battles he won?"

"Yes, my son."

Sigurd continued, "I remember the stories you told me of my birth-father and his special sword. How Odin had plunged the sword into Barnstock, and father was the only man who could draw the sword from the sturdy tree… With this sword by his side, he was invulnerable in battle. Yet, when Odin called father to Valhalla, the gifted sword was broken in two, when father struck Odin's spear. Then, father gave the pieces to you for safe keeping for me. Is this tale true, mother?

Hjordis smiled. "Yes, this tale is true, my son."

"Have you the pieces of father's sword in your keeping?"

"Yes."

Sigurd said, "Then, mother, I confess to you that I am in need of a faithful sword and wish for the pieces of my father's sword and, with them, to have a new sword forged."

"My son, as you are seeking the pieces of your father's sword, as your father said you would, you may have them. And, I believe you are truly ready for them. Your new reforged sword shall be called Gram, as those were the words of your father."

Hjordis went to her special desk, unlocked it, took the fragments that were carefully wrapped in linen cloth and gave them to Sigurd. An aura surrounded him and a phenomenal feeling flowed through him, as Sigurd held the pieces in his hands. He knew this sword was destined for him.

"Thank you, my dear mother. I feel something within these fragments."

"You are welcome, my son. The fragments of this sword are meant for you."

Genuinely appreciative, Sigurd then went directly to Regin with the pieces.

"Regin, have you had enough time to contemplate your smithing?"

"Yes, Sigurd, I believe I have."

"Then take these fragments from my father's sword, and forge me another sword that is worthy of King Sigmund and worthwhile for me to wield."

The exasperated Regin was silently furious. He judged Sigurd as extremely over-demanding and difficult to please, yet Regin restrained his resentment and outrage. He diligently took the fragments Sigurd gave him and went to his forge. He skillfully worked on the new sword and forged a new and gleaming one. When Regin lifted the sword out of the forge, colourful flames leaped and danced from its edges. Regin was in awe as he looked upon it. It was truly something to behold. When Regin was finished, he went to Sigurd.

"Here is your newly forged sword, Sigurd. This one you will find fulfilling."

Sigurd tests the sword Gram, by Johannes Gehrts

He passed the sword to Sigurd, who studied it and then hewed it up and down on the anvil, as he had done with the last two swords. The anvil split at its base. Rather than shatter or break, the blade of this sword remained firm and strong. Sigurd lifted the sword up and admired the blade newly crafted from the pieces of his father's sword. Sigurd smiled, praised the sword, and honoured Regin's work. "This sword is exquisite and truly worthy. I know I have been a hard man to forge for, and you have shown determination and dedication in forging this firm masterpiece, Regin. I am grateful for that, but I have yet another test for this sword."

Sigurd went to the river with his new sword. He carried a tuft of wool to test the blade. At the river he placed the blade into the waters. As he rested the sword-blade in the water, he threw the wool tuft against the current ahead of the sword. As the tuft of wool was carried by the water to the sword, it sliced in two as it ran against the blade. Sigurd was delighted and contented with his newly forged sword. He pulled his sword from the waters, cleaned it off and called his new gleaming metal possession *Gram*, as was foretold by his father, King Sigmund.

When Regin realized that Sigurd was satisfied with the sword and accepted it as worthy of him, he reminded Sigurd of his promise to kill Fafnir. He continued with his reminders. "It is time for you to fulfill your oath to me. I have completed the task of forging a trustworthy sword for you. Remember, there is a loathsome and shameful serpent who awaits the sharp sting of its stroke."

Sigurd had other concerns overflowing in his thoughts and responded, "I will fulfill your request, Regin, but first I have another task I must attend to. To avenge my father and grandfather…"

Chapter Twenty
The Prophecy of Gripir Eylimason

King Gripir Eylimason was a surviving son of King Eylimi, brother of Hjordis and an uncle to Sigurd. He was acknowledged as a scholar, sage, seer and a prophet with extraordinary abilities. Among these strengths and skills was the ability to foresee the future. If anyone came before him, he could foretell their fate. People sought his sageness from near and from afar. Sigurd also wanted his uncle to share his special knowledge with him and to tell him of his own predestined path.

Sigurd made the journey to Gripir's home riding on Grani with Gram by his side. He was greeted at the gates by Geitir, who inquired, "Who are you, young man with a powerful presence?"

Sigurd answered, "I am Sigurd Sigmundarson, the son of Sigmund Volsungsson and Hjordis Eylimadottir, sister to the prophet therein and, therefore, I am a nephew to King Gripir."

Geitir answered, "Wait here, and I will inform him of your arrival."

Geitir went inside and told Gripir that his nephew, Sigurd, son of Sigmund and Hjordis, was at his gate. Gripir was delighted and went to the door. He graciously welcomed Sigurd into his halls.

Sigurd asked, "Uncle, I understand you have the gift of foreseeing one's future… Could you tell me my destiny?"

"Come in, and let us sit together awhile, Sigurd." The two men sat together. "To answer your question, my dear boy, yes… I can reveal to you events of what lies before you, but first tell me the health and news of my sister."

"Mother has kept happy and well. King Alf and King Hjalprek have been kind and gracious, and she lacks for nothing. She recently gave me the pieces of my father's sword, as she said I was now ready to receive them. I gave Regin, my foster father and our blacksmith, the pieces to re-forge into a new sword. He did, and here is my newly forged sword, Gram, the name given to my sword by my father."

Sigurd displayed the sword for his uncle, and they both admired the newly forged sword. When Sigurd put it away, Gripir and Sigurd sat together facing one another, and Gripir began to foresee some visions of times to come for Sigurd.

"My dear Sigurd, I sense within you the need to avenge your father and grandfather, and this shall come to pass. I see all the men of Hunding lying dead and dying, all scattered and bloodied by your newly forged sword, Gram. When the repaying of the Hunding clan has been completed, you will make another journey. You will venture forth with Regin and face the dwarf man's greatest fear. He will step aside, as you satisfy his revenge by slaying his obsessed serpent brother, Fafnir. Yet, the heart of the beast will enlighten you, and nuthatches will warn you of the betrayal by your foster father. Gram will see to the slicing of his head. Fafnir's home, Gnita-Heath, will beckon you, and you will ride therein. Within lies the hoarded gold that speaks to you as it glitters and glistens, and as you gather it up to give to Grani to hold. With brimming chests of gold on either side of Grani, you will venture into an unknown kingdom. I see visions of flames not of Midgard rising to the heavens. You ride through and awaken a dreaming noblewoman. She will trust you and tell you her life story. She will teach you a series of skills, including the wisdom of the runes, every single human tongue and the knowledge of healing. You will learn the healing insights of ages past and present. You will fall deeply in love with the woman, and she with you."

Gripir stopped for a moment and collected his thoughts.

"The woman you fall in love with is Princess Brynhild, the daughter of King Budli and foster daughter of King Heimir. You and she will swear marriage oaths to one another, and you will ride to her foster father's kingdom and visit with King Heimir. You will ask for her hand in marriage. He will be greatly impressed by you and will agree to your request. He will inform you that you must ask her father, King Budli."

Gripir gasped, stopped speaking and heaved a heavy sigh. "Sigurd, that is enough for today, for I do not wish to continue foretelling your fate."

Sigurd sensed something from Gripir and urged him on. "Uncle, there is no other with gifts like yours. Even if you see something grim, please present the pathway that prevails before me."

Gripir gathered himself and continued. "When you are on your way to the kingdom of King Budli, you will stop and rest in King Gjuki's kingdom with the king and his family. Queen Grimhild will be thoroughly impressed with you and will desire you as her own son-in-law. After some nights of rest, unknowingly, you will become her victim. She will give you a magical mead of memory misplacement, and you will forget all about your love for Princess Brynhild and your marriage vows. You will share brotherhood oaths with the sons of Queen Grimhild and King Gjuki, and their golden haired, delicate and delightful daughter, Gudrun, will be offered for you to wed. You will become enamoured, contented and satisfied with her, and you and she will marry."

Gripir stopped a moment. He hesitated but, again, Sigurd urged him on.

"You will become close kin to her brothers, Gunnar and Hogni, and swear oaths of allegiance with them. With no memory of your love vows to Princess Brynhild, you will woo the splendid and spirited Brynhild for your brother-in-law, King Gunnar. You and Gunnar will use the knowledge of shape-shifting, that Queen Grimhild has taught you. Both you and Gunnar will exchange appearances, you to the likeness of Gunnar and Gunnar to the likeness of you. With the appearance of Gunnar, you will spend three nights with Brynhild, with Gram unsheathed between you and her. Upon returning to Gunnar, you will change back into your own shape and Gunnar will change back to his own shape. You will return home to Gudrun with no memory of your past shared love vows with Brynhild. Gunnar and Brynhild will marry and their marriage and your marriage to Gudrun will be celebrated. Your memory of your time with Brynhild will return during the marriage feast. The truth will be revealed to Brynhild. The betrayal will devastate and enrage the woman beyond her senses. She will become obsessed, and vengeance will consume her."

Gripir stopped and slowly said, "Sigurd, I do not wish to foresee anymore."

Sigurd urged him to reveal more.

"I have fore-suffered the sight of your death, Sigurd. That has been revealed to me. Brynhild will follow you, and your wife, Gudrun, will grow forebodingly grim."

Gripir ended his prophecy. Both Gripir and Sigurd sat in silence. Sigurd grew contemplative, as there was an enormous flow of information for him to absorb. He finally turned to his uncle and graciously thanked him.

"My dear uncle Gripir, you have graciously and generously shared your knowledge and foresight with me. Do not grieve for me uncle, for you have done exactly what I have asked of you. You have foreseen and foretold to me the events of my future, and for that I am truly grateful. Although the path before me envisions difficulties and death, there is also, hope, love, wealth, happiness and delight. I know that all lives are filled with sorrows and joys. All men must die at some time, and one cannot defeat one's own destiny. In my heart, I also know that you would have liked to have revealed a more fulfilling and pleasant life for me, if it was foreseen. But, you have told me the truth of your visions, and for that I honour you and I am grateful to you, my good uncle Gripir. It is time for me to journey home. Farewell, uncle…"

Gripir bid farewell to his nephew, and Sigurd rode home. He longed for silence and to remain alone in contemplation of all his uncle had foretold him. However, as soon as he walked through his door, his foster father was knocking. "It is time for you to kill Fafnir, as you have promised."

Sigurd reminded Regin that there were other things on his mind that needed attending to. "You know that I shall do as you ask, my dear foster father. I shall keep my word to you, but first I have a pressing task before me. I must avenge my father, King Sigmund, my grandfathers

Kings Volsung and Eylimi and many of my other relatives and kinsmen who fell before the Hunding family in battle. I must end the lives of King Lyngvi and any other sons of King Hunding."

Chapter Twenty-One
The Avenging of Kin

Sigurd visited his stepfather and grandfather, Kings Alf and Hjalprek. He explained that he had long thought of avenging his father King Sigmund and grandfathers, King Volsung and King Eylimi. He felt that he was ready and asked for their support in the venture.

Sigurd said, "King Alf and King Hjalprek, you both have been kind and generous in raising me as your own son and grandson. You have been open and honest in the nurturing of my well-being and education, and I am grateful for these gifts that you have given me. I feel it is time for me to leave my homeland and find the sons of Hunding, who killed my birthfather and grandfathers in treacherous battles. I am ready to repay them for these deaths and make it known that not all of the descendants of King Volsung have departed this earth. I humbly ask you for support in this venture. Your support would honour me and provide me with a firm foundation for success in this quest and the means to return home."

The kings smiled and agreed with the request of Sigurd, and King Alf said, "Yes my son, we knew this day would come and, now that it is here, we are confident that you are ready to fulfill your quest. We will commence proceedings for your support."

A large force of seasoned warriors was gathered. They practiced and prepared for sea voyages and battles. Splendid seaworthy dragon ships were built, and elaborate and glorious sails were designed. Day by day, the preparations continued until completed. Sigurd and his warriors were given a victory feast and, the following morning, they set sail, as the winds were fair.

After a while at sea, a mysterious storm brewed, and Sigurd commanded each sail to be set higher than before. They sailed beside a craggy headland that stretched out into the sea. There they saw an old man standing alone at the edge of the precipice. His arms where raised high over his head, and his hair was blowing fiercely in the wind. He held a long spear that shone like a lightning rod. The men on the ship were transfixed by this sight. They heard his booming voice, as he asked, "Who is in charge of these ships and these warriors?"

Sigurd heard the old man, as did all the men, and he answered, "Sigurd, son of Sigmund, and the grandsons and granddaughters of Sigmund, and all our warriors are on these wooden ships. We are facing this fierce wind, and this battle with nature may be our last! The waves are higher than our ship, and we are near sinking. Who is asking?"

The old man shouted, "Ah! I have heard this name, and all say that no king's son can equal him. I would like you to lower the sails on one of your ships and take me with you."

"What is your name, old man?"

The old man whispered so low that no one heard. "Hnikar, they called me, when I pleased Hugin and Munin and vanquished Volsung for Valhalla."

Then, with his loud stormy voice, he bellowed, "You may address the old man on this cliff as Fjolnir! Lift me from this craggy rock and allow me passage with you!"

Sigurd brought his ship up alongside of the crag and, as Fjolnir jumped on board, the whirling winds suddenly ceased and all was calm.

When the winds stopped as soon as the strange old man stepped on board the ship, the men were surprised. Sigurd wondered about this man who asked for passage. He had the look of an old and wise sage. Sigurd asked Fjolnir if he knew the ancient omens of the gods, goddesses and mankind. The old man whirled his spear, as it transformed into the form of a staff, and he sat down beside Sigurd. He spoke with Sigurd of omens and advice.

For omens, Fjolnir said, "During a battle, there is good fortune for the warrior, when a sleek black raven is near. A second omen is that when you are outside, preparing for battle, it is favourable when many warriors are before you longing for honour and glory. The third is, if you hear the bay of the wolf, good fortune will follow you."

For advice, Fjolnir said, "No one should fight facing the sun, and knowledge of the battle area will help gain the prize. Those who steadfastly practice swordplay and have learned Odin's battle formation will wage warrior glory. Those whose feet falter while fighting risk a tragic end. Be clean and groomed with a satisfactory meal every morning, for one cannot foresee where one will be when Muni (moon) begins his journey (evening). And, it is dangerous to dash towards one's destiny. And, lastly, it is good to take the stones out of one's shoes."

Sigurd laughed and said, "These are truly wise sayings, and we are honoured that you have shared your knowledge and wisdom with us."

They sailed on welcome winds, and when the land of the kingdom of the sons of Hunding appeared, Fjolnir disappeared. Sigurd and his companions confirmed that the man that came aboard their ship was the AllFather of Asgard, the Ruler of Valhalla, Odin. With this knowledge, they knew that victory would be theirs. They landed and marched with bravery and confidence. They unleashed a fury of fire and iron on the inhabitants therein, killing men and burning settlements and destroying all that they marched through.

Survivors fled to King Lyngvi, shrieking, "King Lyngvi, you and your kin of Hunding have failed us. You lulled us into believing that there was no threat, because you bragged that Volsung and his kin were all dead. You were wrong, for the kin of Volsung have all unleashed an army of seasoned soldiers upon our lands."

As a violent battle unleashed right in front of him, King Lyngvi jumped up and ordered his soldiers into battle formation. Sigurd's sword, Gram, hacked and hewed down many of Hunding's men. Day witnessed a drench of crimson, as the slaughter surged. Sigurd searched and discovered King Lyngvi and confronted him. Words of compensation or reconciliation between the two men were unreachable, and the king lunged his sword at Sigurd, who moved out of the way. Gram detected his target, as Sigurd swung his sword up and down upon the man, splitting his helmet and armoured body in half. He then sliced through Lyngvi's brother, Hjorvard, and all the other brothers, sons and nephews of Hunding. A large part of the remaining army met their fate in the battle.

When Sigurd and his warriors knew all the Hundings had fallen, they ceased fighting. Some rested, while others searched the halls of Hunding. They found treasure, surrendered men, women and children. They offered survivors life by swearing oaths of allegiance to Sigurd. Those who swore allegiance were loaded onto the sturdy wooden dragon ships along with the treasures. The halls of Hunding and all the settlements were set aflame. Nothing of the lives that once lived there remained. Sigurd and his men set up a camp and rested.

When rested, they sailed home on fair winds. They were given a victor's welcome and attended many victory banquets, as Sigurd and his warriors had obtained much wealth and glory. The men, women and children from the kingdom of Hunding had sworn oaths of allegiance to Sigurd and were given the opportunity to receive training as hall or house helpers, farmers, weavers, wood carvers, blacksmiths, boat builders, rune readers and other trades. Sigurd felt that he had finally accomplished his lifelong task of avenging his many elders. He went to rest.

Regin reminded him, "You have fulfilled your quest, as the blood of the slayers of King Sigmund, King Volsung and King Eylimi now reddens the earth, thus pleasing the ravens. You are truly the most victorious heir of all kings!"

Regin continued coercing Sigurd. "It is time for you to smite the dragon and fulfill your promise to me, because now you have completed your task of avenging your kin."

Sigurd said, "Yes, Regin, my promise to you has not escaped my thoughts, and I will fulfill it."

Chapter Twenty-Two
Sigurd Sigmundarson Fafnisbani

Regin was satisfied, when Sigurd rode beside him on the way to the dragon Fafnir's hearth. When they arrived, they saw that it was thirty fathoms high. Regin said that this was Fafnir's cave, and the door was where he slithered out to get a drink of water.

Sigurd was surprised. He could not help but see the vastness of the huge width and breadth of the dragon's lair and accused Regin of lying to him. "Regin, you said this serpent was as large as a worm or lizard, but from the size of his tracks and his lair, he is beyond measurement!"

Regin turned to Sigurd and commanded, "Now that we are here, you better get to work and dig a deep ditch before the water area. When the serpent slithers out for a drink, you will be waiting in the ditch as he passes over you. From there, you will have a clear view of his heart. Let the sturdy sword I forged for you pierce his heart. Your name will long be remembered for the slaying of the dragon Fafnir."

Sigurd was silent, as he remembered the deadly tales about a huge and gruesome beast whose blood was vile and poisonous if it touched one's skin. He also thought that the beast he had heard tales about was Fafnir, the brother of Regin, his foster father. He asked, "Is this your brother you have told me about?"

"Yes, this is where Fafnir lives."

Sigurd said, "This dragon I have heard tales of, but I did not know that your brother was this beast. It has been forewarned that the blood of this dragon is fatal. The blood can kill you faster than his fire. What can protect me from the dragon's blood?"

Regin scorned him. "Sigurd, where is the courage of your forefathers? Faintheartedness does not become you. I have been preparing you for this, but all is lost if you are frozen with fright."

"Regin, you have not told me the truth about this serpent, as you called him. He is larger, fiercer and more deadlier than your stories."

Sigurd grunted and cautiously rode towards the heath. He turned and saw that Regin had disappeared behind a bush. Sigurd began the process of digging a ditch in which to lay and to capture the dragon's blood, when an old man with a long grey beard and a patch over one eye, appeared. The man asked, "Son, what are you doing?"

Sigurd said, "Old man, as you can see, I am digging a ditch."

"And, why are you digging a ditch?" The old man inquired.

Sigurd explained, "In preparation for the demise of the dragon who lives within this cave… It is for me to lay in, and as he passes over me to drink these life-sustaining waters, I will wield my trusted sword into his heart. The ditch is for the dragon's blood, as it flows from the beast's breast."

Marvelling at Sigurd's resourcefulness, the man surveyed the area. He contemplated and then responded to Sigurd. "This dragon has killed many a man, and he is a monstrous beast. One ditch is not enough to hold all of his blood. Your plan is a good one, yet insufficient for this purpose. It is better for you to dig several ditches and, when you are finished, sit in the ditch closest to the water. When the serpent passes over you, thrust Gram into his heart and then quickly jump out, pulling your sword out from above. That way, you will not be touched by his blood."

As suddenly as the man had appeared, the man disappeared. Sigurd felt wisps of wind encircle him, as leaves began circling all around in the air. Little wisps of wind arranged the leaves in many lines in certain areas on the ground. Sigurd was being shown where to dig. He knew he had again been visited and advised by the AllFather. Sigurd thanked Odin for his wise words and for showing him where to dig. He did as the AllFather instructed and dug several ditches in the exact spots where the leaves had fallen. When Sigurd was satisfied with the ditches, he crawled, undetected, into the ditch the AllFather had chosen for him and waited for the dragon.

Before Night rode her chariot over the sky, a loud rumbling sound came from deep within the cave. Fafnir was stirring. He was slowly lumbering to the entrance of his cave to quench his thirst. The rumbling grew louder and the earth shook all around. Sigurd hunkered down in the ditch.

Fafnir emerged from the cave, growled and blew poisonous flames in all directions. He slowly, slothfully slithered towards the water. The earth trembled, quaked and shook, as he crawled forward. Fafnir snarled and, from his nostrils and mouth, blew more poisonous flames all around him. Soon the stupendous serpent was passing over Sigurd, hidden from the view of Fafnir. Sigurd waited for the right moment, took aim at the heart of the serpent and plunged Gram hilt-deep into the dragon's left shoulder. Sigurd quickly jumped out of the ditch, winched the sword out of the dragon's body and took cover. The blood flowed into the ditches, as the old man said it would. The dragon serpent whipped his massive tail, destroying everything in its wake. Fafnir let out a screeching growl, howled and blew flames all around. He thrashed and crashed around, beating his tail on the ground, until he had blown out all his fire. He took in a heavy breath and collapsed, crashing down in a slumped-over heap. He breathed heavily, as he moaned and hissed. In a slow, deep-rooted, angry voice, he demanded, "Show yourself, you who dares vanquish me."

Sigurd believed in all the ancient beliefs, especially the belief that, if a man was about to die and knew who killed him, he could curse him and all his family throughout time. Although Fafnir was a dragon, he had once been a man, and Sigurd wanted to avoid any curse. He answered, "I am no one of consequence and have no family."

Fafnir heard the man. The dragon-man snarled, spit, hissed and coughed. He growled, "You dare strike me, and now you dare lie to me, while I lay dying."

At that moment, something stirred within Sigurd for Fafnir. He came out from where he had hidden and said, "I am Sigurd, son of Sigmund, who was son of Volsung."

Fafnir looked right into the eyes of Sigurd. "I know who you are, and I know your kin."

He then raised his voice an octave higher, "Are you not afraid of me, boy? Have you not heard that everyone fears me and my helmet of terror? You stand there with piercing eyes upon me, yet you know I lay dying, and I know someone enticed you to slay me."

Sigurd answered, "Yes, Fafnir, an iron-minded and stone-hearted one has brought me to you. And, Odin has supported me in this quest, along with these red-blooded, powerful arms that you can see. The sword that has found its way into your heart is called Gram and is the reforged sword of King Sigmund, the gifted sword from Odin.

Fafnir knew who Sigurd and his family were and wanted to insult, taunt and hurt him.

"It surprises me that a war prisoner is so brazen as to approach me. I will make this clear to you, boy, that you have not faced me in a fair battle, as you have snuck around and under me, like a filthy worm. If you had been raised by your kinsmen, then you would have known how to fight me fairly. Instead, you have behaved like a pathetic pawn persuaded to this path by someone else."

Sigurd defended himself. "It is partially true what you say, Fafnir. My mother was taken by King Alf after the war that killed my father and grandfather. I was then unborn. King Alf married my mother and raised me as his own son. I was born a prince and a free person. Not a prisoner, as you may think…"

Fafnir moaned, "Sigurd, I am dying. Heed my forewarning, that the gold lying therein will be the destroyer of your life and the death of you, as it has destroyed my life and is the death of me."

Sigurd was undeterred. "We all die, and we all want to be wealthy while we are alive."

It was another ancient belief that when someone was dying, they could see into the future and into other worlds, and could tell others what they could see.

Sigurd asked, "Who are the norns, that sever the ties between mother and son?"

Fafnir seemed to go into a dreamlike trance. He wheezed and whispered, "They are bountiful, beautiful and strangely unordinary.

Some are from the race of the elves that live in Alfheim… Some are from the race of goddesses, or Asynjur, who live in Asgard… Some are the daughters of the dwarf, Dvalin, from Svartalfheim… Some are of the Vanir of Vanaheim… Some are of the giant clan in Jotunheim, and some are of the fire-beings from Muspellheim."

Sigurd continued, "What is the name of the mysterious island where the fire-beings, along with Surt and the gods, fight their final battle?"

Fafnir responded, "The island is called Oskapt, the unfinished."

Fafnir coughed, opened his eyes and looked again at Sigurd. "My brother, Regin, nurtured his vengeance and brought you to me. But, do not think you have won a victory, boy, for Regin will also cause your death, and that knowledge brings me great joy. He will claim his inheritance all to himself, although he told you the treasures could be yours." He hoarsely cackled at the idea of this turn of fate. "This makes me laugh. Your beloved foster father lied to you, and he will kill you the next chance he gets. The Helm of Terror was mine to wear, and everyone was afraid of me, and I was untouchable. I laughed at their fears and blew poisonous flames all around me."

Sigurd looked upon him, "I have heard of your Helmet of Terror and the few who have owned it. I realize that men are unequal in boldness. Some have none at all…"

Fafnir wheezed and whispered and warned, "Sigurd, son of Sigmund, mount Grani and leave this place, for Regin will find a way to kill you, as he did me."

Sigurd said, "My destiny says I will ride into your den and gain the treasure that was yours."

Fafnir's wounded heart changed even more, and he sighed. Slowly, he said, "Sigurd, let me do something right, while I still live. I see the wrongs I have done. I killed my father with no remorse or grief. I stole the inheritance from my family. I threatened the life of my brother and forced him out of his home. I seized all these sparkling, golden treasures for myself. I also see how this cursed gold seduced and controlled me. This golden obsession has turned me into this vicious and forlorn creature you see before you. Leave now, while you can. If you take possession of the gold, you will have more than enough wealth for the rest of your days. But, you will pay the price, because it will bring about your death as it has brought about mine. You know I am dying and have nothing more to gain. The gold carries the curse of Andvari… Anyone who possesses the gold will die and the gold will be of no use to anyone."

Sigurd listened to Fafnir's last words. "I understand what you are saying, dragon. I know I will die one day and, like many in this life, would prefer to die wealthy. I can see that you are on your way. Farewell, Fafnir, brother of Regin, son of Hreidmar… The giantess Hel awaits you."

Fafnir closed his eyes, breathed out his last breath in a puff of smoke and died.

Sigurd turned and scanned the area in search of his foster father, Regin. He finally eyed him hiding in a nearby bush. The moment Regin realized that the dragon was defeated and Sigurd was searching for him, he jumped out and said, "Sigurd, you will be honoured and praised above all others, as you have slain the dreaded dragon, Fafnir. You deserve the nickname of Fafnisbani, the slayer of Fafnir."

And Sigurd became known as Sigurd Sigmundarson Fafnisbani.

Chapter Twenty-Three
The Nocturne Of The Nuthatches

Regin continued his praising of Sigurd. "Oh, praises to you, my Lord Sigurd, my brave foster son and heir. Praises to you, for today you have brought about the end of the reign of the Helmet of Terror that my brother, Fafnir, wore for far too long. You are the boldest of the bold, the strongest of the strong, and this deed will be proclaimed throughout all the kingdoms and all the ages, now and to come. Everyone will know your name, Sigurd Sigmundarson Fafnisbani.

On the tufts of dried grass that surrounded the monstrous creature, Sigurd slowly wiped the poisonous dragon blood off Gram. He faced Regin and scolded, "Where were you? You were nowhere to be seen, while I faced the vile beast, your own brother, Fafnir. Gram held steady and revealed tremendous firmness and stability, while I used my muscle, might, strength and skills to defeat and dodge this discontented dragon. While I risked my life in this venture of yours, you hid in the bushes, afraid of your own shadow."

Regin reminded Sigurd, "Show me some respect, boy! As your elder, I am thoroughly dismayed, because you need to be reminded, that it was I who forged your steadfast sword with my own hands, the same sword you hold in your hands. And, it was I who led you to the dragon serpent, Fafnir. The beast would never have been defeated without the sword that I forged for you, and without my guiding you to him. And, it was I who advised you how to kill the dragon. Fafnir, the fire-breathing dragon, would have lazily lounged and loafed for ages and ages over the dirty golden treasures, until all would eventually be lost to glittery, golden dust."

Sigurd said, "When men battle, a bold and brave heart serves a man better than a blade."

Then Regin added, "I need to also remind you, boy, that according to the law, when someone kills one's kin, the family must be compensated for the death, or else the killer will be outlawed. Although, I am not innocent in this matter, you, my foster son, have killed my brother, therefore the law states that you owe me compensation for his death or face outlawry."

"What! Regin, now I need to remind you that you are the one who wanted this death and planned for it! You groomed me from the beginning. Trained and prepared me for this killing… You forged Gram with only this purpose in mind. You made me promise to you that I would complete your foul deed, the one you could not do for yourself! You promised me compensation with a share of Fafnir's treasures. And now, you want to hold me responsible for his killing and have me compensate you! You are proving to be untrustworthy, like your kin. What else have you not told me? You need to take your own responsibility!" Sigurd was thoroughly surprised and disgusted by the words of Regin.

Regin made a demand of Sigurd. "I will be leaving you for a short while, as there is something I need to attend to. While I am away, go and slice out the serpent's heart."

Sigurd stood, stunned, as he looked at Regin, yet he did what his foster father asked. As Sigurd cut out the heart of the dragon, he had a closer look at the creature. He sliced off a few of the dragon scales. Some red, some green, some purple, some blue… He then examined the fangs and cut them out. Then, he cut out the dragon's claws. He secured the scales, fangs and claws. He heard Regin approaching from the other side of the dragon. Sigurd was unsure what the dwarf-man would do next. He certainly had been full of unexpected surprises. Sigurd watched, as Regin came around and took some of Fafnir's blood and drank it. Sigurd was aghast. How could he drink the blood? Then, Regin turned to Sigurd and said, "Sigurd, take the dragon heart and roast it on the flames for me, and then we will discuss the compensation." Regin told Sigurd he would be away for a little while longer, but would soon be back.

Sigurd cautiously approached his foster father, sat down before the fire and began roasting the heart of Fafnir over the flames. The juices foamed out, as Sigurd sat roasting the heart, and he tested it with his finger to see whether it was cooked enough. He scorched the skin of his finger on the seared heart and instinctively stuck his finger into his mouth to soothe it. When the blood from the dragon heart touched his tongue, he felt a strange sensation. He began to hear the songs of the nuthatches chirping continuously in the bushes behind him and, to his surprise, he understood what the birds were saying!

Sigurd's senses were enhanced, and he was overwhelmed with his new ability. He listened to the birds as they spoke, in songs, to one another. Sigurd leaped up in surprise, as the birds were singing about him!

The first bird chirped,
"Sigurd is sitting watching
the sustenance sizzling before him.
Wise and strong as he is,
he should see to sup
on the serpent snack all by himself."
The second bird trilled,
"Yes, wise and strong as he is,
he is blinded by his love and trust
for the bloodthirsty betrayer man
with wolf's ears
that hid in our bushes."
The third bird tweeted,
"Ah, Sigurd is listening, my friends.
He must know that, for all the gold to be held by him,
he needs to slice the head of the smith."
The fourth bird twittered,
"Ahh, yes, wise and strong as he is,
he needs to welcome our guidance,
slay the smith and gather the gold.
I can see that Hindarfjall calls to him,

where the skillful and splendid Shield-maiden,
Sigrdrifa, is in a strange sleep.
As strong and wise as he is,
more wondrous wisdom awaits him there."
The fifth bird peeped,
"As strong and wise as he is,
a brother's vengeance lurks in the air.
His wisdom will fail him,
if he softens to the smith."
The sixth bird screeched,
"Yes, as strong and wise as he is,
slay the smith and gather the gold.
Slay the smith and gather the gold.
Slay the smith and gather the gold."

Sigurd contemplated the songs of the birds and thought to himself, *It is true. I have loved and trusted my foster father with all his faults, but I have killed his brother, the dragon beast. And, that dragon beast warned me that Regin is about to betray me. What the nuthatches advised must be right, for I have been given the gift of understanding them. Neither brother shall be the death of me. The goddess Hel shall receive both.*

Sigurd waited for Regin to come back. He was sitting by the fire, when he heard twigs crackling on the ground behind him. He spun around to witness Regin coming at him with his trusty old blade, Refill, yelling words of death towards Sigurd. The act confirmed to Sigurd that the dragon and the birds were truthful and trustworthy. He instinctively drew out Gram and, with one swoop, sliced off Regin's head as he was approaching him. He stood looking at the remains of his foster father. It had all happened so fast. The birds continued singing and praising him for listening to them and doing as they instructed.

Eurasian Nuthatch, by John Gerrard Keulemans

He was devastated by the sight, and went over to the other side of the campfire and sat down. He thought, Regin wanted to eat the heart of the dragon and wondered if he could understand the birds' speech with only a drop of blood from the dragon's heart, what would happen if he ate the whole heart? His foster father wanted to eat the heart. Regin obviously knew something about the power of the dragon's blood and heart that he had not shared with Sigurd. Sigurd did not know what it was, and his foster father could not share any more of his wisdom. What did Regin know about the dragon heart? Sigurd took the serpent's heart, ate some and then stopped. He grew gruesomely grim and put the rest away. He slowly turned and thanked the birds for their powerful wisdom and for their life-saving advice. The young man was too exhausted from the day's events to do anything more. Lulled by the songs of the nuthatches and with Gram and Grani by his side, he soon fell asleep by the fire.

The first beams of sunlight awakened Sigurd. He stretched and rested a moment, while he realized where he was. Regin lay, beheaded and dead, on the ground. Sigurd could not leave his foster father like that, so he silently dug a grave and buried Regin along with his blade. Sigurd was saddened with the realization that Regin had planned to betray him. His own foster father, the man he had loved and thought loved him, had set him up to kill the dragon only to get the gold. He had no intentions of sharing the gold with Sigurd but, instead, had planned to kill him. Even though Regin's last acts towards Sigurd were ones of betrayal, Sigurd had loved him. He stood over the grave and thanked his foster father for all he had done for him over the years and for the teachings he had shared. He beseeched Odin to take Regin on an honourable journey in the afterlife.

Sigurd then turned to Fafnir. What was he to do with the beast? The mighty dragon he had slain the day before had shrunk in size throughout the night, and now had the appearance more of a man than a dragon. He was still huge and too big to bury. Sigurd gathered kindling wood and began placing it all around the dragon. He secured a flame from last night's campfire and placed that all around the dragon. Fafnir was soon ablaze and burned on and on. While the dragon-man burned, Sigurd took the earth that he had shovelled out of the ditches and shovelled it back into the ditches. He covered over the dragon's blood, so that no person or creature could fall into the ditches and drown or harm themselves in the blood. He secured some of the blood for himself. He then shovelled some earth over Fafnir and the dying embers.

Sigurd cleansed himself in the nearby waters. Grani and Sigurd then ate and drank. He looked around, and he noticed that the area that had bemoaned of death and destruction in the morning now had some air of peace. The flames around Fafnir had done their work and had burned out, leaving the distinct odour of burnt flesh. Sigurd secured Gram, mounted Grani and followed the trail of Fafnir into the cave. The lair lay wide open and reeked of a wretched smell. Sigurd covered his mouth and nose with a cloth and rode through the great doors. He found the enormous store of red, white and yellow gold. Grani and Sigurd stopped and stared at the huge hoard of dirty golden objects sparkling and glittering, as tiny rays of sun beams trickled through and shone upon them. Sigurd slid off Grani and looked closer at the objects. He found the infamous Aegis Helm or Helm of Terror. It did not look as horrifying as he had thought it would. He found the sword called Hrotti, a golden coat of chain mail and many other precious things. One by one, Sigurd examined each golden item, cleaned them in the refreshing waters and loaded them into two large, magical chests. He then strapped the chests onto either side of Grani, but when he tried to walk the horse by the bridle, the horse would not budge. He thought to use a whip, but he did not want to hurt Grani. Then, remembering that he had understood the speech of the birds, he thought he might understand the speech of Grani. So, he openly spoke to his horse. "Grani, I see you are not moving. Is this because the load is too heavy?"

The horse neighed, "Sigurd, I am a powerful and supernatural horse, descendant of Odin's prized horse, Sleipnir. I have many means and ways, and one of them is that I will not move for anyone or anything, unless you are riding on my back." Sigurd leapt upon Grani's back, and the horse moved along as if there was no weight upon him. Grani walked along happily, as they listened to the songs of the nuthatches.

Chapter Twenty-Four
Brynhild and Sigurd

BRYNHILD SIGRDRIFA BUDLADOTTIR AND SIGURD SIGMUNDARSON

The nuthatches reminded Sigurd and Grani to ride up to Hindarfjall, and they did. Emanating in the distance, one could see a huge mountain, with multi-coloured flames dancing upon it. The flames arched and bowed like huge rolling waves in a sea of colours. As if alive, hues of blues, purples, greens, reds, pinks, oranges, and yellows, curved, swayed, swirled, and pulsated all over the mountainside. The flaming fire was unlike any fire Sigurd had ever seen. At the sight of the phenomenal flames, Grani and Sigurd stopped and watched a while in wonderment. The fire did not become smaller or larger or burn itself out, nor did it display any other natural qualities known for fire that Sigurd was aware of. The fire flowed upward, illuminating the heavens.

Sigurd and Grani rode up to the flames. He realized the flames did not emanate heat. He looked in and thought he saw something on the other side. The flames did not burn or destroy anything within it. He lifted Gram and gently stroked the flames with his sword. The mystical flames opened with the touch of Gram. Sigurd nudged Gram in a little further and an opening appeared. Sigurd and Grani rode through the flames unaffected. When they rode through to the other side, the flames closed in behind them. Sigurd felt like he had journeyed into a realm without any of the natural qualities of Midgard. They stopped before what appeared to be a defensive wall of shields surrounding some kind of dwelling with a banner raised above it. Sigurd dismounted Grani, and he removed a shield to be able to see what was on the other side of the shield wall. Sigurd looked into what he thought was a sleeping chamber. He gathered his sword and shield and stepped into the chamber. He was mystified when he saw a soldier, dressed in a full array of shining armour, lying asleep. He approached the warrior, listened carefully and heard a heartbeat. The sleeping man was alive! Sigurd wondered who the warrior was, what he was doing there and what the banner meant. He rested Gram and his shield by the bed and, to have a better look, he slowly removed the elaborate ornamental helmet from the head of the sleeping warrior. A long flow of flaming, golden-red hair fell from the helmet, and Sigurd was amazed by the sight before him. The sleeping person he had thought was a sleeping male was an exceptionally beautiful sleeping female!

Sigurd was surprised, curious and smitten. Baffled and bewildered, he looked upon the woman. The coat of mail appeared to be so tight, that it seemed to have grown right into her flesh. He wondered how long she had been sleeping, and if the chainmail hurt her skin. He thought to remove the mail coat from her flesh to relieve her. He grasped Gram and, with tiny gentle strokes, he sliced through the armour down from the woman's neck and out through the sleeves. The metal cut like cloth under the swift slight slashes of Gram. He eased the metal rounds away from the skin. Once the mail coat was loosened, the woman appeared to move and moan.

"Are you waking? It looks like you have slept for years."

Brynhild Sifrdrifa breathed in and breathed out, breathed in and breathed out, in long slow breaths and finally whispered, "Oh! What… What is this?

Sigurd lifted the top part of the mail coat off her and placed it to the side. She moved some more, stretched her form and whispered, "What is this that is so strong that it carved through my coat of mail and stirred me from my spellbound sleep?"

Her words were like a song, and Sigurd was spellbound. He responded, "This is the sword called Gram, that has relieved you from your mail coat."

She stirred more and managed to sit herself up as the back of her mail coat fell. When she fully opened her glistening, green eyes, she queried, "Who are you?"

"The sword that has relieved you is owned by Sigurd, the son of Sigmund, grandson of Volsung, King of Hunaland. I also carry the Aegis Helm, the helmet of Fafnir, the serpent dragon, who hoarded precious gold. And, this is Gram, the sword that has been gentle with you, but was the bane of Fafnir."

From a water basin that was positioned near her, Sigurd washed and dressed the wounds from the metal mesh. There was a long, white robe hanging near, and he helped her put it on. It was like someone, or some entity, had been watching over her and had prepared for her awakening.

Sigurd awakes Brynhild, by Johannes Gehrts

She quivered. "Would you give me your arm and help me up?"

Sigurd tenderly put his arms around her and helped her to her feet. Still dazed and confused since awakening, she was too weak for walking. He helped her to walk.

Brynhild gradually gained more strength and poise and gleefully took in more breaths of the air around her. She expressed her gratitude for being alive, awake and walking. She then exclaimed, "Oh! Hail to the day!!"

Brynhild sat back down on her bed, and Sigurd sat beside her. He gave her a drink of water from an ornamented water jug and asked, "Why were you sleeping in a mail coat, amidst shields, weaponry, and surrounded by those flames unknown to Middle Earth?"

Brynhild sipped the water, contemplated and, as memories flowed back to her, slowly the smile she had displayed dissipated. "Oh, I was once one of Odin's valkyries and attended a battle between two valiant kings, who fiercely fought long and hard. One king, named Hjalmgunnar, was old and wise and a great warrior. He was deeply devoted to Odin and prayed to win the battle. Odin was gratified with him and granted him a victory for that day. The other king was named Agnar, and he was a much younger man. Having valkyrie powers, I saw that no one was protecting him. When I studied the warring tribesmen, I saw that the battle was unequally balanced to ensure protection for everyone. Therefore, in a moment of instinct and to ensure balance, I protected Agnar. But, due to my action there was a grave consequence, for Hjalmgunnar was struck down. Since Odin had granted the victory to Hjalmgunnar, the AllFather became inconsolably furious with me. He roared upon me with a fury of words I had never heard him say before. He let it be known to me and to everyone that I had disobeyed him by letting Agnar live, and that I had also betrayed his word to Hjalmgunnar. As punishment for my disobedience, he stabbed me with a sleeping thorn. He told me that I would never more be a valkyrie nor have valkyrie powers. He also said I would become completely human, would never be victorious in battle and must marry a human."

Odin and Brynhild, by Konrad Dielitz

Brynhild stopped for a moment and, as she remembered, she was shocked by her own words. She slowly said. "Oh, that means I am now only a mortal human!" She looked at her arms with emotion. "My body seems the same, but my upper body hurts where my mail coat used to be."

Sigurd explained to her how he had found her, and how he had cut the mail coat from her flesh, then washed and dressed the wounds. She examined her body, thanked him for his attentiveness and gathered her thoughts to continue her story. "Before the sleeping thorn took effect, I beseeched Odin to not do this, but he had already poked me with the thorn, and that could not be undone. I begged him to protect me in my sleep, as I would no longer have my valkyrie powers of protection and would be exposed and defenceless. As I made the shield wall around my sleeping chamber, Odin gave me the celestial and impenetrable wall of flames for my protection. I also had time to make a counter vow. Since I would become a vulnerable human and have to marry a human, I vowed that I would marry the one true man who knew no fear, who could ride through the supernatural nature of my protective flames, and who would free me from my unnatural sleep."

Sigurd and Brynhild beheld one another, as she slowly said each word. "Sigurd, son of Sigmund, grandson of Volsung…that would be you."

Sigurd was truly astonished with her story and with her words. He was highly impressed with this woman named Brynhild Sigrdrifa. They sat and beheld each other for a while. Finally, Sigurd, seeming to come out of a trance, said, "I am truly fascinated by you and your story. You are beautiful beyond any woman I have ever met. I believe I have heard something of your story before. I have also heard that you hold a wealth of ancient wisdom. Is this true, Brynhild Sigrdrifa?"

Brynhild was delighted. "I do hold some of the ancient knowledge and would be delighted to share this wisdom with you, while you share your wisdom with me. I have been asleep a long while. You can tell me the year and what the times are like now, and I will gladly teach you all that I know about runes or other matters that may please you. But first, let us eat and drink together. I feel sensations like a hunger and a thirst. May the gods grant us a fair day, so that we both may gain profit and renown from each other's wisdom."

Sigurd shared some food, and Brynhild shared some mead. She brought out a drinking horn and sang a beautiful melodic tune. "Let us drink a memory drink to remember this day!" Sigurd and Brynhild both drank from the horn and ate a little.

In the days and nights that followed, Sigurd told her of the times he lived in. Brynhild tried to discern how long she had been asleep. She shared with him her knowledge of runes. Victory runes, ale runes, helping runes, sea runes, limb runes, speech runes, mind runes and book runes…She explained where and how to cut a rune. She made many references to Mimir, as the wise one and to Odin, as the AllFather. Sigurd remembered what Regin had taught him about the runes and shared that with Brynhild. They both enlightened one another.

Chapter Twenty-Five
The Sagaciousness of Brynhild Sigrdrifa

Brynhild made a significant impression upon Sigurd, and he yearned to master more of her exceptional expertise. He confided, "Your knowledge is beyond anything I have ever listened to. You must be the wisest woman in the world. The more I learn, the more I realize that there is more I do not know. I am eager to learn more of your refreshing wisdom."

Brynhild answered, "I perceive that you pursue personal understanding and enlightenment, and it is gratifying for me to satisfy your yearnings."

She continued her wisdom in an enchanting song of the runes and of advice:

The Rune Song of Brynhild

In warfare, call upon Tyr,
the god of justice and war,
once for your protection
and twice to triumph evermore.
Carve runes of victory
upon your sword hilt and blade,
also on your breast plate
for glory in any battle crusade.

Carve an ale rune on your draught horn
and add garlic to the brew.
An ale rune on the back of your hand
and a need rune on your nail will subdue

and protect you from the charms
and harms of lovers pursuing you.

Runes of help and healing can be used
for a mother with her childbearing.
Cut them on the palm, and hold the joint.
Summon the Disir to ease the aching.

For safety in your ships, cut sea runes
on the bow and on the stern,
runes on the rudders and runes on the oars,
runes that the fire did burn.

On the tree, where branches bend east,
cut limb runes on their bark
for healing of sores and wounds,
when the life of a healer you did embark.

To prevent hatred and heartbreak,
speech runes help the law-speaker
bring harmony and understanding,
weaving words like a peace-keeper.

Mimir drank from the Sage's Horn,
and Odin sacrificed his eye,
to learn the wisdom of the mind runes
to cut, identify, clarify and apply.

Sun rides in her chariot driven by
two horses named Arvak and Alsvinn.
A rune is cut on Arvak's ear
and one on the hoof of Alsvinn.
The shiny shield has a rune,
and the shield's name is Svalinn,

who blocks the heat of the scorching Sun,
keeping the earth and horses from burning.

The giant, Hrungnir, owns a chariot,
and runes are carved on the wheel.
The sleigh of Odin has runes cut
on its fetters made of iron and steel.
Sleipnir, the eight-legged horse of Odin,
has teeth with runes that add to his zeal.

Runes can be cut on glass, gold, and iron,
all metals and on ale horns,
wolf and bear claws, eagle and owl beaks
and are found on the nails of norns.

Runes are on Hlidskjalf, the honoured seat of Odin,
and on the point of Gungnir, his magical spear.
Runes are found on the tongue of Bragi,
the god of poetry, a learned skald and seer.

Runes are on the breast of Grani,
the beloved horse of Sigurd.
They are found on Bifrost bridge,
the fairway from Asgard to Midgard.
Runes were given to the gods and goddesses
and spread amongst human kind,
and given to the foresighted Vanir
and, to the Elves, they gave peace of mind.

The runes form an ancient alphabet,
and each one has a meaning all its own.
They were carved on all kinds of metal
and on a variety of wood, stone and bone.

The ancients said for this wisdom to be shared
and to use all runes for good,
to learn from them, and to give them away
to every being and livelihood.

Brynhild stopped for a moment. Sigurd was enchanted. Then she continued with her wisdom song:

When kinsmen wrong you, avenge little,
for it is better to treat them well.
And praises will be raised for your understanding,
endurance, and good will.

The warmth of a wedded woman,
or a desirable damsel under moonbeams,
deserve analysis, as discontent may arise,
because nothing is as it seems.

When a band of unknown men anger you,
best stay calm in these gatherings.
Some men are known to falsify any event
into a raging storm of imaginings.

If a man calls you names, like
'you fainthearted, scaredy cat,'
people who hear may believe these words
and think you are exactly that.

Some may laugh, but pause and conceal
all acts or words of avengement.
Instead, assess the damages done,
and then estimate the cost of a settlement.
Vengeance can wait for another day.
And, if the opportunity does arise,

confront him with his wicked words,
and swiftly slay him for his lies.

She paused again and then, in a captivating melody, continued
with additional advice:

When wandering unknown paths,
be vigilant and watchful,
when nearing the hearths
of creatures known to be harmful.
While walking paths in darkness,
rest not by the roadside,
for the ruthless are known to trick the weary,
especially at Yuletide.

Where there are beautiful women to look upon,
preserve your peace of mind and your sleep
by not permitting the alluring women
to disturb or distract you too deep.

It is foolish to fight with a man
who has had too much mead.
For he spouts senseless speech,
no need to make him bleed.
And, engaging him in a flyting
is a worthless measure
that may lead to injuries or death
and miss being with the einherjar.

If there be trouble at home, persevere with patience,
for it is better to care for your kin,
and save your rage and strength for fighting foes,
rather than battling family from within.

Sworn oaths are sacred bonds
between those who swore the vows.
Oath breaking, or swearing false ones,
ruthless revenge may arouse.

The living need to prepare the bodies
of the departed with respect and care,
for their otherworldly journey to the afterlife
requires special needs and prayer.

Be watchful of the kin of the man you have killed,
as wolves may exist within offspring.
Although one proclaims to be your ally,
the delivery of death he or she may bring.

When Brynhild finished her song of sageness, her foresight began weaving a sprinkling of visions about the destiny of the man before her. "With a glimpse of your future, it sorrows me to foresee disrespect from the blood-kin of your bride" (in-laws).

Sigurd, thoroughly taken with Brynhild, said, "I have never heard or experienced anyone as enlightened as you. You have awakened my soul, my heart and my mind, and I am deeply in love with you. As of this day, I swear an oath that we will be united in marriage."

Brynhild smiled a radiant smile, but then the smile passed. "Sigurd, if I were to select any man from all men in the world to wed, it would be you, as I do love you. Although my foresight is a gracious gift, it is also my fore-sorrow, for it has given me the woe of knowing. Although my visions are incomplete, they reveal another path for you."

"I swear to marry you, Brynhild. I will do all that is required of me. Say you will."

Brynhild and Sigurd swore oaths of love and marriage to one other.

Chapter Twenty-Six
The Man in Brynhild's Eyes

Brynhild and Sigurd sat together and gazed upon one another. The man before Brynhild had long, brown hair that flowed over his broad shoulders, and he had a short, thick, brown beard that tickled her when they kissed. She would giggle, and he questioned her about her laughing. He offered to cut it, but she said she liked his beard the way it was. She ran her fingers over his well-defined face with his high cheekbones and nose. When they were standing together, he stood much taller than her, and he would wrap his strong arms around her in a comforting hug. And, when his piercing deep blue eyes met Brynhild's she melted, as they looked deep into her soul.

He revealed to her that he also had a certain amount of foresight, as he knew of some events before they happened. He felt he had inherited this skill from his mother's brother, King Gripir, the seer and prophet that he had visited before his journey. Brynhild was truly familiar with foresight, being gifted with that, too, as was clearly displayed in her songs, but sometimes she felt it was more like a curse. There were times when she did not like her visions and did not want to know what she was seeing, because she felt helpless being unable to control the event. Destiny always had its own way. She would watch, as events that she knew would happen suddenly happened in front of her. The feeling of powerlessness overwhelmed her, as she could not change the outcome. She disliked the feeling. She had been a vivacious and victorious valkyrie, and a strong and all-commanding warrior woman. The feeling of helplessness troubled her. As a human, she was truly helpless and powerless, yet this did not seem to trouble her, as Sigurd was with her. He woke her, dressed her wounds, helped her walk and become fully awake. She felt fulfilled with Sigurd, and he was her strength. She gave her whole being and her heart to him.

Brynhild was impressed with the armour of Sigurd and with his war gear. He wore a leather buff coat under his coat of golden mail that bore the insignia of a golden dragon. There were also golden dragons embossed on each of his arm-sleeves and on his helmet. When he had come in, he placed his sword and shield by the bed. The shield's top half was a dark brown colour, while the bottom half was a light red. It was all plated with red gold with the image of a golden dragon emblazoned on it. All his weapons were ornamented in gold. The saddle that sat upon his beloved Grani also bore an engraved golden dragon on it. He was well represented as a dragon slayer.

The sword that he had slain the dragon with was the same weapon that had gently sliced through her mail coat, setting her free. Sigurd left it resting beside her bed. He called the sword Gram, and she could see that it was about seven spans long. She knew he was a skilled swordsman.

They spoke of weapons as she, too, had great knowledge in this field, having once been a warrior woman and valkyrie. Together they revealed to one another their weaponry skills. Besides mastering a sword, both knew how to hurl a spear, cast a javelin, bend a bow, hold a shield and ride a horse.

With strong language skills, Sigurd could understand and converse in many languages. He also knew how to give a good speech. What really impressed Brynhild was the fact that he understood the language of the chirping birds and the neighs of his horse, Grani. Grani confirmed that they understood one another, and that he was an excellent horse-rider.

Brynhild admired Sigurd's open mind and his willingness to learn. These traits, among others, aided Brynhild in teaching her knowledge to Sigurd, and they also aided him in his absorption and understanding of the wisdom being taught. Brynhild was content.

Sigurd Fafnisbani, by Jenny Nyström

Chapter Twenty-Seven
The Woman in Sigurd's Eyes

Sigurd was mesmerized by Brynhild Sigrdrifa. Was she real, or was she a dream? He could feel and hear her, and she appeared real. He wanted her to be real. She had been a warrior woman, one of Odin's own valkyries. She had been clad in ornamented gold and silver armour, with the chain mail he had gently sliced through. The helmet he released her from was also ornamented. She had an array of shields, swords and other weapons all around her, ready for use, and he was intrigued by her knowledge of weaponry. He also experienced her special skill of foresight, as she glimpsed into his future. Her sparkling, golden-red hair was accentuated by the long, white gown that enrobed her. Her eyes, oh, her eyes… How dazzling, like emerald gems that sparkled and shone into his soul… He loved her. Her giggling tickled him. Her cheeks slowly filled with a flush of rose. Her skin was fair and her neck a graceful curve. She was lean, firm and well proportioned. When they embraced, he felt a wave of warmth and tender emotion flow through him. He was captivated by her.

He could see that her warrior skills had made her strong and agile. Sigurd had never known a woman like her. A valkyrie with mystical powers… It was like her mystical powers had gently taken him by the heels and flipped him right over! His love for her increased with every passing moment he spent with her. She was the woman of his dreams. Was she real, or was she a dream? Was she from Asgard, the land of the gods? Was he in Asgard? That could explain her strange flames. Had he died, and was she the valkyrie to lead him to Valhalla? He felt a great relief, when she told him she had natural family living in a certain area of Midgard.

Brunnhild, by Gaston Bussière

Chapter Twenty-Eight
The House of Heimir

Brynhild shared with Sigurd about her natural family living in Midgard. She was of this earth! He decided he would visit them and ask for Brynhild's hand in marriage. He expressed this to the woman of his dreams, and she agreed. He bid her farewell and mounted Grani. Leaving the shelter of her hall, her shields, her weaponry, and her surrounding flames, was like being transported from one realm into another realm. Time had taken on a different dimension in Brynhild's realm, so much so that, upon leaving her realm, he became disoriented. He stopped and studied the area he was in. He identified it as Midgard. Grani sensed his unbalance and slowly moved in the direction of Brynhild's foster father. Sigurd relied on the guidance of Grani to King Heimir's estate. The king was married to Bekkhild, a sister of Brynhild, and the couple had one son, whose name was Alsvid.

When he arrived, he could see that Bekkhild was noticeably feminine, with a completely different appearance and demeanour than her sister. She excelled in the feminine skills of the day. She was a devoted wife and mother and worked at fine needlework. Brynhild, on the other hand, had taken up the sword and a mail coat, learned to become a fierce fighter and had been in many battles. She was known as a single and skilled warrior woman, who had thriven in the life of a valkyrie and had been victorious in many battles.

When Sigurd came to the kingdom of Heimir, all the men marvelled at the sight of him and were extremely impressed with his armour that shone brightly and displayed dragons on all sides. He was highly praised and well received. Sigurd made a good impression on everyone who saw him, and he gloried in all the positive attention.

Four men were needed to lift the golden treasures from Sigurd's horse, Grani, and a fifth man looked after Sigurd. Sigurd was held in high esteem. He stayed with Heimir and his men for a long time.

Heimir's men entertained themselves by looking at Sigurd's treasures. Mail coats, helmets, huge rings, golden cups, and a variety of weapons… They had never, anywhere, seen the likes of them. Sigurd enjoyed the attention and the comradeship. He became involved in the skill of teaching the men. He designed lessons showing them how to make their own weapons. He engaged the men in sparring techniques that taught them how to fight. He also enjoyed hunting with hawks, and he shared these skills with the men. Each day they honed their skills, and they enjoyed making their own weapons, sparring and hunting with their hawks.

Sigurd became involved within his present surroundings. Remembrance of the young woman within the flaming circle became a misty memory. When he first rode through the colourful fiery flames, he entered an otherworldly dream-like dimension, where time took on another form. The moments or months with the young woman flew in a flash of desires and colours. When he and Grani rode out from the wild, colourful, flaming circle, he rode into the natural familiarity of Midgard. Within the halls of Heimir, he felt happy, and he had made several friends. He enjoyed teaching the men how to make their weaponry and how to use them. He hunted with hawks and owned several of his own. He also enjoyed teaching and practicing falconry skills with his men. The time with the woman of his dreams seemed to be just that; dreams.

Meanwhile, Brynhild was with his child. She realized her condition and felt the need to be with her family. She no longer had valkyrie powers, was completely human and felt she needed to be with her kin. The life within her was growing, and that filled her with both a euphoria of extreme happiness and an unfamiliar apprehension. She looked around at her shielded bedchamber, her weaponry, her hall and the circle of flames. She sent a messenger bird to her sister, Bekkhild, with a message to send her a horse and some supplies for her journey.

Bekkhild was gladdened to hear from her sister and sent all that she required. Brynhild prepared for her journey. Passing through the flames with ease, she journeyed to the home of her foster father and her sister. Bekkhild and Heimir were delighted to see her, as she had been away for quite some time. They could see a definite change within Brynhild. Her hair was no longer a flaming burst of golden-red. It now was a bright red with gold and white streaks running through. Her eyes, that were like piercing emerald gem-stones, now shone more of a darker jade-green. Not only did her physical appearance seem to have changed, her demeanour seemed to have, as well. She was quiet and gentle, and she took up feminine activities, like her older sister. The household was surprised by her change. Brynhild began embroidering golden tapestries portraying the deeds of her beloved Sigurd. She stitched the slaying of the serpent dragon Fafnir, the seizing of all the golden treasures from the dragon's den, the songs of the birds and the death of Regin. Brynhild sang and was happy and contented, as she prepared for the birth of her baby. She was more than willing to put all of her warrior woman days aside for the love of Sigurd and her child.

The day finally came, when she gave birth to a healthy baby girl, and she had all the help she could ask for. The norns paid their respects and chanted chants that only they understood. One norn was snarly and touched the belly of the baby with these words: "If the husband of this female consummates the marriage on her wedding night, she will bear a male child with no bones." And then she smirked, laughed and disappeared. Bekkhild and Heimir were distraught by the words of the norn, yet they were completely delighted with the newborn baby, and they put the words of the norn out of their minds. The new baby was loved and a name-giving ceremony was held. She was sprinkled with water and named Aslaug. Brynhild and Aslaug, remaining up in the tower halls, were protected, aided and watched closely by the household. Heimir and Bekkhild became foster grandparents to young Aslaug.

Sigurd was unaware that Brynhild had his child, or that she was living in the large estate of King Heimir and Queen Bekkhild. One day, while he was hunting with his hawks, hounds, and men, one of his hawks flew high up into the tower. Flying back to Sigurd, it chirped,

"Come and see! Come and see!" and flew back up to a top window. Sigurd thought the bird was making mischief with him, but he climbed up to fetch the bird anyway. He wondered what the hawk wanted him to see. The hawk perched, chirping his songs, in front of Brynhild's window. As Sigurd climbed up to where the hawk was perched, he looked through the window and gasped. He nearly lost his footing, as a lightning flash of memories penetrated him. He held on, although he was shaken and deeply affected by the appearance of the woman in the room and by all her surroundings. His gaze took in the woman with long, flowing, red hair and her room filled with exquisite golden tapestries of his adventures. He was surprised, startled and stunned by her and all the work around her. Was this woman his dream bride? The woman in the room was in a completely different context than the woman that was in his dreams. Was she real?

His hawk chirped and chirped. "It is her! It is her! It is her!" He came to sense where he was and, with one hand, he held-on even firmer to the building. He outstretched his other arm to his hawk, that then perched on his arm, and he made his way back down the side of the building. Upon returning to his men, he was speechless and became silently sullen, yet serene. Rather than joining his comrades in hunting, fishing, games or conversations, he chose to sit all alone. His friends became concerned by the change in Sigurd's behaviour, and they asked him what caused him to change so suddenly and why he appeared to be brooding.

Sigurd confessed, "I have seen a most beautiful woman, and she lives in the tower."

Alsvid explained, "Oh, my dear Sigurd, you are speaking about Brynhild. She has been living up in the tower. She is my aunt and sister to my mother, Bekkhild. My mother and father are her foster parents. Brynhild and Bekkhild are daughters of the famous King Budli, a remarkable and talented man. You know, the daughters are of imperial and noble birth. Aunt Brynhild arrived a little while after you came, and she has been visiting with my mother ever since."

The woman of his dreams was real… Alsvid was confirming that!

Sigurd looked up to the tower and said, "Alsvid, I desire to meet with her."

Alsvid answered, "Sigurd, my friend, you are best to put her out of your mind and pay no attention to her, as neither you nor any other man will ever succeed in attaining her."

Sigurd continued, "I have my treasures of gold to offer her, and I can give her as much as she desires. I wish to win her love and affections."

Alsvid warned, "Sigurd, my friend, Aunt Brynhild has never allowed any man into her life, as far as I know. She trained as a warrior woman since childhood and was a valkyrie for Odin. Her only desire was to fight and gain great fame in battle. She has been away a long while, though I do not know where, and has recently come here to visit my mother and father. She has stayed up in the tower and has not ventured out since her arrival. I have not seen or heard from her since she came here."

Sigurd listened intently. "Alsvid, you must set up a meeting between she and I."

Alsvid informed, "Dear Sigurd, this may be impossible, as the woman stays up in the tower all the time and has never ventured out."

"Alsvid, you must help me be with her."

Alsvid relented. "All right, my friend. I will see what I can do. Come to the main hall for supper tomorrow night. I will get my mother to invite her down to the main hall for the feast, and I will meet you there. Then, I will escort you to the chair beside her. But, do not expect anything from her."

Sigurd arrived the following day, and Alsvid sat him beside Brynhild.

Sigurd immediately faced her and said, "Beautiful Brynhild, daughter of King Budli, you are the woman of my dreams, and there is love devotion in my heart for you. Tell me you will be my bride and I your husband…"

Hesitantly, she faced him and, as she did, she became transfixed in a daze. "Sigurd, I have foreseen that we are not destined to be together.

My foresight has revealed that you will be betrothed to Gudrun, the delicate daughter of King Gjuki and Queen Grimhild."

Sigurd was stunned. "No, this cannot be. I cannot marry any other woman. You are the only one I want to marry. I swear an oath to marry you and only you."

Brynhild replied, "I swear an oath to marry you. I love you Sigurd."

Sigurd gave the golden ring from the dragon treasure, Andvaranaut, to Brynhild.

"Brynhild, with this ring, I offer marriage to you and only you. This is a gift from the treasures of Fafnir."

Brynhild was happy and pleased, and she and Sigurd again shared marriage vows.

Sigurd asked Brynhild's foster father, King Heimir, for Brynhild's hand in marriage. Heimir was surprised and delighted and agreed with the union. But, the king warned Sigurd that she had trained all her life as a warrior woman and had only recently taken up feminine skills. Sigurd was well aware of that and had seen and been overwhelmed by her beauty and the tapestries she had created. King Heimir also informed Sigurd that he must ask Brynhild's father, King Budli, for permission. Sigurd agreed and made preparations to journey to the kingdom of King Budli.

Chapter Twenty-Nine
Gudrun's Dreams

THE DREAMS OF GUDRUN GJUKADOTTIR

King Gjuki's kingdom was situated fairly close to King Heimir's kingdom and the kingdom of King Budli. The inhabitants of King Gjuki's kingdom lived at the south end of the Rhine River. Gjuki was an exceptionally wealthy and good king. He married a woman named Grimhild, who had charmed him with her specialized magic. The couple were extremely happy. Grimhild bore three robust sons, Gunnar, Hogni and Guttorm. They also had two delightful daughters. The first daughter and the oldest of the children was Gullrond, who lived abroad, was married and had a family of her own. The youngest daughter was Gudrun. Therefore, from the oldest to the youngest child, was Gullrond, then came Gunnar, Hogni, then Gudrun and the youngest of all the children was Guttorm.

As a young woman, Gudrun became terribly distressed by her troublesome dreams. In one of her dreams, she was happily holding a graceful and noble hawk with glittering golden feathers. The hawk was exquisite. As she beheld the hawk, intense and powerful feelings burst forth from within her. She felt like she would rather lose all her wealth, titles and land than lose her beloved hawk. She revealed her dream to her handmaidens, and one of the maidens said she may know what her dream meant. She said, "My lady, I may have an interpretation for your dream."

Gudrun was enthusiastic and said, "Oh yes! Of course, my dear, please reveal what you see!"

"A man of noble birth will ask for your hand in marriage, and you will love him deeply."

Gudrun became distressed, because she did not know who the man was. She asked, "Do you know who this man is or see his face or know his name?"

"I am sorry, my lady, as I cannot see his face, and I do not know his name or family."

Gudrun said, "Oh, thank you for sharing your knowledge of what you do know with me. I am aware that Brynhild Budladottir possesses an exceptional foresight and other special abilities. She also has demonstrated a deep wisdom that has surpassed all others. She shall surely be able to reveal the identity of the man in my dreams. I will visit her."

Gudrun travelled with her maidens to the kingdom of Heimir. She was received with great hospitality, and Brynhild designed some leisurely games for them to play.

Gudrun and Brynhild visited in a private bower in a secluded part of the estate. Rather than participating in any of the games, Gudrun had been subdued, sullen and distracted. She was unable to concentrate on any of the activities. Brynhild asked, "My dear Gudrun, why are you so still and silent and not taking pleasure in any of the merriment?"

"Yes… Pardons to you, fair Brynhild, as you have been generous with the amusements. I have had thoughts and dreams that I would like to discuss with you."

Gudrun hoping that the identity of the man in her dreams might come from Brynhild, asked, "Who is the foremost and greatest of kings?"

Brynhild said, "Gudrun, you are referring to the sons of King Hamund, the great King Haki and King Hagbard, the undefeated."

Gudrun was surprised and asked, "Why do you not declare my brothers?

Brynhild responded, "I mean no disrespect to you or your brothers, Gudrun, but they are all so young and have not been adequately tested. Also, there is one man I know who outshines all others. That, my dear, is Sigurd, a son of King Sigmund, and grandson of King Volsung of

Hunaland. When Sigurd was a young boy, he fought and killed the sons of King Hunding, avenging his father and his grandfather."

Gudrun was surprised and asked, "Where have you learned this? I have not heard of him. What is the evidence of his existence?"

Brynhild said, "I know that, after the battle, his mother, Hjordis, went to the battlefield and found his father. King Sigmund was about to depart to Valhalla, when he told her that she would bear a special son and name him Sigurd. He also gave her the pieces of his sword, which had been a gift from Odin. After King Sigmund died, King Alf found her and brought her to his land and married her with the praises of all his kin and his father King Hjalprek. Sigurd was born there and raised as the king's son and was bestowed with the highest of honours."

Gudrun said, "You have learned a generous amount about this man, and I think it is because you are in love with him."

Brynhild smiled and blushed.

"Yet, Brynhild, the reason I have come to see you is because of my disturbing dreams. They have brought me a generous amount of distress. With your specialized knowledge and unique foresight, I hope that you can help with their interpretations."

Brynhild queried, "Well, then… Let me hear them."

Gudrun told Brynhild one of her dreams. "I dreamt that you and I and all of our friends and maidens were at our palace. We were having a gathering of some kind, and then we all left together on a journey. During our journey, we all saw a glorious, gleaming, golden stag. He was so noble and sublime and surpassed all the other stags. All of us stopped what we were doing, and all of us desired the majestic stag for ourselves. One by one, each of us attempted to embrace the beautiful buck, and he eluded all. Yet, he came willingly to me, and I was the only one able to hold him. The stag filled me with such love and joy, and I was happy and contented, but this did not last. You, Brynhild, on the other hand went into a warrior fighting-frenzy and killed the golden stag right before my eyes. This caused me so much grief and sorrow, that I could not stand it. Then you placed a wolf cub into my arms that spattered the blood of my brothers upon me. The dream has left me stunned. I am so devastated and disturbed by these visions, that I hardly know what to do or what to say. Brynhild, all my dreams have distressed me, but this dream especially. Humbly, I seek your foresight and knowledge for an interpretation of this dream."

Brynhild was quiet and contemplated what Gudrun had told her. She looked deep into her friend's eyes and said. "What I have seen in your dream, and what I am about to tell you, Gudrun, you will not like."

There was silence, until Brynhild spoke again. "Sigurd, the man I just told you about and the same man that I have chosen for my husband, will freely come to you one day. Your mother, Grimhild, will desire him for her own son-in-law. She will give him a magical mead, which will make him forget his love and marriage vows to me. After taking the enchanted drink and having lost all memory of me, he will fall in love with you and marry you. However, your union will not last. You will then marry again, and the next marriage will be to my brother, King Atli. Within this arrangement, you will lose your brothers. I also foresee you killing your sons and King Atli."

Gudrun was more shocked, more horrified and more stunned with what Brynhild had said. Grief and sorrow overwhelmed her.

"Oh Brynhild, how can you say such horrible things! These are gruesome visions! This cannot be the truth of my dreams! This knowledge is far worse than the disturbing dreams I came to you with. Oh, Brynhild, I can barely stand! I do not feel well! I need to go home at once! Gudrun left Brynhild's hall, in the house of Heimir, in a far worse condition than when she had arrived.

Brynhild left the bower where she had been visiting with Gudrun, went to another part of the house and attended to Aslaug. She let Bekkhild know that she would be travelling back to her hall in Hindarfjall to gather the rest of her belongings and bring them to Hlymdal, where she would live and raise her daughter. She prepared a small group of maidens and journeyed to her hall with the supernatural colourful flames. She left Aslaug in the nurturing care of Bekkhild and Heimir and their household.

Chapter Thirty
Sigurd and Gudrun

SIGURD SIGMUNDARSON
AND GUDRUN GJUKADOTTIR

The kingdom of King Budli spread over hills and valleys full of majestic, magical forests and fertile, family farmlands. Budli, being excessively wealthy, was a dynamic and powerful king. He was the noble father of five sons and three daughters. His oldest son had been lost in battle. His next son was named Atli, who grew into an extremely large man, and became a great prince and king and an admirable warrior. But, there was a darkness that surrounded Atli, and he was terribly grim. There were three younger brothers. The three daughters were Bekkhild, Oddrun and Brynhild. All were beautiful in their own ways. Bekkhild and Oddrun had trained in all manner of womanly skills. Bekkhild was married to Heimir and had a family of her own. Oddrun had the ability to assist women in childbirth. Brynhild had trained as a warrior woman and fought in battles, until she disobeyed Odin, and he pricked her with the sleeping thorn.

Sigurd rode with some of his men and all of his gold to King Budli's kingdom to meet with the mighty king and ask for his daughter, Brynhild's, hand in marriage. Before arriving at King Budli's kingdom, he journeyed through King Gjuki's kingdom. While on his quest, he decided to stop with the Gjukung family and rest for the night. He and his men were warmly received and were invited to feast and spend the night. The Gjukung brothers, Gunnur, Hogni and Guttorm enjoyed Sigurd's company and invited him and his men to stay longer.

Queen Grimhild had heard remarkable stories about Sigurd and, now that he was staying within her halls, she desired Sigurd to meet her daughter, Gudrun. Gudrun had expressed extreme distress since returning home from her visit with Brynhild. The mother wanted to help her daughter overcome what was troubling her. She thought that Sigurd could be a good friend for Gudrun. She knew that Sigurd only planned on staying for a short time, and that he would soon leave for King Budli's to ask for the hand of Brynhild. Grimhild observed Sigurd and was earnestly impressed by him, so much so, that she wanted him not only as a friend for Gudrun, but also as her own son-in-law. She contemplated and conceived a plan to compel him to stay with them. She used her magical skills and made a mysterious, magical mead of memory misplacement. At dinner, she personally served the unsuspecting Sigurd the magical mead. He was happy and thankful for her service. Yet, once he swallowed the enchanted drink, he soon forgot all about his beloved Brynhild and his marriage vows.

Sigurd spent days and days of enjoyment riding, hunting and being with the Gjukung brothers. They shared momentous adventures together. They all grew close, and Sigurd loved them like his own brothers. Although the brothers were profoundly powerful, proficient and experts in a myriad of fields, Sigurd surpassed them all in endurance, speed and skills.

Grimhild went to her husband, King Gjuki, and told him to offer their daughter, Gudrun's hand in marriage to Sigurd. That evening, as Gudrun served the mead, Sigurd's gaze followed her around the hall. Her golden hair, sparkling with threads of white and silver, flowed in little braids down her back. She wore a delicately embroidered purple and blue gown. When her deep, sky-blue eyes met his fierce blue eyes, she gave him an inviting smile and he reciprocated. Gunnar took note of this and spoke with Sigurd.

"Sigurd, you know we love you as our brother and want you to stay with us and be happy. Look upon our sister, and you will see that she is beautiful, and she will make you a wonderful wife. We offer you our sister's hand in marriage."

With no memory of Brynhild, Sigurd's eyes beheld the young Gudrun. He appreciated her up-lifting mannerisms, beauty and gentle spirit. He felt an irresistible sense of wonderment around Gudrun. The companionship of the brothers, Hogni and Gunnar, brought him a sense of belonging, of peace and of accomplishment. He accepted the brother's offer, as he was happy and content with his current living arrangements within the halls of King Gjuki.

Sigurd, Gunnar and Hogni swore oaths of brotherhood together. King Gjuki and Queen Grimhild were elated by the proposal and prepared the wedding feast. Sigurd and Gudrun were married. Joyful celebrations permeated throughout the kingdom and the feasting continued. Sigurd gave some of the dragon's heart to Gudrun, and she ate a little. She grew grimmer and wiser.

Grimhild was satisfied with the events that had taken place in their household and, when the wedding feasting and celebrations came to an end, she suggested to her son, Gunnar, that Brynhild, the daughter of King Budli, would be a good marriage match for him. She also told him to go to King Budli and officially ask for her hand in marriage. Gunnar liked this idea.

Chapter Thirty-One
The Proposal to Brynhild

Gunnar agreed with his mother's suggestion of marrying King Budli's daughter, Brynhild. The idea of this marriage proposal was spoken about throughout King Gjuki's kingdom. The brothers and the family agreed that Gunnar and Brynhild would make a marvellous match. Sigurd was unable to remember anything about Brynhild. The memory of the times they spent together was no longer present. Her beauty no longer bedazzled him. Her wisdom of the runes, the special advice and knowledge that she had shared with him, that had filled his soul, were past and hidden memories. He had no remembrance of his love feelings for her or their marital vows. He had given his heart to Gudrun, and she nurtured his heart with her strong love and devotion. His soul was filled with the radiant presence of Gudrun. He beamed happily and contentedly with his new wife. He loved her with all of his heart. He was also pleased for his brother, Gunnar, and supported his decision to marry Brynhild. When the day came for the brothers and their men to ride to King Budli's kingdom for the marriage proposal, Sigurd accompanied them. The traveling would only be for a few days, and he said his farewells to his beloved wife, Gudrun. Sigurd, Gunnar and Hogni, along with their men, journeyed to King Budli's kingdom. Once at the king's household, they were well-received, and the horses were also well-attended to. After rest and refreshments, they met with Brynhild's father, King Budli.

When King Budli heard of the marriage proposal, he quite honestly said, "This is a good proposal for her, yet you will see that Brynhild has a strong mind of her own. She has spent her life training as a warrior woman and a valkyrie maiden. Even if I tell her who to marry, she will marry only the man she chooses. You have my permission, but you must ask Brynhild's foster father, Heimir." The men were satisfied with their encounter with King Budli, and they prepared for the journey to the home of Heimir.

The next morning, Sigurd and the brothers began their journey back to the Gjukung kingdom. At home, they rested a while and then continued on their quest to Hlymdal where Brynhild's foster father, Heimir, lived. Heimir received the group and offered them rest and refreshments. Prince Gunnar faced King Heimir and said, "King Heimir, thank you for receiving our company so well. We have come from the halls of King Budli, and I have been granted permission to marry Princess Brynhild. I now beseech you, King Heimir, for your permission to marry your foster daughter, the warrior maiden, Brynhild."

Heimir replied, "I have heard of you, Prince Gunnar, and of your family, and I believe you would be a good husband for Brynhild. You have my permission. But as you may know, she is strong-minded, and you will need to ask for her permission. She has gone to her hall in Hindarfjall. You may find her there."

The men listened carefully to King Heimir. Sigurd's eyebrows twinged a little, but he still had no memory of her. The brothers and the men set off for Hindarfjall. Once they found the mountain that was home to her hall, they stopped in their tracks and gazed upon the supernatural site. The otherworldly flames blossomed to the heavens, swirling and swaying and encircling her fortress. The baffled men stared at the sight, as none had seen anything like it.

Fearless Gunnar was determined to ride through the flames. He bravely rode his horse, Goti, to the fiery flames, but the horse refused to ride through the fire. Gunnar urged him on, but he would not budge. Sigurd understood the plight of Gunnar and offered his horse, Grani, to ride him through the flames. Gunnar agreed, thanked Sigurd and mounted Grani. But once on Grani, the horse would not budge, because he would only move for Sigurd. Gunnar was frustrated, because he wondered how he could get through the mysterious flames.

In King Gjuki's kingdom, Grimhild had taught the magic of shape changing to Gunnar and Sigurd. Gunnar learned to change into Sigurd's shape, and Sigurd learned to change into Gunnar's shape. The brothers used this skill and changed shapes. Thereby, Gunnar changed into the shape of Sigurd, and Sigurd looked like Gunnar. Sigurd then mounted Grani and, although Sigurd was in the form of Gunnar, Grani knew the person riding upon him was Sigurd. Sigurd then rode Grani through the supernatural fire and into Brynhild's hall.

Once inside, he found Brynhild and her maidens sorting through belongings and packing. They saw the man ride in, and all were startled that someone had ridden through the flames so easily. Brynhild queried, "Who, in Middle Earth, are you?"

Sigurd and Gunnar at the Fire, by John Charles Dollman

Sigurd told her, "I am Gunnar, the son of King Gjuki. I have come with the agreement from your father, King Budli, and your foster father, King Heimir, for your hand in marriage. If you so decide, you are my intended wife, and I am your intended husband. I also have many resources and will pay a generous marriage settlement."

Surprised by his words, Brynhild replied, "Sir, if you have come to speak to me of marriage, let us make conversation, for I hardly know you or you me. Although, I do know of you and your family, I wonder if this is fitting for you to speak to me this way… I must confess, I have trained as a warrior woman and have fought in many battles. I have recently taken up the feminine skills. You may be worthy of me, if you surpass all other men in skills and abilities, and can kill any other man who has asked for my hand in marriage."

Mystified by her comments, Sigurd, disguised as Gunnar, reminded her, "I have the permission of both your father, King Budli, and your foster father, King Heimir, for your hand in marriage. It is known that you made a vow that you would marry the man who rode through the flaring fires surrounding your hall. As you can see, Princess Brynhild, daughter of King Budli, foster daughter of King Heimir, I, Gunnar, son of King Gjuki, have done that."

Brynhild could not argue with that and invited him to stay, so they could get to know one another better. Sigurd stayed with Brynhild for three nights. He had no recollection of his past relationship with her or their marital vows. He was perplexed, when she invited him to her bed. He did not want to offend his brother Gunnar by sleeping with his intended wife, nor betray Gudrun, so he laid the sword, Gram, unsheathed between them as they slept. When she questioned him, he said, "I am destined to honour my marriage vows this way or die."

On the last day with her, Sigurd took the ring, Andvaranaut, from her finger and gave her another ring from the treasure of Fafnir. He rode back through Brynhild's flames, where his companions were waiting. Once back, Gunnar and Sigurd changed back into their own shapes. Sigurd shared the news with Gunnar and the men, that there was a marriage agreement with Princess Brynhild, daughter of King Budli, foster daughter of King Heimir, to marry Prince Gunnar, son of King Gjuki. Gunnar was delighted, and all the men cheered. The group gathered their belongings and journeyed back to the Gjukung kingdom.

While the men were away, it became clear that Gudrun was with child. When Sigurd arrived home, Gudrun told him the joyful news.

He was elated and overjoyed. Sigurd joined in looking after Gudrun's every need, and she was well taken care of. The Gjukung family was excited about both Sigurd and Gudrun's forthcoming baby and Gunnar's forthcoming marriage. The household bustled in preparation for a forthcoming child and the wedding.

Chapter Thirty-Two
Sigmund Sigurdarson

The time came when Gudrun gave birth to a healthy baby boy. Sigurd and Gudrun were joyous and full of love and life. They prepared a name-giving ceremony for their little loved one and invited Sigurd's mother, Hjordis, King Alf, his stepfather and King Hjalprek, his step grandfather. Also invited were the many nieces and nephews he grew up with in the Hjalprek kingdom. All the Gjukung family were present. When Hjordis and Alf heard the news, they were elated and made the journey with their family and some of their household. Getting quite elderly by this time, the journey too arduous for King Hjalprek, so he sent gifts for the new baby. At the naming ceremony, the baby was sprinkled with water and named, Sigmund, after Sigurd's father, Sigmund Volsungsson.

Hjordis was so overjoyed to meet Gudrun, the baby, Sigmund, and Gudrun's family, that she cried with delight. She expressed her happiness at seeing her son doing well. "I am grateful to see you, my son, and your new family, wife and child."

The norns had heard of the birth of the new baby and came to the naming ceremony. They paid their extraordinary respects and chanted continuously over the child.

Hjordis, Alf, the family and household stayed awhile within the Gjukung kingdom and helped with the caring of young Sigmund. Sigurd was happy to see his family from King Hjalprek's kingdom. When the time was right, they returned to their home.

The Norns, by Johannes Gehrts

Chapter Thirty-Three
Brynhild and Gunnar

THE MARRIAGE OF BRYNHILD BUDLADOTTIR
AND GUNNAR GJUKASON

Meanwhile, Brynhild woke with the sun shining into her eyes. She made preparations for everyone to ride back to the home of her foster father, Heimir. Upon arriving, she told him, "Foster father, I have been visited by Gunnar, the son of King Gjuki. He said that he had your and father's permission for my hand in marriage. I have agreed to the marriage, because he has fulfilled the vow I made to myself long ago. I would marry the man who would ride through the protective flames surrounding my halls. Gunnar has performed this feat and, therefore, has proven himself worthy. And in accordance with my vow to myself, Odin and my family, I have agreed to marry him."

Heimir responded, "Yes, the man was here with some of his kinsmen and asked for your hand in marriage, and I agreed. He is a good match for you, Brynhild. Although you have trained as a warrior women, you have recently excelled in feminine skills, and it is good and right for you to have a companion in your life."

Brynhild made a request to Heimir and Bekkhild. "Foster father and Bekkhild, will you keep my daughter, Aslaug, with you and protect and raise her as your own foster granddaughter?"

King Heimir and Queen Bekkhild were joyful, "Yes, our beloved, Brynhild. We are honoured that young Aslaug is with us and are happy to raise the lovely child!"

Brynhild attended to Aslaug. She gave her a note, a picture of herself and a ring. She then left the child with Bekkhild and her kinswomen and rode onwards to her father, King Budli's home. She discussed the matter of marriage with him. "Father, I will be marrying Gunnar, the son of King Gjuki, as he has ridden through my flames. I have left your granddaughter, Aslaug, with Heimir and Bekkhild to be fostered."

King Budli told her, "Dear Brynhild, I love you and want the best for you. The young Gunnar came here with his kinsmen and asked for your hand in marriage. I was impressed with him and agreed. Gunnar and you will make a fine couple."

The marriage feast was prepared in the Budli Kingdom. King Gjuki, Queen Grimhild, and their sons Gunnar, Hogni and Guttorm arrived, along with Sigurd and Gudrun and other kinsmen. They celebrated for days. All were happy and content. Sigurd sat, joyful, beside his wife, Gudrun.

Sometime during the feasting, the effects of the mead of forgetfulness Sigurd had experienced suddenly wore off. He was struck with lightning flashes of memories of his love and vows of marriage to Brynhild. He gasped, his mouth opened, his eyes widened, his heart heaved and his mail coat tightened. In shock, he stared at Brynhild. Paralyzed, he sat motionless. He was unable to speak. He could barely breathe, as more memories flooded through his mind. He realized what his life was like with her, what had happened and what was happening now. His heart heaved again. He excused himself from the hall and went outside to be alone and breathe in the fresh air. Outside, he helplessly threw up, he walked a ways, and then fell to his knees, thinking, " *Oh gods and heavenly bodies, what has happened?!*"

He wept. He beseeched Odin for clarity and called upon his strength and diligence to help gather himself together. For a while, he sat with his head in his hands and taking long, deep breaths. He was flooded with the memories of his love for Brynhild. What was he to do? How could this happen? He had loved Brynhild in the past, but now he was in love with, and married to, Gudrun. He was in love with two women! When he felt some semblance of composure, he took more deep breaths. He gathered his wits and settled himself. He thought that Brynhild must have forgotten her marriage vows to him, as he had forgotten his marriage vows to her. Sigurd sat a little longer and contemplated. He slowly composed himself, slowly got up and slowly stretched his body. He found his way back to his seat beside Gudrun. He had turned pale and sat quietly. Gudrun leaned in. "Is there anything amiss, my beloved?"

He looked at his beloved Gudrun and whispered, "I love you, my beautiful wife."

He leaned in and held her and hid his face in her hair. He did not let anyone know what he had remembered or experienced. He concealed his heart well. He was comforted in the loving arms of Gudrun and his pain eased somewhat. He loved Gudrun and their young son. He tenderly placed his hand on her little rounded belly and smiled. He felt his new child alive within Gudrun, and this eased his inner pain and brought him an inner joy.

After the marriage feasting was over, Brynhild moved in with Gunnar in one of King Gjuki's halls. In a nearby part of the same fortress, Sigurd and Gudrun lived together. Sigurd and Gudrun loved one another and shared everything. He loved and trusted her and could not keep what was in his heart from her. In the quiet of their rooms, he revealed the truth to her about what had transpired between Brynhild and himself. He told Gudrun about the otherworldly flames surrounding Brynhild's hall, and how he rode through them unaffected, how he had found her sleeping and had awakened her. He spoke of the ancient knowledge she had shared with him and of the love and marriage vows they had shared. He had given her the ring, Andvaranaut, as her promise ring. He had asked for her hand in marriage from King Heimir, who agreed. He was on his way to King Budli's kingdom to ask for her hand in marriage, when he stopped to rest in the Gjukung kingdom. It was in King Gjuki's kingdom, after he drank the mead offered to him by Gudrun's mother, that all memories of Brynhild disappeared. There was so much more to tell Gudrun. He had fallen in love with Gudrun and loved her completely. He had no memory of Brynhild, when he disguised himself as Gunnar and rode through the flames. He proposed to Brynhild on behalf of Gunnar, and he unsheathed his sword and laid it between the two of them, as not to betray Gunnar or Gudrun. He took Andvaranaut from her finger and gave her another golden ring. He said his memory returned during the final feasting day of the marriage between Gunnar and Brynhild. His heart was wrenched. He was torn, because he had loved Brynhild, had sworn marriage oaths with her and, unknowingly, had broken his oaths. But now, with all his heart, he was in love with Gudrun, young Sigmund and his unborn child. He sat open-hearted and hurting, yet relieved, that he had told Gudrun the truth. "Though I tell you about the love I had for Brynhild, it is you I now love with all my life."

They sat awhile embraced within a loving hug. They were both quiet, until she spoke. "Thank you for sharing what was in your heart with me. You have shown great love and trust in me by your actions and words. I love and trust you, too. I am curious… Who all knows of the shapes-shifting that you and Gunnar did before Brynhild's flames?"

"Your mother, Grimhild, and all the men who accompanied us," Sigurd confessed. "I did it for our brother Gunnar. He is a good, noble man and a fine match for Brynhild."

Gudrun agreed. He told Gudrun all that he remembered of his life before he had met her. His ancestry, his father, mother, step and foster fathers, growing up with his nieces and nephews, the reforged sword of Odin, the avenging of his family, the killing of the dragon, Fafnir, and of Regin… He also revealed to her the story of the gold and the curse it bore. He brought out Andvaranaut and gave it to Gudrun for safe-keeping. At this point, he found more courage to share with Gudrun the intimate details of his time with Brynhild before he and had met Gudrun. He admitted that, though he had loved Brynhild in the past, he was now deeply in love with Gudrun.

Gudrun listened carefully and sensitively to Sigurd's story. She felt like she had heard something of this before. She deeply loved Sigurd with all her heart. She clarified with Sigurd that she knew nothing of the mead of forgetfulness. She wondered how he was given it and who gave it to him… They lovingly hugged and lovingly kissed and were able to come to some peace within Sigurd's past life story. He loved

Gudrun and was loyal to her and had sworn oaths to her. Gudrun had done the same for Sigurd. Sigurd was satisfied and content to see that Brynhild was happy with her marriage to Gunnar. He came to believe that Brynhild had for some reason forgotten her love and vows of marriage to him as well. The families lived in harmony and happiness in the Gjukung kingdom, and time passed peacefully.

Chapter Thirty-Four
Brynhild Hears the Truth

The people of their respective households bathed themselves in the refreshing waters of the river, Rhine and, one day, Gudrun and Brynhild found themselves cleansing at the same time. They were both washing their hair, when Brynhild waded out further from shore. Gudrun asked, "Brynhild, why are you walking so far away from me?"

She replied, "I am wading over here, because we are far from being equal. You are rinsing your hair at the same time that I am rinsing my hair, and I do not want your rinse water to mix with my hair. My father is the most powerful and noble man, more powerful than your father. And my husband is more courageous than your husband could ever be. My gracious and gallant Gunnar rode through the fiery flames to my hall, while your husband sat ablaze in fear at the sight of my colourful wildfire."

Gudrun was stunned and wounded by her remarks. She thought Brynhild was her close friend, and they were now sisters-in-law. What would spurn Brynhild to say such things? Gudrun could not tolerate the treatment and instinctively followed Brynhild further into the river. She said, "I am entitled to wash my hair further up in the river from you, because my husband is far braver than Gunnar ever was and more courageous than anyone else in Middle Earth. It would be advisable for you to hush yourself and not say such shameful things about my husband. I know he was your first love. With his sword, Gram, Sigurd slew the serpent dragon and the deceiving dwarf, and then he acquired all their inheritance, the gold of Andvari."

Brynhild paused a moment, but refused to listen to the words of Gudrun and continued to glorify Gunnar's deeds. "Greater was the accomplishment of King Gunnar, the valiant, when he rode through the blazing flames around my hall, while Sigurd was a slave in King Hjalprek's halls."

Gudrun felt the sting of her words. She was surprised and hurt by the attitude of Brynhild, and how she was wrongfully portraying the events. Gudrun delighted in correcting her. "Brynhild, you know you speak false words about Sigurd, but say what you will. You truly believe that Gunnar was the man who rode through your flames. Do you not know that it was Sigurd all along? It was he who rode through the flames, only he was disguised as Gunnar. A trick of shape-changing that our mother taught them… Sigurd proposed to you on behalf of Gunnar. It was Sigurd who was lying beside you with his sword, Gram, unsheathed between the two of you while you slept. And, it was Sigurd who took Andvaranaut from your finger, the same ring you received from him as a morning gift. He then gave you another ring from the golden treasures of Fafnir. You can see, for yourself, that Andvaranaut now rests on my finger."

Gudrun lifted up her hand and displayed Andvaranaut upon her finger. Brynhild was now listening and waded towards Gudrun. She grasped Gudrun's hand to have a better look at the ring. Memories flooded into her mind, as she recognized the ring on Gudrun's finger. It was her first ring! It was the ring that Sigurd had given her! In shock, she stood holding Gudrun's hand! She gasped, as the truth of this knowledge seeped into her. She let Gudrun's hand fall from hers. She stood shaking, yet paralyzed. She turned pale and was unable to speak or move. The women exchanged no more words that day. Brynhild then fell into the water, rinsed the rest of her hair and screeched for her kinswomen to assist her. All the women finished bathing and returned home.

At home, Brynhild grew sullen, sad and gloomy, refusing any company. She refused participation in any of the feasts, played none of the games, nor gathered with anyone for anything. She grew gloomier, her skin turned pale grey, and she resigned herself to her room.

Gudrun confided to Sigurd that she had revealed the truth about Sigurd to Brynhild. How he had ridden through her fiery flames disguised as Gunnar, and how he had proposed to her on behalf of Gunnar... She then commented about Brynhild's behaviour. "Since I told Brynhild the truth of these past events, she has been sullen and gloomy and has refused to attend any of the feasts or games or any of the events happening within these halls. She has also ignored all of her wealth and has refused to be happy, although she is with the man she has boasted about and wanted to marry."

Sigurd asked, "Where was she, when she mentioned the man she wanted to marry?"

Gudrun replied, "We were in the river washing our hair, when she said she was married to the man she wanted. She was boasting about Gunnar being the best man in all of Middle Earth, because he accomplished the feat of riding through her supernatural flames. Then, she insulted you, and I was angered by her attitude and disrespect. I told her it was you, disguised as Gunnar, who rode through her flames, and that it is you who is the best man in all of the world. I regret that I may have gone too far with her, but she angered me so. In the morning, I will ask her about which man she wished to marry."

Sigurd replied, "My beloved Gudrun, the truth has now been revealed to her. As strange as this may sound, I am relieved that she knows. But I implore you, Gudrun, do not ask her who she wished to marry, for you will regret knowing her answer."

Chapter Thirty-Five
Gudrun and Brynhild

In the morning, Gudrun coaxed Brynhild to leave her bedroom and retire to their bower. Brynhild was sullen and silent. Gudrun spoke. "Brynhild, my friend… Tell me what ails you."

Brynhild expressed, "You know very well why I am unhappy. Your heart is grim, Gudrun, and your meanness and maliciousness brought you to this."

Gudrun replied, "Do not think these thoughts of me, Brynhild. Rather, tell me what grieves you."

Brynhild responded, "You already know what grieves me. You flaunt your happiness with Sigurd and your concern for me, when you only care about yourself."

Gudrun continued, "Why do you try to provoke me, when I have done nothing to you?"

Brynhild spoke slowly and clearly. "You deny that you have done nothing to grieve me, when you have married the man that I vowed to marry! You will receive your day of reckoning for what you have done to me. The thoughts of you wrapped in his arms, accepting all his attentions, grieves me endlessly, and you have all of his bounty of golden treasures he earned at Gnita-Heath."

Gudrun exclaimed, "Brynhild, I married Sigurd from the arrangement of my father and family. There was no talk of any marriage agreement between you and Sigurd and, if there was, I was not informed of it."

Brynhild said, "Sigurd and I swore marriage oaths to one another long before you met, and this was well known by everyone. You knew of the deception, and I vow to avenge this treachery."

Gudrun responded, "Brynhild, everyone knows you trained as a warrior woman and had little or no training as a wife. I did not know of your vows with Sigurd nor of Sigurd's vows with you. He never said anything about this until his memory came back, and he was honestly distraught. But, by this time we were already married. His memory came back to him during your and Gunnar's wedding feast. He confided in me a little while after you were married. And you are married, Brynhild, to Gunnar, a distinguished, honourable, worthy and good man. With all of your wisdom and foresight, it appears that you are unable to see these truths. You have an exceptional marriage. One that is beyond what you are entitled to… You seem to be revelling in resentment, with vicious thoughts of vengeance running rampant, and this may not be easily contained or softened. I am afraid, Brynhild, that if you continue like this, many innocent people will suffer."

Brynhild expressed, "I would have been happy if Sigurd was my husband, for he is the most fearless and honoured of all men. But, he is married to you, and I am married to Gunnar."

Gudrun said, "Yes, Brynhild, you are married to Gunnar, and he is a forthright and trustworthy man, with an enormous abundance of wealth and power, that you can live and be happy with for the rest of your days. He is highly regarded and well respected. Both kings are gracious and generous, and it is undetermined who is the *greater* king, or even *if* one is greater than the other."

Brynhild reminded Gudrun. "Sigurd rode through my burning flames, and I swore an oath to myself that I would marry the man who could do that. It was not Gunnar, but Sigurd, who rode through the flames, and that is worth more to me than all of Gunnar's wealth and power."

Gudrun justified Gunnar's actions. "Gunnar's horse, Goti, would not ride through the flames. Sigurd's horse, Grani, would but with only Sigurd on his back. Sigurd and Gunnar had learned shape-changing from our mother, Grimhild, and the two men decided together to change shapes. Sigurd, disguised as Gunnar, rode through the flames and, as Gunnar, asked for your hand in marriage. He did this for the sake of my brother and now your husband. And, there is no need to challenge Gunnar's courage, as he did dare to ride through the flames."

Brynhild replied, "Daring is not the same as doing. I see that Grimhild lacks respect for me."

Gudrun said, "Now you turn to our mother with your hostility. She has nothing to do with your quarrel, and she has showered you with love and attention."

Brynhild and Gudrun, by Arthur Rackham

Brynhild blamed her. "She knowingly planned this misery, as she made the mead of memory loss with her magical ways and served it only to Sigurd, so that he would lose all his memories of me and our love and vows of marriage."

Gudrun again was surprised by Brynhild's comments. "How can you say such foul things! You speak false words about mother."

Still, Gudrun wondered, in her heart, if it was her own mother who had given Sigurd the mead of forgetfulness. Was this her mother's doing?

Brynhild carried on, "Do you remember when you came to me with your distressing dreams? This is what I saw, but at that time they were only words and visions, and they did not affect me. But, now that this foresight has truly happened to me, and I am living this nightmare, I find all of this betrayal unbearable. All of you have knowingly shamed and dishonoured me."

She snapped at Gudrun. "The norns have woven grim paths for us all, and my foresight is foreboding. Live and love Sigurd, as if you have not forsaken me. You are unworthy as his wife."

Gudrun said, "I do love Sigurd with all my heart and soul. He is my happiness and my strength. I will delight in his attentions and bask in the sunshine of his love, more than you can ever dream of. No one has ever said that he was your man or too good for me!"

Brynhild grew tired and grave with grieving, and her voice lowered. "Cruel words do not become you, Gudrun, and, when you redeem your dignity, you will be sorry you spoke them. Let us no longer spar with words of hostility and loathing."

Gudrun confronted Brynhild. "You hurled hateful words upon me like daggers into my heart from the beginning, and now you speak of an accord. Am I to trust you, when the arrows of vengeance and hatred shoot from your mouth?"

Brynhild grew fatigued. "Let us rest from this meaningless banter. The silence of the grief and agony in my heart has pained me forever and a day. I foresaw all these events coming, but they were only thoughts and words. Now that the visions have happened, my heart is beyond broken, and I ache through and through. With all my foresight, I did not foresee the agony I would feel. I could sense with Gunnar that something was amiss, but could not determine what it was. But, now that you have enlightened me with these truths, they have cut deeply and have hurt me beyond anything I have ever known. Although you deserve gratitude for the truths you have shared with me, Gudrun, these truths have ravaged the very core of my being beyond repair."

Brynhild was quiet for a moment and then said, "Now, let us turn our thoughts to something else."

Gudrun looked upon Brynhild, as she had never seen her so vulnerable. "These are truths, Brynhild. Yet, few people know this. Sigurd, Grimhild, Gunnar and the men who went with them the day that Gunnar proposed marriage to you… Sigurd told me. I thought that you knew, but realized you did not when you boasted about Gunnar as we were washing our hair. I know as well as you, Brynhild, that your foreknowledge and your forethoughts reach far beyond the present time."

"My foresight never revealed to me the torment, agony and pain these truths would cause in my heart."

The women shared no more words that day. Brynhild became more sullen, somber and silent. She slowly turned from Gudrun and went back to her room. She crawled into her bed, curled up and became motionless.

Chapter Thirty-Six
Brynhild's Grief Escalates

King Gunnar heard that Brynhild had taken to her bed with a strange sickness, so he went to see her. He asked, "Brynhild, my love, what is ailing you?"

She gave him no response and lay still and silent, as if she were dead. Frightened, Gunnar looked upon his wife. Then, he quickly placed his head on her chest to check if she was breathing and if her heart was still beating. Relief entered his whole being, when he heard the rhythmic beating of her heart. She was still breathing. He continued to softly speak to her.

"My dear Brynhild, if you can hear me, let me know how you are, and if there is anything I can do for you or bring you, my love."

Gunnar persisted that Brynhild answer him. She finally stirred, opened her eyes and questioned him in a cold and calculated voice. "Where is the ring that I gave you?"

Gunnar was a little taken aback. What did his ring have to do with her illness?

She continued, "My father, King Budli, gifted me the rare ring. He said you vowed you would die, if you could not have me as your bride. My father graciously asked me if there was any man I would choose for a husband. I had never considered marriage before. I was a warrior maiden and royal ruler of trained troops defending our lands. I felt I was not destined to marry. But, to my bewilderment, my father gave me a choice that day. He said I was either to marry the man he wanted for me or give up all of my wealth. I was torn. How could my father, who said he loved me, put me in such a position? He then pledged an agreement with me, stating that a settlement with him would be more rewarding for me than his rage. I was surprised and furious with his words. I contemplated his words and wondered what to do. Should I accept the man of his choosing and keep my wealth or go to war and kill other warriors causing more bloodshed? At the time, I thought that his sovereignty was all powerful, and I was not given a proper choice, and the only thing to do was to succumb to what he wanted for me. And, I must admit, the thought of losing my wealth struck dread into my heart, as I wanted the wealth. I made the vow to be betrothed to the man who would ride through my quavering flames. I thought that man was you, Gunnar. I thought you rode through the flames, and I gave you the ring from my father. But, now I know that the only man who rode through the flames was Sigurd, son of King Sigmund. You lied to me from the beginning. Our marriage is not a real marriage, because it is based on lies and falsehoods. You, who said you loved me, tricked and betrayed me with all your deceptions. You are neither a king or a conqueror. You knew the vow I made to myself, to Odin and to my family was sacred and solemn. I would love and marry the man who was fearless, the noblest and bravest man born, who would ride through the quavering flames. You let me believe that man was you! Your betrayal is immeasurable and in your self-importance you have no idea what you have done! Sigurd was the only man who rode through the flames. It was he who killed the dragon Fafnir, the betraying Regin and the five kings. Since I am not married to him, but married to you, I am an oath breaker. Your deception shall bring about your death or my death. Your mother, Grimhild, caused this with her wicked ways. There is no woman as heartless as her."

Gunnar knew what she said was true, but he was offended by Brynhild's words about his mother and responded, "Brynhild, what are you saying? These words you have spoken about my mother are unfounded. It is shameful of you to blame my mother, a woman whose position is higher than yours. She has never been the cause of war or bloodshed, unlike you, and she is admired by everyone."

Brynhild continued, "I have been open and honest with you and everyone and have not been the cause of any misdeeds, unlike your mother who attends mysterious and unknown private meetings. I am not like you. You have never taken the time to get to know or understand me, although I understand you thoroughly. You are frail-minded and weak-hearted." She made a loud laugh. "You know I have the skills to smite you where you stand."

Gunnar was startled and stunned, when Brynhild let out a bloodcurdling scream and went into a furious frenzy. Hearing the screams, Hogni and other kinsmen from the household ran into the room. Brynhild grabbed a sword of Gunnar's and threatened him, while screaming words of death. Hogni and the men grabbed and secured her. She screamed and wrestled. It took ten men to restrain her. Hogni put her in fetters.

Gunnar was anguished. "I cannot bear to see her like this. In chains…"

Hogni replied, "I would rather see her in chains, than see you dead, brother."

Brynhild spit at them, squawked, screeched and cackled. "Do not bother yourselves with me being fettered, because, from this day forward, you will never see me happy in your halls. I shall neither attend the feasts, nor drink, nor eat, nor play in any of the daily games, nor sing my songs of runes and advice, nor speak amusingly, nor embroider with golden or colourful threads, nor share any of my ancient knowledge. From this day forward, I am no longer living. I am dead. Dead to you, because of this immense injury you have inflicted upon me. I loved and trusted all of you, and you all deceived and lied to me. It is the most grievous of sorrows that I married you, Gunnar, for now my heart is aching and wrenched beyond repair. Your insincerity has brought about my breaking of my own vow to myself, as I am not married to the right man, the only man who rode through the flames, my one true love, Sigurd."

"Unchain her, Hogni. She speaks the truth, and it grieves me to see her so wretched."

Hogni cautiously unchained her. She rose up and, with the sword, she struck her beloved tapestry of Sigurd and his deeds, then flung the sword away. Hogni retrieved the sword. With her bare hands, Brynhild tore the tapestry to shreds, as she shrieked and whimpered. Then, she opened up her chamber doors and let out a legion of loud lamentations that were heard throughout all the households. When some kinsmen closed her door, she forbade it and burst them back open, as she wanted everyone to hear her. Her sorrows were unrestrained and boundless, and everyone in the stronghold heard her.

When Gudrun heard the lamentations, she asked a kinswoman about Brynhild's troubles. The woman answered, "Today is a dark and foreboding day, as our halls are full of hopelessness and despair."

Gudrun went to speak with the wailing woman. "Brynhild, tell me what ails you, and let me help you feel better. Let us do something cheerful. Let us do our needlework together."

Brynhild squawked, "Nevermore!"

Gudrun could not persuade her otherwise. Brynhild did not eat, nor did she drink, for many days, and an unknown, mysterious madness came upon her. Gudrun went to Gunnar. "Gunnar, speak with your wife, as her lamentations of sorrow pain the whole household."

Gunnar explained, "She will not see me and has forbidden me entrance into her halls."

When Gudrun coaxed him more, he relented and went to speak with Brynhild. He spoke with her many times, but she never responded to him. Gunnar asked Hogni to speak with her. Hogni went and spoke with her, but he also received no response from her. By this time, Brynhild had gone into a deep and dolorous death-like sleep. She would howl and scream in her sleep. The brothers asked Sigurd to speak with her. He only looked solemnly at them and did not reply.

The next day, Sigurd spoke with his wife, Gudrun, after he returned home from hunting. He expressed his concerns for Brynhild. "I know I am not an innocent participant in Brynhild's lamentations and sorrow. But, I believe that this trance she has fallen into is a forewarning. She is plotting a severe vengeance against us, although she may die if she continues like this."

"She is a strange and extraordinary woman with phenomenal insights and abilities, and now that she has slept for seven days, no one wants to awaken her. Sigurd, it is an enormous grief to foresee your death. Go to her and see whether her fury can be quenched with the offer of gold or anything else she wishes that may calm her fierceness."

Sigurd agreed and went to the sleeping chambers of Brynhild. She lay moaning. He went to the windows and threw open the curtains, letting the sunbeams light up the room. He approached her and flung off her bedcovers, saying, "Awake, Brynhild. It is a beautiful day. The sun is shining, and it is time to end this mischief."

Brynhild burst out, "You overbearing brute! I am wretchedly outraged by you and everyone else who has betrayed me. You have all lied to me, and the whole household knew of the deception but me! You and everyone else must see me as a weak-minded fool. You have shamed and disrespected me. I saw that you surpassed all other men, but you must see me as a loathsome fool. I am humiliated and mortified by your treachery."

Sigurd sat down in a chair beside her bed and tried to calm her. "On the contrary, Brynhild… You are wrong, if you think anyone thinks coarsely of you. All have been generous and good to you, and you have also received the husband of your choice."

"No, Sigurd! Gunnar is not the husband of my choice! He did not ride through the flames or settle the wedding alliance with breathless men. I was in wonderment of the man who entered my hall that day. Yet, for a moment, I thought I saw your eyes, but the drapes of destiny prevented the truth from entering into my eyes."

Sigurd reminded her, "I am not more honourable a man than Gunnar or any of the sons of Gjuki. They slew the king of the Danes and a great prince, the brother of King Budli."

Brynhild burst out her painful truths. "Yes, they killed my ruthless uncle, and there are many misdeeds to release upon them, but I do not need a history of my heartaches. You were the one who slew the dragon serpent, Fafnir, the deadly dwarf, Regin, and the five kings. You are the owner of the golden treasures of Andvari, and you rode through the blazing flames to me. Gunnar did none of those things. You were my intended husband, not Gunnar. I have never loved Gunnar, as my heart does not beat with his heart. I despise him and have hidden this hatred from others."

"It is true. I did all those things, and I did not become your husband, although a royal and honourable king compensated your marriage arrangement. It is heartbreaking to hear that you have not loved Gunnar, when he has loved you and has generously given you everything you could need or want and much more. Would not the treasure of his love be more meaningful for you than the treasure of gold? Tell me, Brynhild, what pains you the most?"

"I remember when we met on the mountain and swore oaths of marriage together. I wanted you to be with me and me with you. I had sworn the oath to marry the man who would ride through the wavering flames, and that man was you, Sigurd. You were my intended husband. But, now everything has changed. You and I are not together. You love another and have a wife and a child. I have a husband and, because I married Gunnar, I have broken my own oath to myself. I need to uphold my oath or else die."

Sigurd tried to convince her otherwise. "Live, Brynhild! Stay alive and love both King Gunnar and me. I will compensate you with all my worldly treasures from the bounty of Andvari, so that you live. For I have loved you, Brynhild, more than you know."

"You have delayed too long in telling me of your love. Now that all my sorrows grieve you, I find no comfort in your words. You are far too late. You have tricked, deceived and cheated me of all the pleasures and happinesses of being married to you. Now, I care nothing about myself or my life. I no longer want you or anyone else. All I can see is black, and I do not want to live any longer. I only desire death."

"Brynhild, for years I could not remember your name or even recognize you, and that is my deepest sorrow. My memory came back to me during your marriage feasting, and I was distressed. It hurt me that you were not my wife. I braved it as best as I could, and I was happy because I was able to see you every day, as we all lived together in this household. I would like for you to be my wife, rather than have you die.

I will forsake Gudrun and marry you… Brynhild, will you have me as your beloved husband?"

Brynhild grieved, "Not like this! Not like this! These words should not be spoken! You want me to bed two kings in one hall!! Your lack of respect for me is boundless!! You lie and betray me, and now you want me to lie and betray King Gunnar! Not only that, you will lie and betray Gudrun! I cannot betray King Gunnar, as I would rather die. But I am already dead, as I am an oath-breaker."

Sigurd pleaded, "Brynhild, you are beautiful beyond any woman known. I do not want you to die. Instead, I surrender myself and all that I own, including all of my gold, to you. And, for your sake, I will let my wife, Gudrun, go. Reconsider these thoughts of yours."

Brynhild scowled. "I no longer desire you nor anyone else. I can only see black, and I only desire death. Your offer is shallow. You only offer this, because I distress you. I know you love Gudrun and your son! It torments me, that I cannot secure a sword and stain it with your blood!"

Sigurd shared his foresight. "I know I was the target of a betrayal, and I cannot change that, but, when my thoughts were my own, I did love you. I loved you with all my life. It will come to pass what was earlier foretold, but these events must not be feared. I see that I have but a brief wait, until a biting blade bloodies my heart. But you, Brynhild… You could not ask worse for yourself, because, if you continue on this path you have chosen, you will not live long after me. From here on, there are only a few days of life left for both of us."

She understood. "Your words come from a foresight only known to a few, and they do not come from little distress."

Sigurd's heart broke and his sides swelled so that the links of his mail coat burst. He was grieved by all her words, yet there was truth in her words. He slowly lifted himself up and left.

Sigurd contemplated the words of Brynhild, and then entered the halls of Gunnar. The son of Gjuki asked, "Have you seen Brynhild? Was she able to speak? Can you tell me her affliction?"

Sigurd quietly said, "Yes, Gunnar, she was able to speak. Go to your wife."

Gunnar went to see his wife and asked her, "What is your ailment? Can we mend it?"

Brynhild replied, "I do not want to live anymore. I do not want to live, because both you and Sigurd have deceived, lied and betrayed me. The whole household has betrayed me. And, Sigurd has betrayed you no less, when you let him come into my bed that deceptive day. Now, I do not want to live and have two husbands at the same time in the same hall. This shall be your death or Sigurd's death or my death, because now he has told Gudrun everything, and she has nothing but contempt for me."

Gunnar begged, "Oh Brynhild, my light and my love, please stop these raging thoughts! No one thinks poorly of you. You are praised by all."

Brynhild grew mad and, in a fury, tried to herd Gunnar out of her chambers. "Gunnar, get out! I do not want to see you or anyone else!"

Gunnar stayed by her door.

Chapter Thirty-Seven
The Betrayal of Sigurd

A multitude of emotions seized Brynhild's sanity and senses. She obsessed in her grievous mood of suffering and mourning, proclaiming that all her possessions were despicable and detestable to her. Her land, jewelry, all her earthly belongings, and all her wealth and power were wretched and worthless, because she did not have Sigurd as her husband with whom to share her life. She marinated in the value of vengeance for the vile and vicious betrayal she had endured. Gunnar, again, tried to reason with her.

Brynhild glared at Gunnar with a fierce gaze. She snarled, "You, Gunnar, son of Gjuki… Because of your betrayal, you will lose all your power, all your wealth, your life and me, as I am going home to my own kin and will remain there in deep misery and sorrow."

Gunnar pleaded, "Brynhild, you know that I love you with all my heart. I have offered you all that I own, as you mean more to me than all my power and wealth. Tell me what I can do to appease you or ease your pain."

Brynhild barked, "Kill the wolf, Sigurd, and his wolf cub. Do not leave them alive!"

Gunnar's eyes opened wide, and his mouth dropped. He was deeply distressed by her request. There was a moment of silence, before he spoke… "Odin, I beseech you to let Brynhild come to her true self and senses! You, my love, do not know what you are saying! You know a request like this is impossible and cannot be fulfilled, for I am bound by oaths of brotherhood to Sigurd."

"If you won't do what I ask, then watch me die or leave!" burst Brynhild.

Gunnar retreated from Brynhild, but her words sliced into his whole being. Gunnar wondered which was worse… To break his sworn oaths of brotherhood to Sigurd, or to suffer the disrespectful dishonour of having his wife leave him…?

Gunnar called for Hogni and confided in him all that Brynhild had revealed to him. "Hogni, Brynhild is more precious than anything else in the world, and she is the most esteemed and outstanding of all women. I would forfeit my life rather than lose her. I find myself now confronted with this difficult choice. According to Brynhild, Sigurd betrayed my trust and, therefore, I should desire his death. Yet, according to Sigurd, he placed his sword, unsheathed, between them while they slept. Who am I to believe? But, what if we *did* kill Sigurd? Do you realize, with Sigurd gone, we would gain control of all his golden treasures and all the power too?"

Hogni was horrified by Gunnar's words. "Stop, Gunnar! It is not right to even consider a violation of our oaths with Sigurd. We have substantial support from him. No other kings are our equals, while the King of Hunaland remains alive and well with us. Consider, as well, how beneficial it is for us to have such a powerful brother-in-law and nephew. We will never have such generous and kind kin. But, I can see how this problem arose. Brynhild has stirred this up. Her scornful counsel will only lead us into the ruinous nature of dishonour, disrespect, disgrace, discredit and destruction."

Gunnar could not hear the wise words of Hogni and, instead, he continued in his rantings of intrigue. "We can make this event happen, and I can see a way. We will goad our younger brother, Guttorm, to do the deed. He is young and immature and with limited knowledge. The most important fact is that he has not bound himself to Sigurd with any oaths. Guttorm is free to kill Sigurd."

Hogni groaned, "Oh, Gunnar… This is outrageous and extremely dangerous counsel. Even if, as you say, this deed is done, we will duly suffer horribly for such a malicious betrayal of such a splendid and renowned man as Sigurd."

Gunnar made up his mind. "Either Sigurd must die, or I must die."

Gunnar went back to visit Brynhild. He inspired and encouraged her to rise up out of her bed, to face the bright, sunny day, to use her resilience and be energized.

Brynhild snarled, "You will not enter the same bed as me, until you kill Sigurd."

Gunnar went back to Hogni, and the two brothers whispered together. Hogni gave in to Gunnar's rantings, and they both concluded that the plan could work. Neither of them would take the blame for the death or break their oaths to Sigurd, if Guttorm carried out the deed. They offered Guttorm an abundance of glorious gold, immense power and notable renown, if he were to perform the act. At first, Guttorm was opposed to the idea, because Sigurd had been good to him, and he loved Sigurd as a brother. But, Gunnar and Hogni encouraged him. They concocted a potion from their mother's collection of witchcraft supplies. Grimhild supported them and their decision to go through with the deadly deed. They took snake and wolf meat, mixed with mead and magical ingredients from Grimhild, cooked them all together, and gave the mixture to Guttorm to eat.

After eating the flesh and drinking the potion, Guttorm became like a berserker. As he swore to do the deed, his eyes grew aflame, and he was ready for a fight. His brothers continued telling him that he would earn great renown, respect, honour and wealth.

Sigurd did not foresee a betrayal from Guttorm. The youngest brother boldly went into Sigurd's sleeping chambers and saw the great man laying sound asleep with his wife, Gudrun, curled up beside him. Even with the potion pumping through his blood, Guttorm, could not find it within himself to kill Sigurd, and he left. With the potion inside of him, Guttorm was reeling. He loved his brother-in-law, Sigurd, and wondered how he could possibly kill him… Gunnar, Hogni and Grimhild coaxed him on with promises of wealth and prestige. Guttorm returned a second time to the bedside of Sigurd and, again, he fought a torment within himself. He wanted to kill Sigurd and win great renown, wealth and respect from his family. However, Sigurd had been good to him and, when Guttorm looked in the room, the fierce eyes of Sigurd were staring right at him. Terror filled Guttorm, and he left not being able to commit the act. Gunnar and Hogni urged their younger brother on for the third time and gave Guttorm more of the potion to drink. Guttorm went into Sigurd's sleeping chambers, and saw that Sigurd was sound asleep. Guttorm, red-eyed with the berserk concoction raging through his body, rose his sword high over Sigurd and thrust it down through him and through the bed beneath. With a start from the wound, Sigurd awoke and saw that Guttorm was leaving. He grabbed Gram, that had been laying by his side, and flung it at Guttorm, slicing him in half.

In the arms of Sigurd, Gudrun awoke in horror and torment, as she was drenched in his blood. Screaming for help, she clapped her hands loudly. The man with the mighty spirit heaved himself up in the bed and, with all of his remaining strength, whispered to his beloved Gudrun. "Do not weep my love, for you have your brothers. They are still alive. I know full well why this has happened. Brynhild alone has caused this misery. Your brothers will never find a better brother-in-law to ride with them while hunting or fishing or in the army or in war, nor even such a nephew, if they allow our son to live. It has come to pass, as it was foretold. I knew this would happen, but I denied the truth of it. Brynhild loved me more than she loved any other man, and she has caused this betrayal. I never did Gunnar or Hogni any disservice, as I respected our oaths. If I had known this would happen, I would have been prepared and borne my arms. Many would have died tonight. All your brothers would have been vanquished. I would have been more difficult to kill than the fiercest and wildest of troll bears. I see death is coming for me. Gudrun, I love you with all my heart and with all my life and always will, both now and in the afterlife. You must stay alive, my love. Stay alive, and live your life. Take our son away from here, and protect him if you can. And you, my beloved wife, are with our child. I can see a beautiful girl, and her name is Svanhild. Gudrun, for the sake of our son and our daughter within you, leave this place. Leave and live, my love." With these words Sigurd died in the arms of his beloved. Gudrun wailed in grief.

Sigurd's and Gudrun's household came with the screams of

Gudrun. She was in shock. Ernest, a trusted man of Sigurd, lifted the horrified and crying Gudrun out of their marital bed and gently placed her in a servant's chamber away from the horror. She cried for their sleeping son, Sigmund, for fear that Brynhild may have killed him already. Ernest went to the boy's chambers, gathered him up and then placed him in his mother's arms. They positioned pillows in young Sigmund's bed and covered them over with blankets, to make it look like the boy was still sound asleep. Then they had men watch his bed chambers, while other men watched over the servant's chamber where the boy and Gudrun were. Her kinswomen washed the blood from Gudrun and dressed and comforted her and the boy.

Brynhild had heard the screams of Gudrun and knew the deed was done. She viciously chortled and cackled.

Gunnar saw and heard his wife laugh and cringed. "To think I loved you… The veils of your charms have been lifted from me this night. Unfortunately, I see you as a repulsive vile beast that is fated to die. Although I am far from innocent of this fate, I abhor what we have done. You deserve to watch your own brother, King Atli, slain before your eyes, and then forced to watch while it happens. We must now prepare afterlife rites for our brother-in-law Sigurd and our brother Guttorm."

Brynhild continued cackling. "Nobody can complain that there is not enough killings in this household!" She laughed and laughed and said, "My brother has no concerns for your omens or outrage. I have foreseen him as a magnificent king, far greater than you or Hogni will ever be, and he also lives a longer life." She laughed, then turned to Gunnar and said, "The wolf cub needs to die along with the wolf."

Gunnar refused. "Brynhild, I have loved you with all my heart and all my soul. I have shared with you all that I own, but your actions are too much for me to endure. You must stop this."

"If you do not complete this task, one of my many men will," laughed Brynhild.

Hogni entered and said, "Gunnar, all your wife's seeress abilities and prophecies, that she has foretold to us over the years, have come true. Has destiny been so powerful that it has drawn us into all the predictions, with no other course of action and with us thinking that what has been foretold to us is the right and only way? Why did we not foresee this horror and try to stop this or prevent this somehow? How will we ever be able to atone for the killing of this great and noble man, our honourable brother-in-law, Sigurd?"

Chapter Thirty-Eight
Brynhild Has a Change of Heart

Brynhild had a change of heart and her laughter turned to lamentations. As she realized what she had done, tears burst forth from her eyes, "Oh, what have I done? What have you done? I have killed the only one I have ever loved! My true love…"

She faced Gunnar and said, "I dreamed our bedchambers were chilled with frost and you, Gunnar, rode confidently towards your slayers. Your whole family's destiny is doomed for plotting Sigurd's death. From now on, you all are like me… We are breakers of our own vows. We are all shameful and disgraceful oath-breakers. Do you not remember when you and Sigurd mixed your blood together and became blood brothers? You have repaid him gravely for letting you be a champion, with all the support, strength and honour he so trustingly gave to you. That time, when he came to me in the image of you, all his vows were tested, and he laid Gram between us. But, you thoughtfully planned to wrong him and me. When I lived with my kin, I had all that I ever needed or wanted, and I was happy and contented. I wondered why you three kings came to the fortress. My brother and father privately told me to betroth myself or forfeit my share of the wealth and property. I felt belittled and undermined, as I was never destined to marry. I had trained all my life, not with marriage skills, but as a warrior. I wanted to go to war with them, yet I wanted the wealth more than war. I also did not want to leave a legacy of slaughtering my family. So, I decided it was better for me to marry. Also, Odin told me I must marry a human. Atli asked if I would marry the man who rode through the flames, as I had sworn marriage vows to this man. But, that man was not you, Gunnar… That man was Sigurd, son of Sigmund. From this day forward, your life will wither and shrink and shrivel and, for me, all

I truly desire is death. The norns have woven a wicked and woeful web, and all of this has been foretold!"

Gunnar was torn with both love and hate for his wife. He hugged her and begged her to live and to accept compensation. "Oh, Brynhild… Everything that I have done, I have done for the sake of you. I love you with all my heart and plead for you to stay alive and live and be happy with me. We can live here, be happy and have many children."

"All I desire is death." She was resigned to the fact that this was her destiny. Everyone counselled her to live and be happy but, being possessed with gloom and grief, she drove them away. Steps taken to prevent her goal were unproductive.

The dispirited Gunnar pleaded with Hogni to help him in this matter. Hogni replied, "Gunnar… Think clearly, brother. What benefit has Brynhild ever been to us or brought us? If she thinks she is destined to die, then let her die."

"Hogni, how can you say this about Brynhild! She is my wife! And, she has benefited us by the peaceful alliance with the Budlung kingdom."

Brynhild howled in pain and grief. The suffering woman ravaged her way to where her wealth and gold were stored. She tore it all apart. Then she ravaged into the gold belonging to Sigurd, and her hands found the Aegis Helm. She stopped and stared at it, as it shone upon her face. She put the Helm of Terror on her head and screamed and cried. She demanded that all of her wealth in gold and treasures be brought to her chamber hall. Once her wealth was brought, she sent a message throughout the whole kingdom, that anyone who wanted to receive some of her wealth was to come forward.

"Whoever wants my gold may take it now, and accept the gold as a gift from me. Use it well and wisely in this world. And, whosoever of my loyal men and women who wish to follow me in death may do so."

Gunnar was deeply distraught. He felt that his wife had lost her mind and had gone beyond any rational reasoning in this world. She emanated from another realm and was determined to die and follow Sigurd into the afterlife.

Chapter Thirty-Nine
Gullrond and Gudrun

The following morning, Gudrun had turned pale and was still in shock by Sigurd's death. She sat quietly beside the lifeless body of the man she loved, but she could not cry. Others felt it would do her good, if she could express her sorrow. Many women from all the households tried to help her to voice her grief, but she was inconsolable and unable to do so. All she could do was sit frozen in time. With a dark veil over her head, she remained sitting, numb.

Gunnar and Hogni came to see Sigurd. In their presence, Gudrun declared, "My kin have killed my beloved husband. Now, brothers, when you brave a battle you will learn that Sigurd was your strength and courage, but he can no longer smile upon you with his assistance and support. If he and I had the opportunity to have sons, you would have been fortified and strengthened by his progeny. Now you arc on your own, and that, my brothers, will be the death of you. Now leave us."

Gudrun at Sigurd's Deathbed, by Johannes Gehrts

Many came forth to offer Gudrun comfort, but she was inconsolable and frozen numb. Wise warriors came forth to comfort the grieving Gudrun, but she could find no comfort in their words. Wives of warriors, also, came forth to aid Gudrun. One was Gjaflaug, a sister of Gjuki, who shared her story of grief. "My dear Gudrun, I understand your great sorrow, for I have lost five husbands, three daughters, three sisters and eight brothers." Gudrun was still so overwhelmed from the loss of Sigurd, that she could not feel for her aunt or weep for her or for herself.

Herborg visited and expressed her heavier grief. "Gudrun, I lost my seven sons and my husband, as they were slaughtered in battle. Then, my mother, father and four brothers drowned at sea in a raging storm. A half year later, I was taken as a war prisoner, beaten, disrespected and dishonoured. But, here I am today, still alive, and I have made my way to freedom."

Gudrun heard the sorrowful words of Herborg, but she still was unable to navigate with the iron veil of grief that lay over her, she could not feel or weep. Others came in to see Sigurd and Gudrun. Gudrun was told many tales of how others struggled with the death of their loved ones. She heard the stories of their lives, their grief and their sorrows, but Gudrun was still unable to feel for them or grieve for herself. Nothing seemed to penetrate the dark, iron veil of sorrow that surrounded her.

Finally, Gudrun's sister, Gullrond, came from abroad to console Gudrun. Gullrond sat in silence with Gudrun for a while. She felt that Gudrun needed to see her husband. She got up, pushed the blood-soaked pillows towards Gudrun, and slowly lifted and removed the cloth from Sigurd, revealing his whole worldly body and the full sight of his death wound. His breast and hair were covered in his blood, and the fierceness of his eyes had grown dim. Gudrun slowly stood up and looked upon her beloved husband. Her fragile body began to quake, shaking beyond control, as the horrific site played upon her mind, her heart and her very soul. "Oh, Sigurd, my beloved Sigurd…! Oh! Oh! Oh!"

And, she burst out into a flood of tears, wept uncontrollably and fell to her knees leaning on the blood-soaked pillows. Gullrond knelt with Gudrun, and held her sister as she wept and wept and wept. The shaking of her fragile frame gradually slowed, her tears rested, and they both sat beside Sigurd. Gudrun slowly reminisced about her life with Sigurd. "Oh, Gullrond, my life was so full when Sigurd and I were together. He outshone all other men, as gold outshines all other metal, as the leek outshines all other plants, and as the buck outshines all other animals. Our brothers were jealous of me because of my happiness with Sigurd. They were resentful, because Sigurd was the foremost of them all. He was so much better than all of them combined, and they could not sleep until they killed him."

Gudrun stopped and thought a moment. "I saw Grani, his beloved horse. He made a huge cry, when he saw the death wound of his master. When I spoke with Grani, it was like he was a man and knew everything I said, and that his beloved Sigurd had fallen. He dropped his head towards the earth and grieved over Sigurd like a real brother. Oh, Gullrond, what am I to do? What am I to do? With Sigurd, I felt so good as we sat in our chairs. Now, I feel like a little, lost leaf, floating on a breeze, unsure where or if I will ever land. Our brothers *killed* Sigurd. Do they want to kill *me*, too? And, what about young Sigmund? *What am I to do?* This has been my home, but I no longer feel safe here. I *know* they want to kill our son, for he is Sigurd's heir. I know we have to leave. Sigurd told me to leave. But first, Gullrond, I need to wash him, see to his needs and prepare him for his journey in the afterlife."

Gullrond pondered Gudrun's lamentations and said, "Yes, my sweet Gudrun, let us wash and prepare him. I know your love was the greatest of all loves on this earth, but your life with him has come to an end. I fear our mother, Grimhild, has not been innocent in these doings. I do agree with you, that you and your boy are not safe here and must leave. Gather up, undetected, the belongings that you need, Gudrun. Take young Sigmund and Sigurd's sword, Gram, and we will make our way elsewhere. We will find a safe haven for you and the boy. Sigurd has left this realm and is on his journey to Valhalla, where Odin is rejoicing, because he finally has Sigurd, the boldest and bravest of all warriors. He was too exquisite to remain here in Middle Earth"

Gullrond and Gudrun washed and prepared Sigurd for his journey to the afterlife. According to the ancient traditions, Sigurd's body was prepared with deep love and respect. Everyone said that there was no man of Sigurd's equal in this world, and no man his equal would ever be born again. His name was forever remembered in all the northern lands and kept safe in the Norse and Germanic tongues.

After visiting with Gudrun and preparing Sigurd, Gullrond visited Brynhild. A supernatural madness emanated from the once valkyrie warrior woman. Gullrond had a few words with her but surmised that Brynhild's state of mind was beyond any worthwhile worldly words, so Gullrond bid her farewell.

Chapter Forty
Brynhild's Request

Brynhild spoke her final request to Gunnar. "All those of my slaves and handmaidens who wish to follow me, let them die with me. I want a ceremony, with a huge fire, to be made on a level plane. Place me beside King Sigurd, with a drawn sword between us, like it was the day we lay in one bed and swore marriage oaths to one another. On each side of us, evenly place our men and women, and place two of Sigurd's hawks at his feet. This way, we will be evenly matched, and the entryway to the otherworld will stand open. I will follow closely behind Sigurd with an honourable ceremonial procession. Give your word to me, Gunnar, that you will do this for me."

"Brynhild, my love, I will do as you ask, but it breaks my heart that you choose death rather than to share a life with me. My sorrow multiplies with your request to follow Sigurd into the afterlife and not be my wife in this life!"

"I have my kinsmen and women to prepare me, if you do not. I will do this with or without your consent or help."

Then, Brynhild took her sword out of its sheath and stabbed herself under her left shoulder and fell back into her pillows. For a moment, she lay silent, and then she said, "Now that I am near my death, I can see more of your future. Through your mother, Grimhild's, sweet words, the songs of harmony arise between you and Gudrun, as you are reunited. As of now, she is with child, and her and Sigurd's daughter will be named Svanhild. She will become the most beautiful and fairest of all women born. Gudrun will be forced to marry my brother, Atli, and she will fight against it, but will not succeed. My sister, Oddrun, will become the woman of your affections, and you will happily greet one another in private, and she will love you. You will ask for her hand in marriage, but my kin will refuse you. You will marry another. King Atli will turn against you and will laugh, as he places you into a tomb of serpents. Vengeance will consume Gudrun, as she slays Atli and her sons by him. I see mystical blue and silver waves carrying Gudrun to the kingdom of King Jonakur. He will find her, hear her story, love and marry her. I see they will have royal and honourable sons. Sigurd's daughter, Svanhild, will be sent away to marry King Jormunrek, but darkness hangs over her, as the betrayal of Bikki will deprive her of her life. Gunnar, make sure the pyre is built on a meadow big enough for all of us. Cover the pyre with all of my shields and all of my wall hangings. Gunnar, mists of clouds are settling in. I have foreseen that your race will end, and Gudrun's sorrows will increase. My slash is seething and the wound is opening, and I have spoken my last truths."

Chapter Forty-One
The Funeral of Sigurd

A long and wide pyre was built for all the people who were to be burned. When all the preparations were ready, the body of Sigurd was laid on top of the funeral pyre. A wrapped, childlike form was placed beside him. Brynhild had ordered Gudrun's and Sigurd's son to be killed and, when a carefully wrapped form of a child was placed beside Sigurd, people thought the child was Sigmund, son of Sigurd and Gudrun.

The two halves of the body of Guttorm, who Sigurd had slain, was positioned there. When the fire was ready to be set, Brynhild ordered her chambermaids to take the rest of her gold, as she wanted them to have it. Brynhild wore the Aegis Helm and, aided by her maidens, she slowly walked to the pyre. She was laid down beside Sigurd, with an unsheathed sword between her and the man she loved. She ordered the bondmen and women, and the attendants that were following them in the afterlife, to be placed evenly around Sigurd and herself. In that way, she would have a fine procession following her and Sigurd in the afterlife. When all was ready, she pierced herself through her heart and died beside Sigurd. The pyre was set ablaze. All the bodies were burned along with Sigurd and Brynhild. Gunnar was heartbroken, but he adhered to his wife's wishes.

Few seemed to notice the absence of Gudrun and Gullrond. If anyone asked, they were told the wife of Sigurd was too distraught to attend the funeral or the feasting.

Chapter Forty-Two
Brynhild's Quest

Brynhild and her followers found themselves riding into the afterlife, with the belief that they were following Sigurd. On the pathway, they were confronted by a huge and gnarly troll giantess blocking the passageway. She was thick, like huge, grey boulders, with small dark blue and green sprouts, sticking up all over her body, that could be seen beside a crumpled and rumpled purple, green and blue patchworked dress. Her boulder face had eyes like big, black beetle bugs, and her tangled brownish-green hair had red streaks in it and tumbled past her boulder-like shoulders. Her long, stone arms stood out in front of her preventing anyone's passage. There was a mysterious mist around her. Brynhild had no choice but to stop, although she was in a flurry of a hurry to catch up to Sigurd. She decided her best option was to confront the giantess, tell her life story, while making her quest understood, and plead for passage.

"Oh, great giantess, you have stopped us on our quest. I trust that, if you knew my mission, you would quickly usher me through. Dear lady, hear my story, and understand my needed journey. I trained my whole life as a warrior woman and became a chosen valkyrie under Odin's meticulous watch. In my youth, I unknowingly disobeyed the *One-eyed Warrior* and, as punishment, he struck me with a sleeping thorn, and I fell into an unnatural sleep. He also took away my supernatural valkyrie powers, and I became a human, and also had to marry a human. I was shocked and dismayed. Before I fell into the deep sleep, I asked Odin for help to protect and conceal me. He surrounded my halls with supernatural flames, and I built a shield wall around myself. I also made a vow to myself, to my family and to Odin, that I would marry the man who knew no fear and would ride through my protective otherworldly flames and awaken me. Sigurd was that man, and I loved him and had a daughter by him. We vowed to marry one another. But, he was given a powerful drink of forgetfulness, and he forgot all about me and our marriage vows. He married another. The man I loved wooed me for another man, and I married Gunnar on a foundation of lies and betrayals. Both Sigurd and Gunnar betrayed me. Even though I learned the truth of the betrayal, I still longed for Sigurd and loved him with all my heart and soul. I am overwrought with sorrow and grief, because I was a breaker of my own oath and was not able to be with Sigurd and love him in our lifetime. Now, in death, I plan to be with Sigurd in the afterlife. As you can see, we have a fine funeral procession, and we must hurry to catch up with him. You must let us pass, oh gracious giantess."

With an eerie sounding, gruff and gruesome voice, words came forth from the giantess. "Dearie, you are on your way to the realm of Hel, and if you think Sigurd will be visiting the goddess Hel, you need to think again. A man such as Sigurd would be on his way to Valhalla, as he was chosen by Odin. I heard Sigurd was slain while sleeping, but his sword, Gram, was beside him. He threw his sword, slicing his slayer in half. Therefore, Dearie, he was battling as he died. And, you know that means that Odin has claimed him. You, my dear, will find out your own destination soon enough. You may be fated to find yourself in Folkvang with Freyja and other warriors or in Vingolf. You are welcome to ride where you wish and see where the path leads you. You may find him yet, or may not. Your destiny awaits you."

The giantess laughed a scornful laugh, as she moved aside and let Brynhild and her procession pass. Brynhild continued on her quest searching for Sigurd.

Chapter Forty-Three
The Plight of Gudrun

Due to the death order that was put in place by Brynhild, Gullrond was fearful for the lives of Sigmund and Gudrun. Not knowing who Brynhild's loyal subjects were did not help the matter. Both sisters queried who they could trust, and believed it was too dangerous to continue living in the kingdom of Gjukung. Gullrond, Gudrun, Sigmund, Ernest and a small group of trusted folk gathered up their necessities and set out to leave. Grani came to Gudrun and allowed Sigmund and Gudrun to ride on him. The small band fled into the forest and could not be found. They walked from the mountain for five days. When Gudrun heard the baying of the wolves, she thought of Sigurd and the stories he had told her of his father and his half-brother, Sinfjotli. She thought it would be better to die rather than live without Sigurd, but Gullrond and her companions led her on.

They went deep through the forest, until they came to a huge fortress. It was the home of King Half. They were invited in and stayed within the halls of Thora, the daughter of Hakon. Gullrond saw to the protection and comfort of Gudrun and Sigmund. Arrangements were made for the boy with an extraordinary protection plan and a new identity. All who knew of his existence, felt that he was a target for murder by anyone from the Gjukung or the Budlung kingdoms. It was unclear as to whom one could trust. King Half assigned Prince Thjodrek as the boy's foster father and Thora as his foster mother. Gudrun was grateful for the arrangements.

Gudrun gave birth to her daughter. The baby was sprinkled with water and named Svanhild, as King Sigurd had called her. The norns visited the young baby, and their chantings filled the room. Thora was delighted to be her foster mother, and Prince Thjodrek was honoured to be her foster father. Mother, son and daughter were treated well and generously within the halls of King Half. Gullrond was satisfied that Gudrun's life was now safe, and she returned to her husband and children in her foreign home.

During the time within King Half's halls, Gudrun wove tapestries of the many great deeds and events of her beloved husband, Sigurd, and of the many men and women that fought beside him. The tapestries displayed flashing swords and mighty warriors in mail coats. Her children, Sigmund and Svanhild, learned all about their father, grandparents, uncles, aunts and cousins in the many stories and poems that were told about them. Both children knew their identities and the precautions taken to protect them. Sigmund Sigurdarson was bestowed with the name of Sigurstein Thjodreksson, with the nickname, Siggi. He learned the skills of hunting, sword play, riding a horse, bending a bow, reading the runes and learning languages, as was the way of a prince. Svanhild was raised in the learning of feminine skills. She helped with the work on the embroidery pieces, as her mother embroidered all the objects and ships of the great Kings, Sigmund and Sigurd. Gudrun and Thora also embroidered the battle of Sigar and Siggeir at Fjon in the south. Along with these skills, Gudrun, Siggi, Svanhild and their companions were introduced to the fair games that were common at the time within the halls of King Half. Gudrun began to feel more at ease and was comforted. Gudrun found solace and friendship within the halls of King Half and was very grateful for the friendship of Thora, Thjodrek and King Half. Thjodrek had experienced the death of his beloved, and he and Gudrun empathized with one another. They shared their life stories and the raising of young Siggi and Svanhild. Thjodrek proved to be an honourable man and a good foster father for both her children. Gudrun, with her son and daughter, stayed within the halls of King Half for seven and a half years. She would have spent the rest of her days in the halls, but her destiny called.

Chapter Forty-Four
The Saga of Aslaug

Meanwhile, Aslaug, the daughter of Brynhild and Sigurd, was peacefully being raised within the halls of King Heimir and Queen Bekkhild. When Heimir heard of the horrific happenings within the Gjukung Kingdom, with the deaths of Sigurd, Brynhild, Guttorm, young Sigmund and all the others, he was shocked. Then, there was the disappearance of Gudrun. Both Bekkhild and Heimir were troubled with all these happenings and became afraid for the life of their foster granddaughter, young Aslaug. They feared that, with both of her parents dead, someone may have been ordered to kill Aslaug. They felt they needed to come up with a plan to help protect the young child from harm. Heimir wanted to know the happenings within the kingdoms, but he could not discover any news from where he sat. So, he devised a plan…

One of Heimir's many skills was that he was an avid harpist and luthier. He worked at carving a harp that was high enough and wide enough to hide young Aslaug inside and allowing room for her to grow. He skillfully designed his harp so that it could also be played as a fine instrument. When he finished his project, he was proud of his creation and showed Bekkhild. The beautiful, big harp would become the travel-home for young Aslaug. He would travel around the country, disguised as a poor harp player, and listen to people for any news of any planned attack on Aslaug. Bekkhild was unsure of his plan, but she was enthralled with the harp and how nicely Aslaug fit inside. She felt that her foster granddaughter would be protected within the harp, Heimir would keep her close, and if anyone came to their home to harm Aslaug, they would not find her. Also, Heimir told Bekkhild that he would come home with Aslaug, when he was certain that there was no one out there with an order to harm her.

Bekkhild agreed to Heimir's plan, but made him swear oaths that he would come home with Aslaug as soon as he knew that all was safe. She knew it was the fear of losing their foster granddaughter that drove Heimir to leave their kingdom, taking Aslaug with him, while he was disguised as a poor traveling harp player. On his travels, he called himself Sig and was able to hear what the people were saying about the happenings in the Gjukung and Budlung Kingdoms. He was cautious and careful and listened for any words of threat towards himself or his foster granddaughter. He travelled and played and listened and kept an eye on Aslaug. As time passed, words of threat seemed to fade, but he decided to stay on the road a little longer, listening and travelling and playing his harp with the young girl inside.

One night, he was invited to stay in the home of a poor couple, Aki and Grima. The couple seemed to be a quiet, honest couple and, as Heimir was tired, he accepted the offer. When the couple had a closer look at his harp, they thought that, because of the harp's thickness and size, Sig, the old harp player, must be hiding great wealth inside it. They both wondered about the harp. Finally, Grima convinced Aki to kill the harp player, so they could open up the harp and see what was inside. Aki wanted only to rob the old man and not to kill him, but Grima insisted that he kill Sig and commanded him to do the deed. Aki unknowingly killed a king, King Heimir. When Grima and Aki opened the harp up, they were astounded, surprised and puzzled to see a little girl soundly sleeping, and they were bitterly disappointed to not find any gold or wealth. They regretted the killing of the old harp player. They realized that he was protecting and raising the young girl and, in compensation to the girl for killing her guardian, they raised her as their own. They called the little one Kraka.

The couple knew not who the harp player really was nor anything about the child. And why was she housed in a harp? When a travelling seeress came to the village that was close to where they lived, Grima took Kraka to see her. Maybe the seeress could shed some light upon the little girl. The seeress wrapped the child in one of her cloaks. She placed her hands and staff over the child's head and chanted words known only to her. She slowly moved her hands and staff over Kraka's body. She stopped at her belly, chanted more words and then, slowly, moved on. When the seeress was done, she took the cloak off of the child. She looked into Grima's eyes, and she slowly spoke these words. "From the visions of my cloak, staff and hands, I have seen royalty and norn magic within this child. She is born of royalty. She is the daughter of Sigurd, the dragon slayer, and Brynhild, the valkyrie maiden. The child also carries within her an affliction in the form of a norn womb-curse. It has been said that on the night of her wedding, if her husband chooses to procreate with her, she will bear a child with no bones. This curse can be broken only if the couple wait for another time to consummate their marriage vows."

Grima asked, "Is there any other way to lift this curse?"

The seeress replied, "The only one who can lift the curse is the one who cast it."

Grima thanked the seeress and offered her some soup that she had made from the vegetables from her garden. Young Kraka was afraid of the seeress and her words, as she did not understand them.

As the child grew older, she developed into a beautiful young girl. Aki and Grima were stunned by her beauty and did not want to draw attention to themselves or to her. So, during the day, they covered her face with tar and ash and made her wear a cloak with a long hood. For her own safety, they impressed upon Aslaug the need for her to be all covered up. In the evenings, under the shield of darkness when no others could see her, Aslaug bathed herself in the nearby river.

One evening, the ships of King Ragnar Lothbrok and his companions came in along the coast close to where Kraka lived. Some men, in smaller boats, were sent to the shore. The men were ordered to find an oven to bake some bread. They came across the humble hut of Grima and Aki, and asked the couple if they would allow them to use their oven.

"Kind folk, we have been sent by King Ragnar Lothbrok to bake our bread. We have many provisions we can share, if you allow us the use of your oven to bake our bread."

Grima and Aki were elderly at the time and could not see well but, with hopes of receiving provisions from them, they allowed the men inside to use the oven. Grima was curious and, in a tired voice, asked, "Who is this king, and why is he called "Lothbrok?"

"We are from Denmark, and Ragnar Sigurdsson is our king. He was the son of Sigurd the Ring. He received his nickname, Lothbrok, after he fought and killed a huge and deadly serpent. In preparation to protect himself in the battle with the serpent, he made himself a pair of wide pants made from thick rawhide and covered them with tar and wool. The pants protected him from the bite of the serpent and from the poisonous venom, as neither could go through the cloth to harm him. Due to his hairy pants, no harm came to him, as he bravely fought and killed the serpent. That is why we have given him the nickname of Lothbrok, or *Hairy Breeches*."

Grima laughed, as the men prepared for the baking of the bread. Kraka had finished her evening bath in the river and returned to her home to find the men inside. She was surprised to see them there, but Grima said, "Kraka, help the men bake their bread."

"Yes, of course, mother."

With that, she took off her cloak and hung it up on a hook in the hall. When she entered the room, the men were dumbfounded by her dazzling appearance. Her smile filled the haggard, old, dark room with a brilliant fragrant breath of fresh air and sunshine. Her blue-green eyes shone, as she gracefully took to kneading the dough. The men, mesmerized by her magnificence, followed her every move. When she told the men to watch the bread bake, all they could do was watch her. She was beautiful beyond any other woman they had ever seen. They were all captivated, as Kraka fluttered about the room doing her chores. The men only had eyes for her and, unfortunately, they burned their bread due to their lack of attention to their baking. They had to go back to their ship with burnt bread. When King Ragnar asked them about the mishap of the burnt bread, they told him about the beautiful, young woman in the humble hut.

"We tell you, King Ragnar, this woman is like no other we have ever seen!" All the men blurted out a description of her as being curvy, beautiful, dazzling, magnificent, delightful and radiant, with shining skin and flowing, golden hair! One confessed, "We were all so bedazzled by her beauty, that we burned our bread."

Ragnar's curiosity was set aflame, "Since all of you describe her beauty with such zeal, I wish to see her for myself, but I also want to test her intelligence. A beauty with no brain is no beauty at all. Approach this woman and tell her that the king requests her presence. But, tell her this: when she comes before the king, she must neither be dressed nor undressed, neither eating nor fasting, and neither alone nor in the presence of company."

The men thought these requests were rather unusual, but they did not question their king and did as he commanded. The following morning, Ragnar's men went back to the hut. They gave Aki and Grima a bountiful amount of supplies and then approached Kraka. One said, "Young woman, King Ragnar wishes for your presence on his ship. He has asked you to come before him neither dressed nor undressed, neither eating nor fasting, and neither alone nor in the presence of company."

Kraka thought the requests extraordinary yet interesting. She replied, "Dear men, you will need to give me some time to prepare, as these are strange and unusual requests."

Aslaug thought about the requests for a while, and then knew what she would do. She asked Aki for a clean, unused fishing net. He obliged and gave her a net that she dressed herself in, showing she was dressed but also undressed, as she was not wearing clothing. Her long silken locks flowed to the ground, so her whole body was covered under the net. She gathered up an onion from the garden, cleaned it, placed it in her mouth and bit on it, showing that she was not fasting, because she had food in her mouth, but she was not eating, as the onion was only bitten and held by her teeth. For the last riddle, she took along her pet dog, thereby showing she was not alone, because she was with her dog, yet she was not in the company of any people.

Ragnar Lothbrok and Kraka, by Louis Moe

When she was ready, she went with the men to Ragnar. When the king saw her arrive, he laughed out loud and was truly fascinated and impressed by her creative resourcefulness and her exquisite beauty. "You certainly have done what I have asked, and I am thoroughly impressed. Come and sit by me a while."

The young Kraka sat by Ragnar, and they laughed with one another. He found her beautiful, as his men had said, and he also found her uniquely wise. He thought that she would make a good companion for him. He told her he had been married twice before. His first wife would not leave her country for his, nor resign her rights as sovereign, and his warlike spirit led him back to Denmark. His second wife, Thora, was the daughter of King Herod of Gotland, who died of a fatal illness. He was alone and ready for a companion, and now looked upon young Aslaug as a future wife. He was comfortable with her. She was beautiful and charming and had proven herself very wise. He proposed marriage and, to his astonishment, the young Kraka refused the king's proposal.

"I must admit I am truly grateful for your offer of marriage, and I feel I could have a place by your side. Yet, this proposal comes too early in our relationship. In all fairness, Ragnar, how can I honour your proposal, when I may never see you again, because you are going to war. Might I be widowed before even knowing you?"

"Kraka, my beauty, what you say is true, as we are going on a mission. Yet, love swells within my breast for you, and I believe the gods are with us. I pledge to come back for you and, when I return, will you be my bride and my queen?"

"If you still have your breath within you and your wits about you after this battle quest, I may then consider it."

Ragnar went on his mission and came back for Kraka, as he had promised. While he was away, Grima explained to Kraka all that she knew about her past and what the seeress had said. She cautioned her to delay the consummation of her marriage. Grima gave her all that was in the harp traveling home…a picture of her mother, a letter from her and a ring. When Ragnar returned, he still had breath and his wits about himself, so the couple were married. Aslaug then asked one thing of Ragnar… "Ragnar, I must tell you that, at one time, there was a curse placed upon me. We must wait for the right time to consummate our marriage, because it has been foretold that, if my husband takes me on my wedding night, I will bear a child with no bones. Although we are married, husband, I feel the time is not right for us."

On their wedding night, Ragnar did not want to wait and made love to his new bride. Aslaug gave birth to a son who had a bone deficiency. Since resources were scarce for their clans, the practice was to leave the child alone for a night. If the child survived the night, then the child was worth keeping. The reasoning was *why should one use up resources to feed one who would die anyways?* The resources would be better used by those who were living. Ragnar left the child out for the night. During the night, Aslaug came to him and nurtured him. Aslaug said that the child was born with a bone deficiency because Ragnar would not listen to her. The boy lived through his first night. Both parents loved their son, and he was sprinkled with water and named Ivar. The norns, with their extraordinary chantings, paid a visit.

Aslaug, afraid Ragnar would not return, dreaded every time he left on his expeditions. She called upon all her internal powers and love to weave him a magic shirt that no arrow, spear, or sword could penetrate. This protected Ragnar in all his battles. He always came home to her. Aslaug and Ragnar had three more sons, Bjorn, Hvitserk and Rognvald.

One of the excursions that Ragnar went on was to Sweden, where King Eysteinn was very impressed with Ragnar. Eysteinn wanted Ragnar as his own son-in-law. He wanted Ragnar to leave his marriage with the peasant girl, Kraka, and marry his daughter, Ingiborg, a woman of royalty. "Why should you, King Ragnar, be married to an impoverished girl, when you can be married into nobility? Be a king with me. Rule over this land and its people. Enjoy great wealth. You can gain country, kin, title and great respect. Your life would be much better here with me."

Ragnar liked the idea of being married into royalty. He agreed to dissolve his marriage with Kraka, and then he would come back to Sweden to marry Ingiborg. During this time, Aslaug's power of foresight and three faithful nuthatches told her of the proposed betrayal. When Ragnar returned home to break up the marriage, she revealed to him that he did not have to go elsewhere to be married into nobility. Because, he already was…

"Ragnar, my love, my husband… I have the gift of foresight that stems from my mother and father and their lineages. With this knowledge, I know of your plans to leave me and marry Ingiborg, the daughter of King Eysteinn of Sweden. You desire to marry into royalty and nobility, to gain respect and notoriety. I understand this. Yet, you married me because you loved me. I am a faithful and loving wife for you, and I am the mother of your children. Because I love you and do not wish to lose you or for you to leave, I now choose to reveal to you the true nature of my lineage. You thought that my parents were poor and from the village. But, the truth is that I am not the daughter of Aki and Grima, as you have come to know. I am the daughter of the dragon slayer, King Sigurd, who ranks above all others, as the sun ranks above all the stars. He was the son of mighty King Sigmund, who was son of the famous King Volsung. My mother was Brynhild, the valkyrie woman warrior and shield-maiden of Odin, daughter of King Budli and sister to King Atli. She was the foster daughter of King Heimir and Queen Bekkhild, who in turn, fostered me. After Sigurd and Brynhild died and Queen Gudrun disappeared, my foster grandparents grew fearful for my life. King Heimir travelled with me hidden inside his harp, as he searched for any news from the Gjukung or Budlung Kingdoms. Thinking there was gold inside, Aki and Grima stole my foster grandfather's harp and killed him. They were surprised to find that I was inside and, as compensation to me, they raised me as their own child. My true name is Aslaug, daughter of King Sigurd and Queen Brynhild. All I have is this letter, a picture and this ring. So you see, my love, if you want to marry into nobility and notoriety, you already have. You need not go anywhere else for that."

Aslaug brought out the picture, letter and ring and gave them to Ragnar. Ragnar took them, looked upon them and said, "This is a good story, my love, and your trinkets are intriguing, yet I think you are dreaming, my bright-eyed beauty."

"If you do not believe me, ask Aki and Grima. As a child, they hid me, as best they could, by covering me in tar and soot and making me wear cloaks with long hoods. But, when your men came to our hut, they discovered me. I can prove to you that I am a daughter of Sigurd, as I know from my fylgia and from Odin, that I will bear you a son whose eye will show the resemblance of the serpent that my father, Sigurd fought. We will call our son, Sigurd, Snake in the Eye."

Ragnar was taken aback by the fierceness of her resolve. He kept her trinkets and pondered upon them. He stayed with her, as he loved her, and he wanted to see if her prophesy would come true. When the time came for the baby to be born, the child was, indeed, a boy that had an eye with the shape of a serpent within it. He was named Sigurd, after his grandfather, and his nickname was Snake in the Eye. Ragnar saw the depth of Aslaug's love for him, her sacred spirituality, her vast wisdom and her eternal beauty, so much so, that he stayed with her. When King Eysteinn learned that Ragnar was not going to keep their agreement, he retaliated. A battle ensued, in which King Eysteinn lost his life.

With the secret powerful protection of the magical shirt that Aslaug had woven for him, Ragnar fought and won many battles. When the day came that the secret of Aslaug's enchanted shirt was revealed, his enemies took advantage of this knowledge and took away his shirt. Once the shirt was taken from him, her powers could no longer protect him. It has been said, in stories of old, that King Ragnar declared that all the fierceness and braveness of his sons originated from his beloved peasant girl, Kraka, who was the daughter of King Sigurd, the dragon slayer, and Queen Brynhild, the valkyrie maiden.

Chapter Forty-Five
Grimhild Discovers Gudrun

Meanwhile in the Gjukung kingdom, the brothers of Gudrun, Gunnar and Hogni were blamed for the death of Brynhild, by her brother, King Atli. Even though she appeared to have gone into a madness of her own making and had taken her own life, Atli demanded gold and Gudrun's hand in marriage as compensation for her death.

Trying to appease the king with other women, Grimhild sent Atli an abundance of beautiful and wise women, but Atli would have none of them. He desired Gudrun and only Gudrun. Grimhild sent out messengers and warriors to find out where the rare woman had gone, but there was no word. Finally, she heard that a beautiful woman that fit Gudrun's description was living in King Half's kingdom. Thrilled that Gudrun was found, Grimhild sent her sons, Gunnar and Hogni, to determine whether the woman truly was Gudrun and, if so, to speak with her. When they arrived at King Half's, they were escorted to and welcomed into Thora's halls, where Gudrun was living. Sigurd's son and daughter were secure in one of Thjodrek's halls.

Gudrun greeted them. "Welcome brothers. It has been a long time since we have spoken with one another. What brings you here?"

"Our dearest Gudrun, we are overjoyed to see you. We have been looking for you for all these years. We heard there was a woman living in these halls that fit your description, and we have come to see if the woman was indeed you. Now that we see you, we are overcome with joy that you are still alive, and we are delighted to see you. As you know, we are in need of fulfilling our legal obligations to you as, according to our laws, we are obliged to compensate you for the loss of your husband and son."

"Gunnar and Hogni, there is no need. I relieve you from your obligations. I have all that I need here," Gudrun explained.

"We need to compensate you and will return with a compensation party." Hogni and Gunnar took leave of her. The brothers went back to the Gjukung Kingdom and informed their mother that the beautiful woman living in the halls of King Half was most definitely Gudrun. Grimhild made preparations for a compensation party to travel to King Half's halls.

One day, the messenger came to King Half informing him that the compensation company from the Gjukungs was approaching his kingdom. The Gjukungs wanted to fulfill their obligation to Queen Gudrun and compensate her for the death of her husband and son. Gudrun was aware that the company was coming and made arrangements for their arrival and, also, for the anonymity of the young Siggi and Svanhild.

As the compensation party arrived, many could see from the battlement of King Half's fortress, a sea of five hundred warriors wearing impressive mail coats and polished helmets, and each carrying with them a shield and a sword. Some were carrying banners. Some travelled in their full armour and wore red fur cloaks. Some travelled on illustrious horses, and Grimhild was amongst them. They were an impressive and glorious sight, but Gudrun trusted none of them.

Grimhild and her company were greeted warmly and invited in. All rested, as they were weary from travel. After resting, Grimhild and Gudrun sat together in her bower, and Grimhild brought out a special drink for Gudrun.

"Let us drink together, daughter, in celebration of our being together again. I have missed you so much these long years."

Grimhild gave the potion to Gudrun and, once she drank, she remembered none of her sorrows and grievances. The drink was blended with the energy of the earth and of the deep blue seas and with the blood of the ancestors. An assortment of runes were carved and reddened, with ancient blood, inside and outside of the special drinking horn. Grimhild's words resonated a sweet music, and she said,

"Prosperity and happiness I bring to you, my daughter, for it is so good to see you again. I have come to give you hundreds of special soldiers, as you can see. I have also brought a wealth of gem stones, golden gifts and a fortune of riches from your father's estate. This includes these exquisite rare rings and these treasured wall-hangings delicately hand-woven by skilled and talented Hunnish maids and maidens." She brought out a wall hanging from one of the trunks that had been carried in. "There, my dearest Gudrun… It brings me great pleasure to finally compensate you for the deaths of your husband and son. I have missed you and want to see you happy and married again. You are still young and beautiful and capable of having many more children, my fair daughter. With that said, kindly do as we ask."

"What is it that you ask of me, mother?"

"You will be given in marriage to the almighty King Atli and, with this glorious opportunity, we will strengthen and reinforce our peaceful bonds with the Budlung house. This will appease the king for the unfortunate death of his beloved sister, Brynhild, and you will take pleasure in reigning over all of his kingdoms and his enormous wealth."

"Oh, mother… How can you ask this of me? There is no honour in marrying me off to such a man. I cannot do as you ask."

Grimhild responded, "Daughter, you must not think that way. Our friendly family alliances will be reunited with this union. This is all for the best. I know you were deeply happy and joyous when you were with Sigurd. Think that way, daughter… Think the way you did when Sigurd and Sigmund were alive."

Gudrun lamented, "Oh, mother… Sigurd is forever in my thoughts and in my heart, and he always will be. For, he was glorious and honourable and the finest of all men. And, my young Sigmund… Oh…!"

Gudrun held her head down, as she did not want her mother to see young Sigmund in her eyes.

Grimhild continued, "You have been honoured, daughter, with this proposal of marriage to King Atli, and you will do as we ask, or you will never marry again."

Gudrun agreed. "This is to my liking, as I do not wish to marry again to anyone else. I prefer to stay alone, here with my friend, Thora, After all these years and with all your foresight, mother, can you not see that Atli only wants revenge for the death of his sister? Offering me off to him will only bring agony and heartache to our family and an abundance of hardships will follow. My brothers and I will suffer at his horrific hands. There is no honour with a marriage like this! I beseech you, mother... Do not offer me to this man!"

Grimhild was startled and troubled by Gudrun's predictions about her sons, yet she persevered. "Daughter, do as you are told, and you will be glorified and adored and receive an abundance of wealth and lands, including Vinbjorg and Valbjorg, along with the deepest of our devotions. Your marriage to Atli will be a beneficial endeavour for both the Gjukung and the Budlung families. This, my daughter, is an order, and it would be wise for you to act in favour with your family."

"I realize, mother, that it is my duty as your daughter to do as you declare, but hear me well... This is far from what I want or need, and it is against my own will and better judgment. From my foresight, I only see ruination and heartbreak for you and our whole family."

Grimhild let the warning of Gudrun go. "Let us rest our words and prepare for the journey to King Atli's kingdom, dear."

The women prepared for the journey. Gudrun told her mother she had some business to attend to before her departure. In private, she met with Thora and Thjodrek and told them of her mother's request. She was beyond distressed because, to marry a man against her will, she would have to leave her children, her friends and the kingdom of King Half. Thora and Thjodrek were understanding and empathetic. Thora took Gudrun to meet with Siggi and Svanhild. She was honest with her children and told them what she had to do. They were still young. She did not want to leave them but, in order to protect them and their identity and anonymity, she must. She confirmed that they would be nurtured and safe in the care of King Half and their foster parents, Thora and Thjodrek. She also told them that, if she could, she would either send for them or come back for them. She expressed her love for each child and said her goodbyes. With Thjodrek, she left Grani and Gram for young Siggi. When Gudrun was ready, she met her mother and, with their party, they travelled by horse, by ship and by horse again, until they came to a high fortress in the realm of King Atli. They were well received, and a large banquet was prepared.

Chapter Forty-Six
Mistress Mayhem

Soon after their arrival to the kingdom of Atli, a woman by the name of Herkja, who was one of Atli's serving maids and his number one mistress, spread a slanderous story about Queen Gudrun. Herkja was deeply in love with Atli and desired him to marry *her* instead of Gudrun. She could not bear the thought of Atli being married to anyone but her, and the presence of Gudrun and her party brought her face to face with the fear of losing him. She was overwrought with emotions. She was immensely distressed, severely saddened and excruciatingly jealous. Jealously took over her and reared its horrendous head. She wanted Atli to disregard Gudrun as his potential wife. She told him that Queen Gudrun and King Thjodrek were sexual partners in the Kingdom of Half. Although he listened to the words of Herkja, Atli was surprised by these allegations, and he questioned her on this matter. How did she know this? Who was the source of these words? Herkja made it known that she knew several serving maids in King Half's kingdom where Thjodrek and Gudrun had both resided. She revealed the maids to be the source of this news.

Alti took the words of Herkja and confronted Gudrun with them. She was frightened and dismayed by the statement, and she denied any sexual relationship with Thjodrek. Also, she did not want to bring any attention to the foster father of her son, as King Atli thought her son was dead.

Each woman's story was completely different, and Atli needed to know who was telling the truth. He pondered upon this and decided on a way to discover which woman was telling him the truth. He would use the *boiling water* technique. Each woman would have to put her hand into a pot of boiling water, pick up a gemstone from the bottom of the pot and place the stone on the table. It was believed that the hand of the one who told the truth could place her hand in boiling water and pick up the gemstone without her hand being scalded.

Queen Grimhild was appalled with this technique of lie detection and with the decision of Atli to utilize it. She tried to dissuade him. Seeing this test as madness, she expressed, "My dear King Atli, all human flesh can burn in fire and scald in boiling water, and this is not a test for truth at all."

Atli was set in his ways, and he became annoyed and angered at what he thought was Grimhild's insolence. Gudrun saw Atli's disgust and pulled her mother away from him. She expressed, "King Atli, and my dear mother, I am quite prepared to do as Atli wishes. If he believes that this method will bring out the truth, then I will do as he asks."

He was softened by Gudrun's attitude, but he still would not change his mind. He set a date for the test.

Grimhild and Gudrun met together in their bower and discussed the forthcoming ordeal. Grimhild reassured Gudrun. "Do not worry yourself with this trial, Gudrun, as I have magic that can counteract the boiling water."

Grimhild used her essence and magical skills to weave a woven protective band around the hand of Gudrun. Gudrun was ready on the day of the test. King Atli called the ladies into the chamber of the boiling pot. But first, he told them to draw a stick from a bowl to discover who would go first. He said that Gudrun and her party were guests in his kingdom, and she should choose from the bowl first. Gudrun obliged, put her left hand into the bowl and felt little, wooden sticks. She pulled one out. Herkja was then called forward. She put her hand into the bowl and pulled out another wooden stick.

"Now that you both have a stick in your hand, examine the wood and read out how many strokes are carved into it."

"I have two strokes, my King Atli," Herkja said.

A servant was asked to verify the two strokes, and it was confirmed that there were exactly two strokes carved into the wood. Gudrun looked upon her stick and only counted one stroke, and a servant went to her and confirmed that there was only one stroke carved in her piece of wood. Because Gudrun drew the stick with one stroke, she was asked to place her hand into the boiling water first. Gudrun obliged.

Gudrun slowly walked up to the fire over which the boiling pot hung and stood there. Her right hand was covered with the magical, protective covering her mother had woven for her, although it appeared that her hands and arms were bare. She raised her hand up and slowly moved her hand down into the pot. She could sense the heat of the boiling water, but she was not burned. She picked up a gemstone from the bottom of the pot, pulled it up out of the water and placed the stone on the table beside the pot. She then moved aside, away from the pot, and was relieved. She had proved to Atli and the whole household that she was telling the truth. Then, it was Herkja's turn.

Herkja was afraid and did not want to put her hand into the pot of boiling water, but she had to do the same as Gudrun. Herkja walked up to the boiling pot and slowly rose her hand up and then down into the boiling water, where her hand was scalded. She shrieked in utter pain, falling back onto the floor, screaming in agony. She pleaded to her beloved Atli for mercy.

"You have lied to me, Herkja, and I trusted you all these years. Guards take her away."

Herkja was taken away, and King Atli turned to Gudrun. He said, "My dear Queen Gudrun, I regret to have had to subject you to this test, but I could not tell which one of you was telling me the truth and which one of you was lying. I had to know the truth in this matter. This test has proven to me that you are pure in your words and thoughts, and also that my little serving maid in whom I have trusted all these years is impure in her thoughts, as she has lied to me."

Gudrun and her mother excused themselves from King Atli's presence, stating that this was quite enough for one day. They went to their chambers. Grimhild came to Gudrun's room and removed the magical weaving from the hand of her daughter. Gudrun was relieved that the test was completed, as now Atli would have no cause to interrogate her any further or look upon Thjodrek as a threat. All was well, and they would be left alone.

It was discovered that Herkja did not know any of the servant maids in King Half's Kingdom. King Atli decided the fate of Herkja, his serving maid and prior love interest. Because of her lies and slanderous words against Queen Gudrun, Herkja was sentenced to death in the bog. Gudrun was shocked by this decision and exclaimed, "King Atli, there is no need for this, as Herkja has already scalded her hand in the boiling water, and that is punishment enough!" But, King Atli had his way, and the woman was thrown into the bog and died there. Gudrun had endured false accusations and had been humiliated by his maid and, with the of death Herkja, he considered Gudrun to be avenged.

King Atli called all his household together to arrange a huge marital feast for himself and his bride-to-be. On the day of the feast, King Atli stood up and drank the marriage toast to Gudrun. He expressed his delight and happiness to have her by his side as his bride. Gudrun went through with the ceremony, as was her duty, but her thoughts never laughed with his thoughts, her heart never beat with his heart, and the life she had with him was empty. Gudrun knew, in her heart, that Herkja would have made Atli a better wife than her, as Herkja was lovingly devoted to Atli. The woman that had truly loved him, and would have been happy with him, had lost her life because of him. Gudrun did her duty, but could not find it within her heart, mind or spirit, to love Atli.

Chapter Forty-Seven
Atli's Dreams

King Atli was troubled by his dreams and described them to Gudrun. She listened carefully, as he told her of one dream. "In my first dream, you plunged a fine blade of iron into my heart."
Gudrun gave Atli her interpretation of the dream. "Dreams of iron reveal fire and your wishful thinking of being the best of all men."

"There is another dream for you to interpret. In my second dream, there were two rare and remarkable reeds growing, and I had a strong feeling to protect them. But, to my dismay, they were treacherously torn from their roots and served onto my table for me to eat. I was horrified. Then, in my third dream, two of my prized hawks that were perched on my hand unexpectedly flew away. Unable to snare any game to eat, they flew down into Niflheim, the realm where the giantess, Hel, resides. Their blood-pumping organs (hearts) were blended with the sweetest of nectars, (honey) and I unknowingly ate them. In another dream, the noblest of little offsprings were set down before me, and I reluctantly feasted on their remains. I feel stunned, shocked and sickened by these visions."

Gudrun listened carefully and then, slowly and methodically, said, "These dreams of yours are indeed foreboding and foreshadow that depressing and disheartening deeds will develop for us. And, Atli, they foretell that your sons are destined to die."

Atli shared with Gudrun more of his haunting dreams. "I dreamt that I fell into my bed, unable to move as the otherworld called me, and I learned that my death was devised."

Gudrun coldly commented, "Your dreams will come true for you, and you will know them when they come to pass."

Atli and Gudrun's marriage-life was cold. Gudrun's thoughts never laughed with his thoughts, and her heart never beat with his heart. Although he was respectful to Gudrun, she never loved him. They had nothing in common. Their likes and dislikes were unequal. She performed her marriage duties as was required of her, but nothing more. She bore Atli two sons, Erp and Eitil. Atli was proud to be a father and showed them great affection. But, he secretly obsessed over the gold of Fafnir that had been earned by Sigurd, and was in the possession of Gudrun's brothers, Gunnar and Hogni. Atli desired the gold for himself and thought of a plan to get her brothers into his kingdom. He would invite them to a feast held in honour of Gunnar and Hogni.

Gudrun knew the true nature of her husband and cut a message, in runes, into the ring, Andvaranaut, and tied a wolf's hair onto it. She gave the ring to the king's messenger, Vingi, to give to her brother, Gunnar. The messenger, who was loyal to King Atli, showed him the ring with the message in runes on it and the wolf's hair. Vingi and Atli discussed the ring and the message. The carved runes warned her brothers not to come to the banquet, and the wolf's hair increased the warning. Vingi changed the runes on the ring to make it appear that Gudrun *wanted* her brothers to come.

Vingi set off for Gunnar's hall, and there he met with the brothers. "King Atli has a message for the valiant brothers of his wife Gudrun. He wishes you, King Gunnar, and you, King Hogni, to mentor his sons and look after all his lands and wealth until the princes come of age. He is getting too old for this and wishes for you to succeed him. He has planned a banquet to honour you both, and he intends to bestow upon you great wealth and the finest of gifts."

"Thank you, Vingi, for your message. You may rest yourself awhile before you journey back to the kingdom of King Atli, and we will discuss this development." Vingi was shown to his quarters, while Gunnar and Hogni discussed the message.

"We already have more wealth than any king. With Sigurd's gold, we do not need any of Atli's wealth or land. Why should we bother? This seems unlike Atli, as he has never been generous with us before. What do you think of this ring and wolf hair, Hogni?"

"I am honoured that he would offer us his wealth, kingdom and power, but I do not understand these runes on the ring or the wolf's hair."

At the evening feast, Vingi approached the brothers, and asked if they had come to an agreement. They expressed that they needed more time to consider all the events of the day. Vingi asked to see the ring and pointed out to the brothers that Gudrun, urging them to come to the kingdom of King Atli, had cut the runes herself. Vingi stated, "Atli is old, and his sons are too young, to look after the kingdom. He wants you, the Gjukung brothers, to defend his kingdom, while his sons are unready and still growing. He wishes to grant all authority over his kingdom to both of you, the gallant King Gunnar and the strong-hearted King Hogni."

At the feast, Gunnar and Hogni began drinking mead and became exceptionally drunk. Vingi took advantage of this and kept inciting them to accept the offer of King Atli, as they would gain great wealth, renown and power. The brothers became drunk on the lust for power and the honey-sweet words of Vingi. They agreed with Vingi and swore oaths accepting the request of King Atli.

Kostbera, Hogni's wife, noticed the carved runes on the ring. She was suspicious and asked to examine the runes on the ring more closely. Upon examination, she could see that something else had been cut underneath the existing runes. In the morning, she expressed her concerns to Hogni, and suggested that he need not go to Atli's at this time, but that he could go another time. She said, "My husband, I am not convinced that the runes on the ring are the original runes carved by Gudrun. She is an extremely wise woman and knows the runes precisely well, yet the runes on this ring are sullied. I have seen Gudrun's runes before, and she would never carve like this. I am certain that the runes have been tampered-with, and that the original message that Gudrun gave you has been changed. I think that these runes have been deliberately distorted and altered with deceit and dishonesty. The message on the ring is a false message, and not the one Gudrun intended for you. I would suggest to you, my husband, that at this time do not accept this invitation. You can go another day, but for now, do not go to the kingdom of Atli. I fear, that if you go… it may be your death."

Hogni replied, "Woman, stop your words of nonsense. Atli means *well* for us." Hogni was undeterred and, drunk on thoughts of all the power and gifts he would receive, was ready to gulp up Atli's wealth.

Chapter Forty-Eight
Kostbera's Dreams

That night, Kostbera, the loving wife of Hogni, had terrifying nightmares that disturbed and frightened her. She told them to her beloved husband. "Hogni, please do not go to the halls of King Atli. I have had forewarning dreams that have frightened me. I dreamt that a roaring and thrashing river burst forth through our home, and it destroyed all the great pillars in our halls."

Hogni calmed her. "Kostbera, my love, you know that you have often had gloomy, foreboding thoughts, and nothing has ever come of them. Be at peace, my love. And, do not concern yourself with these dreadful thoughts about King Atli. You know I honour and support all men, unless they prove themselves otherwise. I do not see any reason to refuse Atli, as I believe he will receive us well."

Kostbera insisted. "Hogni, can you not see that companionship is not behind this request? Atli has never before summoned you or Gunnar for anything. Why now? Hogni, I had another dream, and, in this dream, a second river smashed and crashed through our home breaking benches and snapping and shattering your and Gunnar's legs."

Hogni slowly interpreted her dream, as he pointed out to the fields. "Kostbera, look yonder… You see the crops in the fields that stretch out long and wide. That is where you imagined a river. We often stroll about the grounds, while hefty and sizeable pods and chaffs jostle our legs."

Kostbera continued on with her dreams of foreboding premonitions. "I have had numerous dreams, Hogni. I saw the spread from your bed, for no reason, burst into flames, and the ferocious fire leapt out into our hall devouring everything in its path."

Hogni interpreted this dream. "Our clothes are strewn all over the floor of our bedchamber."

Kostbera continued her visions. "A giant and wicked white bear barged in and ravaged your royal throne, and we were all seized in shock and fear, as the bear held us all together in his monstrous mouth."

Hogni responded, "Kostbera, my dear, do these thoughts never cease? A gust of strong wind will come, where you thought there was a white bear."

Kostbera was adamant that her husband take her seriously. "There is one more dream I must tell you, Hogni. An eagle swooped in, here where we are now sitting, and flew through the halls spattering all of us with bright, red blood. The eagle was the likeness of King Atli."

Calmly, Hogni said, "Kostbera, we often slaughter cattle for our food. That is the blood you saw. Do not stress yourself with these imaginings, dear. Atli means *well* for us and will do us no harm."

Kostbera appeared less frantic about her dreams, but she was not comforted by the words of Hogni, nor could she deter him from leaving. Hogni was determined that, with a small group, he and Gunnar would journey to the kingdom of Atli.

Chapter Forty-Nine
Glaumvor's Dreams

Meanwhile, Glaumvor, the wife of Gunnar, was also having troublesome dreams that foretold the betrayal of *her* husband. Similar to the experience of Hogni's wife, Kostbera, Glaumvor cried out loud, as she was terrified by the dream visions. Gunnar, like Hogni, also interpreted the dreams differently than did his wife.

"My dear husband, I dreamt that a big black and blood-splattered sword, with howling wolves at either end, was thrust right through you. The fear of these visions of losing you has overwhelmed me."

Gunnar sat with Glaumvor and calmly gave an explanation for her dream. "Glaumvor, you know the little dogs in the village… They only want to nip everyone's heels, as they walk by. This is all that your dream means."

Like Kostbera, Glaumvor had dreamt more than one dream. She expressed another dream that frightened her. "Gunnar, dark and grim women walked in here, and they all surrounded you and chose you as their husband. They said they were your Disir and were coming for you."

Gunnar tried to soothe his wife and explained, "This dream is not easy to interpret, as this could have many meanings, my love, or no meaning at all. As you well know, no one can avoid death. Do not fret yourself, woman, with these visions, as we will live a long life together with our children. Cast these thoughts aside."

Glaumvor was not comforted. She sought out Vingi and expressed, "You had better be truthful with these messages that you have given us, or serious consequences will come to pass from your visit to our home."

Vingi smiled a vicious smile, as he bowed and said, "All is well, Queen Glaumvor."

Chapter Fifty
Gunnar and Hogni

That morning, it was discovered that other people in both households were also having disturbing dreams. They suggested to Gunnar and Hogni to not journey to the kingdom of King Atli. There was no need to rush, and the journey could be made on another day. Gunnar had already prepared and could not see any reason to delay leaving. He had also been looking forward to receiving Atli's praises, gifts and kingdoms. He had the gleam of wealth in his eyes and could not see beyond that.

To his wife, Gunnar expressed, "I understand your concerns, my love. We will be away for a while, and you are uncertain of the outcome. Your dreams are undeniably disturbing, but Glaumvor, my dear, they are only dreams. I believe all is well with Atli, and he means to honour us rather than to harm us. Let us share, joyfully, in a great sending-off banquet, if it may be our last."

Most of the warriors in the king's retinue remained behind, as Hogni and Gunnar were convinced that they were not needed. They believed Atli had invited them, not to harm them, but to honour them. Solar and Snaevar went on the voyage with their father, Hogni, and with their foster father and uncle, the calm champion warrior, Orkning, brother of Kostbera. They believed they would return home with more honour, glory and wealth than when they had left.

Glaumvor bid, "Farewell, Gunnar, my love, and may the path before you be safe and prosperous."

To Kostbera and everyone, Hogni exclaimed, "Be happy and brave, everyone, whatever happens."

The men rowed and sailed their ships to the kingdom of Atli. When they arrived, they rowed closer to the shore, where their oar pins and straps broke. They had thought that they would be given new ships from Atli and did not secure their old ships. They went farther inland and came to the fortress of King Atli. Expecting a warm and honourable welcome, they were startled to hear loud smashing and clashing sounds, similar to the sounds of a clang of arms being made behind the fortress walls. They wondered what this was and called to those behind the gates, so that they would know that they had arrived. There was no answer from within, and the fortress doors remained closed. Hogni thought that some harm may have come to the inhabitants therein and decided to break through the fortress doors to investigate.

Vingi yelled, "Dishonour will come to pass for you, Hogni, for breaking in. We will soon be looking for a gallows tree to have you hanged from, as you should not have destroyed the front gates."

Hogni retorted, "What are you saying, Vingi? Have you betrayed us and led us into a trap? Do not frighten us with your words!"

The rounded end of their axes landed on Vingi, until he fell and entered the afterlife.

Chapter Fifty-One
The Battle

Once inside the fortress, the brothers were cruelly shown that they were deceived. Atli intended, not to honour them, but to vanquish them. The forewarnings of their wives and members of their households shone true. This realization was an abrupt awakening for the brothers. They had been lured by the enticing and sparkling snare of increased wealth, additional properties and immeasurable power. To their dismay, rather than adhere to the humble dreams and prophesies voiced by their loved ones, they chose Atli's promise of wealth and power and had willingly walked into his planned deathtrap.

Gunnar and Hogni instinctively altered their plans. They swiftly gathered all their men together, ordered them into battle formation and stood strong in the courtyard. Atli came out with fierce warriors ready for battle. The brothers and Atli faced each other in the courtyard, and Atli laughed as he spoke. "Brothers, you have finally arrived. It is time for you to give me the golden treasures that once belonged to Sigurd, now owned by Gudrun, my wife, and thus rightfully mine."

Gunnar replied, "You will never get your hands on the gold, Atli! And, if you battle us, you will find that we are not as easy a kill as you have thought. Rather than fighting us, brother, prepare a fitting feast for us in our honour, as you have promised."

Atli replied, "I have desired your deaths for a long time, as I seek vengeance for your betrayal of your noble brother-in-law, Sigurd, and my beautiful sister, Brynhild."

Hogni countered, "Atli, look around you. It is easy to see that you are not ready for a battle. Come, let us rather retire, and you can prepare a feast in our honour, as were the words of your messenger, Vingi."

When she heard her brothers were present, Gudrun came out. She greeted them warmly and hugged and kissed them and said, "To prevent you from coming here, I sent you the ring, carved with runes, and a wolf's hair. But, you have come, and it has been foretold that one cannot withstand one's destiny. Now, you can see for yourselves that Atli has betrayed you. Before any lives are lost, let us make a satisfactory arrangement."

Sigurd's gold which was in the possession of Hogni and Gunnar, and Atli was prepared to fight for it. Gunnar and Hogni were not prepared to give up the gold, and a resolution was unattainable. Gudrun suggested that they divide the gold up amongst themselves and prevent any lives from being lost by warring. When neither party agreed to that, Atli signalled the beginning of the battle by throwing a spear into the courtyard.

The Battle in Atli's Hall, by Johannes Gehrts

Fighting broke out in the courtyard. Gudrun observed that her brothers were highly outnumbered. She ran inside and called upon Sigurd, as he had taught her how to wield a sword and bend a bow. She tore away her necklace and finery, put on a mail coat, took up a sword and shield and went out to fight beside her brothers. The battle raged on, as Gunnar and Hogni fought through Atli's ranks. Though Atli's men did not want to harm their queen, Gudrun's skilled sword strokes injured many men, and she, herself, became wounded and had to retire to her chambers. Gunnar and Hogni were fiercer foes than Atli had foreseen, and his men were falling. Because a myriad of his men were dying, Atli became distraught.

Atli lamented, "Most of my magnificent army has fallen. From my thirty champion fighters, only eleven remain. My three brothers lay dead in my courtyard. I married into your family, a dominant and dynamic family, and have an elegant and enlightened wife. But, her foresight and knowledge never bettered me, because we rarely found where our thoughts could be unified. Now, most of my men and my family are dead. As the husband of Gudrun, I want the kingdoms and the great, golden treasures that are rightfully mine. The treasures are hers, not yours, and you have stolen them. But, my deepest sorrows are that you dishonoured and betrayed my beautiful sister, causing her death."

Hogni gave argument. "You are the one who has betrayed us! With promises of wealth and power, you lied to us. With your attack on us, you broke the peace first. You are married to our sister and let her fight with us battling you! Now, she is wounded. You have slain my two sons, Solar and Snaevar, and their foster father, Orkning. Your actions are not those of a king. I laugh at your sorrows, and I praise the gods for your misfortunes."

With heavy loss of life, the battle raged on. When all of Hogni and Gunnar's men had fallen and only the two brothers remained, Atli's men were able to seize Gunnar and fetter him. Hogni fought off twenty more men, killing them all, but he, too, was overpowered and made prisoner.

Atli laughed. "Finally, we have you brothers in chains. Your fighting skills are impressive, but now shall we cut out your heart, Hogni?"

Hogni replied, "Do as you desire, as I happily await your decision. I have withstood several severe ordeals long before this one. Although

I am wounded, you will see that my heart is blood red and beats strong and true. Unlike yours, Atli, which is black and steeped in deceit."

Atli's steward, Beiti suggested, "Hogni may be of use to us, as he can tell us where the gold is. It would be better to take the heart of Hjalli, the thrall, and spare Hogni. Hjalli's destiny is to die."

Hjalli heard these words and screamed out loud and ran and hid. He said, "This is a wicked day if I die, as there is no one to look after my herds of swine." Atli's men found Hjalli, grabbed him, and drew their blades, as the man wailed and bemoaned his hardships. "I will do anything, any kind of work, anything! Have mercy on me! I want to keep my life!"

Hogni exclaimed, "I do not want to listen to this man's sobbing and screeching. You need not replace him for me. I can contend with this sport you demand on delivering, better than this man you have bound." The slave was set free and, again, he ran and hid. Hogni was bound in irons and thrown down beside his brother. Atli ordered the brothers to reveal the whereabouts of the gold.

Gunnar said, "You will never see the gold, even if you take the heart of my brother."

Atli ordered the soldiers to recapture the thrall a second time and, this time, they carved out his heart. The heart was brought to King Gunnar and displayed in front of him. Atli laughed and stated, "Here is the heart of Hjalli, the fearful. It is unlike the heart of Hogni, the strong hearted, for this heart trembles. It shivered and quivered night and day when it lay in the breast of Hjalli, the fainthearted."

Hogni was seized, and they sliced out his heart while he was still alive. His hardiness and steadfastness was so powerful that, before he died, he was able to laugh at Atli. Everyone who was there remembered the sounds of his laughter, while undergoing the agonizing and tormenting process. The soldiers displayed the heart of Hogni to Gunnar.

Gunnar grieved and said, "Today, let it be known that the heart of Hogni, the strong hearted, was unlike the heart of Hjalli, the timid hearted. For the heart of Hogni beat soundly and stably, while it rest in his brave breast. The heart of Hogni is also unlike your heart, Atli, which is dirty and disgusting and destined for a dishonourable death. If you seek the gold, Hogni can no longer tell you where it is, because you have killed him and it gladdens my heart to know that you will never find it. I am content, even though we lose our lives, because you will soon lose yours."

Atli ordered, "Take him to the serpent's den."

Gudrun admonished Atli. "May torment and trouble follow you for the rest of your days!"

Gunnar's hands were shackled and secured behind his back, before he was lowered into a serpent den abounding with deadly and venomous snakes. A harp was secured and sent to Gunnar from Gudrun, as he was a seasoned and skilled harp player. Although his hands were bound, he was resourceful and showed great dexterity, as he expertly danced his toes along the strings of the exquisite harp, creating a subduing and soothing music. He played so well, that all the serpents fell asleep under his magical, musical spell. He was able to rest awhile. One giant, venomous viper was not charmed by the calming and alluring music, and it delved into Gunnar, tunnelling its way to his heart. The gallant and good heart of Gunnar strummed its last beat that day.

Chapter Fifty-Two
Oddrun's Revelation

Oddrun, another sister of Atli, had trained as a midwife. As the years went by, she became an experienced and efficient woman in the assistance of childbearing. At one time, Borgney, her longtime friend, confessed to Oddrun of her love for Vilmund, but her father disapproved of the union. Borgney was heartbroken and pregnant with their first child, and Oddrun comforted and assisted with the childbirth. She then aided Borgney's father into the acceptance of his daughter's chosen mate and grandchild. Since then, Vilmund and Borgney were betrothed and enjoyed the birth of many more children, all of which Oddrun helped bring into Middle Earth. On one occasion, it was Oddrun who confessed to Borgney of her love for Gunnar, son of King Gjuki.

She told her, "Long ago, my father commanded Brynhild to train as a warrior maiden. She was happy with that, because she wanted to be one of Odin's valkyries, so, she trained all her young life. Father told me that I would be betrothed to one of the sons of King Gjuki and Queen Grimhild in the south. It would be to either Gunnar, Hogni or Guttorm… It did not matter who. Upon meeting Gunnar, I was excited and loved him, and he loved me, too. We decided that we wanted to marry, and Gunnar went to my brother, Atli, and asked for my hand in marriage. Atli, being the cold and dark-hearted man he is, refused the marriage proposal. He never gave a reason. My breast swelled, as my heart broke. My sorrow was immense, but I carried on with my work, as that brings me great joy. The cruelty of my brother Atli continued, and my heart tore away from my breast even more, when he agreed that my sister Brynhild should marry Gunnar. I loved the mighty prince, and Brynhild hated him. Gunnar was worthy to be loved, and she should have loved him. But, in the end, that marriage turned out to be ill-fated. I met Gunnar again, after the ceremony of the deaths of Sigurd and Brynhild. Gunnar was grieving and found comfort in my arms, and he asked for my hand again, and Atli refused, again. I always wondered why he agreed to Brynhild's marriage to Gunnar and not mine."

Borgney listened and comforted Oddrun. "I see you have suffered, Oddrun, yet I also see that you have been spared, by the gods *and* by Atli, a much worse fate. If you had married any of the Gjukung brothers, you would be a grieving widow. You are much better off being free from them."

"Yes, Borgney, you are very insightful. Atli and the gods have spared me that grief. I see that I was never destined to be with Gunnar or any of the brothers, as I ended up married to neither of them."

Borgney and Oddrun both agreed

"Also Borgney, I have another secret that has pained my heart."

"Well, tell it to me, and your pain will lessen."

Oddrun confided, "As you know, my mother is skilled in a special magic that I do not understand. I know it was she who killed Gunnar. I could not stop her. She transformed herself into a large and loathsome serpent and slid into the pit with Gunnar and the other snakes. Since she was not a natural snake, she was unaffected by the soothing music of Gunnar's beautiful harp playing. She remained awake, while the others slept and Gunnar rested. I saw her and, to my sorrow and horror, she burrowed deep into the heart of Gunnar, and that is how Glaumvor became a widow. I was struck with fear at this sight and could barely perform my duties. And, I am ashamed of myself and my family."

Borgney comforted Oddrun, again. "This is dreadful, dear Oddrun. I sensed there was darkness about your mother, but I could not determine what it was. Also, from this knowledge, I believe that you may be unsafe. Your mother may not know that you know about her. But, if she did, she does have the ability to harm you. It may be wise for you to stay away from your family, Oddrun. Stay with us. I will speak with Vilmund about this, and I am sure he will agree. We have many halls, and I am always in need of help with the children. And, you know our children love you dearly."

Oddrun was grateful for the wise counsel and generosity of Borgney. She would wait for a sign, as she was uncertain of her path. Borgney continued to comfort Oddrun.

Chapter Fifty-Three
Atli and Gudrun

After the battle and the killing of Gudrun's kin, Atli continually boasted to everyone in his household about the slaying of Gunnar and Hogni. He wore the jewel of Andvari, that he took from Gunnar. He was extremely proud of himself, and Gudrun was disgusted.

"I know you take great delight in declaring these deaths to me and to everyone else. But, great grievances and sorrows will come to you, Atli, because you killed my brothers, my nephews and all of their men. While I live, misery and misfortune will follow you wherever you go."

"Gudrun, my wife," Atli laughed, "I am not so hard-hearted and, as expected, you will be highly compensated for the loss of your kin and comrades with anything that you desire."

Gudrun declared, "I have known for a long time that I have not been easy to live with, but I could endure your deeds while my brothers were living. Now that you have killed them, their heirs and their men, a suitable settlement is impossible, because compensation for their loss is beyond measure. Men and women have been forced to submit to your will and, even as your wife, I have had to do the same. Because of this, all of my kinsmen are dead, and I am all alone. All I am left with in this life is you. Although I am not pleased with my present position, I accept my fate and surrender my will to yours. Now a worthy funeral feast must be prepared, so that we can honour my brothers, my nephews, their men, your kin and your men who have all fallen in this sorrowful and shameful battle."

Gudrun's words were sweet and seductive, and Atli believed that Gudrun had submitted to him. She prepared the funeral feast. For so long, she had been forced to play the role of the wife of Atli, and she had two sons by him. She looked upon them and knew they were doomed to die, because those still alive within the Gjukung kingdom would seek vengeance for the deaths of her brothers, nephews and men. While preparing for the funeral feast, she secretly took Atli's sons aside. She hugged and kissed them, said goodbye and silently and skillfully slit their infant throats.

During the feasting, Gudrun sat quietly watching, as Atli enjoyed his meal. When the king asked where his sons, Erp and Eitil were, Gudrun fed him these words: "I will warm your blackened heart, my husband, by telling you. You caused me the utmost grief and sorrow, when you killed my kin and, because of that, you have forfeited your sons. For, on the table before you, are their little white skulls that you have used as your serving cups, You drank the blood of your sons mixed with sweet wine. And, the meat you have eaten was their young hearts roasted and dipped in honey. I hope you have enjoyed your dinner, dear."

Atli was horrified by her words and jumped out of his chair. "Have you gone mad, woman? How can you think of such horrors, and be so cold-blooded a mother as to murder your own sons and then provide them as food for me to eat?"

Gudrun calmly said, "You have brought me endless sorrows, so now my only purpose in this life is to bring wretched agony and dishonour upon you. There are no sufferings that would ever be severe enough for you."

The horrified and angered Atli said, "You should be stoned to death and then burned!"

"I have been appointed a different death. One that you will not be here to see…"

He ordered his men to make a thorough search for his sons in all the chambers and halls of his palace and of the lands of his kingdom. They were not found. Gudrun and Atli departed from one another. Living in her own chambers, Gudrun asked that she be guarded day and night, due to the possibility that Atli might take revenge upon her.

One night, Niflung, one of Hogni's sons, came to see Gudrun, and she was delighted. "Aunt Gudrun, I long to avenge my father, uncle and brothers for their brutal slaying by the hand of King Atli. I know he is your husband, and I do not want to hurt you."

"Oh, my dear Niflung, destiny has sealed us together in thoughts and, soon, in deeds, for I, too, long to avenge our kin. We must stay hidden, so that no harm can come upon us."

The two plotted and planned. One evening, Atli drank and drank and got extremely drunk. He continued to boast of all his skilled killings. He bragged on and on about his murderous conquests, especially about the slayings of Gunnar and Hogni. He did not see the son of Hogni, sitting in his hall, quietly observing and listening. Both Queen Gudrun and Niflung closely watched the drunken Atli. At the end of the evening, Atli stumbled to his bed. Gudrun and Niflung looked at one another in agreement. They met, waited for the king to fall asleep, before they made their way to his bed chambers. Niflung had brought with him a sword. Both Gudrun and Niflung held the sword high above Atli and thrust the sword deep through Atli's chest. Atli awoke from the piercing wound, and he realized, from the extent of his wound, that he was about to die.

"I feel from this gaping wound that no bindings, wrappings or healings can help me survive. Who has delivered my death stroke?"

Gudrun confessed, "One of my nephews, the son of my brother, Hogni, the same brother who you, Atli, the heartless, sliced the courageous heart from. I, too, have been a part of the spilling of your blood."

"It is dishonourable and shameful for you to kill your own husband, when your own relatives gave you to me. I paid a noble compensation with a magnificent marriage settlement. But, you behaved badly wanting to control all the lands that King Budli possessed, and you distressed your mother-in-law to grievous tears."

Gudrun answered, "Atli, even as you die, you lie, for these are all false words. But, I no longer care what you say. I know there has been anger within me, but you have turned my anger into a raging storm of madness. There was never contentment in your courtyards but always a fury of discontented men and women. When I was with Sigurd, there was peace in my life, as I was married to the worthiest of warriors and the most honourable of kings. When I lost him and became a widow, my heart was broken. But, it pained me even more to be given away in marriage to you, Atli, son of Budli, the most cruel and heartless of kings."

"Gudrun, as you stand there lying, I lay here dying. These false words better neither of us. As my wife, prepare my body for the afterworld, with honour and respect."

Gudrun answered, "I will do as you request, as is my duty as your wife. As is fitting for your station in life, you will have a splendid and stately funeral. You will have an exquisite stone burial chamber built for you, and I will wash you in fine-grained herbs and clothe you in handsome finery. Rest assured, Atli, I will provide for all of your needs."

As he released his final breath, Atli looked upon his wife, Gudrun, for the last time. She took the ring, Andvaranaut, from his finger. She did all for Atli, as she had promised. As a proper send off for Atli and his sons, there was a fine funeral and feast. When all she had promised was done, she had a special feast for all of Atli's men, where drink flowed freely throughout the halls. When the men were foolishly drunk, she stealthily sealed all the doors and locked all the king's retainers inside one hall. She went outside, gathered flames from a fire pit and set the hall ablaze.

Chapter Fifty-Four
Gudrun and King Jonakur

While the men were locked inside the devouring inferno, Gudrun, alone, stood outside watching. As the fortress was going up in towering flames, she watched and listened to the screaming men pounding against the door. She stood, unable to move, as she felt the heat of the blaze, yet it was the fiery tormented blaze within herself that caused her to fall to her knees. What was she doing? She felt loneliness bite through her. Her life had been unbearable, and her own death looked good. She no longer desired to live. Sigurd, the love of her life, was dead. Her brothers and most of her family were dead. Her marriage to Atli drove her into bloodcurdling madness. She killed her own sons, she killed her husband, and now she had created a burning inferno that was killing all of his men. The yelling and the pounding slowly ceased. All became quiet, except for the sounds of the scorching flames and the crackling of the falling wood. Feeling unfit for life, she sat for a while. She slowly rose and turned herself away from the wretched blaze. Away from the searing heat of the flames… She slowly dragged herself to the sea. The sea breeze was whispering. The waves were inviting. She waded into the waters, and the coolness doused the immense heat of her flaming inner torment. Her woe drove her to wade deeper and deeper, as she sought to drown herself in the waves. She could be with Sigurd in the afterlife. She yearned for her death and to be with him. Seeking death by drowning, she plunged deeper into the depths of the sea. Ran, the Goddess of the Sea, felt her presence and, knowing it was not Gudrun's time to die, wove a watery ship of waves and gently carried the tormented, weary, woe-struck woman to the shores of the kingdom of King Jonakur.

Gudrun woke and found herself on a shore. She was laying on a beach, soothed by the gentle rolling of waves around her body. The ring was still on her finger. She was attended to and comforted by some unknown people. They carried her into a fortress and nurtured her to health. Gudrun was still a beautiful woman, and her wisdom had increased with her years, although she had grown gruesomely grimmer. She slowly began to heal, was able to eat on her own, dress herself, walk the beach where she had been found, and talk to whomever would listen. She spent long hours looking over the waters and wondering why Ran had spared her life. She eventually took up the art of embroidery. Her tapestries flowed rich in life and colours. Although she remembered her past, her emotional and mental madness was slowly dissipating. King Jonakur spent time with her, talked with her and watched her progression. She was refined, beautiful, gentle, wise and skilled. Over time, he fell in love with her.

The inner torment she had experienced slowly became replaced with a soothing sense of happiness touched with contentment. The king was kind, gentle and loving to her and, one day, he proposed marriage. She was surprised and delighted. Was there a new life awaiting her? She had felt lost and all alone in the world, and now she felt like the gods had granted her a new life, and she was grateful. She wondered if this was why Ran had rescued her and brought her here…She accepted King Jonakur's proposal.

The wedding feast brought his family and friends together. She did not have any of her family or friends present. She became stepmother to Erp, a son from Jonakur's prior marriage. She remembered her own children from her beloved Sigurd, Sigmund and Svanhild. As far as she knew, they were both alive and being raised in King Half's kingdom. Sigmund was living in anonymity. She remembered her two sons by Atli, and was deeply grieved by how they were slain by her own hands. The memories horrified her. Yet, somewhere deeper in her heart, she knew it was more merciful for them to die swiftly, by her hand, rather than to be hunted down and killed by members of her own family seeking revenge. She slowly reconciled with her memories and began the process of becoming something new. Was this forgiveness? She was slowly forgiving herself and experiencing a form of inner peace. An inner peace that became more precious to her than gold or any other material treasures she had ever owned…

The relationship with Jonakur blossomed, and she fell completely in love with him. The couple soon had a son, and Jonakur and Gudrun were overjoyed. They had a name-giving ceremony for their boy, and he was named Hamdir. The norns visited and chanted and chattered over him. The couple was enchanted, and Erp was happy to have a younger brother. Gudrun later gave birth to a second son. He was also given a name-giving ceremony, where the norns chanted and chattered over him. He was named Sorli. The boys soon earned nick names, as they were known as Hamdir, the strong minded, and Sorli, the youngest.

Gudrun shared her life story with Jonakur, as she remembered it. All of her family, her past life with Sigurd, the betrayal of Brynhild, the help from her sister, living in the kingdom of Half, her children being raised there, her being given in marriage to Atli… She found it extremely difficult, but she told her husband of how she killed her sons, Atli and all his men. Jonakur listened. He empathized with his wife, but never judged. He had heard the stories of these horrific events, but listening to her tell her story, in her own words, helped him understand her better. He realized the extent of her sufferings, and he loved and cared for her even more. He believed she had no other choice in her doings, and thanked the gods and Ran for bringing her to him. He loved her.

He shared his life story, and she learned more about him. He had been a warrior king who fought in many battles. He had been married to a valkyrie warrior woman, who gave birth to Erp, before she died from battle wounds. He had also experienced many losses from war. He was now relishing in the peacefulness of his own kingdom and preferred peace over war. The two empathized with one another. They shared in the nurturing and raising of their children. With the three boys, the household was a busy one, and Gudrun loved every minute of it.

One day, Jonakur suggested they send for her daughter, Svanhild, to come and live with them. Gudrun was elated with the idea, and they did. When Svanhild arrived, Gudrun was overjoyed to see her. She introduced her daughter to her three brothers, Erp, Hamdir and Sorli. The children were all raised together in the loving halls of King Jonakur and Queen Gudrun. Svanhild was growing into the fairest of maidens, with fairy, flaxen-white hair and keen, deep-blue eyes. Few dared to face her glance, as her eyes pierced into one's soul, exactly like her father's had done.

Chapter Fifty-Five
The Saga of Svanhild

The saga of Sigurd and his gold became widely known, and many men wanted the gold. A powerful king, named Jormunrek, decided that a way to get the gold was through Sigurd's daughter and, therefore, he wanted Svanhild for his bride.

Svanhild had grown up in the secure halls of King Half, with the protection of the King Half, Thora, King Thjodrek, her brother Siggi, and a trusted household. She now lived in the halls of King Jonakur, her mother and her brothers. She had turned into a beautiful maiden with piercing blue eyes, like her father. Getting to know her new family made life interesting. She was happy and contented. She was well-versed in feminine skills and would make a good wife.

One day, ships arrived to the shores of King Jonakur's kingdom. All were made aware that they were sent from the kingdom of King Jormunrek for the purpose of asking for Svanhild's hand in marriage. Jormunrek had sent his son, Randver, accompanied by the king's counsellor, Bikki, and a large following of trained and gifted men and women. When the company arrived to the halls of King Jonakur, they were greeted warmly, given areas in which to rest after their journey, and a feast was prepared in their honour. At the feast, Randver and Bikki came before King Jonakur and Queen Gudrun and proposed the marriage of Svanhild to King Jormunrek. They presented charming gifts from their king.

King Jonakur and Queen Gudrun at first thought that the proposed marriage would be between Prince Randver and Svanhild, as he was more her age. Gudrun and Jonakur discussed the union and agreed, thinking that the bond with King Jormunrek was suitable, and a marriage settlement was made. On the day of departure, Svanhild, with a splendid following, boarded the boat and she sat beside Randver, her guardian for the voyage.

When Bikki saw the two of them sitting together, he spoke up, as he thought they made a good-looking couple He said, "Randver, you should marry Svanhild. You would be a better husband for her, because you both are young and you could grow old together. As for your father, Jormunrek, he is an old man."

Svanhild, by Jenny Nyström

Randver looked upon Svanhild and found her beautiful and the idea appealing. "Although I do like your idea, Bikki, Svanhild is betrothed to my father, and I must honour his request. We have been sent to accompany her to our kingdom, and that we shall do. Although, when we get home, I can suggest this idea to father, but he may not like it."

During the voyage, Svanhild and Randver became close and spoke with one another affectionately. They developed a liking for one another. Randver informed Svanhild what Bikki had said, about Randver marrying her rather than King Jormunrek. Svanhild liked the idea, and they both agreed that they would like to be married. They decided that when they returned to the kingdom of Jormunrek, Randver would approach his father with the request of his own marriage to Svanhild. When they arrived home, Randver showed Svanhild to her chambers, then went to his own hall and rested. Bikki, on the other hand, immediately visited Jormunrek with these words: "Your son has betrayed you, as Svanhild is his lover."

Bikki had given the king ill-advised counsel in the past, but Jormunrek thought on his words. When Randver was rested, he approached his father with the proposed marriage to Svanhild for himself, but only with his father's permission. When he said this, Jormunrek was indeed suspicious and believed what Bikki had told him. Bikki further persuaded Jormunrek to believe that his son had betrayed him, and the king became irritable, then outraged. Jormunrek charged his son with betrayal and treason and ordered him to be sent to the gallows to be hanged.

While in prison, Randver asked for a hawk to be brought to him, and one was delivered. He took the hawk and tore off all its feathers and sent it to his father, as a message. When Jormunrek saw the hawk from his son, he understood his son's message. He realized that he had stripped his son of all honour and dignity, like the hawk was stripped of all its feathers. He soon realized that, without Randver, he would have no heirs. He ordered his son to be released from prison and to come before him. But alas, it was too late, as by that time, Bikki had already made sure that Randver was dead.

King Jormunrek grieved over his son, while Bikki whispered more unsound advice into his ears, by stating that Svanhild should die a disgraceful death like Randver. The king, in a stricken state, agreed.

Svanhild was placed in the middle of the gate with her arms stretched out, one bound to the right side and the other bound to the left side. Horses where set free to gallop towards her and trample her as they rode through the gate. When Svanhild opened her eyes, her fierce glare made the horses stop, and none would come near her. Bikki realized the fierceness of Svanhild's gaze and had a bag placed over her head. The horses were again forced to gallop through the gate, thereby pounding the life out of the beautiful body of Svanhild and leaving her trodden and dead in the dirt and mud.

Chapter Fifty-Six
The Inciting of Gudrun

Gudrun reeled in agony, when she learned of her beloved daughter's death. Being viciously trampled by the horses of the Goths…! Oh, what a gruesome death for her beautiful young daughter, and what a bitter betrayal of the marriage settlement! She instinctively turned to her old ways of thinking and vowed vengeance. She looked to her sons, Hamdir, Sorli, and Erp, and asked them to help. "My noble sons, you must seek vengeance for your beloved sister, for she has been brutally dishonoured and killed by the King of the Goths."

She stimulated her sons to avenge their sister. She went to the Hunnish storehouse and chose magical mail coats and helmets that were embossed with the insignia of kings and that no iron could penetrate. She also chose an array of fine arms for them to wield. Holding counsel with her sons and their warriors, Gudrun instructed Hamdir, Sorli and Erp on the best method of killing King Jormunrek.

"Wear these mail coats and helmets, as with them, no iron can penetrate you. And, heed this warning, my beloved sons: *Do not use or let any hard pieces of the earth's surface, such as stones or rocks, touch you.*" Gudrun looked upon her sons and continued. "For your best protection, you must go to Jormunrek under the cloak of the darkness of night. Capture him, while he and his households are asleep. Listen carefully, my sons. Hamdir, you must cut off the legs of the king, and in this way he will not be able to get up to fight you. Exactly at the same time, Sorli, you must cut off his arms, and he will not be able to pick up a weapon to wield it against you. And Erp, at exactly the same time as Hamdir is cutting off his legs and Sorli is cutting off his arms, you must cut off the king's head. In this way, he will not be able to call for help. All three of you must work together on your deeds at precisely the same time. Do as I have told you, and you will succeed. Do you understand, my beloved sons?" When Hamdir, Sorli and Erp agreed that they understood the avenging plan of their mother, Gudrun said, "Our beloved Svanhild must be avenged. When the king is dead, leave his stronghold and come directly home. Do not waver. May the gods and the shield of the night protect you. When you come home, we will rejoice in your victory."

As the sons adorned themselves with war gear and mounted their horses, one of them had a flashing premonition. Hesitant and unsure about going against King Jormunrek, Hamdir said, "Mother, I feel we meet for the last time. You will hear the tidings and hold a funeral feast for your sons and Svanhild."

Gudrun hesitated when she heard her son say this. She pondered, *"Why is my son Hamdir saying this? Do we need to make a new plan? No! The plan is a good one. The gruesome Jormunrek killed my beautiful daughter without cause. He must pay for his betrayal!"* She said, "Do exactly as we have planned, my son, and all will be well."

The sons left to fulfill their quest. Erp said he needed to attend to something, and that he would meet the brothers before they got to the kingdom of King Jormunrek.

Chapter Fifty-Seven
Hamdir, Sorli, and Erp

With vengeance on their minds, Hamdir and Sorli and their warriors rode to the kingdom of Jormunrek. Before they entered the kingdom, they waited for Erp. He finally showed himself, and Hamdir and Sorli were relieved to see him. Then, they became confused, as Erp was reciting nonsensical verses, riddles and rhymes that no one could understand. He said, "I can provide you the assistance the arm gives a leg. Also, the guidance that a leg gives a leg… And remember, also, how an arm helps an arm."

The brothers, Hamdir and Sorli, thought that Erp, somehow, had misinterpreted the instructions of their mother and was mixing up everything she had said. Erp continued chattering on with his garbled babble and paid no heed to anything Hamdir or Sorli told him. The brothers asked all their warriors if any of them understood Erp. After listening to the young man, no one knew what Erp was saying. All the men questioned the saneness of Erp's mind, and whether or not he would be capable of accomplishing the tasks ahead. "How can a hand help a foot? Or, a foot help another foot…?"

The brothers were disheartened and discouraged by Erp's disorientated strange words and bizarre behaviour. They were afraid that their half-brother Erp had, some-how, lost his mind. The young men took counsel. They had a job to do, and they needed to have all men present and with their wits about them. While Erp displayed this madness, many believed him incapable of preforming his duties as a warrior. They were fearful that the madman would undermine their quest. They decided that their best option was to kill Erp. The brothers were torn by this decision and needed more time to talk to Erp. They spoke with Erp a number of times but, to their dismay, he displayed no recognition of them nor spoke any reasonable words. The brothers finally agreed that if they were to fulfill their quest, there was no choice but to kill Erp. It was done quickly with no suffering for Erp.

On the rest of their journey, Hamdir tripped and threw out his hand. His thoughts immediately turned to his brother, Erp, and his words. *"That is how an arm helps a leg! Erp was making sense with his words and visions! I would have had a great fall, if it was not for my hand to help me.* He confided this to Sorli.

A little while later, Sorli, misjudged his step and went off-balance. He used his other foot to prevent a fall. Now, his thoughts also turned to Erp, and Erp's words and visions made sense to him. *"That was how a foot helps a foot! I would have fallen, had I not used my feet to balance myself."* He confided in Hamdir. Both brothers now fully understood the words of Erp. They had done their brother and themselves a great wrong.

Upon arrival to the halls of King Jormunrek, the brothers wore the magical mail coats and used the shield of darkness, as their mother had advised. They stealthily entered the sleeping chambers of the king. As the other warriors acted as lookouts, Hamdir cut off the king's legs, while Sorli silently sliced off his arms. Jormunrek still had his head and screamed for help. The brothers realized that they needed Erp to cut off the head of the king, but since they had killed Erp, Jormunrek's head was untouched and screaming. They called for another warrior to do the deed, but help for the king came instantly. Hamdir, Sorli and the warriors were cornered. The brothers fought valiantly with the magical armour protecting them.

"We have dishonoured Erp and ourselves by killing him on the road. His words were wise and right, and ours were unwise and wrong. We needed him to cut off the head of Jormunrek. We have disobeyed our mother. Although we are weary, we are winning a great victory. We have been fighting well and stand here upon many Goth corpses, but all my senses tell me that the norns, and not the soldiers, will determine our destiny."

A one-eyed old man, with wide brimmed hat and a spear, came

before Jormunrek and said, "Your wisdom is immensely lacking, if you cannot kill these little boys."

Jormunrek said, "Then, tell me how, oh ancient one."

"Stone is mightier than iron."

Jormunrek ordered his soldiers to throw down their iron swords and pick up rocks and gravel from the earth and throw them at the brothers. The magical armour protected them from iron but not from stones. Sorli was stoned at the end of the hall, and Hamdir met his fate behind the house. Jormunrek was able to live for a little while, but was horribly maimed and suffered in agony from all his injuries. He lived long enough to regret the killing of his son and of Svanhild, the beautiful daughter of Sigurd and Gudrun. Before he died, he had Bikki killed for his treasonous counsel. Odin was pleased, because now the sons of Gudrun and Jonakur would reside with him in Valhalla.

Chapter Fifty-Eight
The Reflections of Gudrun

Upon hearing the news of her sons' deaths, Gudrun screamed long and loud. Jonakur was overwrought with grief, as Gudrun cried and cried. She lamented, "There has been too much death. Too much suffering… Too much vengeance… Oh, what have I done? What have I done? I should have never let our sons go on this venture of vengeance. Oh, my beloved Jonakur, I have wronged you, and our sons, by sending them on this forsaken journey! The winds of woe enwrap us. The violent violation of our sweet Svanhild stung me, and I sought vengeance for her death. I thought it was the only way. The right way… But, I was wretchedly wrong. All in the name of vengeance, our sons suffered horrible and painful deaths. My heart is broken, as is yours, my love. I have broken your heart by sending our sons to their sorrowful deaths. The overwhelming power of vengeance has once again tore into our souls, minds and hearts."

Jonakur and Gudrun held each other for comfort. He said, "Gudrun, my beloved, this is far from easy to endure. But, know this… Our sons' deaths are not from any wrong-doing of yours. We all thought this to be the right path, as vengeance-seeking is our way. Our sons knew the risks involved and, with honour, accepted the quest. Jormunrek is wounded beyond healing and lays dying. He will not live long. Therefore, our sons have succeeded in avenging Svanhild, and King Jormunrek is well aware of that. From now on, my love, we would be wise to seek a more enlightened path in our future journey, if we have one."

"Yes, Jonakur, you are right, yet we must be watchful. Jormunrek may send his soldiers to avenge him, and the cycle will go on. Unless, we settle a truce with him and his household…"

Gudrun fell into a state of reflection that she shared with Jonakur and their people. "Oh, Jonakur and companions, I have lived in three homes, have been warmed by three hearths, and have been married to three husbands. Sigurd was my first husband, and he was generous, kind and wise. Life was wonderful when Sigurd was in this world. But, we were not destined to last, as was foretold. The norns wove our fates in life and intertwined many miseries. My own mother gave him the ale of forgetfulness and a woman I trusted, and thought to be my friend, mercilessly betrayed Sigurd and me. My brothers wounded me grievously, when they deprived me of my husband by killing Sigurd. The most agonizing memory was being with him, when he was slain in our bed and his blood drenched all over me. And then, death was devised for our son, Sigmund. It agonizes me that I cannot be with him. Heartlessly, by my own mother, I was given the ale of forgetfulness and given away, unwillingly, to a second husband, all for the sake of good alliances between the two families. But, my second husband conspired to gain the garner of gold gathered by Sigurd and then secured by my brothers, and the son of Budli gave us no peace. The sharpest pain cut into my heart, when Atli cut out the living heart of my brother, Hogni. Still not satisfied, Atli devised the most gruesome death for my oldest brother, Gunnar. He had the most hideous of slithering snakes surround to sup on him, but Gunnar was a skilled harp player and lulled the serpents to sleep with his soothing music. It was the wretched shape-shifting mother of Atli who killed Gunnar. With Atli, I had two sharp-eyed boys, but vengeance ripped through my mind and soul and, in a fit of bloody vengeful madness, I chopped off their heads and fed them to their greedy and ruthless father. My soul and mind were tormented. I killed my second husband with the aid of my nephew, and then I killed all his retainers, as the power of revenge ravaged through me.

I was still alive, but I was unfit for life. I had no peace. Only inner torment… I chose to drown within the whirling waves of the sea, but the sea would not have me. Gentle flowing waves held and floated me here, to you, Jonakur, where I lay and rested. Within your household, and with the kindness and caring by you and all here within, I healed, and you loved me back to health. You are a wonderful and good king, Jonakur, and I am grateful for you. You married me, and I was a wife a third time to another nation's king. I continued to heal and to love you, as you shared your love with me. I bore you two sons as legal heirs for our kingdom. Jonakur, I am grateful to you, my husband, for I have lived in happiness, love and peace, and I have found you to be a good and righteous man. I felt secure, and we had my beautiful daughter, Svanhild, sent for, and she came to live with us. Within our halls, our sons Erp, Hamdir, Sorli, with their raven black hair like yours, and my brothers Gunnar and Hogni, and our daughter Svanhild, with her flaxen hair, filled our hearts and days with love and joy. These days were wonderful.

I dressed my only daughter in gold and the finest of linens, and she grew into an elegant, refined, gifted, skilled and beautiful young woman. The King of the Goths desired her, and, with oaths and hopes of an alliance of friendship between our nations, we gave her away to the king. One of my gravest injuries was when my only daughter, your beloved stepdaughter, was mercilessly trampled by the hooves of the Goths' horses. They tied her up and left her alone, trampled and dead in the dirt. I sent our sons to avenge our fairy, flaxen-haired girl and, because of that, they, too, are dead. Sorli was found at the end of Jormunrek's hall, while Hamdir was found behind the house, and Erp was found outside of the fortress. Why could I not foresee that vengeance always finds a way to harm or destroy the avenger? Vengeance seeps into the soul and slowly eats you away. You are wise, my beloved Jonakur, with your words that we need to find another way. A different way… Any other way, but vengeance… I have one more son, who lives away, unknown to the world, and I am afraid of bringing attention to him, for fear of bringing about his death. He remains in King Half's halls. The grievances of my heart are immense.

Today, we build the funeral pyre, as high as the heavens, for our loved ones. All our loved ones, all our woes, and all our sorrows… Let us all bring them here to be burned." Gudrun let Jonakur and her people know what she wanted. She expressed, "Now, all the burdens and sorrows of my heart have been revealed to you, and I release them. I have loved deeply. The sorrows and loss of my loved ones is interwoven into the fabric of my being. Also interwoven is the love I have for them and the gratitude of having had them in my life, if only for a short time. Vengeance has been woven into my life and is a bitter and wretched foe. It has ripped at my heart, scarred my soul, and battered my mind. We have all experienced the painful power of vengeance. We all must let the chains of vengeance go. Let us seek a new and better way for a new day. Today, I let the power of vengeance go. I let it go and think only of the power of forgiveness and love. Be still, and let the flow of forgiveness and love heal our tormented hearts, minds and souls. A heart full of love, forgiveness and gratitude has no room for hate, resentment and vengeance. This was how I found peace of mind and serenity before. This I can do again with your help, and so can all of you. The feelings of resentment, bitterness and the thoughts of vengeance must be stilled, let go of and replaced with the feelings of forgiveness, gratitude and love. Let the goodness of these feelings overflow through our whole beings, our hearts, our minds and our souls. Let goodness wash through us. I let the power of love and forgiveness flow through me. I forgive Jormunrek for the killings of our children. Feelings of forgiveness and love feel better than feelings of hate, resentment and revenge. Somehow, while living in good feelings, I feel better, safer, more secure and more strong."

When it was built, Jonakur and Gudrun came to the funeral pyre, and the bodies of Sorli, Hamdir, Erp, Svanhild and all the young warriors who died with them were placed there. The fire was lit, and all the young people, all the sorrows, griefs and woes, all the feelings of vengeance, resentment and hate… All of this was burned there. A funeral feast was held in honour of all the loved ones. A sadness and the power of love and forgiveness permeated the halls of Jonakur and Gudrun. They, and many others, found peace and healing in these measures. Gudrun addressed her people. "To all our weary warriors and lovely ladies… May your lives flourish, and may love and happiness enfold you all."

Gudrun slowly moved into a private area, and spoke to a form only she could see. "Sigurd, my love, do you remember our promise? That I would visit with you from this world, and you would visit with me from the otherworld…? Let us visit together."

Chapter Fifty-Nine
The Journey of Gudrun and Jonakur

Gudrun prayed to the gods to end the path of vengeance and to end the curse of the gold. She spoke with her husband. "Jonakur, we need to end the curse of the gold. I do not know where my brothers put the gold, but I do have this one ring that I wish to give back to its rightful owner. Also, with all that we have believed about our fate and our destiny, thoughts have come to me that our destinies may not be fixed. Our fates may *not* be woven in iron by the norns and, possibly, *can* be changed. I have held the belief, for far too long, that we can do little or nothing about our destined paths. I have also believed that vengeance was the only way to resolve matters. Now, I believe we can change our fate… our destiny…, and that vengeance is not the way. *Love and forgiveness* is the way. The gold of Andvari and our ways have brought too much sorrow into our lives, and I wish to be free of it all. I let all resentments and vengeance go. And, Andvaranaut… I wish to return it to Andvari and beseech him to lift the curse of death that it holds."

Jonakur loved and listened to Gudrun. He wished for her and himself to find the inner peace she spoke about. He had always preferred peace over war, and he agreed with her request. To fulfill the quest, they prepared for a journey to the falls of Andvari.

To find the falls, Gudrun followed her instincts. It was an easier task than she and Jonakur had thought. Although she had never been in this part of the country before, it was like she already knew the way. Forests opened up to the loving couple, and a pathway was majestically made clear. She felt the loving presence of others, yet none were made known to them. When they arrived to the falls, they marvelled at the splendour and beauty of it all. As Jonakur and Gudrun walked along beside the falls, she called out for Andvari, but he did not appear. They called a while and, still, no Andvari. They gathered up a net that was laying beside the falls and cast it in. As he swam, Andvari was caught. Gudrun spoke with the fish. "Andvari, do you remember the day when Loki came to you and demanded the dwarf's gold that you so diligently guarded?"

"Indeed… He took all my gold, and my precious ring, and left me with nothing. That day, I put a curse of death on the gold. Now, I guard new treasures, which you will never see."

"My good Andvari, we have not come here for your gold. We have come to return to you this ring. From the curse that you cast on this gold, I have lost too many loved ones. I beseech you, Andvari, make it stop. We humbly ask you to lift your curse of death."

Gudrun brought out the ring to show Andvari. It sparkled and glistened. Andvari licked his lips. Gudrun continued, "I remember the day my love gave this ring to me. He told me the story of how he obtained it. It was a part of the vast treasures he acquired from the den of the dragon, Fafnir. He told me about his past with Brynhild, and how he had loved her and gave her this ring. Later, Sigurd retrieved the ring from her, and he then gave this ring to me. In turn, I gave this ring, with a warning, to Gunnar and Hogni, but Atli claimed it. Now, it is with me again. I have loved and lost Sigurd, my daughter, Svanhild, my brothers, and thousands of kinsmen and women. I have let them go. And, Andvari, I confess that, in the name of vengeance, I killed my two sons from Atli, and that I killed Atli and all his men. I felt unfit for life and was about to take mine by the sea, but the goddess of the sea sent me to Jonakur, who is with me today. But, vengeance made us send our sons to war, and they, too, are all gone. Today, I need to freely let them all go, Andvari. Let them all go with love… Andvari, please accept the ring back, as you are the rightful owner. And please, Andvari, lift the curse of death that the gold holds."

When Gudrun placed a gentle kiss on the ring, love formed a powerful, colourful glow around it. She held it out for Andvari and, as he acquired it, the glow of love encircled him. He was uplifted and mesmerized within and without himself. He saw the path of the ring from when it was with him, to Loki, to Odin, to Ottar's whisker, to Fafnir, to Sigurd, to Brynhild, then to Sigurd again, to Gudrun, then to Gunnar and Hogni, then Atli and back to Gudrun, and now to him. As he saw the lives of all who had owned it, he was enthralled. He also saw all of the deaths from the curse, but also the powerful presence of love that shone through, and he was uplifted and inspired. He understood all the experiences of all who had worn the ring before him. He understood the woman before him. A song sprang up from within him, and he sang an enchanting and haunting tune:

> *Love sings and is all around.*
> *Gently whispering a wondrous sound,*
> *A sound so fine, a sound so strong,*
> *in feelings that we all belong,*
> *to one another, the sound so sweet,*
> *embrace each other when we meet.*
>
> *Praises to you for now I see,*
> *the ages, the trials, and the wonders of he,*
> *Sigurd who filled your heart, so long ago,*
> *then broke your heart, and now you must let go.*
>
> *Praises to you for your compassion so deep,*
> *and for the forgiveness that is yours and mine to keep.*
> *I see and can now let go, too,*
> *the curses I spewed and the burdens I knew.*
>
> *You do not know, so to you I will inform,*
> *Gunnar returned the gold to keep you from harm,*
> *before Hogni and him met their doom,*
> *from Atli's hand, before your gloom.*
>
> *Now the gift of gold shines within my realm,*
> *consider my curse uplifted from your home.*

From your loved ones, from your life,
gone from us all! Oh, what a relief!!

With that, Andvari beamed a smile and laughed a delightful laugh. The glow continued around Andvari. He radiated love, joy and happiness. Gudrun and Jonakur were overcome with astonishment and happiness. A great invisible weight slowly arose out of Gudrun, hovered over her for a moment, then dissipated into the air.

"Oh, yes, what a relief! I feel so much better and can humbly see the love that surrounds us. Oh, praises to you! Praises, my dear Andvari… Love is all around, and I see and feel it within and without us all. May the love, peace and joy you feel stay with you and travel with you wherever you may go!"

Jonakur and Gudrun faced each other. Love surrounded them both and they hugged and revelled in the glow of love and relief and the feeling of freedom it brought. He loved her, and she loved him. Andvari dove back into the welcoming waters of Andvari Falls.

Unknowingly, he returned to the form of a dwarf. He was naked and unable to adapt to his new form. Jonakur and his men saw this change. They rescued him from the waters and clothed him. For the night, in peace, the group rested beside the falls.

Dwarf, by Rotox

In the morning, they discovered that their dreams had told them what they would do next. They all had the same dreams! Andvari wanted to stay by the falls and build a home there. Jonakur left some of his men with Andvari to help him. The group gathered up their belongings and journeyed on to the halls of King Half. Love emanated all around and enriched all within its presence. All felt completely safe and secure. All felt it was time for Gudrun to see her remaining son, Sigmund, son of Sigurd.

After their arrival to King Half's halls, Thora came to greet them. "Oh, Gudrun and Jonakur… What a delight to see you! Come… Siggi has just come in from hunting."

Before she finished her sentence, a young man stepped into the room. Gudrun gasped and nearly fainted. Jonakur held her, and they both stared at the young man who had come into the room. The youth smiled with an aura of kindness and love all around him. For Gudrun, he looked like a younger version of Sigurd, with Gram by his side.

Thora spoke. "Oh, Siggi, here you are… Here is your mother, Gudrun, and your stepfather, Jonakur. And, Gudrun and Jonakur, meet young Sigmund," she said with a gentle smile, "your son."

How This Book Came to Be

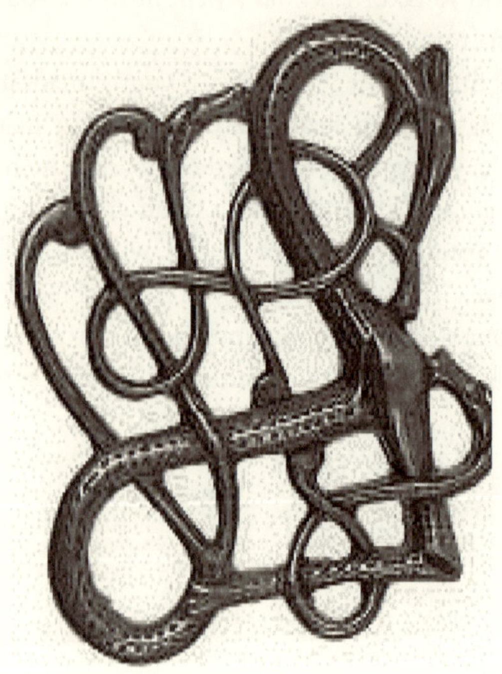

After a graduation ceremony, a colleague once asked me, "How can you wear that?"

I asked, "Wear what?"

"Your brooch…! How can you wear a pagan symbol to a Christian ceremony?

I was surprised by her question. I did not know graduation ceremonies were Christian or that my brooch was pagan. Not knowing what to say, I said, "It is a part of my heritage."

She inferred that by wearing the brooch, I breached some unseen code of conduct. Instinctively, I went into an informative mode and said something like, "The brooch is a symbol of Yggdrasil, the Old Norse

World Tree, which contains the nine mythological realms. This information comes from some of the best ancient literature ever written."

She was interested in learning a little bit about the Norse Eddas, and we left on better terms. Upon reflection, I realized, I had given my first Old Norse Mythology lesson.

The brooch is a replica of Viking art, displayed inside and outside of the UNESCO Stave churches in Norway. The most famous of these churches is Urnes. The picture below shows some of the intricacy and majesty of the Viking art.

A panel at Urnes Stave Church, Norway, a UNESCO World Heritage Site

After the encounter, sharing information about Old Norse Mythology seemed to come naturally to me. I would share with anyone who would listen, not thinking that the stories were pagan, religious, or Christian. Only rather amazing... I felt that people of Germanic or Nordic descent may benefit from knowing something about their own mythology. People seemed to know more about Roman and Greek mythology than Old Norse Mythology. Why was that? I thought of my own experiences before studying the ancient literature. Any knowledge I had of Old Norse Mythology came from Marvel comics and Stan Lee's versions of it. For some people, Old Norse Mythology seemed to be considered somewhat dark or evil, and the internet, with all the misinformation, does not help.

Being a member of the Scandinavian Cultural Centre, I was asked to teach mythology classes. Since I had previously studied Icelandic language and literature, including Old Norse Mythology, Sagas, Children's literature, and Folklore at the University of Manitoba, I agreed. I had also taken and taught Elementary Icelandic language studies at the Centre, so shifting my classes over to Old Norse Mythology came easily. My students were all Scandinavian Cultural Centre members, and said they enjoyed my classes. Eventually, I was asked by a school division to teach in Continuing Education, then a Senior group, and later private lessons. I divided the sessions into Old Norse Mythology 1 and Old Norse Mythology 2. In session 1, students learned about the creation stories, the gods and goddesses and stories about them, Ragnarok and new beginnings. In the second session, we studied The Saga of the Volsungs, the Eddas, and related stories from other sources. The story from this manuscript is scattered throughout several books, with no one source containing all the information for the whole story. And, that is how this book came about. It was written for anyone who would like the whole story in one text and for anyone interested in Old Norse Mythology. Not only was this story handwritten on vellum skins, but remnants of this story were also carved into wood and stone. Throughout the centuries, artists have shared their interpretations of this story, and some of their pictures are shared in this book. The whole history of this story is truly remarkable.

About the Author

Ainsley Bloomer lives in Winnipeg, Manitoba, with her husband. She has two adult sons. She is of Icelandic heritage, and studied Icelandic language in adulthood at the Scandinavian Cultural Centre, and later at University of Manitoba. She ended up teaching Icelandic and Old Norse Mythology in various educational venues. She is now retired, yet her passion for Old Norse Mythology and love of writing, led her to write *A Viking Legend: The Descendants of Odin*.

Sigurd's Story in Wood and Stone

Sigurd's Story carved on wood, From the Medieval Church at Hylestad, Setesdal, Norway.

1. Gunnar, brother of Gudrun, in the snake pit playing the harp with his toes.
2. Sigurd killing Regin. Here he puts his sword through Regin's heart. (in other sources he slices off his head)
3. Sigurd's horse Grani holding the chest of treasures; also shows the birds that spoke to Sigurd.
4. Sigurd roasting the dragon heart, burns his finger thus putting it in his mouth to heal, when juices from the dragon heart permit him to understand the speech of the birds.

5. The Killing of Fafnir.
6. The testing of the sword, Gram.
7. The making of the sword.

Sigurd's Story on Stone, The Ramsund drawing in Södermanland, Sweden (11th-century).

The Ramsund stone was a stone raised by a woman to honour the death of her husband. It contains parts of the Sigurd Saga and runic writings.

A diagram of the Ramsund drawing: Sigurd, the Nuthatches, Regin, Grani, Fafnir, Ótr.

An interpretation of the drawings on the stone:

1. Sigurd sitting by the fire cooking the heart of the dragon Fafnir for his foster-father Regin. When Sigurd touches it, he burns himself and sticks his finger into his mouth. As he tastes the dragon blood, he understands the songs of the birds.
2. The birds warn Sigurd that Regin will try to kill him and advise him to kill Regin. Sigurd slices off Regin's head. (Here Regin is killed by the slicing-off of his head. The wood carvings show Regin being stabbed through the heart. Both the wood carving and stone drawing show Regin being killed.
3. Regin's headless body and his smithing tools.
4. Grani, Sigurd's horse, carrying the treasure of Fafnir, the dragon.
5. Sigurd killing Fafnir.
6. Ottar, the brother of Regin and Fafnir.

The runic inscription reads:
"Sigrid made this bridge, Alrik's mother [and] Orm's daughter, for the soul of Holmger, Sigröd's father, her husband."

This stone was believed to have been made and raised by a woman named Sigrid (Ormsdottir), who built a bridge for her husband, Holmger. The children were Alrik and Sigrod.

In the 11th century, people would often build "bridges" for their loved ones who died. A "bridge" meant a spiritual one to help a soul cross from this world to the otherworld. According to Real Scandinavia, the Swedish National Heritage Board and others, "Medieval Christianity often absorbed pre-Christian legends." The Sigurd legend pre-dates Christianity and, in this stone, Sigrid, the wife of Holmger, built a bridge for her husband's soul, which indicates that she or he or both were Christian. Christian stories also suggests that the killing the dragon Fafnir (bad) by Sigurd (good) may correlate with the Christian story where the Archangel Michael (good) battles

Lucifer, the Morning Star, also known as Satan (bad). Both are *good vs. bad* scenarios. But, that is another story…

This stone is an example of one stone with the Sigurd Saga on it. There are many others, all pre-dating Christianity.

Sigurd Stones Wikipedia https://en-academic.com/dic.nsf/enwiki/6906171

Appendix 2
List of Characters and Genealogy

***Descendants of Odin are *italicized*:**

Odin + Katrin – have a son, *Sigi Odinsson.*

Sigi Odinsson + Sigurros Bjornsdottir – have a son, *Rerir Sigason.*

Rerir Sigason + Sigrid – have a son, *Volsung Rerison.*

Grimnir (giant) + unknown giantess – have a daughter, Hljod.

Volsung Rerison + Hljod – have twins, *Sigmund* and *Signy,* and 9 more sons, *Rerir, Sigi, Helgi, David, Bjarni, Fridrik, Thor* and, the youngest, *Metusalum.*

(The twins) *Sigmund Volsungson* + *Signy Volsungsdottir* – have a son, *Sinfjotli.*

Signy Volsungsdottir + Siggeir - have two sons, *Vili and Ve,* and *two unnamed children.*

Sigmund (son of *Volsung*) + Bjorghild – have two sons, *Helgi* and *Hamund.*

Hamund Sigmundson + Kristjanna – have two sons, *Haki and Hagbard.*

Sinfjotli (son of *Sigmund* and *Signy*) + Osk Sigurbjorg Thorsteinsdottir – have a girl, *Emily.*

Helgi (son of *Sigmund* and Bjorghild) + Sigrun Hognadottir – have three sons, *Viglundur, Andres, and Trausti,* and three daughters, *Ila, Steinunn and Julia.*

Hogni + unnamed wife – have three children, Bragi, Sigrun and Dag.

Granmar + unnamed wife - have two sons, Hodbrodd and Gudmund.

Hunding (feuds with Sigmund) + unnamed wife – have two sons, Hjorvard and Lyngvi.

Sigmund Volsungson + Hjordis Elymisdottir – have a son, *Sigurd.*

Eylimi + Kimberlee - have a son, Gripir, and a daughter, Hjordis.

Hreidmar + Runa – have sons, Fafnir, Ottar, and Regin, and daughters, Lyngheid and Lofnheid.

Hjalprek + Kathi – have a son, Alf, who married Hjordis (widow of Sigmund, mother of Sigurd) and a daughter, Shelly.

Budli + unnamed wife – have five sons, one named Atli, and three daughters, Bekkhild, Brynhild and Oddrun.

Bekkhild + Heimir – have a son, Alsvid, and are also foster-parents to *Aslaug*.

Gjuki + Grimhild – have Gullrond, Gunnar, Hogni, Gudrun and Guttorm.

Sigurd + Brynhild – have a girl, *Aslaug*.

Aslaug + Ragnar – have five sons, *Ivar, Bjorn, Hvitserk, Rognvald, Sigurd* (nickname: *Snake in the Eye*).

Sigurd (son of *Sigmund*) + Gudrun – have a son, *Sigmund* and a daughter, *Svanhild*.

Gudrun + Atli – have two sons, Erp and Eitil.

Gudrun + Jonakur - have two sons, Hamdir and Sorli. (Jonakur had a son, Erp, from a previous marriage.)

Hogni (brother to Gudrun) + Kostbera – have three sons, Solar, Snaevar and Niflung.

Genealogical chart
by Dustin Geeraert

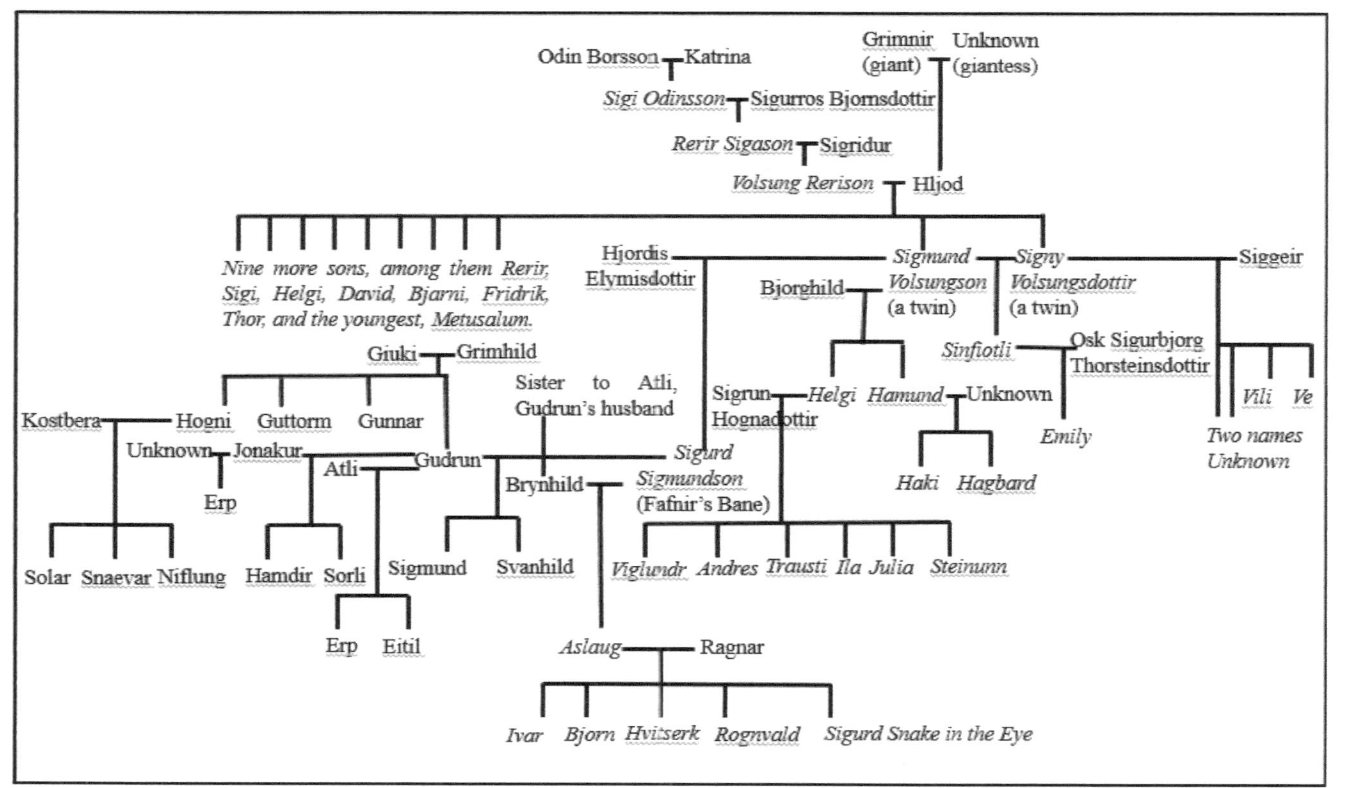

Annotated Glossary

A

Aegis Helm (Ægis Helm), the Helm of Dread or Terror Helmet, owned by Hreidmar.

Aesir (Æsir), plural of As, (Ás), meaning male Norse gods, live in Asgard (Ásgard).

Agnar, the king who fought with King Hjalmgunnar, to whom Odin had promised victory. But, Brynhild protected Agnar causing Hjalmgunnar to fall. Odin, then, punished Brynhild.

Aki, spouse of Grima. They both killed Heimir for his harp, thinking the harp contained gold. But, it contained a child. They fostered the child, whom they called Kraka.

Alf, son of Hrodmar, challenged mythological Helgi to a dual and killed Helgi.

Alf Hjalpreksson (Álf Hjálpreksson), son of King Hjalprek of Denmark. He became a king, found Hjordis, the widow of Sigmund, married her and became stepfather to Sigurd and his nephews and nieces.

Alfheim (Elf-home), one of the nine realms of Yggdrasil (the World Tree). Elves live there.

Alfhild, the favourite wife of King Hjorvard.

AllFather, another name for Odin.

Alof, married Atli. She was the daughter of Earl Franmar, who was earl to King Svafnir.

Alsvid (Alsvið), son of King Heimir and Bekkhild.

Alsvinn, meaning "the swift," is one of the horses that drives the chariot that Sol (sun) rides in.

Althing, Icelandic parliament.

Andlang, spiritual heaven, 2nd heaven to the south, long and wide.

Andres, a son of Helgi and Sigrun (an author-given name; he is unnamed in sources).

Andvara Falls, location where the dwarf, Andvari, lived and kept his gold.

Andvaranaut (Andvari's gift), the name of the ring of Andvari, from the dwarves' gold, a magical ring that produces more rings. This was the same ring that Loki took, and Odin placed on the whisker of Ottar to complete the ransom.

Andvari, the dwarf that was turned into the likeness of a fish, known as a pike, and guarded the dwarves' gold.

Angrboda (Angrboða), giantess, spouse of Loki, mother of Hel.

Annar, meaning another, second husband of Night.

Arvak, meaning "early waker," name of one of the two horses that guides the chariot that Sol (the sun) rides in.

As (Ás), god (singular).

Asgard (Ásgarð), name of the city of the gods, God-earth, world of the gods.

Ask, the first human male.

Aslaug Sigurdsdottir (Áslaug Sigurðadóttir), daughter of Brynhild and Sigurd. Regarding source materials for her story, she is mentioned in The Poetic Edda, The Prose Edda, The Saga of the Volsungs, The Fostering of Aslaug, The Tale of Ragnar Lothbrok, The Saga of Ragnar Lothbrok, and The Lay of Kraka.

Asynjur, female goddesses living in Asgard.

Atli Idmundsson, son of Earl Imund, who was earl to King Hjorvard. He married Alof.

Atli Budlason (Atli Buðlason), king, some have referred to him as Attila the Hun. In this story, he is brother to Brynhild, Bekkhild and Oddrun, and brother-in-law to Gunnar, second husband of Gudrun.

Aud, meaning wealth, son of Naglifari and Night.

Audhumla, a primeval cow, is the second creation and nourishes the first creation, Ymir, with her four teats of flowing milk. She licked the salty primordial rime and revealed the first god, Buri.

Aurgelmir, the frost giants' name for the first being, a giant known by the Aesir as Ymir.

Austri, meaning East, the name of the dwarf that holds up the Eastern
part of the sky (Ymir's skull).

B

Barnstock, the tree inside Volsung's hall that Odin thrusts a sword into.
Some say Barnstock is part of Yggdrasil, the mythological World
Tree.

Beiti, steward of King Atli.

Bekkhild Budladottir (Buðladóttir), sister to Brynhild, Oddrun, and
Atli, married to King Heimir.

Bergelmir, the frost giant who survived the flood, saved himself, his
family and household. All frost giants and giants are descended
from him and his family.

Berserker, one who fights in a frenzied, rage-like state and is not afraid
of death. This state was, possibly, induced by rituals or drugs.

Bestla, daughter of Bulthorn, a frost giant, who married Bor.

Bifrost, name of the rainbow bridge joining Asgard and Midgard. The
bridge was guarded by the god, Heimdal.

Bikki, adviser to King Jormunrek, who had Svanhild and Randver
killed.

Bjarni, a son of Volsung and Hljod (author-added name; unnamed in
sources).

Bjorn (Björn), father of Sigurros, father-in-law to Sigi (author-added
name; unnamed in sources).

Bjorn (nickname) Ironside (Björn Ragnarsson), son of Aslaug and
Ragnar.

Bondwoman, a female caregiver to a member or members of a royal
family, a slave girl or woman. Loyalty is expected.

Bor, son of Buri, the first god, married to Bestla. Father of Odin, Vili
and Ve.

Borghild, wife of Sigmund, mother of Helgi and Hamund, stepmother
of Sinfjotli. She killed Sinfjotli and was banished.

Borgney, was a friend to Oddrun and was assisted in childbirth by Oddrun.

Bragi, son of King Hogni, brother to Sigrun and Dag.

Bredafonn (Breðafönn) "Bredi's drift," name of snow mound where Bredi was found.

Bredi (Breði), a thrall of Skadi. He was killed by Sigi.

Breidablik, meaning Gleaming Far and Wide, the home of Baldur, son of Odin and Frigg.

Brett, warrior King of Hunaland (author-added name; unnamed in sources).

Brynhild Sigrdrifa Budladottir (Buðladóttir), sister of Atli, Bekkhild and Oddrun, daughter of Budli, lover of Sigurd, wife of Gunnar.

Budli (Buðli), a king, father of Brynhild, Bekkhild, Oddrun, and Atli.

Budlung, (Buðlung), was the name of Budli's family line and kingdom.

Bulthorn, father of Bestla, grandfather of Odin, Vili and Ve.

Buff coat, a coat made of animal hide. It was worn under armour to help protect the skin from chaffing caused by the metal armour.

Burgundians, a tribe or group of tribes living in Germania, now a part of Poland. They were documented as a "barbaric" tribe that moved west to become Burgundia, which is now a part of France.

Buri, the first god created. He was licked out the clean, frozen ice by Audhumla, the she-cow.

Busiltjorn (Busiltjörn), name of a river.

D

Dag, brother to Sigrun.

Dain, a stag, living in Yggdrasil, that aided Sigi.

Day, a god, son of Night. He rides the chariot containing the sun and drawn by the horse, Skinfaxi, thus creating daylight.

David, son of Volsung and Hljod (author-added name; unnamed in sources).

Delling, shining and bright, third husband of Night, father of Day.

Disir (dís) singular, (dísir) plural, a goddess or priestess, a female guardian spirit who follows every person from his/her birth and only leaves him/her in the hour of death (Cleasby-Vigfússon dictionary). Also: spiritual beings believed to exist and decide a person's fate.

Dowry, the accumulation of wealth a woman brings to her husband in marriage.

Duneyr, a stag living in Yggdrasil, aided Sigi.

Durathror, a stag, living in Yggdrasil, that aided Sigi.

Dvalin, a stag, living in Yggdrasil, that aided Sigi.

Dvalin, chief of the dwarves.

Dwarves, lived in groups in Svartalfheim. As per the Norse Creation myth, each of four dwarves, named Austri, Vestri, Nordri and Sudri (East, West, North and South), hold up a corner of Ymir's skull, thereby forming the heavens.

E

Eikyhrnir, a stag that stands near Valhalla. Its horns drip dew that flows down to the Well of Hvergelmir.

Einherjar, the name of warriors, who died in battle, called to Valhalla to fight alongside Odin during Ragnarok.

Eitil Atlasson, the name of Gudrun's son with King Atli.

Eirik, the man who had ruled Hunland, while Volsung and his descendants were away.

Elivagr, the name of the combined eleven primordial rivers that gushed from the well, Hvergelmir in the early creation period.

Embla, meaning Elm, the name of the first human woman, who was created from drift wood.

Emily, daughter of Osk and Sinfjotli (author-added name; unnamed in sources).

Ernest, a trusted man of Sigurd (author-added name; unnamed in sources).

Erp Atlasson, son of Atli and Gudrun.

Erp Jonakursson (Jónakrsson), King Jonakur's son, Queen Gudrun's stepson.

Eylimi, a mythological king, father of Svava, father-in-law to Helgi Hjorvardsson.

Eylimi, a famous king, father of Hjordis, father-in-law to Sigmund.

Eysteinn, a King of Sweden, who wanted Ragnar to marry his daughter, Ingibjorg.

F

Fafnisbani, nickname for Sigurd Sigmundarson, meaning the bane of Fafnir or the killer of Fafnir.

Fafnir (Fáfnir), son of Hreidmar, brother of Ottar, Regin, Lyngheid and Lofnheid. He killed his father, banished Regin, coveted the gold, became a dragon and was killed by Sigurd.

Fetch, a spiritual being or guardian spirit associated with a family. Fetch is also associated with the Disir. It was thought that the family fetch (or, in Old Norse, Fylgia) appeared before the death of a hero.

Fimbulthur, one of the eleven rivers gushing from the well of Hvergelmir formed at the dawn of creation.

Fjolnir (Fjölnir), another name for Odin, the old man who appeared to Sigurd.

Fjon (Fjón), the place name for where there was a great battle, as depicted in one of Gudrun's embroideries.

Fjorm, one of the eleven rivers gushing from the well of Hvergelmir formed at the dawn of creation.

Flyting, a type of verbal battle or exchange of insults which occurs in Old Norse literature.

Folkvang, the warrior maiden's afterlife, governed by the goddess Freyja. According to The Poetic Edda, Freyja receives half the battle-slain in Folkvang, while Odin receives the other half in Valhalla.

Franmar, Earl to King Svafnir, father of daughter, Alof.

Freki, one of Odin's wolves.

Freyja, member of the Vanir race, goddess of love, war, magic called seithr (seiðr). She receives one half of the slain into her realm called Folkvang.

Freyr, member of the Vanir race, god of fertility, twin brother of Freyja.

Fridrik, (Friðrik), son of Volsung and Hljod (author-added name; unnamed in sources).

Fridsteinn, (Friðsteinn), an honourable and knowledgeable horseman in King Hjalprek's kingdom (author-added name; unnamed in sources).

Frigg, goddess of fertility and of the home and hearth. The wife of Odin.

Fylgja, the family spirit.

G

Gautland, a place name, Götaland (Swedish) also Gothia, Gothland, Gothenland or Gautland, considered to be in the southern tip of what we now call Sweden. Inhabitants are called Gautar or Geats.

Geitir, the greeter at King Gripir's gates.

Geri, one of Odin's wolves.

Giant (see also Troll), a primordial, ancestral being often opposed to gods and heroes. These vast creatures come in a chaotic variety of forms, and they have many conflicting characteristics and abilities.

Gimle (paradise), at the southern end of heaven, the brightest and most beautiful hall, which survives Ragnarok and becomes part of the new afterlife world, a place where the good and righteous dwell.

Ginnungagap, a yawning abyss, which has been described, in the dawn of the Old Norse creation stories, as the great void and as being freezing cold.

Gjaflaug, sister of King Gjuki.

Gjallabru (Gjallabrú), the name of the bridge that crosses over the river, Gjoll, on the way to the area of Hel in the realm of Niflheim.

Gjoll, one of the eleven rivers gushing from the well of Hvergelmir formed at the dawn of creation. It flows through the area of Hel.

Gjuki (Gjúki), king and father of Gullrond, Gunnar, Hogni ,Gudrun and Guttorm.

Gjukung (Gjúkung), the family line and name of the kingdom of King Gjuki.

Gladsheim, a part of Asgard that houses Valhalla and Hlidskjalf.

Glaumvor (Glaumvör), second wife of King Gunnar.

Glitnir, meaning Radiant Place, has walls, columns and roof made of red gold, and is the hall of Forseti, the god of law and justice.

Gnita-Heath (Gnitaheið), the area where Fafnir, as a dragon, made his home and guarded the gold.

Goths, widely-settled tribal groups.

Goti, King Gunnar's horse.

Grafvitnir, father of serpents or snakes.

Gram, Sigurd's sword, reforged from the pieces of the sword that was given to Sigmund by Odin.

Grani, Sigurd's horse, descendant of Sleipnir, Odin's eight-legged steed.

Granmar, a king and father of Hodbrodd and Gudmund.

Grima (Gríma), spouse of Aki, who raised Aslaug.

Grimhild (Grímhild), wife of King Gjuki and mother of Gullrond, Gunnar, Hogni, Gudrun and Guttorm, she knew witchcraft and how to shape-shift.

Grimnir, a giant and the father of Hljod.

Gripir Eylimason (Grípir Eylimason), brother to Hjordis, king, uncle to Sigurd, a prophet and seer, could see the future.

Gudmund (Guðmund), brother of Hodbrodd, son of King Granmar.

Gudrun Gjukadottir (Guðrún Gjúkadóttir), daughter of King Gjuki, married Sigurd, Atli and Jonakur, mother of Sigmund Sigurdarson and Svanhild Sigurdsdottir, Erp and Eitil Atlason, Hamdir and Sorli Jonakarson.

Gullrond Gjukadottir (Gjúkadóttir), sister to Gunnar, Hogni, Gudrun and Guttorm.

Gungnir, the name of the magical spear of Odin.

Gunnar Gjukason (Gjúkason), brother of Gullrond, Hogni, Gudrun and Guttorm. He married Brynhild and Glaumvor, and was killed by Atli.

Gunnthra, one of the eleven rivers gushing from the well of Hvergelmir formed in the dawn of creation.

Guttorm Gjukason (Gjúkason), youngest brother of Gullrond, Gunnar, Hogni and Gudrun. He killed Sigurd.

H

Haenir (Hænir), a member of the Aesir, a friend of Odin and Loki. Variations of his name include Hænir, Haenir and Hoenir.

Hagal, foster father to Sinfjotli and Helgi Sigmundarson.

Hagbard (Hagbarð), son of Hamund, a foremost king mentioned by Brynhild.

Haki, son of Hamund, a foremost king mentioned by Brynhild.

Hakon (Hákon), father of Thora, a woman who lived within King Half's halls and sheltered Gudrun after death of Sigurd.

Half (Hálf), the king who received Gudrun and company after Sigurd died.

Hamal, son of Hagal.

Hamdir Jonakursson (Hamðir Jónakrsson), son of Queen Gudrun and King Jonakur.

Hamund Sigmundarson (Hámund), a king mentioned by Brynhild, Sigurd's half-brother, the second son of King Sigmund and Borghild, who became king in his mother's country and has two sons, Haki and Hagbard.

Harbard, another name for Odin, who was disguised as the ferry man, took Sinfjotli.

Hatafjord, the fjord where the giant, Hati, lived.

Hati, a grizzly giant.

Hati Hrodvitnisson, a monstrous wolf chasing the Moon.

Hatun (Highmeadow), the land given to Helgi Sigmundarson.

Heavens, (There are 9 heavens) Andlang, Valaskjaf, Folkvang, Gimle, Gladsheim, Vingjolf, Himinbjorg, Valhalla and Vidblain

Hedin (Heðin Hjörvarðarson), son of mythological King Hjorvard and Alfhild, stepbrother to Helgi Hjorvardsson.

Heidrun, a goat whose teats produce the mead that the Einherjar drink in Valhalla.

Heimdal, the god who guards the Bifrost bridge.

Heimir, a king, foster father of Brynhild, who gave himself the name of Sig, as he portrayed himself as a poor harp player (author-added name: Sig; unnamed in sources).

Hel, the half-living, half-dead giantess, ruler of an underworld realm that is also called Hel, aka Niflhel, in the realm of Niflheim. She was a daughter of Loki and the giantess Angrboda.

Hel, the area of Niflheim where the goddess, Hel, dwells,

Hels-gates, the gates before the area where Hel dwells:

Helgi Hjorvardsson (Hjörvarðarson), favourite mythological character of King Sigmund, who he named his son after.

Helgi Sigmundarsson Hundingsbani, son of Sigmund and Borghild.

Helgi Volsungsson, son of Volsung and Hljod. (author-added name; unnamed in sources).

Helm of Terror, Helmet of Terror or Dread. See: Aegis Helm.

Herborg, the woman who speaks to Gudrun about her sorrows.

Herkja, the mistress of King Atli.

Herod, King of Gotland, father of Thora, who was the second wife of Ragnar Lothbrok.

Highmeadow, (Hatun), the name of a piece of land given to Helgi Sigmundsson.

Himinbjorg, home of Heimdall, the watchman of the gods.

Himinvangi, Heaven's Slope, the name of a piece of land given to Helgi Sigmundarsson.

Hindarfjall, a splendid mountain, surrounded by supernatural flames, where Brynhild slept.

Hjalmgunnar (Hjálmgunnar), a great and wise king.

Hjalprek (Hjálprek), King of Thjod, father of Alf and step-grandfather of Sigurd and his nieces and nephews. He hired Regin as a smith.

Hjalli, a thrall in Atli's kingdom.

Hjordis Eylimadottir (Hjördis Eylimadóttir), married Sigmund and was the mother of Sigurd.

Hjorvard (Hjörvarðr), a mythological king (the father in the Tale of Helgi Hjorvardsson).

Hjorvard Hundingsson (Hjörvarðr Hundingsson), son of Hunding, brother of Lyngvi.

Hlidskjalf (Hliðskjalf), the name of Odin's seat, or (hásæti Óðinns) Odin's throne, where he sits and looks out over the nine realms. Odin is the only one allowed to sit on it, though his wife Frigg has been known to sit on it. Freyr once sat on it, but with consequences...

Hljod (Hljóð), a wish-maiden of Odin, daughter of giant Hrimnir, who gave Rerir and Siguros a fertility apple, the wife of Volsung. (The children of Volsung and Hljod were unnamed in the Eddas, and unnamed characters have been given names in this story by the author).

Hlymdal, the name of area where King Heimir and Queen Bekkhild lived.

Hnefatafl, "The King's Table," a Viking chess game.

Hnikar, another name Odin used.

Hodbrodd (Hoðbrodd), son of King Gramnar, was betrothed to Sigrun.

Hogni (Högni), king, father of Sigrun, was killed in battle by Helgi. Hogni betrothed Sigrun to Hodbrodd, but she married Helgi Sigmundarsson.

Hogni (Högni Gjúkason), son of King Gyuki, brother of Gullrond, Gunnar, Gudrun, and Guttorm.

Hraesvelg, a wind eagle.

Hreidmar (Hreiðmar), a dwarf, father of Fafnir, Ottar, Regin, Lyngheid and Lofnheid.

Hrid, (Hrið), one of the eleven rivers gushing from the well of Hvergelmir formed at the dawn of creation.

Hrimfaxi, a horse given to Night from Odin. She rides Hrimfaxi around the worlds every 24 hours.

Hrimgerd (Hrimgerð), giantess, daughter of the giant Hati.

Hrimnir (Hrímnir), a great giant.

Hringstead, the name of a royal Danish residence on the Island of Zealand (Sjælland).

Hrodmar (Hroðmar), the king who pursued Sigurlinn and killed her family.

Hrotti, sword of Hreidmar.

Hugin (Huginn), Thought, one of Odin's ravens.

Hunaland (Húnaland), the name of the area in Europe where the human family line descended from Odin originated. Some believe this was in the south, where France is today.

Hundingsbani (the Slayer of the Hundings), the nickname given to Helgi Sigmundarson.

Hunding, a king that King Sigmund was feuding with.

Huns, Hunnish (Hún), a group of people in Eurasia.

Hvitserk Ragnarsson (Hvítserk Ragnarsson), a son of Aslaug and Ragnar.

I

Idmund, earl to King Hjorvard, father of Atli.

Idunn, (Iðunn), a goddess who gives special apples to the gods that keep them young.

Ila, a daughter of Helgi and Sigrun (author-added name; unnamed in sources).

Ingibörg, daughter of King Eysteinn of Sweden.

Island of Zealand, Sjaelland (Sjæland), a Danish island.

Ivar Ragnarsson, a son of Aslaug and Ragnar.

J

James, a warrior King of Hunaland (author-added name; unnamed in sources).

Jonakur (Jónakr), a king, married to Gudrun.

Jormunrek (Jörmunrekr), (Iormunrekk), The Gothic king who killed Svanhild, Sorli and Hamdir (children of Gudrun).

Jotunheim, the eastern realm within Yggdrasil, the World Tree, and home of the frost giants, giants, trolls, ogres and other creatures.

Julia, a daughter of Helgi and Sigrun (author-added name; unnamed in sources).

K

Katrin (Katrín), a human loved by Odin, the mother of Sigi (author-added names).

Kathi, a queen and wife of King Hjalprek, mother of Alf and Shelly (author-added names: Kathi and Shelly).

Kenning, a poetic phrase used instead of a direct reference to a name a person or thing.

Examples:

"Steed of the sea" is a kenning for a "ship"

Blood kin of your bride (in-laws)

Blood pumping organ (heart)

Blood snake (sword)

Fire of the well (gold)

Muni begins his journey (evening)

One-eyed warrior (Odin)

Son of Budli (King Atli)

Stallions of the sea (ships)

Sweetest of nectars (honey)

Kimberlee, wife of Eylimi and mother of Gripir and Hjordis (author-added name).

Knefrod, another name for Vingi, a messenger in King Atli's Kingdom.

Kostbera, wife of Hogni, sister-in-law to Gudrun.

Kraka (kráka), the name given to Aslaug by Aki and Grima. *Kráka* means crow. The word *krakki* means child, and *kraki* means an underwater sea creature, cf. the kraken. *Krakinn* means *a* tall, thin person, cf. Hrolf Kraki.

Kristjana, wife of Hamund (author-added name).

Kynfylgja, the family spirit. (also see fetch).

L

Leiptr, one of the eleven rivers gushing from the well of Hvergelmir formed at the dawn of creation.

Lofnheid Hreidmarsdottir (Lofnheið Hreiðmarsdóttir), sister of Lyngheid, Regin, Ottar and Fafnir, and daughter of Hreidmar and Runa.

Loki, known as a god of mischief. Loki was of the giant race and was a childhood friend of Odin. Ancient texts have referred to Odin and Loki as blood brothers, having sworn oaths to one another. Loki had shape-shifting abilities, meaning he could change his shape into other forms. He was known as a trickster. Sometimes he helped the gods, and sometimes he harmed them. In this story, he helps Odin and Haenir.

Lyngheid Hreidmarsdottir (Lyngheið Hreiðmarsdóttir), sister of Lofnheid, Regin, Ottar and Fafnir, and daughter of Hreidmar and Runa.

Lyngvi, a king, the son of King Hunding, who wanted to marry Hjordis.

M

Mani, Moon.

Metusalem, son of Volsung and Hljod (name given by author).

Midgard (Miðgarð), Middle Earth, where humans live.

Mimir, the knowledgeable companion and confidant of Odin. Mimir's Well is named after him. Mimir was the wisest and most intelligent god, and he shared his knowledge with anyone who would listen. The Aesir and the Vanir (another race of beings) were in a never-ending war. They both decided to end the war and give each other hostages. Mimir, Haenir and possibly other gods were sent to live with the Vanir, while Njord (god of the sea) Freyr and Freyja (children and twins of Njord, the god and goddess of fertility) were sent to the Aesir. The Vanir became sick of listening to Mimir's wisdom, so they cut off his head. Odin brought his head to remain at a life sustaining-well. Odin would visit the well and speak with Mimir's head. (This is another story.)

Mundifaeri, (Mundifæri), father of Mani, the moon and Sol, the sun. He married Sol to a man named Glen that angered the gods.

Munin (Muninn), Memory, one of Odin's ravens.

Muspelheim, a fire realm, where Surt and the fire-beings live.

N

Narfi, a giant, father of Night, dark and swarthy,

niðgjöld (see wergild), payment in compensation for insults or a death.

Nidhogg (Niðhögg), dragon snake, lives in Niflheim

Niflheim, (meaning dark world, dark home, or realm of darkness), one of the nine worlds of Yggdrasil.

Niflung Hognason (Niflung Högnason), also spelled (Hniflung), son of King Hogni and Kostbera, nephew of Gudrun. He helped in the killing of Atli

Niflungs, descendants of Niflung Hognason.

Night, a female spiritual being, daughter of giant Narfi. Odin gave her and her son, Day, two horses (hers is named Hrimfaxi) and two chariots and set them up in the sky to ride around the earth every twenty-four hours.

Njord (Njorð), member of Vanir race, god of the sea, father of twins, Freyr and Freyja.

Nordi (Norði), North, the name of the dwarf that holds up the north part of the sky (Ymir's skull).

Norn, a female spirit known as a weaver of fate. There were many types of norns. There were the three norns of Yggdrasil, Urd, Verdandi and Skuld (Past, Present and Future). There are norns specific to childbirth, where they visit a child upon birth and spin the fate of that child's life. Some believe that there were norns specific to the dwarves, asynjur deities, elves, giants, fire-beings, humans, and all creatures living in Yggdrasil. Pleasant norns could weave a good life, while nasty norns could weave misfortune into one's destiny.

O

Oddrun Budladottir (Oddrún Buðladóttir), sister of Atli, Bekkhild and Brynhild.

Odin (Óðinn), the chief Norse god, known as god of the slain, of prisoners, of cargoes and of hanged men. He has many names, aliases and epithets: AllFather, Fjolnir, Grim, Gangleri, Harbard, Hnikar, High, Just-As-High, and Third.

Orkning, foster father and uncle of the sons of Hogni and Kostbera, Solar, Snaevar and Niflung, and he was the brother of Kostbera.

Osk Sigurbjorg (Ósk Sigurbjörg), a lovely woman married to Sinfjotli. (author-added name; unnamed in sources).

Oskapt (Óskapt), the name of an island where Surt and the Aesir will fight at Ragnarok.

Ottar, son of Hreidmar, brother of Fafnir, Regin, Lyngheid and
     Lofnheid, who was in the shape of an otter. When killed by Loki,
     his death was compensated to his father Hreidmar by Odin, Loki
     and Haenir. This compensation is known as Ottar's Ransom or
     Fafnir's Gold.

P

Pledges, an activity in which men or women would pledge to do
     something (similar to swearing an oath).

R

Ragnar Lothbrok (Loðbrók meaning "hairy breeches"), the nickname
     of Ragnar Sigurðsson, son of King Sigurd Ring. No relation to
     Aslaug, was husband of Aslaug (different sources suggest
     differences in Ragnar's wives and children).
Ragnarok, the Norse mythological end of the world, referred to as The
     Final Battle.
Ran (Rán), goddess of the sea.
Randver Jormunreksson (Randvér Jörmunreksson), son of King
     Jormunrek. Randver loved Svanhild and was killed by Bikki.
Ratatosk, the squirrel that runs up and down Yggdrasil, the World Tree,
     is known to spread gossip, to the inhabitants up in the branches of
     the tree, and in the roots of the tree.
Refil, the name of Regin's sword.
Regin Hreidmarsson (Regin Hreiðmarsson), son of Hreidmar and
     Runa, brother to Lofnheid, Lyngheid, Fafnir and Ottar, and foster
     father to Sigurd.
Rerir Sigason, a king, unable to have children, until visited by a wish-

maiden who gave him and his wife an apple. He was the son of Sigi.

Rerir Volsungsson, a son of Volsung and Hljod (author-added name; unnamed in sources).

Rhine (Rín), the name of a river and, also, the name of the gold of Andvari (the Rhine Gold).

Rhine Gold, Gold of Andvari, owned by Hreidmar, Fafnir, Sigurd, and then the Gjukung brothers. Gunnar put the gold into the Rhine River.

Rimur, (Rímur), ancient poetry performed while chanting.

Rognvald Ragnarsson, son of Aslaug and Ragnar.

Runa (Rúna), wife of Hreidmar, mother of Lyngheid, Lofnheid, Ottar, Fafnir and Regin (author-given name; unnamed in eddas and sagas).

Rune (Rún), an Old Norse alphabetical symbol that can also have a meaning of its own.

S

Saehrimnir (Sæhrímnir), a magical boar, is killed and eaten every night by einherjar and becomes alive again every day.

Saga, a story or history.

Samuel, a prince who was cast under a spell and donned wolf skin (author-added name; unnamed in sources).

Seeress, a woman with special insights and abilities, who may perform a specialized magic.

Seer, a male with special insights and abilities, who may perform a specialized magic.

Shape-shifting, when someone takes on another form, or when a creature changes shape into another creature, also known as skin-changing or transformation.

Shield Maiden, another name for a valkyrie, who uses her special abilities to shield warriors.

Shelly, daughter of King Hjalprek and Queen Kathi, sister to Alf (author-added name; unnamed in sources).

Sig, the nickname King Heimir gave himself, when he was portraying the role of the poor harp player (author-added name; unnamed in sources).

Sigar, a trusted friend of mythological Helgi Hjordvardsson.

Sigar, a king. Gudrun embroidered his adventures.

Sigarsholm, the secret location of a golden sword. Svava told Helgi Hjorvardsson where it was.

Sigarsvoll (Sigar's Fields), name of a plot of land given to Helgi Sigmundsson.

Siggeir, King of Gautland.

Siggeir, a king. Gudrun embroidered his adventures.

Siggi, the nickname of Sigmund Sigurdarson (author-added nickname).

Sigi Odinsson (Sigi Oðinsson), the first person documented in the line of Odin's sons, was a tribe member, killed a thrall, was banished, protected by Odin, father of Rerir and became King of Hunaland.

Sigi Volsungsson, son of Volsung and Hljod (author-added name; unnamed in sources).

Sigmund Sigurdarson (Sigmund Sigurðarson); aka, Sigurstein Thjodreksson, son of Sigurd and Gudrun, nickname: Siggi (author added the other name and nickname).

Sigmund Volsungsson (Sigmund Völsungsson), son of Volsung and Hljod, twin brother to Signy.

Signy Volsungsdottir (Signy Völsungsdóttir), twin sister to Sigmund, daughter of Volsung and Hljod.

Sigrid, wife of Rerir (author-added name; unnamed in sources).

Sigrun Hognadottir (Hognadóttir), daughter of King Hogni, a valkyrie, married Helgi Sigmundarson. (The number and names of children of Helgi and Sigrun were unwritten and unnamed in ancient texts, so these are provided by the author.)

Sigurd Sigmundarson (Sigurð), son of Sigmund and Hjordis.

Sigurd (Snake in the Eye), son of Aslaug and Ragnar.

Sigurlinn, daughter of King Svafnir, a beautiful woman, who married King Hjorvard.

Sigurros (Sigurrós), translated as "Victory Rose" and also as "Sigi's Rose," married to Sigi, mother of Rerir (author-added name; unnamed in sources).

Sigurstein Thjodreksson, the other name given to Sigmund Sigurdarson, nickname: Siggi. (author gave the other name and nickname).

Sinfjotli Sigmundarson, son of Sigmund and his twin sister Signy, half-brother of Helgi, Hamund and Sigurd.

Sjaelland (Sjæland), Zealand, the main Island of Denmark. The original name was possibly Selund.

Skadi (Skaði), owner of thrall named Bredi. He declared Sigi an outlaw and banished him.

Skinfaxi, the horse given to Day by Odin to ride around the worlds every twenty-four hours.

Skoll, a monstrous wolf who chases the Sun.

Skuld, the norn of the future, "will happen."

Sleipnir, the name of Odin's eight-legged horse.

Slidr, one of the eleven rivers gushing from the well of Hvergelmir formed at the dawn of creation.

Snaefjall (Snæfjall), Snow Mountains, land given to Helgi Sigmundsson.

Snaevar Hognason (Snævar Högnason), son of Hogni and Glaumvor.

Sol (Sun), brings light to the earth.

Solar Hognason (Sólar Högnason), son of Hogni and Glaumvor.

Solfjall (Sólfjall), Sun Mountain, land given to Helgi Sigmundarsson.

Sons of Grafvitnir, serpents living in Niflheim along with Nidhogg.

Sorli Jonakursson (Sörli Jónakrsson), brother to Hamdir, son of Gudrun and Jonakur.

Spa Woman, (spákonur) singular form of spaewomen, another name for shield-maiden or valkyrie. The term comes from spádísir (prophetic female guardian spirits), which can refer to dísir, spiritual female beings that include valkyries, norns, female deities or goddesses.

Spaewoman (spækona), or Protector in Battle, another name for valkyrie, shield-maiden.

Span, a unit of measuring distance using the hand, the distance between the tip of the thumb to the tip of the little finger.

Special apples, in Old Norse Mythology, were special immortality apples gathered by the goddess, Idunn, who gave the apples to the gods. These apples kept the gods alive and young. These apples may relate to the special gift of a fertility apple from Odin to Rerir and Sigrid.

Steinunn, daughter of Helgi Sigmundarson and Sigrun (author-added name; unnamed in sources).

Stulka, meaning girl.

Sudri, (Suðri), South, the name of the dwarf that holds up the south part of the sky (Ymir's skull).

Surt, a fire-being (the god of fire), who dwells with his fire-being sons and daughters in the fiery realm called Muspelheim. They are destined to appear and burn the world during Ragnarok.

Svafnir, a king, the father of Sigurlinn.

Svalinn, the name of a shield that shields the earth and mountains from the deadly heat of Sol (the Sun).

Svanhild Sigurdsdottir (Sigurðardóttir), daughter of Sigurd and Gudrun.

Svartalfheim, dark home, a world where dwarves live. There appears to be some connection between the dark elves and the dwarves, as some believe they are the same beings.

Svava, a valkyrie, the daughter of King Eylimi, who married the mythological Helgi Hjorvardsson.

Svol, one of the eleven rivers gushing from the well of Hvergelmir formed at the dawn of creation.

Sybil, a sorceress who changed shapes with Signy (author-added name; unnamed in sources).

T

Terri, the mother of Osk Sigurbjorg, mother-in-law to Sinfjotli. (author-added name; unnamed in sources).

Thjod (Þjoð), the land where the realm of King Hjalprek was.

Thjodrek (Þjodrek), a king, who lived in King Half's hall, was friend to Gudrun and foster father to young Sigmund and Svanhild.

Thor, (Þór), god of lightning, thunder and fertility.

Thor, (Þór), a son of Volsung and Hljod (author-added name; unnamed in sources).

Thora (Þóra), a trusted handmaiden of Hjordis.

Thora (Þóra Hákonardóttir), a friend of Gudrun, who lived in King Half's halls and was foster mother to Sigmund and Svanhild.

Thora (Þóra), the daughter of King Herod of Gotland and second wife of Ragnar.

Thrall (þrall), a slave. Thralls were compelled to work and were not free to travel. They were one of three social classes in early Norse society along with freemen (farmers) and warriors (aristocracy). These legal and occupation-based distinctions are mythically explained in a poem, "The List of Rig."

Thorstein, the father of Osk Sigurbjorg, father-in-law to Sinfjotli (author-added name; unnamed in sources).

Tracy, a prince who was cast under a spell and donned wolf skins (author-added name; unnamed in sources).

Trausti, a son of Helgi Sigmundarson and Sigrun (author-added name; unnamed in sources).

Troll, a large and disturbing being often associated with supernatural dangers. It is common in Old Norse Mythology and Scandinavian Folklore that, when the sun shines on a troll, he or she turns to stone. Some turn to stone and explode.

U

Urd (Urð), the norn of the past, "has happened."

V

Valbjorg (Valbjörg), the lands offered to Gudrun by King Gjuki to marry King Atli.

Valaskjalf (Valaskjálf), Silver Roof, one of Odin's halls, where Hlidskjalf sits.

Valhalla, one of Odin's halls, where the slain warriors, einjarnar, go.

Valkyrie, a mythological female warrior or spiritual warrior woman, also called shield maiden, because she uses her powers to protect chosen individuals. They were also known as "Choosers of the Slain," when they were responsible for taking those fated to die in battle to Valhalla (Hall of the Slain), one of Odin's halls. Some are human and marry human men.

Vanaheim, one of the nine realms of Yggdrasil, the World Tree, home of the Vanir.

Vanir, a group of warrior deities that live in Vanaheim, who are sometimes identified with the elves and have a specialized magic.

Varinsvik (Varinsvík), meaning Varin's Bay, the land area where the giantess Hrimgerd wanted to meet Earl Atli.

Ve (Vé), a son of Bor and Bestla, the brother of Odin.

Ve, the name of Signy and Siggeir's second son, named after the brother of Odin (author-added name; unnamed in sources).

Verdandi (Verðandi), the norn of the present, "happening now."

Vedrfjolnir (Veðrfjölnir), the name of a hawk which stands between the eyes of the eagle atop the tree Yggdrasil.

Vestri (West), the name of the dwarf that holds up the west part of the sky (Ymir's skull).

Vid, (Við), one of the eleven rivers gushing from the well of Hvergelmir formed at the dawn of creation.

Vidblain (Viðbláinn), meaning Wide Blue, the third heaven. Only light elves live there.

Viglundur, a son of Helgi and Sigrun (author-added name; unnamed in sources).

Vilheim, the brother of Borghild (author-added name; unnamed in sources).

Vili, a son of Bor and Bestla, the brother of Odin.

Vili, the name of Signy and Siggeir's first son, named after the brother of Odin (author-added name; unnamed in sources).

Vilmund, the husband of Borgney.

Vinbjorg (Vínbjörg), lands from King Gjuki's kingdom offered to Gudrun to marry King Atli.

Vingi, a messenger in King Atli's kingdom, also known as Knefrod.

Vingolf, the hall of the goddesses.

Volsi (Völsi), the ancient god of fertility.

Volsung Rerison (Völsung), son of Rerir and Sigrid, named after a fertility god, Volsi. With the help of a special apple, he was conceived, yet the pregnancy was said to last six years.

Volsungs (Völsungar), a group of people related to Volsung Rerison.

Voluspa (Völuspá), meaning Seeress's Prophecy, is an ancient poem in the book called *The Poetic Edda*, where information about Old Norse mythology is revealed.

W

Well of Hvergelmir, located in Niflheim, under the third root. Eleven rivers flow from the well, and their names are: Fimbulthul, Fiorm, Gioll, Gunnthra, Hrid, Leiptr, Slidr, Svol, Sylg, Vid, and Ylg.

Well of Mimir, named after Mimir, the most intelligent of the Asgardians, who was beheaded in the war with the Vanir. His head is kept alive by the life-sustaining Well of Mimir, and Odin seeks his wisdom there.

Well of Urd, located in Asgard under one of the roots of Yggdrasil.

Wergild, a compensation for taking a life. If someone killed another and declared the killing, then the death was considered "manslaughter," and the punishment was a wergild, or a payment to the grieving family for their loss. The payment could include land, sheep, cattle, food, material goods, coins and thralls, as long as the value equaled the social standing of the person who died. If the killing was not declared, and the killer was discovered, then the killing was classified as a "murder," and the punishment was "exile," or "outlawry," from the family unit or village. Classified as *vargur í véum*" or "a wolf in the sanctuary," outlawry was often a death sentence, because of the harshness of the environment and weather, made it difficult for one to survive alone. Moreover, bounties could be put on outlaws, and they could be killed-on-sight by anyone. Wergild has also been referred to as a Niðgjöld, with nið referring to slanderous speech to another person, which also required compensation.

Wish-maiden (*Óskmær*), a female being associated with Odin. Some can change shape. Odin sent the wish-maiden, Hljod to deliver the fertility apple to Rerir and his wife.

Y

Yggdrasil, the name of the Old Norse World Tree.

Ylfings, the wolf clan, descendants of Odin.

Ylg, one of the eleven rivers gushing from the well of Hvergelmir formed at the dawn of creation.

Yule (Yuletide), the winter solstice season, similar to our Christmas season.

Further Reading

The verse from *Völuspá* (*Seeress's Prophecy*) is translated by Ainsley Bloomer and Ryan E. Johnson. The author consulted numerous sources while preparing this book for publication, in some places quoting from previous translations, but most often paraphrasing information from multiple (sometimes conflicting) sources. Characters not named in the original sources have been given names and descriptions by the author. The information from this manuscript comes from the sources listed and the author's imagination. Those interested in learning more are encouraged to consult the following works:

Author unknown. *The Lay of Kraka (Krákumál).* https://lyricstranslate.com/en/krákumál-crowsong.html

Author unknown. *The Poetic Edda.* Translation by Carolyne Larrington. Oxford University Press, 1996.

Authors unknown. *The Sagas of Icelanders.* Preface by Jane Smiley. Penguin Books, 2000.

Author unknown. *The Saga of the Volsungs: With The Saga of Ragnar Lodbrok.* Translation by Jackson Crawford. Indianapolis In. & Cambridge Hackett Publishing, 2017.

Author unknown. *The Saga of the Volsungs.* Introduction and translation by Jesse Byock. University of California Press, Berkley and Los Angeles, California, 1990.

Hólmarsson, Sverrir; Sanders, Christopher; Tucker, John. *Concise Icelandic – English Dictionary Íslensk – ensk orðabók.* IDUNN-Reykjavik, Iceland, 1989.

Crossley-Holland, Kevin. *Norse Myths.* Penguin Books, 1982.

Lindow, John. *Norse Mythology: A Guide to the Gods, Heroes, Rituals, and Beliefs.* Oxford University Press, New York, 2002.

Merchant, Francis P. 1928, *Tale of Ragnar Lothbrok // Icelandic Saga //* 13th Century. Patreon.com/voicesofthepast

realscandinavia.com

Sigurd Stones. Wikipedia https://en-academic.com/dic.nsf/enwiki/6906171

Skaptason, Jón. ritstjóri, *Ensk- íslensk Skóla Orðabók. English- Icelandic*

Dictionary. Örn og Örlygur. Printed in Iceland,1986.

Sturluson, Snorri. *Edda*. Translated and edited by Anthony Faulkes. Everyman, London, 1987.

Sturluson, Snorri. *The Prose Edda*. Translated and edited by Jesse L. Byock. Penguin Classics, 2005.

Marcussen, Wanda. "Medieval Stave Churches of Norway." *Brewminate*, October 11, 2020. https://brewminate.com/medieval-stave-churches-of-norway/

Morris, William. "*The Fostering of Aslaug*." The Earthly Paradise, 1870.

Thorpe, Benjamin. "Of Ragnar and Aslaug." Northern Mythology, Comprising the Principal Popular Traditions and Superstitions of Scandinavia, North Germany and the Netherlands. Lumley. pp. 109–113, 1851.

Zoëga, Geir T. *A Concise Dictionary of Old Icelandic*. University of Toronto Press, in association with Medieval Academy of America, 2004.